The Wyvern's Apprentice

— A NOVEL —

BRENT SNYDER

Fulton Books
Meadville, PA

Published by Fulton Books 2023

ISBN 979-8-88731-587-4 (paperback)
ISBN 979-8-88731-588-1 (digital)

Printed in the United States of America

Prologue

Tÿr'Ynyn slept poorly. It was hot, and her nightclothes stuck to her body as she tossed and turned in her restless sleep. Dreams plagued her constantly this night. She would wake from one, only to fall back into another. Dreams of faceless, phantom people she'd only heard of in tales to frighten children to make them behave. The people were a feared family from islands in the seas far away. The family, the Inbröttiös—people who were said to kidnap children and take them from their villages, never to be heard from again. There were rumors that these people were inbred, and that was the nicest rumor. Cannibals was another, and every bad thing that Tÿr could think of was going through her mind as she dreamed. Tÿr was running through her village with these monsters on her heels. The more she ran, the worse her legs felt. They were turning to jelly as she tried to run from these shaggy-haired people. She couldn't really see their faces, only open mouths with large, pointed teeth. Breath came harder and harder, and she seemed to be getting closer to the ground as she moved. Tÿr dared a glance back, and a clawed hand was swiping at her face. Tÿr sat straight up in her bed. Sweat ran into her eyes as she tried to gather her bearings. The dream had been so real she was sure that she was caught.

Outside it was noisy from the men in the village. They were working through the night to bury the village's guardian and chief healer. An ancient wyvern, which had served as healer and magiq user and protector, had passed earlier in the day. The wyvern's human partner had performed several ceremonies on its body as was custom. The heart was removed carefully, as were the teeth, the eyes, and several buckets of its blood. All these would be used in rituals and magiq items for the healers' supply. Powerful potions were made with wyvern parts, and they were very valuable. Some were used to make anesthesia for surgery. Others were used to make very expensive potions that usually only royalty could afford. Many parts were used as armor.

Tÿr laid her head back on the bed as she listened to the men digging in the field outside the village. The men of Vennex worked tirelessly to dig a hole large enough to hold the body of their former protector. The wyvern had served the village for nearly three hundred years, and she was massive. Aaxtagara had reached ancient status for a wyvern when she reached seven hundred years of age. She was four hundred when she came to Vennex as its protector. Now she lay dead, and the corpse she left was almost seventy feet, and that didn't include the three-foot spike on the end of her tail.

Master carvers and craftsmen would bid on it to see who would win the honor of carving the statue that would adorn the palace of the emperor. All pieces that were removed and not used for the carving would be saved and brought to the human healer left behind. The spike was jet black with a metallic-rainbow sheen and could be used for more magiqal potions. The healer was hoping to fetch a great deal for the spike as it can support him and buy his supplies for many years. Even though the sky was always light on this part of the planet, it wasn't terribly bright right now. The planet was beginning to slingshot back to the suns, where it would get brighter and hotter as the first summer season began.

Tÿr got out of her small bed and walked to her window. The three suns were still far enough away they didn't cause the grueling heat of summer, but the temperature was still warm enough to cause her to sweat. She could see the men in the field if she looked to the side of her house. *They must be miserable*, she thought, *but at least it isn't summer*. Even during the night, it was unbearable.

The planets she lived on were called Peyda Kirin and Peyda Noirin. They were connected by a thick section of land where she lived. She was grateful that she lived on this part of the planets. The smaller of the two planets that were connected was called Peyda Kirin, and it was made up of mainly desert, according to the studies she received in school. Peyda Noirin was larger and situated behind the other, so much of the front of it was in shadow, as was the mass of land her people inhabited. Anyone who lived in this section were called mid-dwellers. In the middle, there were more seasons than on either of the planets.

Peyda Kirin faced the tri-sun system and was mainly covered with desert. Peyda Noirin was behind and always faced away from the suns. It was covered in violent seas and thousands of islands. She knew there would be no more sleep for her, so Tÿr went to her trunk and pulled out the clothes she planned to wear for the ceremony. She figured that maybe she'd go watch the men finish the enormous hole needed to bury the old wyvern. These events rarely took place as wyverns had incredibly long life spans. Most people hadn't seen the ritual as the last wyvern to die was over 150 years ago, at least according to the records kept by the people of the planets.

Tÿr lived in a small cottage on the property of her father's brother. Her uncle was the magistrate of Vennex and had a huge amount of land. Her parents and her grandfather all had places on the property. When she came of age, her uncle had a cottage built for her. It was nothing as fancy as the manor he lived in with his young wife, but she was happy.

One day, when her parents were gone, she would own the house they lived in. During the day, she usually helped her father at his shop. He was a furniture maker, and she helped with the carving on special orders. Tÿr learned carving when she was ten, and by the time she was eighteen, she was as good as her father. At least that was what the people of Vennex said. She often went to help the healer and the wyvern in her free time. They would send her on errands to deliver salves and potions or out to the fields or woods to collect herbs for use in medicines.

What she wanted to do was be a healer like Kuired, the healer for Vennex and the surrounding areas. He had worked with the now-deceased wyvern, Aaxtagara, for around thirty years. Unfortunately, women were never chosen to be healers, and she was too old to start. The wyverns were the ones that chose the new healer apprentice, and they were usually ten years younger than she was. She didn't feel that twenty-three was too old, but there was so much to learn. Kuired had allowed her to assist with many of the preparations and rituals that went into healing. Even Aaxtagara had seemed to be pleased with her work, as pleased as any wyvern could seem.

As Tÿr neared the grave site, she felt an emptiness in the pit of her stomach. Even though she wasn't sure a person could ever be close to a wyvern, she had a great fondness for the creature lying before her. The once-shining, deep-blue scales were dull, and she could see everlasting places where scales were missing. She knew of the tradition of removing certain pieces of the dead wyvern, but it seemed like such irreverence to do it. She also knew that if it wasn't done, raiders from villages near and far would come looking for prizes to sell on the black market. The dynasty of wyverns that Aaxtagara had come from would post guards over the grave of their fallen family member for weeks to keep the grave-robbing to a minimum. She knew this was just the way of life and death, and many in her village would think her ridiculous for getting upset over what they considered a wild beast. It made her heart heavy to see the great bulk of Aaxtagara just lying there.

It was getting time for people to begin rising from their sleep. Though the suns never really set on this part of her world, Tÿr could tell that in less than an hour, people would be up and bustling about. Birds were beginning to fly around. Some dove down to try and feed on the huge wyvern carcass. She tried to shoo them away. Some of the men looked up with fondness. Most everyone liked Tÿr and knew she was friendly with the wyvern. Others simply shook their heads, not so much in disgust but in exasperation that a person could care for a beast. A great deal of these men were farmers and looked at animals as servants of humans. It was the farmers' way.

The pile of blue earth that sat near the body of Aaxtagara was huge. It would remain there until the whole ceremony was over. Most of the villagers didn't know what to expect. No human alive on either planet had ever witnessed a funeral rite in their life. Even the magistrate and the council had to look up the procedure. The only person who was sure of anything was Kuired. He'd been briefed by the great wyvern before she died. He had let Tÿr know some of the things that would happen. One thing was that Aaxtagara's entire dynasty would arrive shortly before the ceremony to pay their respects. He did tell her that they would help to cut down on the grave-robbing, but hadn't said much more than that. He was very stricken with grief at the death of his partner and mentor. They had been together every day for over thirty years. Never had Tÿr heard a cross word between the two, though they didn't speak a lot.

Tÿr felt she had done enough standing around. She figured her parents would both be awake by now. Both were early risers, which was where she got it. She turned from the huge pit and the wyvern and began to walk back to her parents' home. If she was in time, maybe she could wrangle some breakfast. As she neared the house, she could see the familiar blue-grey smoke lifting gently from the chimney. If there was smoke, breakfast would be close behind. As she reached the door, she could smell the kettle of qafi. Qafi was the breakfast drink in her country. Many of the older people drank it throughout the day as well. Most homes kept a pot on the fire in case any visitors stopped in. Qafi came from the qii tree. It was abundant in the mountains and forests on the peninsula she lived. Everyone drank it. It was nutritious and had many vitamins, and you didn't have to be rich to drink it. The trees grew everywhere and produced the seeds year-round. Even babies were given qafi to drink when there wasn't anything else. Tÿr opened the heavy front door to the cabin and saw her mother preparing breakfast. There were strips of wild-hog meat frying in a pan over the fire and a cauldron that had boiling water to make the mash, cut-up pieces of a wetland, grass-root cormel called Zea tricasia, also known as Z-tri—not a favorite of Tÿr but her mum usually had some berries or mushrooms and wild onions to mix with it.

"Hi, Mum," Tÿr said as she walked over to the lady working at the fire.

"You're up early, m'dear," her mum replied. "Grab some qafi and sit. It's nearly ready."

Tÿr grabbed her usual mug and a cloth to grab the handle of the kettle. She poured herself a very full cup.

"You don't want any honey for that?" her mother asked. "How do you drink it without sweetening it?"

They had the same conversation every morning and since Tÿr could remember. Tÿr liked the bitter flavor of the qafi, but nearly everyone drank it with some form of sweetener, usually honey. Tÿr had never liked honey, even when she was young. Her two best friends could eat it straight from the hive, but she thought it revolting. As a child, Kuired had recommended that she take honey with a home-distilled spirit, and she hated it. To this day, the smell of honey made her gag.

Tÿr sat back on her stool and drew in the smell of the qafi. It made her taste buds scream. Slowly she put the cup to her mouth and drew in the bitter liquid. This was what she liked most of all, sitting in her mother's kitchen with a mug of qafi while breakfast cooked. Her dad would soon come in from his shop. He'd probably been out there for an hour or more. As she waited to eat, she thought about the upcoming ceremony for her friend. *Yes, friend,* she thought. They had been friends. Aaxtagara didn't say much, but they had gotten close, especially in the final year. She smiled to herself as she remembered her friend, and that was when she decided that she would go to Kuired and ask to help him. He would surely need help now that it was just him.

Tÿr must have had a particularly determined look on her face because her mother noticed and asked, "There's that look. What's going on in that head of yours, lass?"

"Huh? Oh, I was just, uh, it's nothing," she said, shaking her head.

Her mum had a knowing look as she smirked. "Okay, if you say so. Why don't you go fetch your da so we can eat?"

The young woman thought about telling her mother but thought better of it. She knew that she'd get a mini lecture about how being a healer was a man's job and that her father liked having her help at the shop. *Yes,* she thought, *best I keep this to myself.*

She got off her seat and walked out of the cottage and to the shop. She could hear her father humming as he worked. Helping around the shop was nice, but she just wanted more.

Chapter 1

The day began with the suns in the sky, but as the time for the ceremony drew close, clouds blew in from the sea. It set the stage for the somber occasion. The entire village of Vennex was in attendance. There were also people from other countries that Tÿr didn't recognize. Even the emperor was there in his finest robes. They were just waiting for her uncle, the magistrate, and Kuired, the village healer. They would both partake in the ceremony to honor Aaxtagara. Then the wyvern dynasty that Aaxtagara had belonged to would also do something. No one really knew what to expect.

Tÿr glanced around to see if she could find her two friends. She wondered where they could be. She was sure they wouldn't miss this for anything. Her friends, two brothers, and her had spent almost every day together since they were young children. Danior was the older one, a year older than her and his younger brother, Gordian. Gordian was twenty-one and cared for his older brother as he was blind. The three were inseparable, and if one was in trouble, they all were. She tried to see over the heads of the crowd around her, but she was too short to see very far. Tÿr hoped that Gordian and Danior were close. Gordian was very tall, and she'd have no trouble spotting him. After a minute, she gave up though. The palankeen litter bearers had set the emperor down and were standing at attention as they waited. A light rain began to fall as everyone stood around. There was almost complete silence among the joyless crowd. Even the bright clothes of the emperor seemed dim.

Movement from the village drew everyone's attention. Tÿr's uncle and Kuired were walking toward the crowd. Kuired was wearing a bright-red tunic that Tÿr had never seen before, and he was carrying his staff. He only used the staff when performing difficult magiq or healing. Týr began to look around. Where was the group of wyverns? She figured they would be here already. Many of the others gathered around the giant pit must have been thinking similar thoughts as they were looking around too. Týr glanced at the people who had assembled there and realized how many people she didn't know. Now that she was paying attention, she could see just how many people were there. There were more than double the village's population. What a crowd!

She also began to feel a bit underdressed. Most everyone was there in their finery. She hadn't understood what a huge deal this ceremony was. There were dignitaries from neighboring villages, as well as people from other countries. Some of the attire was completely foreign to her.

In the distance, Týr heard what sounded like a rustling noise. It was growing louder and louder, and people began to look around. Kuired and the magistrate reached their spot in front of the gathered crowd. The rain had begun to fall a bit harder as the two stood solemnly behind a small platform that Týr hadn't noticed before. People were looking up into the sky as the flapping noise raised in volume. Týr looked skyward and was startled to see the sky filled with wyverns of all sizes. Some were smaller than Aaxtagara, and there were several that dwarfed even her. Even though the skies were filled with dark rain clouds, the scales reflected the light that there was, and the water made them sparkle like jewels. The older creatures had deep-blue scales that reflected colors like purple and orange and pink. The younger wyvern scales were the palest blue and almost opalescent. Many of the larger ones were missing all or parts of their black tail spike. Great green wings beat the air as they neared. It was almost majestic as, one by one, the large, winged serpents landed softly. It was incredible to Týr how quietly the huge creatures could land. She had expected the ground to tremble beneath their limbs as they sat down but was amazed at the grace. Siolad Týr watched as the winged guests landed and folded their wings down to use as front limbs. Kuired stood at his side, all the while barely moving. Rain dripped from his face as he waited for the crowd to settle down. The arrival of the wyvern dynasty was an awe-inspiring sight. Tÿr wondered what the village would ever do if that was an invading force. There were at least fifty of the enormous lizardlike reptiles. The crowd seemed to drink in the atmosphere as well, realizing that this was a once-in-a-lifetime event. Most people didn't really think they would ever have another chance to witness an event of this magnitude.

When the wyverns had settled on the ground around the crowd, both the magistrate and healer took a step up the platform. Kuired raised his staff, and silence fell immediately. The head of the staff began to glow a bright red, and the healer spoke directly to the largest wyvern.

The crowd listened intently as Kuired began.

"Almighty Ghra'zhenn, I come before you today with the deepest sadness. Your sister has passed from this world and into the next. Please accept the sympathy of the people of the village of Vennex. We mourn the loss of your sister, Aaxtagara, and appeal to your creators for a swift and blessed crossing."

The wyvern paragon dipped his massive head in acknowledgment. Tÿr watched intently as her uncle stepped forward. Siolad Tÿr took the glowing staff from the other man on the platform as he, too, spoke to the wyverns.

"Mighty dynasty! As is tradition, I ask that you lay to rest your loyal servant. Aaxtagara served us with dignity and the utmost loyalty. She will be sorely missed by our village. I pray her fair winds on her final voyage."

All the wyverns dipped their heads in unison. The occasion was a very solemn one, and even the young children in attendance seemed to know this as hardly a word escaped any of them. Tÿr brushed a tear away from her cheek. She had known the wyvern her entire life and had come to call her a friend, despite the fact that there had only been a handful of words exchanged between the two of them. Wyverns were not known as verbal creatures. They could speak, but rarely chose to.

Siolad Tÿr continued to the wyvern dynasty, "Please lay to rest your sister in your custom as is fit for her station."

Tỹr's uncle passed the staff back to Kuired, and immediately the beautifully carved head ceased to glow. The magistrate turned back to face the crowd.

"Please step away from the grave site. The wyverns will now entrust the body of their beloved sister back to the earth, which will hold her body for eternity."

There was a bit of confusion from the people gathered. They glanced around at each other. No one wanted to give up their place at the side of the burial place, but as the wyverns began to approach, they decided it was better to move. The emperor's palankeen carriers cleared a place in front of everyone else, and the other dignitaries tried to squeeze in around him. Some villagers yielded to them, but others stubbornly refused to surrender their spots. It was their town's fallen healer and protector after all. When everyone had finished moving back, some of the larger wyverns gathered around Aaxtagara. They used their heads or hands on the ends of their wings to move the corpse into the great pit. Even with the steady rain, a cloud of blue dust rose from the bottom of the grave as the body hit the bottom.

All the wyverns circled the grave, peering in at the deceased. The paragon began to speak in the deep, guttural language of the wyverns, Cmok. The crowd watched in rapt attention, listening as the ancient wyvern spoke. When he finished what Tỹr figured was some type of eulogy, he looked around and spoke to the crowd.

"And now we send the spirit of our dear sister, Aaxtagara, to her place among our beloved ancestors."

As soon as he finished, he turned back to the dead body. One by one, the throats of the wyverns began to glow. Then, in unison, they opened their large mouths, and blinding white fire shot at the corpse in the grave. Within just moments, the body was reduced to a smoking black lump and ashes. With this, the wyverns backed away from the hole, and the village men stepped forward with their shovels. They immediately began to fill in the grave site. *Wow*, thought Tỹr, *that was fast*. She wasn't sure what she had expected, but she'd figured that it would last longer.

Siolad Týr stepped back up the podium and called for the crowd's attention. With his hands raised, he cleared his throat and began to speak once again.

"Today I am afraid I have more sad news to bestow on my village of Vennex. After speaking to our beloved village healer, Kuired, I have been advised that he will be departing our village to seek new endeavors. A village in the forest nearer the planet Peyda Kirin will be the benefactor of his knowledge and talents. He feels that he cannot stay any longer now that his longtime friend and mentor has passed on."

Shock ran through Týr's chest. She had not seen this coming at all. She had visited Kuired following the death of Aaxtagara, and he had never mentioned any of this to her. He had been down, but she never imagined that he would leave. A weight fell on her chest too. Not only would she be losing a friend but she would also be losing her chance to train as a healer. Týr immediately felt bad for these selfish feelings, but she would be losing her chance.

When the magistrate finished talking to the crowd, Kuired stepped back up the podium.

"My friends, it is with a very heavy heart that I find that I must leave the village of Vennex. When my mentor passed on, I took it as a sign, and I have spoken to the village of Yelliton, who has found itself without a master healer. I will be leaving almost immediately to take up the post. Before I go, I have organized with the magistrate to hold a tournament to help decide a new apprentice healer. This apprentice will train under the instruction of Vennex's new wyvern protector."

At this, the group of wyverns opened, and a young wyvern of approximately twenty-five feet moved forward. Its scales were still light blue, signifying it to be under two hundred years old. It was slender in build and moved gracefully toward the podium, where both the magistrate and Kuired stood. Its black eyes glittered brightly despite the dark rain clouds above. As the young wyvern moved to the platform with Týr'Ynyn's uncle and Kuired, the healer continued to speak.

"In two days' time, the young men in the village who wish to apply for the position of apprentice will gather at this memorial site.

Together with myself, your new wyvern protector and the magistrate will gather to select the young man most worthy of this honored position. It is a task that will be very difficult, and the sacrifices will be great. The eventual post of master healing requires extreme devotion to oneself and the village under his care. Everything must come second to him once the profession has been entered. Friends may need to come before family, or even self. It is difficult and at times extraordinarily tiring. Please only consider yourself for this career if you intend to devote the rest of your life to serving people. There are even times when you may need to help wild creatures. Oftentimes this position can feel thankless, but for me, it has been the most rewarding thing I have ever chosen to do."

Tÿr felt some jostling and nudging coming from behind her as she stood listening to the village master healer. She turned and came face-to-face with her friends.

"Hey, Tÿr beer!" Gordian said in a low voice.

Tÿr knew Gordian had meant to whisper, but she also knew that there was nothing in his physical makeup that would allow him to whisper. He was loud, the same as his mother. Danior was much quieter and held up his hand to wave.

"Hey, Tÿr!"

"Where have you guys been?"

"Looking for you." Danior smiled. "It's terribly hard to see you in this crowd."

"It's terribly hard for you to see anything, you idgit," she joked back. "In case you've forgotten, you're blind."

"I knew there was a reason I couldn't find you."

Tÿr and the boys joked about this all the time. It was okay for them, but if anyone outside their little group tried it, they would have to deal with the three of them, and Tÿr knew from experience that Danior could hit pretty hard. They only ever play smacked each other, but she was sure that if he was mad enough, he could do some real damage to anyone or anything in his path.

"Have you been here the whole time?" Gordian again attempted a whisper. Several people looked to see who was talking.

"Yes, I have," Tÿr responded.

"I think I may try out for the apprenticeship," Gordian stated matter-of-factly.

"Shh!" Several people turned to shush him.

"Yeah, keep quiet for a minute, Gordi. I want to hear what Kuired is saying."

It was a sure sign that Gordian thought a lot of Tÿr'Ynyn because he immediately quieted. He usually listened to her or his older brother. The trio of them got on so well there were hardly ever any disagreements, and if they did argue, it was usually over when Gordian made some type of inappropriate comment. Tÿr glanced at Danior, who shifted his head to hear better as well.

Kuired mainly explained the rules of the upcoming tourney. He said that it was open to anyone who felt like their life was leading them into a path of service. When he concluded his speech, he thanked the wyvern dynasty for their participation in the ceremony of his departed friend and mentor. He also thanked them for the appointment of the new wyvern. It turned out that the new protector and mentor's name was Varanus and that he and the paragon would also take part in the choosing of the new apprentice.

"What do you mean?" Tÿr asked Gordi suddenly, in the softest voice she could produce.

"What?"

"What do you mean you're going to enter the challenge?

Gordian stared at his friend for a second before his face broke into a huge grin.

"Of course, I'm going to try. You should too, Tÿr!" he told her.

Danior snorted his amusement. "You're way too old to sign up, and besides, who's going to help me?"

Tÿr, too, was laughing quietly. "I'll take care of you, Dani, but there is no way Gordi will ever stand a chance. You know he's too old. You have to start the training to be a town physician when you're ten or twelve."

"I could do it!" Gordian said defiantly. "I'm smart enough. I used to help Kuired too, if you'll remember!"

"Yes, you did, and you're plenty smart, but you are too old!" Tÿr shook her head in exasperation.

Danior didn't even try to hide his amusement. He, too, knew his brother could do it, but he also knew that he would never like it. Gordian was rash sometimes and did things more on a whim and to prove he could than because he truly wanted to.

Gordi had set his chin, but when he saw the amusement on the faces of the other two, he joined in chuckling with them.

The trio noticed that people were beginning to stir and talk now. The ceremony was over. Tÿr wanted to run and catch up to Kuired. She couldn't believe that he was leaving. He must have taken the death of Aaxtagara much harder than she thought.

Why didn't he say anything to me? I thought he liked it here. Why does he have to go now? All these things were running through her mind. She tried to see if she could spot Kuired by the podium, but he was nowhere to be seen. It was as if he had simply vanished. Tÿr knew that he could do some basic magiq, but she had never seen him just disappear.

"Come on!" she yelled as she grabbed Danior by the hand and practically pulled him off his feet.

"What's going... Where are we going, and why must we run?" Danior yelled after her, trying to keep his footing.

"Just hurry!"

Gordi was keeping up with them by holding his brother's other hand. "Tÿr!"

"Just keep up," she yelled back over her shoulder.

Danior was peddling his feet as best he could in the situation. It wasn't the first time Tÿr had ever dragged him behind like this. It didn't make it easier though. They weaved in between people as Tÿr dragged them toward the platform that her uncle and the healer had occupied just minutes before. Rain still drizzled from a grey sky as she ran, pulling her friends behind impatiently.

"Hey, watch it!"

"Look where you're going!"

Cries and reprimands from several people in the crowd bombarded them as they wound their way forward.

"Oy! Watch out!"

8

"I'm trying!" Danior yelled back over his shoulder. Both boys laughed as they ran on.

Tÿr finally spotted her uncle talking to some people she had never seen. They were dressed in desert garb and talking animatedly to the magistrate. He seemed to be amused by what they were saying because he laughed at almost everything they said. Tÿr figured one of them was probably a high magistrate or lord high magistrate. The clothing was hard to decipher because on Peyda Kirin most everyone in the desert wore the same type of clothing. The main difference was in the cleanliness of it. Near the midlands, there were more water sources, so garments were washed more often. Much depended on the water source and the distance from it. Still, there were caravans that pulled huge wagons filled with massive containers of water. They traveled to the farthest reaches of the desert planet.

Another determining factor on the station of people was the brightness of their clothing. The lower the station, the more faded the garb. Leaders and people in positions of power always had bright clothing. They rarely spent time in the suns, and so the fabric didn't fade as much.

"Uncle Siolad, Uncle Sio—"

Her uncle raised his beefy hand to cut her short. He was still listening to the dignitaries from the desert and chuckling politely. The foreigners talked with a unique accent. Their skin was well-tanned too. The suns often darkened the skin of Kirin-folk.

When the gentleman with the long yellow headscarf finished speaking, Siolad Tÿr turned to his niece. "Tÿr, what can I help you with?"

He put his chubby hand on her shoulder as he waited for her to respond.

"Lord High Magistrate Chinastri, may I present my niece, Tÿr, and her friends."

Chinastri nodded politely to her and the brothers. Tÿr gave a quick wave and turned back to her uncle.

"Uncle Sio, have you seen Kuired? I've been trying to locate him, but he seems to have disappeared. I looked one second, and he was here. I glanced away, and now he seems to have just vanished!"

9

"He went back to his dwelling. Now, don't you go bothering. He has more important things to do than entertain you three!" Her uncle smiled, but the twinkle was not in his eyes.

"Uh, okay, thanks! Talk to you later, Uncle!" She turned her back on him and began to pull Danior along again. This time he almost fell.

"Hey, psycho, warn me before you do that again!" he called up at her. He didn't think that she even heard him, and the three began to snake their way toward Kuired's home. Again, people had to jump back or twist out of her way.

"Leave him alone, Tÿr!" her uncle called out as they ran toward the healer's home. "Just let him finish what he's doing!"

Tÿr threw up her hand in acknowledgment but continued her determined trek to see Kuired.

Chapter 2

Danior and Gordian were already standing outside Tÿr's parents' house when she strolled up from her cottage. The morning was bright and completely clear. No cloud marred the sky.

"Hey, guys." Tÿr waved as she joined them.

"You're going to the tests, aren't you?" Gordian queried.

"Wouldn't miss them!"

Tÿr walked past the brothers and opened the front door. Smells of wild-hog meat and Z-tri with onion and mushroom accosted her senses as she entered the home.

"Something smells wonderful!" Danior yelled out as he followed his brother and Tÿr inside.

Elmky turned to greet her daughter and her friends as they entered the cooking area.

"Hello, boys! Lassie! Are you headed down to the tourney this morning?"

"Of course, Mum. We don't want to miss this. Maybe I'll try out."

"Yeah, me too!" Gordian added.

Her mom rolled her eyes and shook her head, exasperated. "Now, you both know that you're too old to try out. Besides, lassie, you know girls aren't allowed!"

Tÿr objected immediately. "Nowhere does it say that girls can't enter. They just don't. A woman can do the job as well as any man!"

"That may be true," Elmky agreed, "but no young lady has ever been chosen. There's simply no sense in trying."

Tÿr let it drop. If she didn't, her dad would be in to join her mum's side, and she'd end up missing the tourney. The family "discussions" could go on for hours once her father got his feet under him. She could see that Gordi was dying to join in, so she put a hand on his shoulder and discreetly shook her head. He took the hint and closed his mouth. The trio of them hopped on stools and watched as Tÿr'Ynyn's mum finished the meal. They discussed the upcoming event quietly as they drank their mugs of hot qafi. Tÿr watched Gordian spoon honey into his mug. The thought of drinking it that way made her physically ill. Within minutes, Seryth Tÿr walked in from his shop. Her dad glanced at the trio of them on the stools and broke into a big smile.

"Good morning, my dear." He nodded to Tÿr. "Boys."

Danior raised his mug in greeting, slopping a bit on himself.

"Oh, dang it!" he said, wiping it off his pants with his hand.

"The boys are going to join us for breakfast if that's okay, Mum."

Elmky smiled at her daughter. "Don't they always. I hope there's enough."

Tÿr rolled her eyes at the boys. Her mum always worried about having enough food at every meal, and she always ended up throwing some out. Elmky Tÿr had just made a habit of making enough to feed the boys every morning. She was worried that they didn't get enough to eat at their own home. The boys still lived with their mother. Their father had died a few years back, and she liked to keep them around for company and to help with things around the house. She usually fed them before they came over to Tÿr'Ynyn's parents', but Gordian had an insatiable appetite and could eat for hours if left to himself. Danior just really enjoyed Elmky's cooking.

"So are you three heading down to the field for the healers' tournament?" Tÿr's father asked.

"Yes, sir," Danior replied. "Gordian thinks he could make it as a healer, so I'm going just to watch."

Seryth Tÿr gave an incredulous look at Gordian. "You're way too old to try out for that, son. They won't even let you try. If I know my brother, he's already made up his mind. I believe that wife of his has been putting a bug in his ear about choosing her son. He just turned fourteen. I told him that the boy was too old at fourteen. If I remember the lad, he's about as sharp as a marble."

The trio laughed at this. Tÿr knew that her dad didn't much care for his brother's wife. She was stuck-up and looked down on anyone in the town that couldn't do something for her. Even Tÿr's mum smiled politely. She didn't like it when her husband bad-mouthed his brother's wife. She didn't much care for her either, but she would never admit it openly. Elmky tried to be nice to her sister-in-law, but the woman made it very difficult sometimes. Tÿr got off her stool and got the cloth to grab the kettle. She was sure this was probably the third of the morning already. Her dad could usually drink an entire kettle by himself before the morning meal. Her mum drank qafi too but usually sipped one or two cups over the course of the morning.

"Here you go, Da," Tÿr said as she handed him another mug.

Seryth Tÿr smiled as he took the mug. He always used a mug in the house, but he had a larger tankard that he kept in his shop. His wife hated his tankard because it was grimy and always covered in sawdust. She refused to let it in her clean house. Tÿr helped her mum dish out the mash to the men in the room. The pot was still over half full. Her mum had worried needlessly. Everyone took their hog strips and pulled them into pieces and then tossed them into their bowls of mash. Everything helped to flavor Z-tri. Elmky got up from her seat at the bar and went to her pantry. She brought back a small bowl with chopped green herbs in it.

"Does anyone fancy some fresh herbs?"

"Yes, please!" both boys said in unison.

In Vennex herbs with a meal were a treat. Tÿr often went into the woods to collect them. Her mum sold herbs at a stand in the village square each day to bring in a little "pocket silver," as her mum called it. Anyone could go into the forest or near the Ajenti River to pick them, but most of the villagers either didn't know what to look for or didn't care to. Her mother's business could bring in a good amount of silver on some days. It just depended on the herbs she found. Some were quite rare, and so they fetched a decent price.

Elmky Tÿr also had some fowl around their property that she fed and then collected the eggs. Some of the eggs, too, brought in a fair amount. A few of the rarer birds' eggs were delicacies in Vennex. Eggs were not often served in her parents' house. Her mother hated the smell that they gave off when cooking. Tÿr loved forest hen eggs if they were fried in hog fat and then put in the morning mash, or if they were boiled and crumbled in. Her dad really liked eggs as well, but if the boys were there to eat with them, her mom's profits took a dive. Gordian could easily eat twelve, and Danior could eat half as many. If her dad had six, that was two dozen eggs her mum couldn't sell. They usually only got them for the morning meal if her mum had any left over from the day before. She refused to sell the old eggs.

Tÿr spent the entire meal steering the conversation away from that morning's tournament. She had to elbow Gordian in the ribs several times before he finally cottoned on. Danior knew immediately after the first time he heard his brother grunt from the sharp elbow in the side. By the fourth time, he was attempting to stifle his chuckling. When the five of them were finished eating, Tÿr jumped up and collected the bowls for her mother and put them in the washbasin.

"We hate to eat and run, but we want to be there when the thing starts!"

The brothers took their cue and stood up. They thanked Elmky for the delicious meal, as they always did, and practically ran for the door. Elmky Tÿr sighed and waved as the trio sped from the cottage to the field. Her husband smiled at her and got up to pour himself another mug of qafi.

The trio wasted no time getting to the field where the tourney would take place. They barely slowed to wave or greet anyone on the way down. There was already a small crowd gathering near the site where Aaxtagara was buried. Tÿr saw the honor guard posted at the grave site. Sometime between the funeral ceremony and this morning, a small wooden pavilion had been erected next to the deceased wyvern's resting place. Tÿr and the boys slowed as they passed it. There was a plaque on one of the pillars that held the pergola's slatted roof up. There had also been some type of vine planted at the base of each pillar. Tÿr thought how nice it would look when the vines had grown over a couple of seasons. She recognized the vine as a flowering type of ivy that many people planted on trellises. When it was in full bloom, the yellowish-orange flowers would be amazing. There were three long tables set in the field with two short stools in front of the middle one. On top of the tables sat many different things under covers. On either side of the tables, two of Tÿr'Ynyn's uncle's own guards stood with their staff bolines in their hands—long-handled weapons with a large, crescent-shaped blade at the top and three long prongs on the opposite end. Obviously, they were ordered there to keep curious villagers or hopeful apprentices who wanted an advantage away. Tÿr steered the boys away from the gathering crowd and as close to the front of the tables as she dared.

"That's close enough, you three. You must remain fifteen feet back from the tables at all times!" The guard closest to them sneered.

He was the same age as they were. They had all been in classes together when they were younger. He hadn't been pleasant then either. The trio of them despised him. He had only gotten the position as guard to the magistrate because his father had pulled some strings for him. It didn't go anywhere to popularize him with his former classmates nor the rest of the town. He had been a bit of a bully in school, and now he got paid to be an ass.

"Whatever, R'auva," Gordian said and made a rude gesture to the young guard.

R'auva started to say something, but Gordian turned his back on him and grinned at Tÿr. Others in the small crowd seemed to think Tÿr had a good idea, and so they, too, moved closer to the tables. The trio grew restless as people gathered around them. Danior did not do well in crowded situations. Even though he couldn't see, he often said how he felt boxed in. Gordi made sure people didn't get too close to them, and the guards in front didn't let anyone step in front of the three.

Luckily, the gathered village didn't have to wait very long. Within just a short time, the sound of flapping wings from above filled the air as two wyverns began their descent to the field. They both landed on the blue earth with a slight puff of sand. Tÿr recognized both wyverns on sight. The largest was the paragon of the dynasty that had led the wyvern part of Aaxtagara's ceremony, and the much-smaller one was the incoming protector of Vennex, Varanus. The two stood in stark contrast next to each other. Varanus was so much lighter in color than the ancient one. Most of the crowd had been watching the arrival of the winged visitors; they hadn't noticed Kuired or Siolad Tÿr arrive. The two men walked over to greet the large, reptilelike creatures. Kuired was walking with his long staff. Tÿr'Ynyn took this as a sign that this meant that some type of magiq was sure to be employed. She loved watching the healer use magiq. It fascinated her above all else that he did. When things were in place, the four walked over to the tables. The men took places behind the stools at the middle table, and the wyverns stood off to their left. Kuired raised both hands, and the staff in his left began its familiar glow. The villagers silenced straightaway.

"Friends and families of Vennex, distinguished guests, we are gathered here to choose your town's new apprentice healer," he began.

He went on to again explain the hardships of the job and the sacrifices required. When he had finished, he called the wyverns up near the tables and made introductions.

"I'd like you to join me in again welcoming the paragon wyvern from the dynasty called Achkrih and your town's new mentor, protector, and mediator to the paragon, Varanus."

Cheers sounded immediately. The welcome was well-received, and the people appeared to want the new protector. Vennex did have its own militia under the command of Siolad Tÿr, but they were mainly used to keep roving beasts and thieves and other problems in check. They did, on occasion, need to actually fight for territory disputes, but they were few and far between. Dani and Gordi's father had lost his life serving in the Vennex militia while attempting to fight off a group of rogue wyverns from a distant wyvern dynasty.

When Kuired was done with the introductions, he called the entrants forward. The magistrate walked out of the crowd and came back toward the tables, leading his son, Sämir, with hands on his shoulders. One other lone boy followed with his mother. Tÿr knew of the boy, but not much about him. She had already guessed that her cousin would be the winner of the tournament whether he deserved it or not. Despite the fact that he wasn't the smartest, Tÿr knew her uncle escorted his son to the front of the eager crowd as an intimidation scheme. She, too, was sure that Siolad Tÿr had been talking to Kuired privately about giving his son the prestigious position. Tÿr also knew that Kuired was a very fair and impartial man, so there was a slim chance the other boy might win. As the two boys took their places in front of the tables, the magistrate went back and sat on his low stool. It had been fitted with a large cushion. No doubt for his large backside, Tÿr knew. Then in a surprise move, Kuired looked directly at Tÿr'Ynyn and gestured her to come forward. At first, she thought she was mistaken and glanced around to see who he had meant. But when he pointed at her again and called her forward, there was no doubt. Tÿr shot a panicked look at her friends before jogging to the front. Gordi just shrugged and gave her a gentle push forward.

"What's going on?" She heard Danior ask his brother. She was already out of earshot to hear the response.

She approached the healer with apprehension. If her parents were here, they would bother her about joining this tourney for weeks. She relaxed a bit when Kuired simply asked her to remove the covers from all the items on the tables. There was a little bit of disappointment as well, but she knew she'd never have a chance if her cousin was competing for the spot. Tÿr went down the tables, uncovering each object. She recognized everything under the lids, from the plants to the stones and potions in the little bottles. She returned to her spot in the front of the crowd next to her friends when she had finished. Her uncle also moved back to his padded stool behind the table, next to the healer. The wyverns stood and watched as the event began to unfold. Then Kuired called order again. His staff was still in his hand, but resting on the ground at his side. The headpiece still glowed a warm crimson.

"I now call the village to order and declare the tournament officially begun." Kuired then looked directly at the two boys standing in front of him and asked, "Do you both pledge to enter this contest with the village's best interest at heart, and do you pledge to put its needs above all else as long as you serve as its apprentice healer?"

Both boys nodded and mumbled an affirmation. The boy turned and looked at his mother, as if to let her know that he no longer required her presence. She nodded once and patted his shoulder fondly before turning and finding a spot in the front of the silent crowd. Kuired began by bringing the boy up to the table where he could talk quietly. He told Sämir to go stand next to the wyverns. Sämir looked at his father, who nodded slightly, and then he walked toward the two huge, lizardlike beasts. Apprehension was written all over the youngster's face. He'd never been so close to a wyvern, let alone two. The paragon eyed him critically as he took his place near, but not too close to them. Tÿr watched as her cousin moved to his spot. It almost felt like the wyvern didn't like her cousin very much at all either.

"The first part of this examination is in general knowledge of ingredients and common items used by the typical healer. It is simply to see how much you know already. It is not a pass-or-fail exam. It is used to show us how great your knowledge in healing is at the present time. If chosen, you will learn all of these things within the first year of your training. The training period for your apprenticeship will last approximately twenty years. Some people finish sooner, and some a bit later. This is your final chance to bow out with no consequence. Do you, Elluur, son of Ellärr, wish to continue?"

Kuired's voice boomed through the crowd. The boy stood as straight as he could and answered, "I wish it."

Elluur, that was his name, Tÿr thought. His father was another who died around the same as her friends' father. Almost fifty men had lost their lives in that conflict. The village watched as, one by one, Elluur attempted to identify the items on the tables. Tÿr tried to will the answers to him just to keep her cousin from winning. Her cousin, Sämir, wasn't the nicest person in the village, and she personally hoped to have someone smarter than him should she require medical attention in the future. Kuired would name different herbs or crystals or salves and ask Elluur to identify the proper item on the table. Tÿr would nod slightly as the boy got to the correct object or component of a salve or potion or would try to imperceptibly shake her head if he reached for the wrong one. More than once she looked up and thought she saw the wyvern paragon looking directly at her. Often the wyvern Varanus would throw out a question to the boy as well, things like, "Where would you locate that herb in a forest?" or,

"What are the main uses of that crystal?" Questions that Tÿr knew the answers to.

The boy answered several of the questions correctly, but he also missed a fair amount as well. Each time he missed a question, her uncle would fake a sympathetic smile and then glance toward his son and give him an imperceptible wink. Siolad's smugness incensed Tÿr. The boy was doing his best, and for her uncle to make all those ridiculous faces in front of the village really made her angry. It was as if the choice had already been made and this tournament was just a formality. Sämir would do no better when it was his turn. Hopefully, that would knock the grin off her uncle's pompous face. The question-and-answer session went on for practically an hour before Kuired was satisfied. Other than the odd question during the exam, the pair of wyverns sat and watched stoically, barely moving at all. Tÿr'Ynyn was sure that the paragon, Ghra'zhenn, kept looking at her, but it was so hard to tell. He hardly moved his head, and his eyes were pitch black, making it impossible to see where he was looking. On the rare occasion that he or Varanus did move, he would stretch his long neck close to the junior wyvern and quietly whisper something to him. Most of the time, the younger creature would just nod or say one or two words back to his leader.

It was Sämir's turn now. He strutted to the tables with a big, goofy grin plastered on his face. He seemed to know something that the crowd didn't. Tÿr noticed that his cocky strut to the tables didn't faze either of the wyverns. They sat without one sign of emotion. Wyverns were hard to read on the best of days, but today Tÿr was sure that they almost appeared bored. Apparently, his birthright held no sway over them. Tÿr just hoped that they had enough authority at these proceedings to choose the best candidate, not the one with the best pedigree. Her cousin began, and it was clear that he had absolutely no knowledge about any of the items on the tables. He missed eight of the first ten identifications. Kuired, who was usually unreadable, even began to show his amazement at the boy's total lack of knowledge. He had glanced at the magistrate at one point, and her uncle could only shrug his shoulders. Embarrassment was easily read on Siolad Tÿr's face now. The gloating smile had suddenly faded. Then after a couple more questions, the second boy began to answer the questions correctly. He didn't miss any of the next twenty identifications. Kuired had even asked a couple of trick questions, and though the boy took several extra seconds to answer them, he managed to even get them correct. Gordian tapped Tÿr on the back, and she found him with a puzzled look on his face.

"What's up with this?" he asked in a voice that he thought was a whisper.

Tÿr shrugged her shoulders, as puzzled as he was, and mouthed, "I have no idea!" She glanced over at the wyverns, who were both as still as statues. Their giant figures dwarfed the boy. It was then that Tÿr'Ynyn spotted something off to her left in front of the crowd. Sämir's mother, her aunt Ellysse, stood in front of the village like she often did on major events. Tÿr saw that she was gesturing to her son. What the crowd obviously thought was contemplation on the boy's part was stalling until his mother told him which item to choose. How anyone else didn't notice this was beyond Tÿr. The girl turned back to her friend who was standing just behind her. He was tall enough to see over her and his brother's head. She inconspicuously told him to look over at her aunt. It took a second, but then he caught on.

"Is something wrong?" Danior asked the other two. "What are you whispering about?"

Gordi went to speak, and in his excited state, Tÿr put a finger to his lips before he accidentally yelled it out. That was the last thing she needed to deal with. She leaned in to Danior's ear and quietly told him about what her auntie and cousin were up to. His grip tightened on her arm. He had begun to hold onto her because his brother had moved behind the two others so they could see and didn't take up so much of the front row. Tÿr really wanted to shout out to Kuired and the wyverns to stop the contest. It was completely unfair to the other boy, and no one else saw, or if they did, they didn't care. Kuired was getting ready to begin another group of identifications when Ghra'zhenn spoke.

"Honorable Kuired." He turned to her uncle. "Magistrate, I believe we have seen enough."

Tÿr's uncle's face broke into a great smile.

"You may send these boys away. I believe we may have found a better choice for this position," the wyvern stated matter-of-factly.

Siolad Tÿr's face looked like someone had let out the air from it. The smile had gone as fast as a thunderclap. The magistrate rose from his cushioned seat to protest.

"Respectfully, Mighty Ghra'zhenn, the contest isn't over. How can you decide this so rashly?"

The man was struggling to keep the anger and sarcasm from leaking into his words. His face had turned a deep shade of magenta and was clashing horridly with his yellow-and-violet tunic.

"It is apparent that neither of these young men have enough knowledge to continue on to be an apprentice of this honorable position," Ghra'zhenn stated simply. There was no malice or disdain in his voice.

"Now, just you see here!" the magistrate spat, slamming his hands on the table. "My son has the right to take on this apprenticeship. He has the breeding, and he—"

"Magistrate, I'm afraid your son wasn't answering his own questions. The lady behind you has been directing his actions for the past answers. I cannot, in good faith, allow him to continue."

Again, there wasn't any anger or even accusation in the wyvern's statement. Just the facts. The magistrate, furious, started to spit out more venom when Kuired raised his hand to quiet the fuming man.

"Are you certain that this has been happening, Mighty Paragon?" he questioned the ancient wyvern.

"It has," Ghra'zhenn affirmed. "Varanus and I have been watching this as it has unfolded. The lady was coaching the boy on which items he needed to identify."

"Which woman?" the village magistrate asked as he turned back to see of whom the wyvern was speaking. His face fell even more as it stopped on his wife.

Tÿr would have bet anything that her uncle's face couldn't have gotten any darker, but she would have been wrong. The magenta gave way to a deep purple.

Many people in the crowd began to whisper loudly now. Phrases like, "spoiled brat" and "because his dad is magistrate!" and "who do they think they are?" assaulted Tÿr. She almost felt bad for her uncle, but he didn't seem to feel any remorse nor did he appear to believe the wyvern.

"That is utterly preposterous! My family would never be caught doing something like that!"

The bad feelings left her immediately. If they had been caught, just take the punishment. He wouldn't be making any supporters by trying to let his family get away with it. It was the way he worded it too. "His family would never be *caught*!"

Kuired seemed to be ignoring the large man having a fit next to him and turned back to the wyverns.

"You said that you had another in mind for this position. May I ask who you are speaking about?" he asked the giant lizards.

The crowd appeared to hold its collective breath as they awaited the paragon's response. Danior cocked his head to the side, the way he always did when he was listening for something.

"What did it say?" he questioned quietly.

"Shh!" Gordi and Tÿr hushed him.

"What's going on?" he continued. "I can't hear anything!"

Again, the pair tried to quiet him so they could hear the wyvern's response. Slowly Ghra'zhenn turned his large, viper-shaped head to look directly at Tÿr. Her heart skipped a beat or two. What was going on?

"Please bring forward the young lady in the front row, just there." Ghra'zhenn raised his winged hand and pointed a clawed finger straight at Tÿr.

The crowd all turned to see who the giant paragon was pointing to. Puzzlement ran throughout the villagers as they realized that the wyvern's choice was a girl and that she was over twice the normal age of a usual apprentice.

"What the..." Gordi gasped.

"What?" Dani begged. "Hello, blind man here!"

"Oh my, Dani, the wyverns just chose Tÿr!" Gordian ejaculated.

"Gaunt ghosts' gusset!" Danior spouted.

Gordian chuckled at his brother. He rarely cursed, so he made up his own version of phrases he thought would be offensive.

Kuired pointed to Tÿr and motioned for her to come forward. She swallowed and passed her blind friend to his brother. *What in the world is going on?* Tÿr thought as she began her walk to the front of the crowd. She could feel each eye on her as she slowly walked up to Kuired. *What were her parents going to say?*

Tÿr'Ynyn could hear mumbles and questions being tossed around behind her. Her uncle was glaring at her when she made it to the two men now standing in front of her.

"What is going on here?" her uncle snapped to Kuired. "I thought we had discussed this. My son should be the one standing here in front of us right now. Not this…this girl."

Tÿr felt like she had been slapped in the face. Her uncle was not what people would call genial, but he had never spoken of her like this before. She had always gotten on with him in the past. The wyvern paragon lowered its head to Siolad Tÿr.

"This young woman is the choice of my dynasty, Your Honor." Sarcasm dripped from the wyvern as he said *Your Honor.* "Your offspring has neither the knowledge nor the dignity to serve this village. Should you choose to refuse our appointment, we will also pull our support out of the village of Vennex as well."

Tÿr's mind was spinning. *How is this happening? Did Kuired talk of me to the wyverns?* Then her mind fell on her father and how the relationship would be with his brother and his family after this.

"Varanus and myself sat and watched the entire proceedings this morning," the giant wyvern continued. "This girl knew every answer to every identification that was asked. I've also been told that she is intelligent and caring."

The magistrate could hardly contain his rage. He was mere seconds from a full-blown fit.

"My son"—he was attempting to keep his voice even—"is every bit as smart as any girl in this village. No *woman* has ever held the post of master healer, and I'll be damned if it happens while I'm magistrate of this town!"

Kuired put his hand on Siolad's arm to try to calm him down.

"Magistrate, please take care of what you say before you say something you'll come to regret!" Kuired's voice was amiable yet stern.

Tÿr didn't know if it was the healer's voice or if he had worked some quick magiq, but her uncle seemed to compose himself some. He nodded and then sat down on his low stool as if his legs were going to lose function if he didn't.

A million things raced through the girl's mind. This was her dream come true, but really not the way she had seen it happening. Again, she imagined the looks she was going to receive from her parents, mainly her da.

"Tÿr'Ynyn, our honored guests, the two wyverns who have joined our village for the day, and myself would like to ask you some questions. Depending on your answers, you will be offered the apprenticeship of healer. Will you answer our questions?"

"I will!" she almost shouted. Tÿr hadn't meant to sound so eager to accept the task. She had completely meant to answer as if she was as honored as she felt, but the words just poured from her lips.

Kuired cocked an eyebrow, showing the slightest bit of amusement. He knew how bad Tÿr wanted this, so he allowed the minor outburst from his young friend. Apparently, the magistrate was so upset he stood back up. He waddled over to where his wife and son were standing. He grabbed the boy's wrist and breathed the words, "Let's go!" to them. He had attempted to keep it quiet, between the three of them, but his voice echoed throughout the gathered crowd. The three testers waited for the magistrate and his family to hurry back to the village. When they were out of the picture, all three turned back to the girl.

Questions came quickly. Each was more difficult than the former. Tÿr knew how to answer most questions that were posed to her. Every answer she gave built her confidence too. Kuired would smile and nod at each correct answer. If she wasn't sure of the correct answer, she would give her best guess and finish the answer by saying that she would make sure to find out the correct answer as soon as she was done with the questions. That, too, made the healer smile. Even Varanus, who had kept a perfectly impassive face, winked at her once. The questions came at her for two solid hours before Ghra'zhenn thanked her for her cooperation and called the tourney to a halt. He raised to his full height, which was very impressive.

"Villagers of Vennex, after enduring questions designed to test her basic knowledge in the art of healing, your town's favorite sister is now offered the position of apprentice healer!"

The enormous creature lowered his wedgelike head to Tÿr's level and spoke directly to her.

"Tÿr'Ynyn, of the village of Vennex, daughter of…" Ghra'zhenn glanced at Kuired.

"Seryth Tÿr and Elmky Tÿr," Kuired finished.

"Do you agree to take this position of honor and to put all else before your needs?" Ghra'zhenn stared straight into her eyes.

"And"—Varanus had taken a step forward—"will you accept my teachings and use them to aid your skills and techniques as you embark on this long journey for the period of at least twenty years?" Varanus, too, seemed to be staring into her soul. The eyes, although black as pitch, held such emotion.

Tÿr nodded as she affirmed her oath to serve this village, or another like it for the rest of her natural life. She somehow knew this was the path meant for her. The fates would not have laid it at her feet if it were not meant for her. *What are Dani and Gordi going to say?* she thought as she stood there. *I wish more profound things than this would come to me now. How am I going to tell Mum and Da? How can I ever face my uncle again?* Over and over these petty things plagued her thoughts, and she simply wished she had something more profound to say. *What if they ask me to say something?*

To her great relief, the smaller wyvern bowed his head and said loudly, "Let all here present be aware that Tÿr'Ynyn has accepted the offer and has also passed the tests set forth by your master healer and myself. She will henceforth be known as Apprentice Tÿr'Ynyn of Vennex. Please raise your voices in welcoming your village's new healer!"

Tÿr felt heat in her cheeks as she flushed. She was not one for all this attention. She turned as cheers rose from the villagers gathered in the field. The noise was deafening. She smiled shyly as she looked for her two friends. There they were, still standing in the front row. She was certain that she could hear Gordian above everyone else. She looked around the crowd and then stopped suddenly. There, a short distance from her friends, stood her parents. Her mother had tears running down her cheeks, and her father had his arm around her shoulders, trying to console her. *Everything had been going so well too*, she said in her mind. *Dinner tonight should be fun.* She let out a little sigh but then caught herself. No woman had been a healer in over fifteen generations. This wasn't an occasion for sorrow. Today was a day of celebration. She had done what everyone, including her parents, thought was impossible. Tÿr was trying to soak all this in— her appointment to the apprenticeship, her uncle and his rotten son disgraced. People would be talking about this for a very long time. She turned to talk to Kuired. She really wanted to thank him for his faith in her. She wanted to make sure he knew that she wouldn't let him down and tell him before the crowd got to her, but he was gone. There was absolutely no sign of him. He'd been there just moments ago.

Ghra'zhenn bent his head near her. His deep, raspy voice said quietly, "He has gone, young one."

"Excuse me then. I have to talk to him!" she responded to the ancient one.

"You can't, my dear. He has gone and won't be back. He asked me to give his pardon and offer his congratulations!"

"But I needed to thank him myself!" she blurted out.

"He'll be back again soon, my dear. This is your day, and he wanted you to enjoy it."

Tÿr felt a twinge of sadness. Kuired was the entire reason she was where she was today. But Ghra'zhenn said that he would be back. She would definitely talk to him then. Dani, led by Gordian, was walking up to join her. Others from the village seemed to have similar ideas. The boys made it moments before the crowd swallowed Tÿr'Ynyn and her best friends.

Chapter 3

Tÿr'Ynyn was given three weeks to get the affairs of her life in order. She used four days and was ready to go on to her new position. Varanus had gone into the mountains to await her training. When she arrived to meet up with him, the pair would set out to find suitable living quarters. She kissed her mum and dad on their cheeks and left their cabin to meet the young wyvern. Both Dani and Gordian had to run to keep up with her as she led the quest into the mountains to find her new mentor. The brothers pelted her with questions as they walked out of town and into the woods toward the Ajenti River. They would follow it to the foothills where she would bid the boys farewell and continue the trek alone.

"We'll be able to visit all the time, right, Tÿr?" Danior asked her, puffing along at the rear.

"I'm not sure. I would think so. I mean, I'm going to be very busy, but I want you guys to come see me whenever you can."

"You can count on it."

Gordian led his brother along. Danior held one of his arms with one hand and a crooked walking stick with the other.

"I want you boys to visit my parents all the time too! You're just like sons to them. I don't want them to be lonely. I already talked to Mum, and you can go eat with them every morning if you want."

"Speaking of eating..." Gordian cut in. "I could use a little something right now!"

"Really, Gord? We just left! You ate before we set out, and I might add, you went back for more, three times!" Tÿr teased him.

"But I'm a growing boy!"

"Yeah, growing sideways."

She heard Dani snort.

"Keep laughing, brother, and I'll leave you here until I come back through!" Gordi told his older sibling.

"Please, I could follow you the entire way," Danior quipped back. "First, you're louder than an entire militia walking over dry twigs, and second, you smell!"

"What do you mean I stink? I bathed last week!" Gordi snapped back indignantly.

"At no time did I say stink," Danior continued. "I said smell. You must have eaten half a hog this morning. I can smell the grease on your breath!"

Tÿr couldn't see Danior's face behind her, but she could tell he had a huge smile as he continued to mess with his brother. Then!

"Hey, what the…"

"If you think you can follow me so well, then do it!" Gordi laughed. He had removed his arm from his brother's grasp and walked several steps ahead.

Dani was completely unfazed. He simply used the walking stick to feel his way forward, and in seconds, he had reached the place where the other two were standing. He grabbed his brother's arm again.

"See, I told you I could smell you!"

Tÿr set her pack down and fished around inside for a moment before she came out with a linen bag. She pulled out two paper-wrapped *cyclopean owl* eggs for each of them. Her mother and her had found a pair of nests a few weeks back and had been collecting the eggs ever since.

Cyclopean owl eggs were her very favorite eggs, and they were a treat to have as they were hard to come by. Usually, her mum would sell the eggs because they fetched three silver pieces each, but her mum told her that it was a special occasion and that she wanted to give her daughter a treat to have on the way.

A cyclopean or cyclops owl was a strange bird. It was the largest raptor on the planets with a wingspan of over fifteen feet across. It was so named for the large yellow eye that sat just off to the right side of its hooked beak. Huge, razor-sharp talons adorned each clawed foot, and the feathers were so black they appeared blue in the bright sunlight. The cyclops owl was the only bird of prey that was safe to consume its eggs. It only fed on small, nonvenomous creatures, so the eggs or meat didn't contain any residual toxins. Many people found the eggs to be too rich and strong-flavored, but Tÿr and the boys were used to them. Owl eggs were a favorite treat of the trio because they didn't get them often. Tÿr's mom sold them whenever she could because of the price they brought in. The boys were happy to find that their friend had even thought to bring a small saltcellar along. Eggs were good by themselves, but with a sprinkle of salt, they reached the realm of incredible.

"You've thought of everything, haven't you, Tÿr beer? The only thing that would make this better is some fresh, cracked..."

Pepper. Tÿr produced a small cloth sack with a string tied around the neck. Gordi knew this sack from their many adventures into the forest. This was her herb-and-seasoning bag. She really had thought of everything. They spent a few minutes eating their eggs before setting off again. The woods were thick, but the undergrowth was sparse. There were a fair number of leaves covering the blue ground, but very little plant life, save for the trees. The light didn't really reach the forest floor enough for other things to grow. Birds flitted in and out of the branches above their heads, and the occasional beam of light found its way down to the floor. They followed a leaf-covered path that ran parallel to the river. The forest mainly consisted of qyrry trees, transplants from the slopes of the Piral Volcano. The volcano boasted thick forests of the unique tree. It was the only place on either planet or the shift that the plant could grow. Its tough-shelled seed must be dropped into the boiling lava of the volcano to burn away the shell and allow it to germinate. When the lava hardened and cracked as it reached the cool streams or rivers, the seeds washed up on the shores of the Ajenti River. Birds and animals would spread the now-viable seeds around the area and create the magnificent forests. The trio stopped walking for a moment.

"Does anyone see the path? It seems to have disappeared!" Tÿr was looking around to find signs of the trail.

Gordian began kicking leaves aside to find the telltale signs of the trail. Blue dust clouds rose in small puffs as he continued searching. Dani began to move leaves around with his walking stick in order to help too. Tÿr had walked off in the direction of the river. She returned a few moments later.

"Let's go a bit closer to the river. We need to keep moving so we can reach the foothills of the mountains by nightfall."

The three travelers moved closer to the sound of the rushing river. They could hear the rapids moving swiftly through the trees. Soon they were back on track and moving toward the mountains. Tÿr estimated that the trip would last into the afternoon. As long as they kept moving the way they were, she felt there would be no reason that they wouldn't.

Danior began a round of pub songs as they wound their way through the trees. It helped to pass the time. Gordi patiently led his brother through the forest, guiding him over the rough terrain and tree roots that had made their way to the surface. An injury this far into the woods would not be good.

The trio had walked for a couple more hours before mentions of hunger and food began to crop up. Gordian was the first to bring up his need to eat, and Tÿr heartily agreed with him. Danior said that he could go on for a while if he needed to, but when they halted, he ate as much as any of them. Tÿr'Ynyn's mother had sent along a good amount of food: a small half wheel of hard cheese, several smoked sausage links, and a dozen individual loaves of bread. They knew that they would be able to find fruit bushes near the water. Each of them carried a goatskin that had been filled with a sweet red wine.

It didn't take them long to fill their bellies and get moving again. Every once in a while, they would see a wild animal scamper away from the hidden trail. Mostly there were spotted squirrels or the odd fox. Nothing to worry about for the time being. As they neared the mountains, they would have to keep a watch out for larger animals, like white and river bears, wolves, and a couple types of wildcats.

None of the travelers had any real protection with them. They all carried hunting knives on their belts. They knew never to go into the woods without some type of protection. Even a hunting knife with an eight-inch blade would serve as some protection, as long as they didn't come across a female white bear and her cubs. The cubs would prove little trouble, but a nursing mother would be more than a match for the three of them.

When the trio finally reached their destination, it was midafternoon. Other than the little mix-up earlier, the trek had been uneventful. They decided to make camp for the night near the edge of the Ajenti River. The banks weren't steep, so they could set snares in the water in hopes of coaxing some fish to bite the lines. Fish would be a nice change. Tÿr's mum hated fish, so she wouldn't even let it in the cottage.

All three dropped their packs at the campsite and sat for a rest. It wasn't late, so they wouldn't need to set anything up. Besides, the most that they had to do, other than set fishing lines, was unroll their sleeping mats. They never took tents on their excursions. It was just extra weight. A sleeping roll and a light blanket would suffice. Gordian set to work, putting out lines in the river, while his brother and Tÿr'Ynyn searched for dry sticks and other wood to burn in a fire. Danior carried a small hatchet on the trip to cut up any larger pieces. They didn't need a lot of this type of wood. Qyrry wood was very dense and burned for a long time.

When Gordi was done with the fishing lines, he moved back to their makeshift camp and began brushing away the leaves and seedpods of the trees to make a firepit. They had all been camping in the woods so often they each had regular jobs and knew what had to be done. In less than an hour, they had a hot fire burning, and they sat to wait and see if they would snare any fish. After the long trek, a few good draws on the goatskins were in order. They all lay back on their sleeping rolls and fell asleep in just minutes.

It was only an hour or so before Gordian woke up, his stomach sending urgent hunger messages. He smiled at the other two as they laid sleeping. He figured he'd let them sleep until he checked the lines.

The other two were awake and sitting up, chatting quietly, when Gordi returned with ten fish. Danior's job came as they prepared to eat. He had a knack for fileting fish. The other two figured that it was because he was used to using his hands to feel for everything. He could read things, provided the letters and symbols were slightly raised or carved into something. His fingers were so sensitive none of them had ever found a fish bone in any filet he had cut. He was a master with a sharp knife, and he was best at getting the biggest filets off the fish. Once he proved how good he was, the job had become his permanently.

Dinner was eaten with gusto, and the boys even roasted a couple of sausage links over the fire when the fish was consumed. The trio had all intentions of leaving half their wine for the next day, but it was going down so easy, and they had the Ajenti River right next to them for fresh water. They stayed up until late into the night. It never got dark at this time of year especially. The Kirin-Noirin shift fell into the shadow of Peyda Kirin, but with three suns, it never got totally dark. It did get dusky when the planets were farthest away from the tri-stars in their 965-day year cycle. Right now, they were just going into their first of two summer seasons, so the light was still prevalent.

Týr enjoyed the night with her friends. She didn't know the next time she would see them, so she wanted to make the most of it. They drank and laughed and talked until none of them could keep their eyes open. One by one they drifted off to sleep, with a nice set of coals in the firepit.

Týr was once again running from one of the filth-covered Inbröttiös family members. She looked for a place to hide, but any available hiding spot was gone. Trees disappeared from the land in front of her. The largest piece of cover was a small bunch of grasses. She only saw open plains in front of her, with the matted-haired man closing in on her from behind. She felt the familiar heaviness in her legs beginning to set in. Glancing behind, Týr wanted to see how close her attacker had gotten. When she turned back around, the scene changed, and she was in a huge building. The other end was so far she couldn't see the far wall. It was dark down the length, but there was some form of ambient light that allowed her to see enough of the long passageway. Týr wanted to risk another glance back, but she could literally feel the breath of her assailant on her neck.

Reaching for her hunting knife, the girl resigned herself to fight. She could no longer keep up this pace. Her hand felt for the hilt of the knife, but it was not there. Her progress slowed even more in shock, and she reached down with her other hand. *Did she strap the blade on her other side?* Nothing!

Crack!

Smash!

Her feet broke through the wooden floor of the great hallway. She had to pull her feet up high to get them unstuck from the jagged floor. She could literally hear the cracking of the wood as her boots shattered the floor beneath her. Panic began to overtake her. She couldn't run. She had no weapon. Her breath was caught in her throat.

Crack!

Tÿr was awake and breathing hard! She glanced around, half expecting to find her imaginary assailant behind her still.

Standing near the fire were four figures she didn't know. They were breaking branches and tossing them into the firepit. A good little fire had begun burning again. None had noticed that she was awake.

"Gordi!" she yelled.

Gordian sat straight up on his mat, reaching for the blade he kept under the head of the roll. His brother was still asleep on her other side. The four figures standing near the firepit dropped to a crouch, holding wicked-looking, curved daggers made of lachtrys. Lachtrys was a clear blue stone, often favored for dagger and knife blades or arrow and spearheads. The way it formed made it extraordinarily tough, and its scarcity made it very expensive. Often lachtrys blades were reserved for royalty and others who could afford it. The closest figure turned and grabbed Gordian by the head, the dagger at his throat.

"Get off him!" Tÿr screamed.

Danior began to stir but simply turned back over and went back to sleep.

"Stop right there, little lady," the dark figure hissed.

Tÿr'Ynyn was in tears. She was frightened and suddenly angered beyond all reason as she saw her friend being held at knifepoint.

"Get off of him now!" A growl came from somewhere deep inside her chest.

The other hooded figures had moved to grab her and Danior, who was still half asleep and had absolutely no idea what was going on.

"Hey, Tÿr! Get him off me!" he yelled.

"Stay still!" the girl called back to him.

"Listen to your friend," the dark leader's velvety voice oozed back at Danior.

"What the… What's going on here?"

"Just stay calm, and nothing will happen." The apparent leader continued, "We saw the smoke from your fire and thought we'd share its warmth."

Tÿr knew that this wasn't true. It was plenty warm out. The winter season was over as the first summer had just begun, and it was nowhere near cool now anywhere on the Kirin-Noirin shift. Luckily for them, they were still close enough to the triple solar system for it to be warm and light out. In one hundred more days, the entire daytime would have been in partial dusk because of the position of the planets to the suns. But now it was plenty light out, and the strangers were easily visible. The three strangers moved the trio of travelers over to one side of the fire, opposite the leader.

"Now, if you help us with what we need, you'll never see us again, and we'll leave you the way we found you."

Gordian looked like he wanted to respond, but the knife on his throat kept him from saying anything. Tÿr was afraid for his life. She could see how sharp the blades that these thugs carried were, and it would take no effort at all to slit her friend's neck.

Danior, not realizing the gravity of the situation, was the first of the trio to speak. "What do you want?" His voice trembled slightly.

"We need food," the hooded stranger said. "If you have any, we will take it and be on our way. If you make any sudden moves or try to stop us, you will die," he said simply. "Do you understand?"

"We have no money!" Tÿr pleaded. "Please don't hurt us!"

"I'm not in the habit of repeating myself, girl. We require food. That is all. Do you have any?"

"In my pack," Týr pointed.

The large man pointed to one of the others standing watch on the three helpless captives. "Go check," he ordered.

It seemed that some of the malice had left his voice, and he almost appeared to relax without forfeiture of his control over the situation. The lackey moved over to Týr's pack and upended it all over the blue dirt. Her clothes and other belongings were strewn about without care. The hooded thug rifled through the items and came up with the food. He opened the wrapped package, took out one of the sausages, and lowered his hood to cram it in his mouth. Týr's breath caught in her chest. The man had a small tattoo on the hollow of his neck, the mark of an assassin. Everyone in the midlands knew the symbol—a wolf heart with a curved knife blade pierced completely through it. These men belonged to the assassin sect called Amsälja Vrasës. They were thugs, thieves, and murderers who would hire themselves out to the highest bidder. There wasn't anything too vile that the sect wouldn't stoop to do, and there were always twenty-three. When one left or was killed, another fell in to take their place. Týr tried desperately to get Gordian's attention, but he was frozen in place. She couldn't even see the rise and fall of his chest. Danior, too, was stock-still, but she could see that he was attempting to hear as best he could. The reputation of these men was such that she would do almost anything they asked if it meant keeping her friends safe.

"Put your hood back up!" the leader snapped at the other as he saw the look on Týr's face. "Do you want them to run back to the authorities?"

One of the other assassins spoke up, "We should just kill them and be done with it. That way we don't have to worry about any of—"

"Shut it!" the leader snapped back at him. "We don't just kill for a bite of bread."

The other man looked as if he had more to say but thought better of it. Tÿr relaxed slightly but was still very concerned for her friends. The one thug still held his curved blade to Gordian's throat.

The leader turned to Tÿr'Ynyn. "Is this all the food you have?"

"Please don't hurt my friends," she pleaded with him again.

"I won't ask again!" Fury was rising in his voice.

"Please, sir, I'm just scared!"

She heard the other assassins chuckle at these words.

A cool female voice with a foreign accent drawled, "You're smarter than you seem, pretty one."

The leader was losing his patience with the entire situation. Before he could speak, Tÿr blurted out, "Yes, that's all the food!"

The leader of the assassins looked at her for a moment and then nodded to the man who still hadn't replaced his hood. The thug moved over to each of the boys' packs, dumping them on the ground as well. He kicked the things around with the toe of his boot and then shook his head back at his leader. "All right, let's go."

Before he left, he stared directly at Tÿr. "If you try following us or try anything stupid, we will kill you without even thinking about it. Do you understand me?"

Tÿr nodded immediately. She wanted them gone, and if this did it, she'd agree to almost anything.

"Pray that our paths do not cross again, little beauty," the hooded lady drawled in an unfamiliar accent. "Next time you might not be so lucky!"

With that, the four assassins turned and left the campsite.

Danior looked around. "Are they gone?"

"They're gone, big brother," Gordian told him. He rubbed his neck where the blade had been pressed against it. A fine line of blood had beaded up. "I'm bleeding," Gordian said matter-of-factly.

He showed his hand to Tÿr'Ynyn, who rushed over to inspect his neck. Upon closer inspection, she saw that it was a superficial cut. The blade that the assassin carried was made of lachtrys and extremely sharp. Luckily, the thug had not put much pressure on the skin. Tÿr cringed at the thought of what could have been.

"What in four types of hell just happened?" Danior asked. He was still half asleep.

"We were just robbed," Gordian told him.

Tÿr was attending to the scratch on his neck. She had gone back to her belongings that were spread on the ground and returned with a small ceramic jar of salve. It stunk to high heavens, but it took the sting away instantly. Tÿr had made a batch before leaving in case any of them had an accident along the way.

"Did you see who they were?" Tÿr hissed.

Gordi shook his head. "I was busy playing statue. If I had moved, no amount of your ointment would work to fix the cut."

Tÿr knew he was right. Those people were not anyone to cross. They were lucky to have escaped with their lives.

"When that one man took his hood down, I saw an Amsälja Vrasës mark on this throat. Just here." She pointed to the hollow spot on the front of her own neck.

"Gaunts!" Danior said knowingly.

"Indeed." Tÿr nodded.

"You're sure you saw the heart and dagger?" Gordian asked. "I mean, they had hoods and—"

"I'm positive. There's no mistaking that mark," Tÿr said sternly. "Plus, they were all carrying lachtrys blades. The lachtrys was a stone that came from the Anbry Mountains, more specifically, the Piral Volcano. It was harder than diamond and could hold an edge sixty percent longer than any metal on the conjoined planets. It didn't chip and rarely broke. And its most advantageous quality is that it was extremely light. The perfect material for an assassin's blade. The blades were usually made by skilled magiq users and very expensive. Often blades were passed down from one generation to another, or in the case of these assassins, more likely stolen or taken off a dead corpse."

Gordian looked around. "Did they get all of the food?"

Tÿr nodded. "Yes, everything. That food was going to be for you boys to eat on your way home tomorrow." The boys could hear the loathing in her voice.

"Hold on a minute," Gordian told them and hurried off toward the river.

"Gordi! Come back! What if they're still around?"

Tŷr would have run after her younger friend, but she didn't want to leave Danior by himself. The two of them waited, and luckily, they only had to wait for a short time. He came back, carrying a bunch of fish on a rope. He held up the fish to show them as he neared.

"I forgot I still had the lines in the water! There were fish on all but one. That means we have two apiece and one left over! Anyone hungry?"

"I could eat."

Tŷr smiled and shook her head. "Do you boys ever think of anything other than your stomachs? We nearly died just a few minutes ago, and you want to eat."

"I'm always hungry." Gordian smiled. "I reset the lines so we have something to eat in the morning. I'll never get to sleep now. I need to relax for a bit." He had raised his hand to his neck without realizing it.

"Did they take the goatskins?" Danior asked. "I'm parched."

Tŷr took his and her goatskins to the river to fill them with the crystal-clear water. The Ajenti River was a sacred river on the Kirin-Noirin shift. It was the only water anywhere on the shift or the planets that was clean enough to drink straight from its banks. The open seas of Peyda Noirin were fresh water but had to be boiled before drinking. All other rivers, and streams and lakes too, had to be treated before consuming. The Ajenti River was a phenomenon. The water could flow in either direction depending on the position of the planets to the three suns. All water flowing into the river instantly purified and was made potable. No one on the planets knew the reason behind this curiosity. There were many tales and fables that tried to explain it, but nothing had ever been proven scientifically. Tŷr returned to the camp, and Danior was sitting down, cutting the fillets off the fish. She hadn't thought about food until Gordian had mentioned it. Now she could taste the smoky fish, cooked perfectly over the fire with long, pointed sticks. She sat the goatskin next to Danior and walked over to her pack. The contents were still scattered on the ground next to her sleeping roll. She gathered up the items and shook them out before putting them back into the pack. She was looking for something specific. There! She spotted it. The little bag that contained her herbed salt. It tasted so nice on the fish.

She wished they still had the wine. She could use a nip after the night's excitement. Instead, she'd have to settle for water.

"Hey, guys, they didn't get the salt!" She held up the little bag.

"Hot damn!" Danior exclaimed.

Tÿr knew that the boys' mother didn't have much money, and salt was considered a luxury. Many families went without it, but since Tÿr'Ynyn's mother sold things in the village square, she had connections that could get her good deals on small amounts of salt. They would place the large crystals of salt into a mortar and grind them together with different herbs. Her favorite combination was wild tarragon and basil. The delicate flavors were good on practically everything. Danior placed the filets on a piece of canvas that the trio used to prepare food. Tÿr seasoned them and helped spear them on the roasting sticks. The fire was burning nicely and would provide even heat to cook the fish.

"I really wish we hadn't drank all of the wine!" Gordian said out of the blue.

"I was just thinking that too," Tÿr agreed. She thought for a moment and then said, "Hey, we're in the woods. I bet I could find some plants to make tea with."

"Then why are you still sitting here?" Dani teased. "Get cracking!"

"Are you going to help me find them?" she joked back. "I can show you what they look like!"

"I'll show you something. Here!" Danior made a gesture. He tried making a rude gesture, but never actually having seen it, he didn't get it quite right.

"Well!" Tÿr said in mock disgust. "You better hope your mother never finds out that you just did that."

Danior just giggled. He'd heard what the gesture was a hundred times as it was one of his brother's favorite rude gestures to throw at people that he felt deserved it. He also knew that Tÿr would never mention it to his mother. Tÿr grabbed Danior by the hand, and they wandered off toward the river. Their chances of finding the herbs to make tea with would be better where the trees were thinner. Tÿr never made Danior hold her arm like he held everyone else's. She liked to hold his hand. Walking with him was special, and after tomorrow, it would be a while before they could do it again.

They walked near the river and enjoyed the calming effect it had on them. The rushing water always made her relax. They returned to the campsite a short time later, carrying a handful of leaves and grasses. Gordian was minding the fish. Tÿr got back into her pack and brought out a pot. It wasn't huge, but it was big enough to make tea for the three of them. She emptied her goatskin into the pot and placed the herbs in to cook at the side of the fire. By the time they had finished eating their late-night snack, the tea would be finished steeping. Tÿr had chosen many herbs for their flavor, but she had also spotted some that would help relax and put them back to sleep. She was still nervous about going back to sleep after what she had awakened to last time, but she let the herbs take effect, and soon she was ready to go back to sleep. She bid the brothers good night once again and lay back down on her bedroll. Sleep came almost immediately.

Chapter 4

Morning arrived faster than the trio of campers would have liked. They all woke up at about the same time. Danior was last to rise. He had always enjoyed his rest. Gordian had been to the river and returned with a few more fish while Tÿr had gone down with him to look for some fruit bushes. She had taken their cups along to fill. She returned with the little metal cups overflowing with small green berries that Gordian recognized as *chartreuse fox cherries*. They were a favorite of the brothers. Their mother often would splurge to buy a small amount to split for pudding after weekend suppers. She never had this many though! Gordi was going to savor every one too, even if they made him sick.

"Look!" Tÿr shouted out, holding the cups out.

"What is it?" Dani asked quietly. He was still trying to wake up.

"Fox cherries!" Gordi replied back to his elder brother. "Lots of them!"

Danior's smile widened. Fox cherries only grew in the wild near water sources or in boggy ground. Vennex had the river that ran past, just outside of town, but the berries were usually picked pretty clean. Some people had tried to grow fox berry bushes, but never with any luck. The plant would grow and thrive for a few seasons but would never produce any fruit. Eventually people gave up. They had been spending lots and lots of money to propagate the small, treelike bushes, but there was no luck with the production of fruit. Eventually they would cut the bushes down and dig out the multistumped trees to make way for better crops. For some of the farmers, the hit had been one from which they never recovered.

The three travelers sat and ate their midmorning meal slowly so they could spend as much time together as possible before they parted and went their separate ways. The boys were subdued as they ate. They were both very happy for Tÿr, but this would be the first time in their lives that they wouldn't be together every day. Tÿr, too, reflected on how much she would miss her friends. This was a giant step for her to take, and despite her melancholy mood, she was very excited to begin this new chapter in her life. When their small meal of fish and cherries was over, Tÿr hugged the boys and told them to get going. She was worried that they would be too tired and hungry to complete the journey by the end of the day if they didn't get going now. She, too, still had a trip to complete, and she wasn't exactly sure where she was going.

Before continuing on, Tÿr went down to the river. Now that the boys had gone, she decided to bathe quickly before she went on to meet Varanus. The water was cool and refreshing. She felt so much better getting the layer of blue grime off her body. The water only kept the blue cloud of dirt for a second before it cleared. It was one of the wonders of the Ajenti River. Any dirt or cloudy water instantly cleared when it touched the sacred waters. The girl started to emerge from the cooling stream when a movement from the bushes froze her in her tracks. She slowly lowered herself down into the water. If those thieves or assassins or whatever they were had come back, she was in trouble. Tÿr's eyes were locked on the spot where she had seen the rustling. In just moments, a long nose and dark-brown eyes emerged cautiously, followed by long ears. It was a *shift fox*, a small creature no bigger than a common cat, with long, coarse brown fur and a bushy blond tail. Males were solid brown. They were generally shy animals, not often seen by humans because of their skittish nature.

"Hi, little girl," Tÿr greeted the shy fox. She moved slowly as she got out of river.

The fox seemed curious and watched from the bushes at the side of the moving water. Her ears stuck straight up, listening intently for any sounds of danger. The soon-to-be healer got dressed quickly. She remembered that there were still some scraps of fish at the side of the firepit. She gathered them up and slowly approached the little animal. Stopping about ten feet in front of the shift fox, Tÿr tossed the scraps of fish over to the inquisitive animal. It was definitely hungrier than it was nervous because it walked directly over to the fish. It sniffed it one time and then began to eat, deciding that the human girl posed no threat.

Tÿr walked back to the spot she had left her pack. She tied her sleeping roll to it and started to lift it on her shoulders. Then she thought about food. What would she eat later? She had never been to the place where she was to meet her mentor, so she had no idea how far it was yet. Would there be things to eat along the way? She sat her pack back down and got her cup again. A few more berries would keep her going throughout the rest of the day. She was used to eating only two meals a day anyways. She had never really had a big appetite. Berries in hand, Tÿr went back to her traveling pack and loaded it high on her shoulders. Numerous trips into the woods had taught her it was easier to carry the pack higher up on her back. Without glancing behind, she began the final stage of her journey.

It was at least another two hours before she would come within sight of the mountains. Had the forests not been so dense, she could have seen better where she was. Tÿr kicked at the leaves that covered the makeshift trail. Many people had traveled through here from Vennex and beyond to the *Keltainyn Sea*. It was the only saltwater sea on the planet, and it was completely landlocked on Peyda Kirin.

The Ajenti River flowed from Keltainyn and down through the entire isthmus. Many mountain streams flowed into the Ajenti along the way as it flowed into the *Xëchys Sea*. Both large bodies of water on either end of the isthmus could flow into the Ajenti River. Depending on the water pressure from either sea, the sacred river could switch directions. Tÿr had walked for about a half hour, not thinking of much of anything. She let her mind wander and just took in the scenery as she continued her trek along the river. At some place, she knew she would have to cross. There were bridges at intervals along the river, but she didn't know if there would be one near enough to where she would have to cross.

The rendezvous spot with Varanus was on or near Mesthysta Point, in the middle of the Anbry Mountains. Methysta Point was not one of the shift's tallest mountains. Piral Point was over fifteen thousand feet taller. And some of the nonvolcanic hills were even larger. Methysta was unique because it was rich in many gems and minerals, some that could not be found anywhere else on the planet. The mountains contained many rare things that Tÿr figured would come into play for her training. This way, they would be able to walk out of their home and collect most of these things without extended day trips. Becoming a master healer wasn't just about knowing all the parts of the body. It sometimes required knowledge of magiq and folk remedies. It also included knowing more than just human physiology. People also brought in sick or wounded creatures. Sometimes it even required the healer to go out and treat the person or animal or whatever was in need of treatment. Being a healer was more than a full-time job. It was a lifestyle.

Tÿr knew that when she had accepted the position, she would be accepting a single and sometimes lonely lifestyle. As a healer, she would never be able to dedicate herself to the job and another person as well. Taking a partner would be out of the question. There just wouldn't be time. When she had been little, Tÿr had always assumed she would have two children. When she and the boys had played house as youngsters, she was always the female and Danior the male in the partnership. Gordi had always been the friend of the two. She had two rag dolls that had been her children, and Dani had always played the part of the father. Tÿr had always pictured the boys in her life, and that was just how it was. It felt so odd to be leaving them on this new adventure of hers.

Tÿr's mind wandered all over the place as she continued on toward the mountain destination, but it always ended back on the boys and her. She was really going to miss them and hoped that they would be able to visit her often.

A soft rustling behind her caused her to stop and listen. Her hand moved down to the knife on her belt. She heard it again from behind her. Every sound made her nervous since they had been accosted by the band of assassins. How they had made it out of that situation without more than a scratch still amazed her. She tried not to think about it too much. Things like that could really end up messing with a person's mind if they continued to dwell on what could have happened. The crumpling of leaves was closer this time. It was too light to be a human, she thought. Before she had a chance to do anything else, the small brown head of the female fox from the campsite poked out from some long grasses growing in some small shrubs along the path. Tÿr smiled and let out a sigh.

"Hello again!" she said gently.

The fox looked up at her expectantly, as if to reply back. The fox's body emerged even farther from the safety of its hiding place.

"What are you looking for?" Tÿr asked.

The little fox cautiously approached even closer. Tÿr was amazed at how brave the little female was.

"Are you still hungry?"

The girl moved her hand very slowly to her cup at her waist. She took out a few of the green cherries and held them out to the small animal. The fox's nose was sniffing the air prudently. She didn't seem scared of the girl at all but was still moving with utmost wariness. The little brown creature was close enough to touch, and Tÿr had frozen in place. She didn't want to spook her new friend. This was an amazing moment that she would remember always. Finally, the tiny fox abandoned all caution for hunger and quickly snatched a single cherry from the girl's hand. She chewed once and then grabbed another. Tÿr couldn't believe her luck. Things like this didn't happen near the village. The larger foxes that lived around Vennex were considered pests and were usually hunted down by farmers or young boys. They had become skittish and didn't usually get near humans for fear of their lives.

As the little shift fox reached for its third berry, Tÿr gently reached out touch its head. At first, it wanted to pull back, but as it realized that it wasn't in any danger, it allowed the girl to touch it. Hunger had won out over its trepidation. Tÿr stayed crouched down. She didn't want to make any sudden movements to frighten the small animal. Soon she realized that the issue probably wouldn't come up. The fox had come up to her and was sniffing at her hand, looking for more of the fruit. The pair of strangers sat in the forest and ate the shift cherries together.

Tÿr didn't know how much time had passed. She didn't care. This was an experience she was not going to miss. The young fox had now climbed onto her lap and was eating out of her cup, smacking away happily on the fruit. The shift fox ate her fill while Tÿr'Ynyn petted her shaggy fur. It looked much softer than it was. Fur like this was mostly for protection. The shift fox spent most of its life in the forest, hunting in dense undergrowth of brambles and sharp sticks. This fur coat was designed to keep the pointed impediments of the thick forest from penetrating its soft skin beneath. The pair of unlikely friends sat together for almost an hour. The fox let Tÿr pet her and rubbed up against her chest. It was if they had been old friends.

Tÿr began to feel the twinge of hunger and suddenly remembered that she needed to be moving on. She popped a few of the remaining berries in her mouth and walked down to the edge of the river. From where she stood on its bank, it didn't appear to be moving very fast, but Tÿr knew that the river was a very quick-moving stream; and if she were to go in past her knees at this spot, she'd be pulled back downstream rapidly. The small fox had followed her and moved forward to dip its head in the cool waters for a drink. Tÿr followed suit. Kneeling down, she cupped her hands and drew the refreshing waters to her mouth. There was no odd flavor to the water. It was pure and delicious, quenching her thirst instantly. When she had sated herself, she got back to her feet and readied herself to finish the last bit of her journey. She didn't have to be there to meet the wyvern for a couple of weeks, but she was so excited to begin the new chapter of her life she had taken no time at all to set her affairs in order and set out for Methysta Point. She wasn't sure when the wyvern would be there even, but she liked to be early and settle in before jumping into her intense training.

The reflections on the water proved helpful as she could see mountains in the river's clearing upstream. They were still a fair distance away, but they were in sight. Tÿr figured that it would take about two hours until she reached the first of the mountain footholds. From her instructions, she would be searching for the second major peak. It was rumored to be slightly different from the ones surrounding it. There were great deposits of purple amethyst through the mountain, along with many other more-valuable stones and gems. Amethyst was the most prevalent though. There was supposed to be so much it colored the mountain from the normal blues of the land to lavender. Tÿr loved amethyst. It wasn't especially rare or valuable, but she loved the deep purple colors of it—purple being her favorite color in general. The girl smiled to her new friend and bid it farewell as she continued her trek.

She'd be glad to find her destination. The boys and her had gone into the forests on overnight camping trips many times, but this was her first sojourn into the deep woods by herself. She wasn't sure what she would do if she came across more trouble on her way but found herself thinking that it wouldn't help to think like that. If she let those feelings surface, she'd never let herself go anywhere. Every so often, Tÿr'Ynyn would look behind to make sure that she was still alone and not being tracked; and each time she'd glance back, the little blond tail would stop and stand straight up in the air. The fox was following her.

"What are you doing, little girl? You should go back to your home!" Tÿr would tell the little creature. It would appear to listen to her for a minute, but as soon as Tÿr turned to go back down the path, the fox would continue following her. After three or four tries, Tÿr gave up and realized she was going to have a traveling companion for a little while at least. As Tÿr walked, she began to search for more things to eat. She didn't know where the next meal was going to be coming from, so she wanted to be prepared. She still had a couple of fishing snares too, as long as she stayed near the river. Since it didn't get dark for the night hours, she could keep going as long as she wanted as long as her legs didn't give out. Tÿr continued walking throughout the afternoon, her friend following at a safe distance the whole time. She decided that she would only go for about another hour. Her legs were sending her brain extremely tired signals as she trudged along the path. Luckily, there weren't too many obstacles on the trail that needed to be navigated.

The qyrry trees were incredibly strong, so there weren't many large branches on the forest floor. A healthy qyrry tree didn't really shed many branches. They were hearty and disease-resistant for the most part. Qyrry wood, even from dead trees, burnt for a long time because of how dense the wood was, one of the main reasons it was favored for weapon handles. Another tree, the *taipuva*, was a close cousin to the qyrry, but it couldn't have been more unlike its hearty cousin. The wood was so soft even large branches bent with ease. The main use of the taipuva was the making of *bësoms*. A bësom was a broom made from the taipuva tree branches, tied around an oak or other hardwood handle. Though the qyrry tree would have made a great handle, its wood was generally reserved for weapon-making or furniture. Furniture made and carved in qyrry wood was extremely expensive because the furniture makers would have to sharpen their knives after every two or three cuts. The furniture was usually purchased by royalty or the very wealthy. Even though Tÿr's dad liked the money that came from the sale of a custom qyrry piece, he rarely made any because it wasn't really worth the amount of time he put into it. Tÿr and her mother both had wardrobes made from the tough wood, and Tÿr's bed was also made from qyrry. Both had been presents from her father for her birthday one year.

Tÿr smiled at the thought of her father. She hoped the brothers would stop by and keep him and her mother company. Her smile grew at the thought of the boys showing up every morning to have the morning meal with her parents. Her mum would love the company.

Tÿr'Ynyn was just at the point of stopping for the night. Since she wasn't even expected for a couple of weeks, she wouldn't be late if she stopped to rest. She removed her traveling pack and set it down on the leaf-strewn ground. The blue dirt still poked through in some places.

Tÿr noticed that the trees weren't quite so close together here, and toward the edge of the river, there were hardly any. There were some areas of closely grown shrubbery and grasses in dense clumps around some of the trees, but fifty yards from the water, the trees formed a good-enough canopy should it decide to rain while she slept.

Food was a priority. She found the snare lines in the pack and set two in a deep pool that wasn't racing as fast as the rest of the river.

Tÿr knew that fish often came into these deeper, calmer pools to rest and feed. She had easily found some grubs just under the surface of the dirt, feasting on the roots of the sparse grasses that grew in the shade here. The girl had finished throwing in the last line and looked around to get a feel for her surroundings. She wanted to make sure she had an escape route should the situation require it. She also needed to mark the direction in which she was heading. Tÿr rarely got turned around, but she wanted to make sure she didn't end up backtracking. As she took in the scenery around her, she found that she was closer to the mountains than she expected. Just up the river, it made a sharp bend; and in the clearing in the trees, she saw that the terrain began to rise. And just past the bend, she could see a large, fallen qyrry tree leaning all the way across the river. The Ajenti wasn't terribly wide this close to the steep mountains.

"That's where I'll cross," she said to no one in particular. Then she remembered her little friend. "Do you think that looks like a good place for us to go across?" Tÿr had resigned herself to the fact that as long as she gave the little creature food, it would follow her. Besides, she'd grown fond of it in the short time that they'd spent together. She kind of liked the company. "Well, little one, change of plans. We aren't that far from our destination."

The little fox looked at her curiously, as if it was trying its hardest to understand what she was saying.

"You know," Tÿr said to the little shift fox. "I can't continue to keep saying *you*. You need to have a name to if you're going to continue traveling with me!" Tÿr thought for a second.

"Rævii!" she exclaimed suddenly. "That's it! What do you think?"

The little fox looked at her quizzically. It was trying so hard to comprehend what she was saying.

"Come here, Rævii," she called to the little one. Its tail twitched with amusement, and it jumped forward. "Come on!" Her hand was outstretched to the fox. It paused briefly and then bounded up to her hand to sniff it. "You want something to eat, don't you? Why don't you come with me, and we'll find some fruit and maybe even get a couple fish if we're lucky!"

The little fox came closer and rubbed against her bent leg. It really was a sweet animal. It had probably never seen a human before and didn't have any reason to be scared. Týr sat and rubbed the dense, rough fur, and the fox stayed right at her knee. It was practically purring. As her hunger got the better of her, Týr went and checked her lines in the river's cool water. Before she even got to the sticks poking into the blue banks, she could tell she would have meat for dinner. Both lines were moving up against the lazy current. Before taking the fish off the lines, she foraged around the immediate area for some dry wood to use for a small fire. She'd eaten raw fish before, but preferred to have it cooked. When the fire was burning nicely, Týr went back to the water and brought out the two fish. Her new companion followed close behind. The little fox seemed to be hungry as well. It turned out to have quite an appetite as well. The fish cooked quickly over the hot coals of the fire. Týr had removed the heads and tails and tossed them to Rævii, who ate them in no time at all. She moved over to nuzzle Týr, as if to tell her to hurry up. She licked the remains of the fish off her brown, furry face.

"It's coming, greedy! Give it a moment!" Týr laughed.

She broke up the fish for the fox. She needn't have worried though. It was gone before she had finished two bites of her own. The little fox had eaten the skin, scales and all. The human girl pulled the skin off her fish and tossed it to the hungry little fox, and it was gone as quick as it had landed.

"Change of plans, Rævii! We're going to continue on to the mountain. We'll be there in another hour or two, and then we can rest."

The fox chirruped to her human. She was ready to do whatever the girl was going to do as long as it meant getting all the food that she'd been receiving. Týr cleaned up the area and kicked dirt over the fire. She was ready to finish up the final leg of her journey. She didn't know what she would find at the end, but in the worst case, she could at least come back down to the river to catch some fish for her and the young fox. It would probably get old really fast, but it would sustain them for the time being. Between the fish and the berries, she could scrounge, and they'd be able to eat until they met up with the wyvern.

The pair left their dinner site and moved toward the mountains. This time Rævii walked next to Tÿr'Ynyn. They proceeded to the spot that Tÿr had seen with the downed tree. Tÿr reached down and picked up the little fox to help her across the river. She placed it on top of her pack, and the fox settled down between the pack and Tÿr's shoulders. The girl maneuvered between the branches of the fallen tree. It was a testament to the strength of the tree. It hadn't broken and fallen. It appeared that a great wind had toppled the ancient tree, roots and all. Tÿr walked carefully to make sure she didn't trip and fall into the water. The fox rode along without a care in the world, and when they finally reached the other side, Tÿr dropped back to the ground and reached up to take her furry passenger down. The little fox playfully nipped at her fingers, and so Tÿr allowed it to continue riding on her shoulders. It was so small the weight was practically inconsequential. Tÿr just shrugged and moved forward. The violet peaks of her destination were clear in her sight now. If she continued at the pace she'd already been going, they'd be there in just a bit over an hour. Then she would rest, and she would have no trouble falling asleep this evening. Tÿr planned to camp at the foothills of Methysta Point. Tomorrow she'd be rested and could scale the mountain to the peak if needed. She wasn't sure where they would be staying. Varanus hadn't been entirely clear about it. Perhaps he didn't know either.

Because of extensive mining on Methysta, there were sure to be many caves and openings that would be perfect to serve as a home. They would protect from the elements and could be easily heated in the cooler months. As the conjoined planets grew farther from their trio of suns, the days and especially nights could get frigid. In the higher elevations, snow wasn't unheard of, even during the warmer seasons. Rævii stayed on the traveling pack for a good deal of the final leg of the trip. Toward the end though, she grew restless, turning circles on Tÿr's shoulders in the little area by the traveling pack. Tÿr gently sat the shift fox next to her on the ground, and they each got a drink. Tÿr drank first from the goatskin, and then she cupped her hand and filled it with water for Rævii. The fox lapped the water thirstily and then shook the excess of from her mask. The two continued, both on foot. Tÿr slowed her pace. There was no need to rush.

The mountain was close as the companions had covered a lot of ground in the past hour. The ground was beginning to slope up toward the peak of the mountain. Trees weren't quite as thick as they were on the flat earth, and Tÿr could see that only a couple of thousand yards above them, the ground plateaued enough for them to make camp there for the night. Tÿr had plenty of water for the evening and began to climb up and away from the Ajenti River. She thought she could hear the trickle of water in front of her somewhere. She would look for a mountain stream as she climbed higher.

The girl and fox had to veer from the path that cut its way along the side of the river to ascend the mountain. Terrain became tougher as they strayed from the path. Bushes grew close together, and the branches wove tightly. Tÿr found a long, straight qyrry branch lying on the ground. She figured it would make a good walking stick. It looked as if someone else might have used it for that very purpose. There weren't any qyrry trees around this far up from the river, and this particular stick had all its bark removed.

It was now part of the warm season, and the stick would come in handy for flushing out odd creatures from the undergrowth, especially snakes. The shift had many venomous types of snakes, and the most dangerous of these was a variety known as the *screaming brush viper*. It was extremely dangerous to people who didn't heed its shrill warning. When scared or threatened, the snake took a large gulp of air into a sac in its throat and expelled it through its hollow tongue. It made a shrill, whistling sound that could be heard from a long way. The viper hardly ever bit a person because the venom was used to hunt small creatures, and it needed the toxin to kill them so it could feed. It took several days to replenish this poisonous serum, so it was cautious about using it. The viper much preferred to give its incredibly loud warning than to strike. Tÿr didn't want to take any chances though. Even a tiny drop of the venom would kill her new friend, and not much more would be deadly for her. The eight-to-ten-foot adult snake could easily consume an adult fox.

Tÿr and the shift fox climbed the gentle incline as it led to the plateau. She poked into every bush and shrub and clump of grass they came across. Tÿr figured the fox would also warn her of any danger. They managed to climb the incline quickly. The undergrowth had thinned, and at the plateau, there were only a few trees. Nothing as tall as qyrry trees. These were small, dense trees that were volunteers—trees brought to the area as seeds spread by animals like birds. Tÿr even spotted a deep-purple, variegated-leafed pear tree. Pear trees didn't grow in Vennex, so Tÿr was excited for yet another treat. There were many things that the villagers just couldn't propagate, and unless they traveled, or vendors came to Vennex, they never got to try many of the things. Tÿr would have to remember to bring some of the pears back to her parents. She knew her dad liked pears, even though they gave his stomach fits. He always ate too many. One of the good things of living on the shift was the temperature. It was generally nice for most of the year. Only at the farthest part of the planet's revolution did it get too cold. Even then, there wasn't much snow on the shift.

Peyda Noirin, on the other hand, was a different story. On the tight arc at the end of the elliptical revolution, the sea-covered planet experienced heavy snows and ice flows in the seas. The waves would rise to tsunami force and could devastate islands in its wake. Generally, the population was much lower in the islands than the continents, so the death toll was lower, but still, people insisted on living on some of the smaller islands. As Tÿr got closer to the pear tree, several brightly colored birds took to the air in the direction of the peak. All over on the ground were sparkling bits of purple stones. Tÿr understood how the mountain had gotten its name. Mythesta was the ancient Peydan word for the purple crystal called amethyst.

On the far side of the pear tree, Tÿr mistook a long, curved object for a branch. She was reaching up to pick a couple of the juicy fruits when a startling screech assaulted her ears. The shrill sound only took seconds to recognize. The curved stick, upon further examination, turned out to be a seven-foot viper. Its head twisted around to stare directly at Rævii. The fox halted, and every hair on its small body stood on end. Tÿr grabbed the fox and jumped back several yards. She got out of the viper's striking range. Vipers were pretty much one long bunch of muscles. The strike of the viper was said to be similar to being hit with a pickax. Grown men had been knocked over by a strike to the chest in past attacks.

Týr knew that the snake could strike at a distance equal to its body length. She wanted to shoo it away with her walking stick but knew it wasn't long enough to do the trick. Suddenly this didn't seem like the perfect place to make camp after all. If she could get rid of this snake, it could possibly come back and cause issues for her and her little companion. Týr thought about trying to sneak up on the viper from behind, but short of using the little fox as bait, she didn't know how to distract it. Despite being on high alert—her nerves sharp as the edge on a blade—Týr also noticed how beautiful the snakeskin was. The larger splotches of color were heptagonal in shape. The center color was a deep green surrounded by dark-brown outlines. The underside sported chevron stripes of black that pointed at the angular head. The head was pale yellow, very large, and contained two sets of three-inch-long fangs. And the other end was black and forked. Týr picked up some of the round black stones and tossed them at the viper. One came extremely close to its head, and it struck out at it. The blow seemed to stun it briefly. The little fox danced around her shoulders with anxiety. Týr threw another rock at the snake and struck it below the head. It spun to see what had touched it. Týr'Ynyn knew that there was no way that neither her nor Rævii could stay the night here if the snake wasn't disposed of. She threw several more rocks at the now-coiled snake. One of the rocks smashed into one she had previously thrown and cracked open to reveal dark-purple, glittery crystals inside. An amethyst geode.

Týr looked around and found some more decent-sized stones to toss at the coiled snake, and as she was searching, another slithered out from the low bushes near the pear tree trunk. She was puzzled by the fact that the birds had been sitting so quietly in the tree before they had arrived. Normally, snakes were mortal enemies of birds. Apparently, the birds hadn't felt threatened in the branches. From above their heads, in the direction of the mountainside, a loud, flapping sound filled the air. Týr's head shot upward to see a wyvern dropping from the sky. It landed with a dull thud on top of both snakes. The first snake was completely flattened, but the other was caught under the hand on the wing of the giant pale-blue lizard. The armored scales on its body shone with different colors of the rainbow as it grabbed the still-slithering snake off the earth. The snake thrashed back and forth in the winged hand but couldn't do more but bite at the scaled armature of the wyvern's wing.

"V…Varanus?"

The wyvern dipped its large head to acknowledge the girl and then threw the snake into its open mouth. One quick bite, and the snake was in two. Varanus swallowed its remains in one.

"Tÿr'Ynyn! I'm pleased to greet you doing so well!"

Tÿr relaxed. The little fox peered out from behind the girl's head at the enormous creature standing before them.

"I, too, am happy to see you!" Tÿr exclaimed. "Thank you for your assistance."

The great wyvern dipped his head again. "You have arrived earlier than I expected. Luckily, when those birds came flying up the mountain past me, I figured there must be some sort of intruder on the mountain. That is when I decided to drop down and take a look, as it were."

"Well, you have perfect timing!" Tÿr told her mentor. "Eventually, I might have gotten one of those vipers, but then the second one came out. I wasn't ready to take them both on by myself."

Varanus nodded politely.

"Are you and your young companion hungry? I have been out and caught a small wild hog. If you can see to a load of wood, we can cook part of it, and you'll have a nice, warm meal of roast hog to eat."

Tÿr didn't realize how hungry she was until Varanus had mentioned eating. She knew that Rævii would eat whether she was hungry or not, so she dropped the little fox and her pack on the ground and set out to find some wood for the cooking fire. Varanus followed at a distance behind her to keep from spooking the small fox.

"I didn't anticipate the extra mouth," Varanus told her with mild amusement in his voice. "Am I to gather the little female will be staying with us during your training?"

"I would like that very much," Tÿr told the large, scaled creature.

"As long as its care doesn't interfere with your duties and training, I see no reason to disallow it," the wyvern continued.

"I will be fine," Tÿr told him matter-of-factly. She had already gathered up a large armful of dead sticks.

The wyvern used its hind leg and scraped down into the blue dirt and left a large depression behind. This was to be the firepit. Tÿr began to break the wood into manageable-sized pieces. She had gathered some feathers and leaves to use as kindling to start the fire. Tÿr had gone back to her pack once a nice-sized pile of wood was gathered. She was trying to find her flint and steel to get the fire started.

"Is there anything I can help with?" Varanus asked her.

"I'm just grabbing a flint to start the fire," Tÿr responded back.

"Just stay where you are!" Varanus directed her.

His throat bloated only slightly and began to glow. He appeared to hold his breath only for a moment before a fine line of white fire came from its mouth. The fire was burning hot in just a matter of moments. Tÿr put her flint and steel back in a side pocket of the pack. Instead, she unsheathed her hunting blade and set out to dress the pig for cooking. Varanus had caught a nice-sized wild hog. Tÿr and Rævii would eat well this night!

"Tomorrow we will move up to a cave that I have chosen to use as our home and training area," Varanus told Tÿr as she collected some pears from the tree.

She sampled one as the wyvern continued to talk to her. It was delicious. Tÿr'Ynyn had cut the meat she figured she would be able to eat that evening and speared it on a long stick she cut from one of the other trees on the plateau. She made sure to get extra for the shift fox. Tÿr wondered if the little creature had ever eaten hog before. She doubted that the two animals had ever even crossed paths before. The fox was so shy, and the hog could be dangerous with its sharp tusks. The little fox sat near the fire as the meat cooked. The smell had entranced the small, doglike animal. It would surely enjoy its meal this night.

Varanus didn't speak the common tongue fluently but managed to convey everything it wanted to the apprentice. Tÿr learned that the wyvern had spent every day since its departure from Vennex on the mountain. It had made several flights over and around the mountain to check to see if Tŷr had shown up. Tŷr told him how glad she was that he chose the perfect time to help remove the slithering threat from the area. Varanus became amused as Tŷr spoke to him. After hearing his broken use of the language, she sometimes fell into the same pattern. She would catch herself and apologize. Varanus told her not to worry about it as he chuckled to himself. The two talked about how Tŷr's training would progress; how she would not only learn healing for people and creatures but how she would learn different magiqal spells and potions to aid in healing and other things the pair would come up against. Tŷr was also surprised to learn that Varanus intended to teach her to use basic weapons like swords and knives and also the long-handled or staff boline. The latter was a weapon of many of the militias that defended cities across the Peydan planets. He would also teach her to use magiq to form a blade from the magiqal stone called lachtrys. This part excited Tŷr more than almost anything.

When the meat had finished cooking, Tŷr took it from the fire. She had an eating bowl in her pack. It would be easier to feed Rævii from it, and that way, the young fox wouldn't end up eating a bunch of the blue sand with her meal. Tŷr had taken an entire side of ribs and part of the loin meat. Her mother had showed her how to butcher a hog when she was younger. Whenever they got one in, they had to butcher it quickly and cook it or smoke it to preserve the meat.

Varanus had taken the remaining parts of the wild hog away from the fire to eat it away from Tŷr. He was concerned that she would find his eating habits unsettling. She just laughed and told him not to be ridiculous. He still dragged it back from the fire, although the girl could hear every bone shatter as he crunched the entire remaining bit of the hog, tusks and all. Tŷr had cut up the meat for Rævii to eat easier. She had also sliced up some pear to go with it. The spotted yellow fruit was crisp and refreshingly tart. Even after all the work Tŷr had gone through to cut up the meat for the fox, the little creature dragged each piece out of the bowl and ended up eating it off the ground.

Tÿr ate until she literally couldn't handle one more bite. As she cleaned the rib bones, she tossed them into the fire. Tÿr didn't want to risk attracting any other animals to their campsite while she slept. Varanus had already told her that he would keep watch overnight so she could sleep. She washed everything down with a long pull of water from her goatskin. It was still ice cold and as fresh as when she had filled the container. Varanus sat across the fire from Tÿr and allowed her to question him about the apprenticeship, things she could and couldn't do. She found that she was free to do what she pleased, and he would keep her on track. He had no trouble if the boys wanted to come and visit or stay for a few days at a time as long as she continued her studies and stayed on top of her training.

Tÿr could feel her eyes began to droop as they sat and talked. Varanus shared that this was his first time as a mentor and that he was eager to begin the training as much as she was. Soon Tÿr was going in and out of consciousness. She was missing complete fragments of statements. Then she was only catching a word or two every now and then when her head would fall forward and snap her back awake. Eventually Varanus's voice ceased to speak. He could see how tired she was, and he just let her drift off to sleep. He moved over to her and used his wing hands to lay her down on her bedroll. Something like a shock sped through his limbs. It was the very first time he had ever touched a human.

Chapter 5

Varanus was the first to move around in the morning. He had already been out and hunted some mountain hares for Tÿr to eat when she got up. Rævii had slept, curled up on Tÿr's chest the whole night. Now she was up, and curiosity had gotten the better of her. She dared a few feet closer to the wyvern. Varanus chuckled. He stayed still as the fox came ever closer to him. His last laugh had brought Tÿr out of her dreaming, and she sat up sleepily.

"It's okay, little girl. He's safe!"

Tÿr was amused the way the little fox would scamper three steps forward and two back. Eventually the fox abandoned caution and ran up to the pale-blue, winged lizard. Varanus put his hand down on the ground, and the fox climbed up his wing. It made little, excited, barking noises as it got closer to the giant head. Determining that there was no danger, Rævii climbed up the wing and onto the long neck. It stopped to rest on the wyvern's head.

"It looks like you have a new friend." Tÿr pointed out to Varanus.

His face smiled, or what Tÿr considered a smile. "I think she only likes me because she knows I brought food with me."

Tÿr noticed the rabbits on the ground near the firepit. "Varanus, you didn't have to do that! I can get my own food!"

"Oh, I intend to let you once we begin training, but I was already out, looking over the mountain to make sure we had no uninvited visitors. Those poor hares never saw me coming."

The girl could hear how pleased the wyvern was. "Tomorrow I get food for us then!" Tÿr told him.

"Understood," Varanus replied.

Tỹr got up slowly. She could feel the ache in her legs from the last two days spent walking. She reached down for the hares and got her knife out to skin them. She tossed the fur onto the flames that were now dancing happily on the firepit again. Varanus must have gotten some more wood too. Tỹr only put one rabbit on the fire to cook. She didn't want Rævii to get too used to getting cooked meat, or else she wouldn't eat anything but cooked meat. If anything were to happen to Tỹr'Ynyn, the little fox wouldn't be able to feed itself if it only got used to getting prepared food.

"Are you going to eat, Varanus?"

The giant lizard shook his head slowly.

"You need not worry about me. I eat large amounts of food at one time and can then go for a week or longer before I require more."

"You speak very well, Varanus!"

"Thank you. I have had many years to practice. My paragon has trained me since I was very young. I was always to be a mentor. You are my first, so this will be a great learning experience for both of us."

Tỹr immediately felt a kinship with the young wyvern. Even though he was eighty-three, he was just a juvenile. In wyvern years, he was actually younger than she was. Tỹr and the young fox finished their morning meal and were ready to embark on their new life. Varanus had already scraped dirt over the firepit where smoke still seeped through the dark-blue earth, a large, reptilian footprint in the place where the fire had been burning just minutes before. Tỹr walked to Varanus, carrying her furry little passenger.

"How much farther is it to our destination? Should I bring some fruit along to eat? Will there be food up near the cave?" Tỹr's mind was racing now. She wanted to make sure that she would be able to feed Rævii and herself.

"Fear not, my young friend. Your needs will be seen to. You will have all you need to eat each day. As far as the distance to the cave entrance, it is about five thousand feet straight up the side of this mountain."

Tỹr glanced up toward the top of the mountain. It was almost straight up after a couple of hundred yards. Little glints of light sparkled all over the face of the cliff, obviously crystals of amethyst or diamond-like quartz poking out from the sheets of rock. She hoped there would be a path that led up to the cave. She had never scaled such a steep mountain face before.

"Fear not, Tÿr," Varanus started. "You won't have to climb anymore. I have a much-quicker way to get us there."

Tÿr gave him a quizzical look.

"We are going to fly," the wyvern said simply.

Tÿr could feel her mouth hanging open. That was not what she was expecting. The highest she'd ever been was in a qyrry tree in the forest just outside of Vennex. She felt her toes tingle at the thought of flying anywhere.

"If you're ready, we can go now."

Tÿr was amazed at the ease that the wyvern talked of flying, almost like he assumed everyone had done it at one point or another.

"Varanus," she began. "I've never flown before. Am I supposed to ride on your back? How do I hang on? I have to hold the fox to make sure she doesn't fall."

"Whoa, take it easy, my friend. It is a very simple thing to do. I am large enough to lift you and your belongings. I believe I could carry you and your two friends without so much as losing my breath," he said.

"But how…" She let the question just fall.

"I have a harness that has been made of the fibers of a type of palm tree on the island where my dynasty resides. The fibers are very strong and will hold you easily. There are places to hold on, so you will be completely safe!"

She breathed a little easier. He seemed sure of this harness, and the wyvern had yet to give her any reason to doubt him. Varanus turned and went to a large clump of opaque stones. From behind, he pulled out a large harness made of something like hemp rope.

"If you could assist me, we can get this around my middle and attach it under my belly. All you'll have to do is climb on and grab the straps. In just a minute or two, we'll be there, and you will have saved yourself half a day's climb."

Tÿr considered this for a moment and resigned herself to take her first flight. Varanus told her where to place the harness on his back. He helped her pull the long straps around his underside. There were large wooden toggles to fasten it in place. There were two large bags attached to the harness, one on either side of the wyvern's body.

"You may place your traveling pack inside one of those bags. It will make the trip easier for you," the lizard told her.

Tÿr slipped the pack down into the bag and fastened the bag closed with the toggle. Then she tightened her belt around her tunic and created a little area for the shift fox to ride in. She could snuggle down in against Tÿr and keep safe.

Tÿr had considered picking up some of the amethyst crystals that were just lying around all over the ground. The geode that had broken open was so pretty, but Varanus told her that there would be plenty up above. The cave where they would be staying was an abandoned mine, and there were more amethyst than she would know what to do with.

She called the little fox over to her, and it ran playfully up to her outstretched hands. "I have to put you in my tunic for a few minutes. It will be over before you know it."

Rævii purred like a cat and allowed Tÿr to pick her up. Tÿr'Ynyn tucked her down into her tunic, against her chest. The little fox turned once and snuggled up next to Tÿr's warm skin. Varanus instructed Tÿr how to mount the harness. She chose her seat carefully as the wyvern's hard plates ran down either side of its head and met just behind its neck to form a row all the way down to its tail. The seat of the harness sat on the plates but gave some padding to insure a modicum of comfort to the rider. Tÿr talked down into the front of her tunic to reassure the shift fox, who had already closed its eyes to go to sleep. Obviously, Tÿr was more nervous than her hairy little partner.

"Hold tight now," Varanus instructed his apprentice.

He unfurled his enormous wings and beat the air. Tÿr held on as tight as she possibly could. Her stomach was all aflutter. And she felt as if she left it behind as they rose into the air. All she could hear were the sharp flapping of wings and the rushing air. They hovered for a moment, and then the wyvern shot up into the sky. Tÿr grabbed the straps and pulled her body closer to the back of the back of the wyvern. She was amazed by how smooth his scales were. They always looked very sharp and rough, but they were the exact opposite. They were cool to the touch and felt almost like glass beneath her hands. The flight was fast, and Varanus was gentle as he climbed up to the cave. Tÿr was getting used to the flight by the time they reached their destination. Varanus flew them up and over the ledge and then sat them down directly in front of the dark cave opening. Tÿr's legs felt weak as she stepped down on the ground. She put her hand against the wyvern to steady herself for a moment.

The wyvern's head turned back to face the girl. "How did you enjoy your first flight?"

Tÿr could hear the glee in his voice. He had really enjoyed taking her on her first trip through the air.

"I'm not sure exactly. It might take some time to get used to." Tÿr smiled weakly.

When she put her hand in to remove the shift fox, it was still sleeping. She pulled it out and hugged it close. It still didn't stir. Tÿr took the little fox into the cave and laid it down on a pile of leaves that had blown in. Varanus had already begun to unlatch the toggles of the harness. Tÿr returned to assist him. They pulled the harness off, and Tÿr walked into the cave as well. She took out her pack and set it aside too. She took a few moments to let her eyes adjust to the darkness of the cavern. It was huge. She couldn't see the back of it because it went so far into the mountain. The first thing she noticed, other than the size and darkness, was how much cooler it was inside than it was out under the suns. It got even darker as the outline of the wyvern appeared in the opening. The doorway was so large Varanus didn't even need to duck down to walk into the cave.

"How do you find your accommodations? Will this place be acceptable for our living arrangements?" the deep, rasping voice asked.

"Oh, this is fine." Tÿr replied.

"I am pleased that you think so. There are a few things that will have to be done so I, too, can inhabit the cavern."

Tÿr looked at the wyvern and waited for him to finish. Her head semicocked to the side.

"The first and most important thing for me is some type of heating device. I am cold-blooded and will require warmth, especially as the planet travels farther from the three suns," Varanus continued. "We will need to build a forge, and I will instruct you how to construct a type of furnace for warmth."

Tÿr had never used a forge to make anything, but she was anxious to begin the construction as soon as she could. The girl's eyes had adjusted to the dim lighting. She decided that she would need to invest in some lamps to help illuminate the cave. Toward the center of the cave, there was a large stack of stone piled over four feet high. Tÿr couldn't tell what exactly the dark rock was, but it just looked heavy. The cavern was larger than Tÿr had first thought. The posterior of the cavern went back far enough that she couldn't see the rear wall, but it appeared to go back indefinitely. Varanus stood up to his full height.

"The ceiling in here goes up way beyond my head. When we have the furnace in here, smoke shouldn't be an issue. I believe that when this mine was dug, ventilation shafts were cut in to allow toxic gasses to escape, so that will help as well."

Varanus seemed pleased with his choice of their new home. Tÿr would be able to build something to sit on. She had worked with her father enough in the shop to have experience to build simple furniture. The girl knew she'd eventually have to try a bed as well. The cave floor was sure to be cold, and the chill would creep throughout her whole body by the morning if she slept on the floor too long. Even though it was still quite warm outside, the cave was at least twenty degrees cooler where she stood in the main cavern. Tÿr guessed the temperature was even cooler deeper in the mine. This gave Tÿr a great idea. If the mine was much cooler down lower in the earth, she could actually make a place to store foods and medicines that spoiled easily. Food wouldn't go to waste as often! The possibilities became endless. Even her parents didn't have refrigeration in their cottage. That was something reserved for royalty or the wealthy—generally deep cellars that took many man-hours to dig and then build out of the native blue clay.

"Would you care to look around?" Varanus asked her.

She noticed that he had something long and narrow in his wing hand. He held it to his mouth as his throat glowed briefly. A bright flame shot at what was now apparently a branch. It caught on fire immediately, and a soft orange glow flickered to life in the blue rock mine. Tÿr could see that rock had been hewn from the walls as smoothly as possible. She took the makeshift torch and walked around the cavern. It was actually larger than she had thought it to be. Two shafts ran off in different directions at the back of the large cavern.

"The one thing I must ask is that you don't go wandering through the tunnels by yourself. I haven't been able to get back in as far as I'd like. I don't want you to get lost!" Varanus said with concern.

"I wouldn't feel comfortable going in by myself anyway," she told him. "Maybe if my friends come to visit, I'll try it then."

"That would be wiser," the gentle creature said simply.

Firelight reflected in the endless black of his eyes. Tÿr was beginning to love the sound of her mentor's voice—the deep timbre that was a bit raspy and a bit rumbling, almost an echoing roll. It was soothing and mystical at the same time. At times, Tÿr couldn't help but stare at Varanus's scales. The way they reflected even the torch light was magiqal. Rainbows on each scale reflected back at her. Each scale was like a thin slice of one of the types of rock that the planet was comprised of—a luminescent feldspar. The whole of the planet was made out of blue rock, feldspar, and lapis lazuli. There were the feldspar and also large mountains of turquoise and chrysocholla. When the mountains of rock broke down, it formed the unique blue dirt that covered the whole planet, except for one large island in the Qelibar Sea. The island was Berdæra. It had formed from a mysterious reddish-brown volcano system, and the entire island and muddied waters surrounding it were a deep bloody red. Most of the rock was volcanic in nature, with red-orange carnelian forming from the hot lava below the surface. The island's nickname was the bleeding island.

The bleeding island's rich, volcanic soils boasted incredible plants and birds. There were over thirty varieties of exotic hummingbirds alone. Some had tails that were twenty times the length of their body, and others were small enough to be preyed on by larger insects. There was even one breed that was as black as night from the long beak to its tail. The *midnight hummingbird*. It was the size of a squirrel hawk, but even though it was fairly large, it still beat its wings so fast they were a blur. The flower varieties on Berdæra were almost unlimited. Týr's mom often got flowers from the island to sell at her stall in the village square. Týr's absolute favorite flowers were the orchids. She marveled at how varied the same species could be—from one simple petal to huge, ornate flowers bigger than her head. Týr felt a pang of guilt. She had been so busy and occupied with the trip and the occupancy with the sect of assassins she had barely thought about her parents. She hoped, too, that the boys had made it back to the village without any incident. She also wondered if the boys had shown up at the cottage for breakfast that morning. These thoughts made her smile, but she missed them all at the same time.

Varanus's voice broke her out of her reverie. "I already have brought in a pile of iron from a neighboring hill," the wyvern told her. He gestured with his winged hand at the pile of rocks in the center of the great cave. "I'd like to begin making an oven or furnace for heat while it is still warm. That way, we will have it in the cooler months."

"That sounds like a good idea," Týr responded. "Will you need the heat in this cave now?"

"I am able to go out into the sun for heat right now, but as the planet leaves the warmth of the suns, I will need the heat. This part of the planet isn't as warm as my home."

The two stood around and got to know each other. Týr heard about the place that Varanus came from, how there were over one hundred wyverns in the dynasty that he came from. He also told her about the years of training he had received in order to mentor her in her training. The two talked back and forth for two hours before they even realized it. Týr felt she actually understood her mentor better after speaking to him about almost everything. Varanus also felt he had a better grasp on his apprentice as well, where she was in her studies, things she already knew, and things that she would only require "brushing up" on. Varanus was confident on his choice for the first lady apprentice in many generations.

It was already midafternoon when they decided that they should get to work. Rævii had slept most of the time the pair of healers had spent talking. It was when they quieted that she began to stir. Tÿr watched the little fox go out of the mine and walk around on the ledge. She obviously had business that needed dealing with, so Tÿr let her go. She knew the furry creature would be back in shortly. Sure enough, in less than a minute, Rævii walked back into the cave and strolled right up to Varanus, all misgivings gone. The fox didn't flinch as the wyvern gently stroked the shaggy fur. Varanus was very kind to Tÿr's pet. Tÿr could see a certain fondness had grown toward her traveling companion.

Tÿr decided that until they had a way to build the heating device for the cavern, she would build a fire. She took out her hunting knife and went to the center of the large chamber. Near the pile of what she had learned was iron, she bent to the cave floor and began to dig in the packed dirt with her blade. Little by little, she chipped away pieces of dirt, and she brushed them out of what was the beginnings of a depression.

She continued working on a firepit while Varanus went down the mountain to find some wood. He made several trips and came back each time to break the longer pieces into nicely sized ones, suitable for burning in the firepit during the nighttime. Tÿr had dug a good-sized pit when Varanus finished his final trip below. She finished scooping out the loose dirt and then helped to put wood in it for the fire. She found that she was hungrier than she had been for a while. Digging in the hard, earthen cave floor was tough work. Tÿr wiped sweat off her brow and went out into the sun. She decided to have a pear or two until she and Varanus would eat an evening meal. She wiped the blade of her knife off on her pant leg, leaving a faint line of blue dust on it. Rævii followed close behind her, hoping to nab a bite of the sweet pear. Varanus joined the other two in the sun. He had stayed behind to start a fire in the newly dug firepit. Little fingers of smoke snaked their way out of the front of the mine opening as he emerged to join them.

"I believe we must go into a town for some supplies and tools we will need to build our heating device. Do you have any place you would prefer to go?"

Týr didn't need any time to think about it. "Could we go back to Vennex? I know where we could go to get some of the things we might need!"

Týr felt excited at the prospect of seeing her friends and parents so soon after leaving. They would be surprised to see her. This would give Týr a chance to let the brothers know that they could visit anytime they chose. It helped to make her training seem not so lonely. Varanus agreed that they could go back to Vennex for some of the supplies. They would also be visiting another town. Varanus told her some of the tools that she would require, and she knew that some she would be able to get from her father's shop. He had extras of many things. Some were even the tools that she used when she assisted him in the shop.

Týr told Varanus about her idea for possibly using the caves to refrigerate certain food items and medicines they would make. Varanus agreed that this was not only going to be time-saving but a very well-planned idea. Týr could tell that the suggestion had impressed her mentor. Coming from where he did, in a more-temperate climate toward the edge of Peyda Kirin, he hadn't used refrigeration to preserve either food or anything else. They had been forced to eat what they had and make what they needed each time it was required. The caves would prove to be very useful once they had the chance to explore them and map the layout. It would also prove useful should they ever encounter unfriendly visitors in their new home. They could hide their belongings or themselves if they had a map of the old mines.

Every once in a while, Týr would spot a particular piece of amethyst on the ground or in the cave that caught the light just right. She'd pick those crystals up and slip them into one of the pouches that she wore on her belt at her waist. It didn't take long before she could feel the weight of it begin to tug at her midsection. She wasn't exactly sure what it was about the purple and lavender crystals that she liked so much. She did enjoy the color, yes, but it was more than that. It was almost like each little crystal contained a tiny world of its own deep inside. Some of the crystals appeared a bit cloudy, and she didn't pick up many of those. It was the ones that were extremely clear that attracted her. The deep-purple hue was just something beautiful to her. Varanus was right, the gems were everywhere, and she was going to collect each one that spoke to her.

Tÿr remembered that Kuired sometimes used crystals and other gems in potions or salves for people. Many had magiqal properties. Although Kuired had known how to employ magiq in his healing, he often didn't use it because many of the older villagers were superstitious and didn't want nor did they allow any magiq of any sort in their homes. Tÿr smiled at that thought. Even though the older people in the village didn't like what they called "new magical medicine," they would change their tunes if their loved ones didn't respond to their old home remedies or traditional medicine. Then they would beg Kuired to use anything to heal them or their loved ones. *People could be funny*, Tÿr thought to herself. They wanted nothing to do with anything new no matter how well it worked, until they were knocking on their own coffin lid.

"There is another town that is approximately an hour's flight to the south of Vennex that I'd like to visit. It is a bit larger, and we might be able to find a few more things that we can use for making basic medicines," Varanus explained to her. "Do you think you will be able to endure such a flight this soon?"

"I'll do it," Tÿr said passionately, "because it has to be done. There are many things in my training that I may not like to do, or want to do, but I agreed to do this and devote my life to this. I will be fine."

"I appreciated those words. I may have to remind you of them before your training is complete," Varanus told her.

"I believe you probably will. I'm not some faintheartedlike waif though. I can do this, and I will make you proud of me!"

"I believe you will." The wyvern nodded. "When the paragon and I recommended you for this mission, we did so because you were by far the most knowledgeable at the trials that day. We knew it wouldn't be the most popular choice we would make, but I firmly stand by my decision. You will complete the training, and I believe that you will be the greatest healer your village has seen for millennia!"

Tÿr was taken aback by the directness by which her mentor spoke. He wasn't giving the most popular choice, only the most logical. Just hearing him speak this way about her helped give her confidence a boost. It would also make it that much harder to quit when the tough times came and she wanted to throw in the towel. Varanus had never seen her work. He'd never known anything about her except for what she'd told him, yet his confidence was high. Maybe he had spoken to Kuired about her. Whatever the case, she would do her best to see that his confidence was not misplaced. She remembered the look on her uncle's face when she had been chosen over his son. She would prove him wrong as well, and she would do whatever it took to do it. The magistrate had tried to make her feel like the wrong choice simply because she had the nerve to be born as the "wrong" sex. If justice ever prevailed, she would be the one who saved her uncle's life someday. Tÿr caught herself. That man would not turn her into the thing he had said her to be. She would be better than he could ever imagine and succeed. That alone would be enough to keep the venom out of his mouth.

"I am going to flush out some dinner for us," Varanus told her. "I'll want to keep my energy up so we can fly to our destinations tomorrow."

"I'll continue to watch the fire then," Tÿr told him. "I will eat whatever is chosen for me then," Tÿr said. "I'm pretty hungry as it is, and Rævii and I are just hungry enough to eat most anything."

"I will see what I can find," Varanus told her, and without another word, he spread his large wings and shot up into the air.

Tÿr wanted to clap her hands and shout. It was completely amazing to watch him fly into the afternoon sky. He banked hard to the left and then dove straight down the side of the cliff. The sight was magnificent. Tÿr though to herself, *I'm glad that I won't have to see that thing drop out of the sky at me.* There would be no escape for anything unlucky enough to be under the shadow of the hunting wyvern.

Tÿr was wandering around the blue cliffs with Rævii at her heels. She was just looking to see what there was of use around the opening to the mine. She spotted some mint growing in a clump of yellow grass. *This will come in useful,* thought Tÿr. She loved to have a bowl of minted pears for pudding after her supper with her parents. Pears were always a treat for her, and now there was a tree right in front of the mine entrance!

Tÿr'Ynyn also found some wild basil growing near the edge of the plateau's edge. Wild basil was one of her favorite herbs because it was so versatile. It could be used for sweet or savory dishes. Her mother would often serve it with mint on different fruits or mix it with butter to slather on fresh biscuits. Tÿr figured that pears with mint and basil would be a great idea for dinner. Basil was in the mint family of herbs and gave a unique flavor to fruits. She grabbed a handful of herbs and returned to the cavern to get her cup. Tÿr muddled the herbs with her fingers in the bottom of the cup, bruising the leaves. Delightful, minty aromas rose from the cup. Her fingers stained green as she mashed the herbs. The little fox was sitting next to Tÿr as she prepared the pears. Its little nose was sniffing the air as the herbs were being crushed. Tÿr smiled down at her new pet. The smell of the herbs made Tÿr think of her mother's kitchen at home. Rævii poked her head from between Tÿr's arms as she finished mixing the pieces of pears. The little fox sneaked a piece and backed up to eat it.

"Do you like that?" Tÿr asked her.

Rævii responded by moving forward to grab another mint-covered pear. The girl stroked the fox's rough fur as it ate the pear slice. She offered the animal another piece, but it didn't take one. The fox seemed to be saying that it knew there was meat on the way and it was going to eat its fill of whatever the wyvern brought back. The tender moment between the human and fox was broken by the flapping sound of wyvern wings. Varanus rose above the edge of the plateau with his rear claws literally full of dead animals. One of the rear feet carried two wild hogs, and the other held several smaller creatures. Tÿr spotted a couple of hares and an owl and something she wasn't familiar with. Varanus dropped the bodies of the animals in a pile before landing next to the two on the ground.

"Wow! That's a lot of meat!" Tÿr exclaimed.

She remembered what she had told Varanus about getting her own food. So far, the only food she had gotten were pears, and they hadn't proven that difficult to hunt. Tÿr examined the pile of dead animals. There was only one creature that she wasn't familiar with. She had seen it before but had never eaten one. It was a *squelle*, a rodent-like creature with two white stripes circling its middle. Adults had several white spots on the hind quarters. Tÿr had never eaten one because most people in the villages didn't eat them. They were scavenging creatures whose meat tasted much like what they had been eating prior to their death, making them unpopular meal items for villagers. People who lived in the rural settings tended to eat whatever was unfortunate enough to wander near, so they were used to the unsavory tastes of the squelle.

"What would you like to eat tonight?" Tÿr asked the wyvern.

"I have already eaten while I was hunting. I was concerned that my eating would upset you."

"Don't be silly," she told the giant lizard. "You couldn't upset me. It's just eating after all!"

Varanus smiled as best he could and nodded. "I will bring the meat that you aren't going to eat into the tunnels of the cave. It should keep fresh in there for a while."

Tÿr chose a wild hog and began to cut it up as the wyvern moved the pile of meat into the mine. The fox stayed right next to her as she worked on dividing the hog into sections for easier cooking. Tÿr felt bad that Varanus thought he needed to eat away from her. The cracking of bones would take some getting used to, but it didn't disturb her. It was just nature. When the meat was stored in the tunnel, Varanus came back out and stood, watching Tÿr carve up the meat.

"Are you sure you wouldn't like some more to eat? There is more than I can eat in a week. Maybe two."

"If you're sure," Varanus told her. "I'll save you the trouble of cutting any more from that hog."

Tÿr grabbed the other half of the hog and dragged it over to Varanus who picked it up and, in two quick bites, swallowed it. "I'm really not going to have to eat for a while," the giant told her. A deep, rumbling belch erupted from the depths of his gut.

"I want to make sure you don't get weak on our trip tomorrow," Tÿr said with mock concern.

Varanus chuckled. "You need not worry about that. I ate the day before as well. I shouldn't need to eat for a few days at the least, but I'll share something with you. I enjoy it. Especially wild hog. It has incredible flavor."

Varanus got serious then. His voice lowered a bit as he continued speaking. "We really do need to begin training. You have had a little time to get acclimated to our new home now, so after you eat, I will ask you to perform some basic magiq for me."

Tÿr felt a panic wash over her. She had never done anything close to magiq before.

"Varanus, I feel I must be completely honest with you. I have never tried to do magiq on purpose or by accident. I'm not sure how to even try!"

The wyvern raised his wing-hand. "It's okay, my friend. I will teach you. I just want to see what your propensity for magiq may be. I will explain the theory, and you will attempt. It will be a way for me to judge how far you are, or yet need to grow."

Tÿr was feeling a little more relaxed. After all, it was only her first day. She didn't want to let her mentor down though. As she gathered the stack of meat, the girl noticed a clump of weeds. She recognized it as *western rat weed*. Her mom had taught her to identify the plant as a youngster. It was one of the first plants she could identify easily back then. Rat weed was a great plant for keeping unwanted pests from any area. The plant caused allergic reactions in all rodents, so they didn't stay around long enough to cause any trouble. She would come right back and harvest most of the plant and spread the leaves around the tunnel near the food. At least she'd be able to keep unwanted visitors out of her food supply.

When she finished her meal and Rævii was satisfied, the fox went and laid down on her bedroll. She had unrolled the sleeping mat on the floor near the fire so she would remain warm in the cool cavern. This would be the very first time that Tÿr would sleep in the darkness. From her home position on the Kirin-Noirin shift, often the suns would be in a position that the planets would shade the shift; so there would be a twilight feel, but it never actually darkened at night. From her studies in school as a youngster, her teachers explained that the twin planets didn't rotate as many others did. That was part of the explanation for the curious gravity on the Peyda planets. As the planet revolved around its triple solar stars, however, it wobbled a bit. This was what the cause of semitwilight came from. It also explained the reason of the dangerous waves on Peyda Noirin as the planets swung around the tight, elliptical orbit. The gravity pulled extremely hard on the seas' waters and caused extremely large tidal waves and tsunamis. Some of the smaller islands could be wiped clean after being hit by the rogue-traveling mountains of water. All travel via water came to an end during the peak of the cool seasons. Only master sailors even attempted to sail then. It was just too dangerous. Varanus was waiting by the entrance of the mine when Tÿr exited.

He sat, perched patiently on his haunches. "Are you ready to begin?"

"I am, Master," she replied formally. She didn't know the etiquette for her position, so she figured that *master* was a good title for him.

"We need not be so stuffy, Tÿr," he told her gently. "My name is fine. I am always called Varanus by everyone, and I don't plan to use a superior title just because I will be training you."

"Yes, Varanus, I will if you wish it."

"I do. Please show me how you would make light from one of the crystals of amethyst on the ground. It is best if you use a chunk of geode or a nice double-terminated crystal."

Tÿr had absolutely no idea how to produce any flame. She picked up a large purple crystal from the ground. She quickly inspected it. It had been sitting there for as long the mountain perhaps. The stone was deep purple and was almost completely clear. Tÿr hoped that the stone she had chosen would not be damaged by the learning tonight.

It was almost too pretty to use. The first thing the wyvern asked of his apprentice was to create light. He told her that she would often need to have light while working indoors where a torch was impractical or she wouldn't have one. Tÿr didn't have any idea what to do. She concentrated as hard as she could. The crystal was warm in her hand, but she didn't have any idea what she needed to do. Did she need an incantation?

After a few minutes of trying everything she could think of, Varanus asked her to attempt to light a small fire on a stick. Again, she began to concentrate. Varanus saw how she screwed up her face, but he sat there impassively, without moving a muscle. Finally, Tÿr's shoulders slouched.

"I'm sorry. I just don't know what I'm supposed to do. I don't know where my magiq is supposed to come from. Does it come from within me? Does it come from an external force?"

Varanus could tell that his apprentice was disappointed. "Do not feel badly," he said softly. "Not everyone can perform magiq. Some healers go for their whole lives without it."

"But I want to be a great healer," Tÿr pleaded. "I truly believe that I will be able to do my job better if I can use magiq."

"It may come to you in time," he said calmly. "But as I said, it may never happen."

Tÿr was disheartened at this news. Kuired had been able to use basic magiq to help his healing. She resigned herself to the fact she might never be the same type of healer as Kuired, but she also decided then and there that she would not rest until she had tried her best.

"Is there something you can suggest to help me concentrate or find the magiq around me?" she asked him.

Varanus was already impressed by the types of questions the apprentice was asking. She didn't ask him to show her things nor did she ask for alleged magiqal items to help. She asked where it could be found and how to concentrate the energy for use. Varanus explained how he could use the magiq, how he could conjure fire not just from deep inside his throat but at his fingertips. He demonstrated how to do it several times to her. He tried to tell her how he felt when he was doing it. Tÿr listened intently, her fingers flexing each time he caused flames to appear.

"I have taught you everything I can think of. I've shown you several times," he continued. "Now, if you are willing, I would like you to attempt it again."

Tÿr was afraid he was going to ask her that. She had listened to every word he had said though. She would try to duplicate his feelings. If she couldn't use magiq, it would be a huge blow to her morale and self-confidence.

"Try to feel the energy enter your head and pull throughout your body feel it gather and pulse in your hands and then into your fingers. It concentrates there and explodes out. Please try the stone again. Make it glow!" Varanus's voice rang with confidence and with a commanding presence.

Tÿr felt something she hadn't before. The doubt was gone. She suddenly felt that this was possible. She took the double-tapered crystal and held it in her open palm. This time she wouldn't squeeze it like before. That might have been something that had helped to distract her before. Tÿr cleared her mind of anything but the crystal and the energy she meant to transfer to it. She wasn't entirely sure, but she thought she felt something. Eyes shut tight, she concentrated harder than she ever had her whole life. She wasn't exactly sure what she was supposed to be feeling. That was when something broke. Not in her head but in her chest. She felt as if a strap that had been restricting her breathing had snapped, and she could finally draw in a full breath of air. Exhilaration was as close as she could to describe the feeling. Tÿr dared a quick peek through one of her closed eyes. Though not bright, there was a light deep inside the crystal. The more intense the feeling grew, the brighter the glow. Her other eye snapped open.

"Varanus!"

The wyvern sat, watching the girl with the crystal. He was sure that he had chosen correctly now.

"It's glowing!" she practically yelled. That was the thing that stopped it. The crystal went plain again. "But it was working, I swear it. Varanus, did you see it?"

"I saw it!" he said.

Even he could hardly contain his excitement. This was just the first time. Now that she had figured she would be able to duplicate it more easily, he would ask her to perform this simple task over and over in the weeks to come, adding one or two things to learn every week.

"Can you repeat it?" he asked eagerly.

Tÿr held out the amethyst again. She could still feel the energy flowing through her. It only took a few seconds before a faint light glowed in the heart of the purple stone again.

"Very good. That will do for now. How do you feel about trying something a little more difficult?"

Tÿr felt like she could do anything at the moment. "Yes, let's do it. What do you want me to do next?" she asked. Tÿr slid the crystal into her pouch on her hip. She would keep this for something special. It held sentimental value now. It was the first thing she had ever performed magiq on.

"I want you to pick up the branch I gave you and try to set it on fire. Do exactly what you did for the stone," he told her.

Tÿr retrieved the little branch and held it out in front of her. Again, she felt energy surge through her. She wasn't sure exactly how she would describe it, which was why Varanus probably had trouble telling her. It wasn't bad at all. The closest she could think of was if she had drunk too many mugs of qafi—the feeling that it gave her, but not the jitteriness. It was pure energy. This time Tÿr could feel the energy. It swirled throughout her head. The feeling was much stronger now. Did healers always feel this way? There was power to be had. Could a person use it properly? Tÿr remembered tales that she and her friends at school would talk about, powerful magiq users that chose to use their magiq to gain power over individuals and countries. Some of the magiq users were infamous people from the past who had misused their power to harm people and seize control of governments. Those were stories that were told as fantastic stories on playgrounds of schools. Tÿr hadn't heard of a magiq user since from before her birth. Many people were very skeptical, although, of magiq. Powerful magiq users just didn't exist anymore as far as she knew. The most that anyone used magiq was to heal or help people, and they were carefully watched and controlled by the governments of all the planets' countries.

Almost as soon as she thought of the stick catching fire, the tip began to smoke. Curls of black drifted above her head. Rævii came out to watch her friend. The smoke had mesmerized the little furball. Embers began to glow and consume the ends of the stick, but no flames ever burst to life. Tÿr tried not to let it get to her. She was pleased enough that she knew she would be able to do some magiq in the first place.

"Very good," Varanus told her. "You have done enough for this day. You have managed more than I could have hoped for. Today you have experienced your *awakening*. This is what the wyverns who can perform magiq call the ability. Congratulations!"

"Awakening is the ability to use magiq?" Tÿr asked the mentor.

"The awakening is when a creature first performs any type of magiq no matter how small or large. Yours has been very successful and is very exciting to witness. Many wyverns of my dynasty have never been part of an awakening. You must be truly gifted. I predict that your life as a master healer will be great. You will be remembered for a long time. The last awakening witnessed by a wyvern was your predecessor, Kuired's. You and he will be the planets' only magiq-using healers!"

Tÿr was surprised by these words. She just assumed that all healers used magiq to aide them. Certainly, there were tales of healers from the past with the ability.

"I believe we will leave our training for tonight. You will find that magiq can take a lot out of you. You may feel shaky or even hungry again. You have done wonderfully this evening. Congratulations on your awakening!"

Tÿr felt a stab of disappointment, but she, too, felt hungry. Even with all the meat she had consumed during the evening meal, she could feel herself growing shaky from what she assumed was lack of food.

"Is it okay if I choose to continue practicing for a while before turning in? I'd really like to see if I can do more with what I've learned."

"There is no need to ask permission to train yourself. You may do so at any time you see fit. Just remember what I told you about using it too often. You most likely are beginning to feel the effects of using magiq already, aren't you?"

Tÿr nodded. She would roast a bit more to eat and try again. She truly was wanting to be the best possible healer that she could be. She knew that using magiq would aide her in that quest. The girl smiled. The thought of her cousin doing any of this was laughable. He was spoiled, and from all the rumors around Vennex, he didn't accept orders well from anyone, even his father. She was sure Varanus had chosen the correct person for the apprenticeship.

Tÿr and Rævii ate some more after roasting some meat over the fire in the cavern. Tÿr hadn't realized how much that little bit of magiq had drained her. She savored the cooked hog that she had cut from the second in the tunnel. There was plenty enough to share with the fox who wouldn't let her go anywhere without her, as long as she held the meat. Tÿr had gotten out her little bag of salt to season the meat well before she cooked it. Rævii had tried crawling up her arms as she cooked the meat on the long stick. She had to set the little animal down next to her several times as she cooked. The herbed salt seemed to act as an attractant for the furry little creature. It began to drool freely as the meat cooked. The two girls sat and ate. Tÿr wanted to get back to the magiq. She was excited to find out how much more she could do, all with the power of her mind. The concept was amazing to her. The little brown fox ate the final bits of the hog and then licked Tÿr's fingers clean.

"You can't still be hungry," the girl teased. "You ate nearly as much as I."

The fox chirped playfully to Tÿr as the girl ran her hand down the shaggy coat. Eventually its full stomach got the better of it, and it laid down on Tÿr's lap. Varanus came near the fire as well.

"I wanted to tell you that I had you use the amethyst from the mountain. It is not one of the easier stones to work with. Many of the old magiq users chose to work with quartz. They are in the same family, but quartz seems to work better as it has less impurities. The next time we are near a place that is known for containing that stone, we will find you a piece to carry with you. I believe you will find it much easier to work with. That will also be a part of your training. You must learn to cut and shape different stones to obtain the most power from them. This is an old art that must be relearned. Too many healers have shunned magiq. Magiq that could have saved lives. You will begin a whole new generation of healers with magiq. Your friend Kuired's knowledge is limited in this area. I foresee that you will surpass him one day."

Tÿr let all this sink in. She would double her efforts to use magiq. She couldn't let her mentor down now. Not after all this confidence he had placed on her. The three of them sat around the fire until Tÿr was too tired to pay attention anymore. She moved from the side of the fire to her bedroll. The area around the firepit was nice and warm. She didn't grab her blanket. It was nice enough to sleep without. Besides, Rævii moved over to her and curled up next to her, putting her furry head on Tÿr's arm. Tÿr laid on her back, arms at her sides. She was exhausted. The little magiq that she had managed really had worn her out. Thankfully, the second meal of nothing but protein helped to bring her back from the brink of total exhaustion.

"Varanus? What is your home like? You're from nearer the desert planet, are you not?"

Tÿr was anxious to hear of the wyvern home and of the workings of the dynasty, how the paragon was brought into power, and how they others responded to him. The whole idea of a creature other than a human having a form of government and a hierarchy was fascinating to her.

"Well, there isn't a lot to tell. My dynasty lives on the side of a volcano in the Keltainyn Sea. The volcano is known as *Thunder Mountain* in the common tongue, or in the local dialect, *Ÿkkynnÿk*. The climate is very warm, especially during the months when the planet is closest the *Trë Suns*. It is even warm deep in the caverns and caves in the side of the mountain. We spend our days…"

Tÿr never heard anything else. Her body, tired from the day's events, gave out, and she dropped off into a deep, dreamless sleep. She didn't move the entire night, sleeping better than she had in a long time. She woke to the lapping of the fox's rough tongue on her face.

Chapter 6

Tÿr was completely rested when she rose from her sleeping roll. Even the hard ground in the cave hadn't bothered her. One thing she was going to see to was getting a cot. Her father had built some for customers who had backed out of the deal at the last minute, and he had been stuck with the six cots. Unfortunately, they hadn't paid anything for them, so they had been a bit of a waste according to her father. If people ever went into the woods for hunting trips, they just took a sleeping mat or even just a couple of blankets. Cots were too heavy to be carrying around all over while they hunted. The whole transaction had left a bad taste in her father's mouth, and he changed his policy on paying for the work before he started on it. He would bend the rule for good customers and only require a down payment for them. He even made his own brother pay up front. He like to tell Tÿr that his brother had more money than the gods and he could afford to pay. Tÿr thought it was because her uncle had become, what some villagers called, a right bastard.

Tÿr had seen what the money and power had done to her uncle. He was not how she remembered from when she was younger. He had been one of her favorite people in the world. Then it all changed when he met her aunt. She had never been kind or even pleasant. She was demanding and had her uncle running in several directions at once. She knew why too. Her aunt was very pretty. Not in the traditional way by any means. Her nose was a bit too slender as was her jaw. The cheeks weren't as high as some and her lips not as full. She was the perfect type of wife for an important man like her uncle. She had insisted that he run for the position of magistrate, and when he was elected to the position, everyone that had helped him make his climb was left by the wayside. Anyone who didn't fit the bill of being deemed important enough to her aunt was basically ignored.

As a youngster, Tŷr didn't understand why her uncle didn't come around to their cottage anymore. There was no more bouncing on his knee or playing outside at the cottage. Her aunt had turned him against his own brother, and Tŷr realized that she had resented the woman for that. Now her uncle was every bit as nasty as the woman he had partnered with. Tŷr didn't feel proud about this, but she couldn't wait until she could go back to Vennex and show off even the tiny bit of magiq she had learned. She knew that her cousin would not have been able to do anything close to what she had managed the night prior, not without his mother whispering answers into his ear anyway. The girl felt another stab of guilt at these feelings of ill will toward her uncle. She missed the days when he was still his happy-go-lucky self.

Varanus was not in the cave when Tŷr looked around. She walked out of the cavern to find out when her mentor wanted to leave. She was ready as soon as he gave the word. She was anxious to get back to Vennex to see her parents and her two best friends. Varanus was not out on the small plateau surrounding the mine entrance either. Tŷr decided to look for more rat weed to scatter in the tunnels. She couldn't abide the furry menaces. They seemed to be able to go anywhere and get into things even if they were sealed. The thought of sharing a cave with the foul rodents was most distasteful. There were several more clumps of the herb growing around the flattened ground. She found one clump right at the edge. With her arms full of the green herb, she went into the mine again and dropped handfuls of the rat weed all around the cavern and down both tunnels. When her arms were empty, she went back out and into the light to pick a few pears to take along her upcoming trip. As she was choosing the largest pears, she heard the now-familiar sound of wyvern wings. A shadow crossed above her, and the figure of her mentor settled on the ground near the entrance of the mine. Rævii watched interestedly as the wyvern came to rest gently on the plateau. The little fox seemed to be asking why she hadn't been invited on the flight.

"Did you enjoy a restful sleep?" Varanus asked his apprentice.

"I did, thank you. Did you have a restful night?"

"Alas, I did not sleep very much. I did rest as you fell to sleep, but I needed to speak to my paragon. I needed to tell him of your ability and that you are further along than even he had assumed you would be. He had hoped that you would have some magiqal abilities but had no idea that you would show such promise. Your knowledge of plants had already impressed him greatly."

Tÿr was amazed by this. "You flew all the way to Ÿkkynnÿk Mountain during the night?" She was shocked that her mentor could have traveled such a distance in so little time.

"No," Varanus shook his angular head. "Ghra'zhenn, my paragon, is in residence at the northern end of the Anbry mountain range. He will remain there for the next two years to assist should I require it and watch over things here. He has taken great interest in you, Tÿr'Ynyn!"

Tÿr felt about a hundred different things all at once. Pride, curiosity, and exhilaration were some of the feelings that bombarded her. When a wyvern took an interest in a human, it was a special thing; but when a paragon wyvern did, that was amazing. Tÿr had to make damn sure that she didn't let any of them down. Varanus had been carrying a large pack when he landed, but Tÿr hadn't noticed at first.

"What do you have there?" she asked, pointing to the large cloth bag.

"I picked up a few things I thought would be nice for you."

He twisted the toggles on top of the black bag and opened it up. Despite the fact the Varanus's hands were located on the middle-bend section of his wings, he was very nimble with them. Tÿr had seen him pick up the smallest pieces of crystals from the ground. He could also snap large branches as if they were nothing. As Varanus unpacked the bags, he told Tÿr that the plans to go to Vennex would be postponed by an hour or so. She didn't care as long as they were still going. The wyvern pulled several smaller bags from the large one, along with at least ten bottles of something that Tÿr assumed was wine.

"What is that?" she asked.

"Ah, have you never heard of sweet wyvern wine?"

Tÿr had heard of it. She'd known people who had drunk it before. It was a very strong wine made of *desert dragon fruit*. The fruit was said to ferment on the trees as it ripened because of its high sugar content. Wyverns often ate the fruit for many of their ceremonies. The visions it induced were said to be intense. Many people had died from eating too much of the fruit as it had toxic effects in large quantities.

"I have heard of dragon fruit wine, but I've never tried it," she told him.

"I myself do not drink the wine," Varanus told her. "I do, however, enjoy dragon fruit when it is at its peak ripeness. Eating too many can produce some severe hallucinations, so I just have them as a treat once in a while," Varanus continued. Each blue bottle had a cork stopper dipped in wax to preserve freshness.

"So are we going to be leaving now, or is there going to be a delay this morning? I planned to bring some pears for Rævii and myself to eat on our way."

"A good idea. We will be gone until after the evening meal. We will find you a place to go in the villages. If you get hungry while we are there, I will drop you outside of the village proper as many people don't take kindly to a wyvern strolling the main square of their cities. On that note, we should also leave the fox here as well. I fear that its safety may be in danger if we bring a fox into a city where there are many farming people. Foxes tend to be known as bird killers, and the farmers might mistake our little friend for a common bird killer."

Tÿr nodded. That made good sense to her. She had grown very fond of her pet fox and was not going to lose her because of their prejudices. Varanus continued to unload the pack that he had returned with. One thing looked like a small pillow filled with straw and other grasses.

"I brought this along for the fox to sleep on," he said, handing the cushion to Tÿr. There were tools and bottles of wine, the cushion, and a box of small clay jars with lids. There were also the smaller bags in a pile next to the other items. "I've brought these jars for storing herbs and salves that we may need. This way, we have some way to organize our supplies."

Tÿr noticed that many of the jars were different colors, or had different-color lids to go on them. She understood how clever this was. She could store different items in each of the jars, and as long as she memorized which jar contained which supply, the system would work well for her. She also understood that there would now be the need for shelves. After working in her dad's furniture shop, she had learned how to build and carve many things. She could easily make some shelves for the tunnels and the cavern to help keep things in order. The apprentice helped to move everything into the cavern. She placed the cushion near her makeshift bed so Rævii could sleep on something other than the hard floor, or her, should it choose. The wine she put in the tunnel by the meat. It was cool in the tunnel and would be a perfect place for the wine to keep. The other things she stacked near the wall between the tunnels. She made sure that the tools sat on something to keep them off the sometimes-damp cavern floor. She didn't want them to rush or get dull. When she returned outside to talk to Varanus, she was surprised to see the huge form of Ghra'zhenn sitting next to him, and they were deep in conversation.

"Hello." She waved to the paragon. "How are you feeling today?

The air came alive with the larger wyvern's deep, booming voice. "Tÿr'Ynyn, it is a pleasure to see you again! Your mentor has told me about your ability. Would you be able to show it to me?" the huge lizard asked her gently.

"Of course. It's really nothing. Once I learned the little trick to do it, it is quite easy," she said proudly.

"It is by far a little trick, young one. Many healers go their entire lives without so much as a flicker. Varanus said your crystal actually glowed for longer than just a moment. That is truly amazing for your first attempt. I foresee greatness from you! Please never make light of your ability to use magiq. It is an incredible gift to be sure."

Tÿr was sure that she had just been admonished, but the giant was so caring and decent when he spoke she wasn't completely sure.

Varanus spoke up, "I'd like you to try using this crystal. I located this piece of quartz while I was out earlier."

He reached his hand out, and Tÿr took the crystal from him. It was a piece of crystal-clear quartz. It tapered on each end, and on the inside of it, she saw what looked like two exact, smaller versions of the stone growing inside the larger piece—one inside, the other inside the large piece. It refracted light in her palm, and rainbows shone on her face and in the eyes of her mentor.

"This is beautiful, Varanus!"

"Yes, it is, and I believe that you will be able to use your magiq better with this piece. Please show Ghra'zhenn what you can do!"

Tÿr held the stone tightly in her hand at first. She began to concentrate as hard as she could. A sharp pain shot through her left temple. Without thinking, she brought her hand up to her head.

Varanus grew concerned. "You're working too hard. Let the energy flow back into you like it did last night."

Tÿr took a deep breath and relaxed the grip on the quartz. Immediately the tingling sensation began in her head. Energy began to fill her chest and move down her arms. Not bothering to close her eyes, she stared at the glassy crystal on her palm. The center of it began to show some signs of energy. And then the next crystal on the inside showed life, all at once; it was as if someone turned the crystal's switch. It began to glow brightly, much brighter than the amethyst had. Even her hand seemed to be alight. Tÿr looked over at the pair of wyverns who were watching her raptly, wound up in the moment. She looked to Varanus, who in turn turned to look at Ghra'zhenn. All three of them wore smiles, though the largest by far belonged to the human girl.

"Astounding!" was all Ghra'zhenn managed to say. It was clear that he had not been prepared for what he was seeing.

Varanus was as proud as he could have been. "This is going to change the dynamic of things I believe," he told the paragon. "We may end up with our hands full at some point."

Ghra'zhenn nodded.

"This changes things, but for the better. We knew it was possible, but not this soon!"

Varanus was excited about something that Tÿr didn't understand. He wasn't willing to tell her yet though. He and the paragon walked away from Tÿr, who let the light fade from the stone in her hand. She knew that this would now be a lucky stone that she would carry everywhere. At least, that was her plan, if her mentor didn't take it back from her. Tÿr was a bit confused by the conversation between the two wyverns. She approached them as they talked in hushed tones.

"Varanus, you were correct, this crystal is much easier for me to use. I wanted to give it back." She stood with her hand outstretched.

Varanus cut his conversation off with the paragon. "No, Tÿr, I brought that for you. In time, we will incorporate it into a staff for you to use, similar to the one your friend, Kuired Gÿann, carries."

Tÿr had to think for a moment. She knew Kuired's name, but hardly anyone used his second name when referring to him. People didn't take a second name until they reached the age of thirty-five. It was a tradition that people on the Kirin-Noirin shift and many of the islands on Peyda Noirin has adopted. At one time, it was tradition on both the conjoined planets, but the desert dwellers had dropped the tradition a few centuries before. Now they either chose one or two names depending on their desires at the time. Generally, if a child had two names, they were from the desert. There was one exception to both rules, and that was on the *Open Hand Archipelago*. That particular group of islands was home to a "family" called the *Imbröttiös*. The Imbröttiös family chose to have as many as several names, all with the surname Imbröttiös. They were a feared family that often inbred among themselves. When the gene pool became too murky or they ran out of breeding adults, the family sent out raiding parties that would travel all over the planet to kidnap and bring more people into the family. It was overseen by a cruel yet shrewd old man called *Ekaj Joonts Laynn*. He was incredibly distrustful of anyone not related to himself and hated magiq. Any of the Imbröttiös from the third generation or younger could be instantly identified by their lack of earlobes.

Tÿr's mind had wandered for a moment. She quickly came back though. The quartz crystal was hers. It sparkled in her hand like a huge diamond. The prism effect was still throwing rainbows around the plateau. Tÿr put the crystal in her pouch with the others she had collected. She was already trying to think of what her staff would look like. She had always admired Kuired's, though she had rarely been allowed to touch it. He was extremely protective of it. Tÿr let her mentor finish talking to his mentor. They only continued for a couple of minutes before Ghra'zhenn announced that he had to be going. He said that he had many things to do, including a flight back to the island of the dynasty. The huge wyvern gently touched Tÿr on the head and told her how glad he was that he had chosen her for the position. He also told her that he planned to spend more time with her during her extensive training.

After Ghra'zhenn left the training team, Tÿr helped Varanus attach the harness for her to use for the flight. He also took the large bag that he had used earlier. Tÿr made sure that her pet fox was nestled in her new bed. She left a small pile of sliced pears for Rævii to eat and went back out to prepare for her flight.

As she climbed on her mentor, it struck her that she had never really flown before. Sure, she had ridden up to the plateau, but she was always close to something. Now she would be high above the ground without the comfort of anything near her. Suddenly her stomach was in knots. She held on tighter than she would probably need to. Varanus checked this time to make sure she was ready, and then without pause, he lifted up. The ground pulled away from the pair quickly as the wyvern's strong wings forced them off the earth.

In mere moments, the cavern had vanished from Tÿr's vision. Below her was the Ajenti River sparkling like a jewel in the middle of the thick forest. The rise and fall of the wyvern's wings were disconcerting for Tÿr'Ynyn. In no way was the flight smooth, like she had hoped it would be. She held on with every ounce of strength she possessed. Luckily, the ride to Vennex wasn't as long as Tÿr thought it would be. There was no twisting path or rough ground to traverse. From above, she spotted the opening of the fields surrounding Vennex, and as they descended, the tops of buildings in the town came into view. The descent was not a gentle lowering but a dropping by many feet at a time. Tÿr's stomach was in her throat as they got closer to the village. She tried to hold her composure when they finally landed, but in reality, she was very glad to be on the ground again. Her legs were jelly when she disembarked from her seat on the harness.

Despite her discomfort from flying, she was very excited to be back in Vennex. It had only been a few days since she had left, but it seemed longer. Many things had happened since her departure, and she was excited to tell her parents and her friends about them. She was especially excited to tell Danior and Gordian that Varanus would allow them to visit whenever they wanted.

The walk from the field to her parents' cottage didn't take her any time at all. She practically sprinted the whole way there. Varanus was careful where to go so as not to spook the villagers. He knew from tales in the dynasty that humans could still be superstitious and possibly mistake him for one of the fearsome dragons of old. Though there hadn't been tales of any dragons in many years, he didn't wish to risk upsetting the villagers. If they were scared, they might be provoked to attack; and though he could take care of himself, the damage would be done if any human were injured in a showdown between a villager and himself. The wyverns had spent centuries portraying themselves as benevolent creatures, and even if humans attacked him first, the damaged would be permanent. All that the wyverns had worked toward would be lost.

Tÿr'Ynyn's visit at her parents' cottage got her a meal and time to visit. She was able to get some of her tools from her father's shop and also took one of the cots that had never sold. She finally knew it was time to be on her way. She and Varanus still had one more town to visit before returning to their home. Tÿr met up with Varanus and delivered what she had gotten from her father. There was still one last stop to make here. Varanus was gracious and never made her feel rushed. She did make it a quick visit to the brothers' cabin. They were very excited to see her. They told her about their return trip and about what had happened the day they had been home. She listened intently but told them that she had to go. She also let them know that they were welcome to come and visit whenever they wished. They seemed very excited by this, though they didn't want her to leave them again. Tÿr kissed and hugged them and left to join Varanus again.

Danior and Gordian were not the only friends Tÿr saw that day. When they left Vennex, they flew to the town of Yelliton. Yelliton was a much-larger town than Vennex, with a more-diverse group of shops and places to purchase supplies. Tÿr wasn't sure where all the money was going to come from because Varanus had a large list of things he wanted to purchase. It turned out that he had several gold and silver pieces in a pouch tied to his hand. Most of their time in Yelliton was spent finding things they would need to put the shop together in the cave. Varanus wanted to assemble a large variety of shelves for ingredients of potions and medicines and salves. He also wanted to make sure that Tÿr had her privacy. They ordered a load of cut wood to be driven to the mountain. Varanus would bring it up to where Tÿr could make the shelves and other things required. After they had gotten their orders placed, they went to locate Kuired. They found his healer shop on the outskirts of the town. He had affixed a sign to a post in front of his cabin that said, "Master Healer's Quarters."

Kuired appeared happy to see Tÿr. They chatted about her new position and other things before Varanus suggested that they should get going. The two of them bid Kuired goodbye, and they were again on their way. The trip back to the mountain was easier for Tÿr. It was still uncomfortable to be up so high, but she didn't have a death grip on the straps this time. She had found a way to fly more comfortably. By laying close to the wyvern's neck, the wind didn't assault her as much, and she didn't feel like she was fighting the flight. The trip lasted longer than the trip to Vennex as they were about an hour farther away. Still, the time went quickly, and they were descending toward the cave sooner than she expected.

Chapter 7

The trips the previous day had done a world of good for Tÿr. She was still flying high from her success with magiq. She was also pleased that she had the chance to let her friends know that they could visit her anytime on the mountain. In fact, Varanus said that he would even make trips around Vennex and back to see if the brothers were in the woods traveling to the mountain.

Last night, for the first time in a few days, Tÿr had slept on a cot instead of the ground or the hard, cavern floor. Rævii didn't know what to do at first when Tÿr had gotten on the cot, but Tÿr lifted the young fox up to lay down next to her. The fox snuggled with her for a short time, but then she decided to jump down and sleep on the soft, grass-filled cushion. The girl had already decided that she would save the feathers from any birds that they had for dinner. She could then stuff the cushion when it got too thin after the grass broke down.

The morning activities went along smoothly. Tÿr was anxious to begin her training. Even though twenty years was a long time to learn things, she wanted to begin as soon as possible. She felt that she would have a better chance of learning what she needed to if she was younger. Her mind felt sharp, and her magiq had agreed to work with her thus far. She knew much about healing and about harvesting herbs and plants for tonics and potions to help her villagers should they fall ill, but the magiq was what really garnered her attention. She wanted to be able to help people with it, sure, but shoving that smug look off his uncle's and aunt's face and cramming it down their throats, that would really be worth it. True, it was completely selfish to wish this upon her own blood, but she was completely fed up with the snobbish attitude of her aunt and boorishness of her uncle. She couldn't really blame the pale, little toad of a son that they had raised. He was a product of the environment. It didn't necessarily excuse the behavior, but it definitely explained it.

Magiq was going to aid her in creating elixirs and potions and other things that all medical science couldn't alone. It was also good to be a magiq user to offer charms to keep disease and harm at bay. Magiq was still something of a taboo among the older villagers, though the younger generation didn't mind if a healer employed it. Varanus was sitting outside the mine entrance when she walked out. She noticed that he had dug a hole in the earth where the previous firepit had been. Now there were rocks surrounding the circle. It looked like her mentor had made another firepit, one outside.

"We already have a firepit, Varanus. What's this one for?"

"The one inside is simply for cooking and warmth. This pit outside is for melting iron and other things. We are going to need to make the oven to warm the mine inside, and without any breeze to fan the fire, it won't get hot enough."

Near the fire was a large pile of wood broken into three-foot sections. Obviously, the wyvern had been busy while she had been asleep.

"What will we be doing today?" she asked her mentor.

"Today is when I will get an idea of exactly how much you know about basic healing. Now that we have ingredients, I will have you make several different types of potions and elixirs. What is made correctly, we will store in the tunnel to use when the need arises. Are you up for this challenge, or should you require another day or two to get organized?"

"I require no more time. If I do well with this, may we practice more magiq? I want to become sufficiently practiced in something more than making a stone glow. I know it will come in handy sometimes, but what about something else that will be more useful?"

She thought of all the mixing of potions that she was going to end up doing and figured there had to be some type of spell that might be useful for that. Týr knew that some potions actually had to be stirred or mixed in a certain direction before reversing the direction. These could be tedious and extremely temperamental potions and ointments. Her mind also went back to the time a few days prior when those thugs robbed them on the path.

"Varanus, I wanted to ask you about something. I know magiq can be helpful for when I need light of want to make fire, but what about if I'm attacked?"

Varanus grew very solemn. "Why do you ask this? Has something happened to you?" His voice was riddled with deep concern. "Has someone used magiq against you in the past, child?"

Tÿr shook her head vigorously. "No! It's nothing like that, but on my way to meet you here, my friends—you know, the brothers you met yesterday—well, we were robbed by a group of assassins from the Amsälja Vrasës sect."

If Varanus hadn't been paying attention before, his head snapped to attention at the mention of that. Though Amsälja Vrasës wasn't the most notorious of the deadly assassin sects, they were enough to cause a great deal of concern for the wyvern. "Amsälja Vrasës! You're completely sure?"

"Yes, the leader had the wolf heart with a blade through it just here." She pointed to the hollow place in her neck.

Varanus nodded. "That definitely sounds like them. It was a six-valved heart, not just a four-chamber one?"

"Oh, it was definitely a wolf heart. Four main veins above and two below. There's no mistaking it."

"Okay," he said, putting out a hand. "This is going to take some thought. If Amsälja Vrasës is moving this far from the sewer that they call home, we could have some problems."

"That is why I thought it might be better to learn some defensive magiq, along with the other…"

Varanus contemplated for a few moments without even moving. This was going to be sanctioned by him if he taught her this. She was too valuable to risk losing—he decided in the end—so he would teach her some basic magiq defensive spells that she could at least use to block or get out of danger. Varanus still needed to discuss this with his paragon before committing to much magiq ahead of his schedule.

"When you have completed the basic potions and elixirs."

Tÿr felt that this was completely acceptable and agreed to it immediately. "I accept!" Tÿr said without needing to hear anything more.

With that, Tÿr'Ynyn's training began in earnest. She made every salve that Varanus had asked of her. She made sixteen different elixirs as well. Many could be made from similar ingredients, so Tÿr made them as she went on, cutting down her work as much as she could. Her father had always explained that she should work smart and not hard. She had completed most of the potions in good time. Varanus was again very impressed.

By the time Tÿr felt hunger gnawing at her stomach, she had completed over forty different items that she could use should the need arise. About halfway through the potions, Tÿr had an idea. Some of the potions needed to be stirred so many times one way and then the other way. If the amount of stirring wasn't followed exactly, the potion could be ruined; it could end up being something completely different, which meant sometimes it could be dangerous. The only way she would know would be to give it to someone. With her reputation on the line—and not only that, in some cases a life—she was not willing to risk it. Sometimes the potions or salves or whatever mix she was working on would change colors after being mixed so many times in one direction. This helped her to keep count, but other times, the elixir was simply clear. She had an idea.

"Varanus? Is there a way to mix potions faster and keep track of the turns of the spoon? I'm so worried that I could undermix something or give something and extra stir. Is there a way to do this quicker and more accurately?"

The pale-blue lizard chuckled quietly as he sat, watching her mix one of her last salves. The object of the stirring wasn't the speed; it was to make sure the healer or apothecary paid attention to the thing they were making. Speed had nothing to do with it, unless it said to stir for exactly eight or ten minutes. Without a time limit, one could stir it in a flash. It was about following instructions.

"I have been expecting this question." He continued to chuckle, but not mean-spiritedly. "Ghra'zhenn said to expect this from you, and he is hardly ever incorrect."

Tÿr didn't know whether to be pleased or if she was just being a predictable human. "How do you mean, Master?"

"My paragon said to expect this question from you because he predicted that you would be clever enough to think to ask it!"

This time Tÿr blushed, though she was trying desperately to keep her composure. Varanus could see the conflict in his apprentice's face. On one hand, she wanted to be good, but she was worried about feeling good when she had done as she wanted.

"Never keep yourself from being proud of your accomplishments, Tÿr'Ynyn. When you do well, you should feel proud and celebrate your triumphs. So often people aren't told that they have performed well, and that can lead to resentment." Varanus continued, "My mentor told me to expect great things from you already when he chose you back at your village. It is good to be humble, but celebrate your greatness too!"

Some of the pink left Tÿr's face. She wasn't always praised. By her parents, she grew up knowing that she had done a nice job when she had done something exceptional. But during her schooling, she was too busy fighting the boys for position. Girls weren't forbidden from learning, but it was never easy for them at all. Tÿr would use what little power she had as a healer to help young girls of the village to advance themselves as well. She had been given this chance to prove herself more than just a breeding member of the village. In fact, with the job of master healer, she probably wouldn't have time for that at all.

When all her work was done, Varanus kept his word and set out to teach her a bit of magic, things that could assist her in her potion-making for now. He would go to the paragon while Tÿr slept and discuss anything more difficult, like protection spells and the possibility of making her own staff that would act as a conduit to charge the magiq and focus its power. Her mentor oversaw everything that Tÿr did. He didn't watch over her shoulder, which would probably make her nervous, but he watched to make sure she didn't make a mistake as she worked. Tÿr's batch of medications grew. After finishing each one, she would store it in a jar so she could find it easily. It was a huge help to have them color-coded.

They ate after all the work she had done. Rævii was happy to have her friend all to herself again. After their food had settled, Varanus asked Tÿr to produce a light in her crystal without touching it. Tÿr was able to do this almost as soon as Varanus had said the words. It was glowing in her pouch before she took it out.

"Very good!" Varanus complimented. "Now make it go dark, and I want to see how quickly you can do it again. Wait until I tell you."

She dimmed the quartz and then, on his word, brought back to shining life. It was even more brilliant this time. They practiced this for a bit longer before he had her try something completely new— fire on her hand. He instructed her to allow a small flame to hover over her palm. It took a couple of tries. The first time she lit her hand on fire, but as it was a magiqal flame, it didn't burn. It only took a couple more tries before a perfect flame hovered in her hand. Without prompting, Tÿr made the flame float between her hands. Varanus was very pleased. He continued to have her manipulate the flame. First, he had her divide it and hold one in each of her hands, and then he had her try more difficult things, like making it hover in the air—first in front of her, then above her. That was when Tÿr got an idea.

"Master, may I try something?"

"Proceed," the wyvern commanded.

Tÿr concentrated, and then the flame shot at the firepit. Burning wood pieces were blasted out and spread around the ground. The wyvern stared into the pit.

"I believe you now have one defensive spell at your disposal," he said.

Rævii had come to see what all the excitement was. She rubbed up against Tÿr's leg as if to congratulate her too. The apprentice reached down to pet the little fox. The smile on her face couldn't have been bigger. She reached out her other hand and willed the flame back to her. Without hesitation, the flame pulled out of the firepit to settle back on her outstretched hand.

Chapter 8

Tÿr's ability as a healer grew at an astounding rate. In a short time, she was able to do things that master healers could do. Ghra'zhenn had also taken an active role in her training as well. He was spending more and more time at the cavern, as were Tÿr'Ynyn's two best friends. The first visit they had ever made was done unaided by Varanus. He had been spending more and more time flying between his paragon's second home and the mine. With Tÿr's new abilities growing so quickly, he had many things to report.

One day, Tÿr had been studying large tomes that Ghra'zhenn had brought for her to use. They were ones the wyverns had rescued from certain destruction in different towns and villages from over the entire two planets. She had heard some rustling coming from over the side of the plateau. And voices. She was sure she had heard voices. Immediately she was on alert and held handfuls of fire, prepared to shoot them at any would-be assailants. The apprentice had walked to the edge to sate her curiosity. Varanus had taught her to always have the upper hand in situations of attack. That was when she heard the two brothers talking as they scaled the side of the cliff face.

Danior's hand had been the first to feel his way to the top as his brother helped him reach the plateau. "Grey gaunts! How much farther can it be? I'm so tired I don't know how much longer I can do this!"

"You'll do it because there is no other choice," came Gordian's voice from below.

Tÿr quickly doused the fires from her hands and kneeled to pull her friend up to the plateau. Gordian struggled for a moment before he finally managed to push himself up and over the top as well. Both the boys then moved from the edge and dropped their traveling packs, followed shortly by themselves.

"Thanks, Týr beer!" Danior breathed deeply as he laid on the blue earth to rest.

Gordian removed his goatskin and took a long drink before passing it to his brother.

Týr moved over to grab both their packs. "Get off the ground, you two! I've got beds for you to kip down on!"

Over the past few months, Týr had requested many more loads of sawed lumber to build a few things out of. She had made some beds that Varanus had gone out and provided feather mattresses for. He had also gotten some thick blankets for when the weather began to cool as the cooler season would start soon. The boys followed Týr into the mine entrance and to their waiting beds.

"Gordi says your hair has gotten long," Danior said from behind her.

"It has a bit, I suppose," Týr said over her shoulder. "You haven't seen me for almost four months."

"I haven't seen you ever!" Dani joked back.

Týr had really missed the boys, but she was almost ashamed to admit that she had been so busy she really hadn't had the time. It was so good to have them here now!

Gordian was impressed to see the inside of the cavern. It was much larger than he had thought it would be. There were many rows of shelves lining the back of the cavern, with bottles and jars of all shapes and sizes on every shelf. There were also racks where herbs were drying. Some hung in large bunches while others were laying out in piles. It helped give the smoky-smelling cave a fresh scent as well. Many of the cut plants had large, drying flowers. In the center near the firepit were four beds all made up with blankets and large pillows. A complete luxury for the boys. On the other side of the cavern was a large, circular metal device that stood over ten feet tall. There were vents cut into the bottom and top, and this, not the firepit, was where the pleasant warm of the cool cavern was coming from.

"What on the Peydas is that thing?" Gordi asked, pointing to the large metal thing.

"That is our forge and furnace. Come, I'll show you!"

Gordian could hear the pride in Tÿr's voice as she explained how Varanus required the heat to survive, as did the paragon when he spent time here. She explained how she and Varanus had constructed the huge heating device from the ore that Varanus had provided. Both boys sat in rapt attention as she told them everything she had accomplished in the short time that they had been apart. She even gave them a brief demonstration of a couple of the magiq triumphs she had mastered. They were truly impressed, but they were also tired from the long trip they had just come from.

"How long are you planning to stay?" Tÿr asked before she let them rest.

"We haven't really decided," Danior replied. "Would a week be allowed?"

"Just one?" Tÿr asked in semi-mock disappointment.

"We don't want to be any trouble," Danior answered. "We were just missing our time with you, and we finally had a chance to come. If a week is too long, we can…"

"A week is fine!" the girl told him. "You are welcome here anytime, and I'm sure Varanus would have no problem if you stayed longer."

"We will see, Tÿr beer," Gordian concluded. "Right now, though, I just want to take a rest. The mountain didn't look as high as it actually is."

"Okay, just lay down, and when you wake, we can eat. What sounds good to you two?"

"Oh, you know Gordi, he'll eat a boot if you put the right gravy on it."

Tÿr knew that wasn't far from the truth either.

"We brought some fish too if you would like a change of pace from pears," Gordian said, smiling.

Tÿr had told them about the large pear tree outside the cavern that had the nicest fruit. She knew pears would be something the boys didn't often have, and she had meant to save some for them, but the tree barely got low on the delicious fruit. In the moderate climate on the mountain, the trees were practically evergreen and always produced pears. Once the boys were in their beds, Tÿr went back outside to continue studying. Their arrival had been exactly what she needed. Her spirits, though not low, were lifted higher now that her friends had come.

The tome she was reading was explaining that there were many ways to control fire. She had already learned many of the ways to employ the fire to work—from warming to lighting to destroying in large blasts. The passage she was reading explained that fire could be split into many separate flames and used to target multiple targets at once. This particular tome was one of Tÿr's favorites. It contained many defensive maneuvers to aide in the suppression of enemies. She absorbed the words as she read. There had already been spells that she had learned, which aided her in potion-making, spells that could be instructed to stir or mix things in a particular order or direction; and upon the employment of the spell, it would happen in the blink of an eye. Things that had taken hours to prepare were being completed in just minutes. According to both wyverns, she was ahead in her training.

Tÿr tried to spend an equal amount of time in the magiq tomes and the medical scrolls. She used the many diagrams and charts to memorize body parts and positions. It wasn't just the human body either. She memorized animal charts as well. Being a healer was going to require all physiologies—from human to every animal on the Peyda planets. Ghra'zhenn had already told her that her talents were proving to be amazing, and if she continued on the path she had set, he would also be recommending that the wyvern dynasty use her as their healer. Her skills would outweigh his if this accelerated path of learning continued. Tÿr was not about to let Varanus nor Ghra'zhenn down. She studied hard for many hours each day; sometimes she only got three or four hours of sleep. Varanus had warned against this, for he was concerned that she would get burned out and then she would be more likely to not want to learn as much. Tÿr made sure that when she was so tired, she did get rest. There was no real set schedule on becoming a healer. Most people took the entire twenty years of studying and practice to become comfortable enough to continue alone. Tÿr was sure of her abilities now, but also knew how far she had to go. This path she had chosen could possibly be expedited, but practice and technique would make her a great healer, not just memorizing journals.

The apprentice continued reading in the thick tome, going over everything more than once to absorb the information. When the words began to melt together, she decided to set the huge book down. She was getting hungry and knew the boys would be as well. She almost jumped out of her skin. Varanus was sitting on the ground next to her. She had been so deeply involved in her studies she hadn't even heard her mentor return.

"I hope I didn't scare you!" he said quietly.

Tÿr'Ynyn had to suppress a startled yell. "Good gaunts!" she mimicked her friend. "When did you get back?"

"I have been here for a short time," the wyvern answered her. There was no amusement in his voice. He could see a slight glowing on the skin of her hands. She was seconds from casting a fireball. "I should have made my presence known when I landed," Varanus explained to the still-shaken girl.

"I swear I'm going to get you a bell to wear around your neck."

Varanus's teeth shone in a smile. "But how will you get me to wear it?" he teased.

"You'll sleep sometime," the girl joked back.

The two joked together for a few minutes. Tÿr had really gotten comfortable around her mentor. They were both learning together as they were both comparatively young for their species. At one point, Tÿr had become overwhelmed by fits of laughter as she tried to explain certain parts of human physiology to Varanus. He had been taught much, but to hear some of the issues coming from a human, it had seemed unbelievable. The more he couldn't grasp, the funnier it was to Tÿr. By the time she had been able to explain the point to him, they were both laughing.

"By the way," Tÿr told her mentor, "we have company for a week or two if you don't mind."

"Who is it?" he asked curiously.

"Dani and Gordi."

"Ah, delightful," he replied. "You could definitely use a break in your studying! I don't want you to become burned out on everything. You have certainly earned a respite!"

"Oh, thanks, Varanus! I won't have any problem. I've decided to rotate the things I'm learning so they don't become boring for me. I've tried to do as much human physiology as I can digest. In between, I practice my magiq. I've gotten quite good."

"I have been observing you. Your magiq is far beyond what I could have thought possible. Many healers never accomplish what you have in their whole lifetime. Ghra'zhenn has taken a tremendous interest as well, as you know."

Týr felt pleased with her progress. She had never thought that she would be a magiq user in her life. The fact that it came so easy was something very pleasing to her. The girl decided to stop her studying for the night. It was time to celebrate and spend time with her friends. She grabbed the huge volume and walked it to her bed. When Týr walked into the cavern, Gordian was just sitting up in the bed. He smiled at her as she put the book down.

"Hey, Týr beer, I brought a bottle for us tonight. While your master—"

"He isn't my master, goofy!"

"Whatever he is, do you think he will mind if we crack a bottle?"

"Not if you brought him a bottle!" Týr could see the wheels turning in her friend's mind.

"Are you serious?"

"I'm not sure, actually," she said thoughtfully. The amount of wine that it would take the wyvern to get drunk would probably be astounding, nothing that the boys could have carried anyway.

Gordian nudged his brother to wake him. "Hey, sleepy, wake up. It's time to celebrate!"

"What are we celebrating?"

"Being here!" Gordian told his brother.

"Is it morning already?"

"It's time to get up and have a cup of wine!" Týr told him.

Danior sat up and stretched. He hadn't even taken off his cap before laying down. He removed it and scrubbed his hands through his already-messed-up hair.

"What do you want to eat?" Tÿr asked them.

"What are the choices?" Dani asked. He was having trouble waking up.

"We have some wild hog that we could cook with some herbed salt, or we have the fish you brought, or…" She continued, "We have some squelle too if you'd like to try that? I've actually come to enjoy it."

The boys decided to try the squelle. They had plenty of fish on the trip to the mountain, and they trusted Tÿr. Gordian went to his pack and pulled out a wooden box.

"Here!" he told her as he walked out of the cavern.

She looked at him curiously. Gordian just smiled as he walked past her and into the light. Tÿr opened the little wooden coffin and was pleasantly surprised. Inside the box were chartreuse-green berries. Fox cherries! Tÿr's heart leaped. She had been thinking about the berries for a week or two. She loved the pears, but the cherries would be a great change of pace for the day. Tÿr loved that the boys had thought of her.

That night began a two-week session of studying in the morning when Tÿr finally managed to get out of bed. She and the boys went through many bottles of wine. Varanus had gone back to Yelliton to get several more bottles of wine for the trio as they easily emptied bottle after bottle of the fruity, weaker wine.

On the last night of their visit, Gordian had said that he wished that they had something stronger. Varanus took this as his cue and went into the tunnels to retrieve a couple of his strong, wyvern-made bottles of dragon fruit wine. Tÿr chuckled when the wyvern walked back into the cavern, carrying the three wax-dipped bottles. She knew her friends, and they would want to drink fast and hard, and experience had long since taught the apprentice that it just couldn't happen that way. Tÿr'Ynyn had done it only once. The hangover that had resulted was something she wouldn't likely forget for a long time.

The biggest problem was that the wine was sweet and went down like candy syrup. The punch that followed was terribly painful.

Týr was correct. Gordi had started a juvenile drinking game that many of the younger generation played in the pubs in Vennex. Danior had eaten a large meal and continued to eat the crunchy, crusted bread that Varanus had gotten in the village a day earlier. His stomach had a good base to drink with. Gordi, on the other hand, had completely ignored the bread, opting for two bowls of fruit instead. When it was time to pass the bottle, Gordian drank like it was the last thing he'd ever have. Týr sat on the ground, watching him down more than he probably should. She didn't care; they deserved a fun night with some drinking at night and a huge bunch of regretting when they awoke the next day. The night went on just about the way she expected it to go.

After only one and one half bottles, Gordian was a basket case and loved everyone, to include the wyvern. Varanus was just as amused as Týr by the younger brother. He didn't seem to heed the warnings very well. Gordian asked Týr to show him some of her magiq, and she obliged, for a little while. He was fascinated by everything she had done. He even asked her to teach him to do some, but the wine had a good hold on him, and there was no way he could have figured any of it out.

Morning hit with the force of a runaway delivery cart. Danior, while he had consumed a lot of wine, had done so responsibly. His brother had not. Týr tried not to laugh as Gordian tried to get out of his bed, his head never coming more than a couple of inches off the pillow.

"The female and the blind guy are in better shape than the healthy young guy? Say it isn't so!" Týr said in mock delight.

"Ooh, not so loud," Gordian said. "I've got something stomping through my head! What was in that wine?"

"It was just a little dragon fruit wine." She smiled sheepishly. She knew all too well how the stuff could make one feel. She had drunk way too much on her first time out too.

The fun continued throughout the visit, but sadly, their final day at the cavern came, and the boys had to go back to Vennex.

The boys promised to visit soon and then climbed aboard Varanus. Tÿr watched until the wyvern was out of sight.

"Well, that's that," Tÿr said. "Time to get back to the books." She went in for her huge volume.

The past couple of weeks had been a fun break, but Tÿr wanted to get back to her studying. She was coming up on the sections about making magiqal objects and was anxious to attempt making one to help her with her spells. The giant tome explained that an object that was infused with magiq would help concentrate the actual force and allow the user to focus the energy onto something or someone. As she read the words, she found it so incredible that she could follow the thought. Only three or four months prior to this, the concept would have been as foreign to her as the wyvern's mother tongue, Cmok.

When Varanus returned, Tÿr would approach him about constructing her own magiqally infused staff. As easy as the magiq had come to her, she was very excited to see what it would be like after it was amplified. Reading was difficult in the beginning because everything was so detailed and in-depth, but as she learned more, the reading became easier to understand and absorb. Not only that, it was so interesting, and she wanted to read each word to make sure she didn't miss anything.

Varanus let her study while he rested. When he was done, he asked her if she would like to learn another magiq spell. She had found several on the pages that she was reading, but none were labeled. Many were scrawled on the margins of the book. Varanus had made sure to warn her about trying things that she was unfamiliar with. Many healers and magiq users had come to unpleasant ends by trying things they hadn't practiced or known about. Sometimes things were written in the books, and it wasn't even sure if the entire incantation was complete. All recipes for certain disaster. When questioned about the construction of a staff, Varanus gave his approval and told her that he would oversee her as she built one to suit her specific needs. Until then, he was going to help her with a new bit of magiq.

The new magiq that she was to learn was to manipulate energy so she could move items without touch. This could help her when something large would need to be lifted higher than she could physically or to speed up the process of moving several items at the same time. The wyvern explained it to her first and how she could employ the magiq once she had mastered it. The theory part of the instruction took longer than it had in the past. He wanted to make sure she understood everything well before attempting to try it.

As usual, it didn't take any time before she could lift a small item off the ground and set it back down where she got it. Her gestures were corrected when they weren't exact, and she was told to retry. It only took one or two corrections before she was able to move multiple things. She could set them down on top of each other to form stacks. They were using pieces of crystals that were laying around the plateau.

When she had mastered the smaller objects, she moved on to different sizes and different shapes, stacking them by rotating them to fit together nicely. She was able to take larger stones and balance them on top of stones much smaller. She would continue to balance the pile while moving other stones. To complicate things, Tÿr also lit some of the crystals on fire. Varanus had her stack the crystals one on bottom that was lit on fire with two crystals that weren't. Then she'd add another one that burst into flames on the way to the stack. Varanus did this quickly to see how well she managed under pressure. Time after time, she performed everything he asked her to.

Finally, after two straight hours of assaulting her with patterns of crystals, Varanus called a stop to the training. Clouds had begun to roll in on the mountain from the east of the isthmus. When storms came from the east, they were generally stronger than other storms. The black clouds could end up staying for several days to even weeks, depending on the concentration of water in them and the direction of the prevailing winds.

From the look of the skies, Tÿr was sure that rain was on the way, and it would be intense for a bit, at least. The rain began in earnest. Sheets fell and blew around the cavern entrance. A constant mist hung around the open doorway as the storm beat down on them. Tÿr was not going to miss the opportunity to bathe. The cool water was refreshing as she stood under the open grey skies. She brought her soap and started with her clothing, making sure to get the blue dirt stains out. The rain pelted the soap bubbles off her as fast as she could create them. When she was satisfied that she had cleaned her clothing well enough, she disrobed and continued to wash herself. The water was no cooler here than when she bathed in the river. Rævii stood in the doorway and watched as her friend washed herself. Tÿr had attempted to get the fox out to bathe with her, but the shaggy animal was having none of that nonsense.

Tÿr grabbed her tunic and pants that she hung on the branches of a pear tree and walked back into the warmth of the cavern. She had gotten used to bathing in front of Varanus who, still turned away when she was nearby. He wasn't bashful, but it was a sign of respect. There was a small trickle of water leading from the doorway down to the firepit. She moved a rack closer to the fire and hung her wet clothes over it. It would take an hour or two with the fire burning as it was. The rain had refreshed her, and she was clean. Two days of dirt and grime washed by the rainwater. Now she slipped into clean clothes and was ready to continue training.

Varanus had told her that they could begin construction on her staff the following day, but she felt energized and wanted to start immediately. If the wyvern was tired, he never showed it and agreed to assist her.

"The first thing you will need for the staff is the actual body of the staff. There are several different choices for you to decide on, but I'm assuming that you will use the one you have been using as your all-purpose stick?"

Tÿr nodded. "This has meaning, and I read that items that have a personal connection with the user work the best."

"That is true," Varanus agreed, nodding his large head. "You have carried that staff since you arrived. I have never used a qyrry branch, so I'm afraid that I won't be able to advise you on the ability of it."

"I feel drawn to it, and I believe it is asking to be used," Tÿr told her advisor. She held out the long, thin piece of wood. "Besides, it is so strong and still bends." She demonstrated by putting the end under her foot and pulling up sharply. The stick bent but didn't make a sound as she distressed it.

"The first thing I will have you do. Set it aflame. Mark the wood with the fire, but don't allow the fire to consume it."

The apprentice followed the instructions. She laid the stick on the cavern floor, and immediately a deep-red fire engulfed the staff. She watched the wood to make sure that the flames didn't actually burn into the dry wood. Týr had been practicing before this—fire that didn't completely burn the subject it covered. When the wood was colored a deep, rich ebony brown, Varanus told her that it was good enough, and instantly the flames dissipated. The girl picked up the staff cautiously and found that it was barely hot to the touch.

"Now, you will have to decide what design you wish to use for the top. This is only limited by your imagination. Do you have any ideas?" he asked his apprentice.

"I know exactly what design I'd like, but I'm not sure how to go about doing it," she told Varanus.

"Well," began her instructor, "you will draw it out, and then you will decide what materials you will use. I will recommend some metals that work well, or at least have done in the past."

She described that she wanted to put a pair of wyvern wings spread open, yet sheltering her quartz crystal. Varanus let her finish describing her idea before asking.

"Why wyvern wings?" he asked curiously.

The fox had come to sit between the student and teacher, as if to say she didn't want to take sides, so she would sit in between them both.

"I love watching your wings as you fly," she told the wyvern. "They are so powerful and majestic at the same time. And then, if you need to, you can use your hand to do something so delicate. Your wings can be used to describe magiq."

Varanus thought about it for a moment before thinking what a perfect choice for the crystals would be. He was certain that she should continue to use the piece of quartz that he had given her, but there were so many stones and crystals to use. In the end, he decided that he would teach her how to cut lachtrys to make a perfect generator stone. It was already powerful with magiqal energy, and so it would definitely be beneficial in her training and work.

Together the pair flew down to the river as they had almost every other day to allow her to bathe, but this time, Tÿr collected a container full of dark-blue clay from near the Ajenti River. She would use this to make a mold of the wyvern wings for her headpiece. She used the quartz crystal she had been given to measure a space in between the wings so it would represent the wyvern's body.

Varanus explained that crystals would behave differently when heat was applied, giving them more or different power. Tÿr spent several hours carving the wings exactly how she wanted them, even adding the delicate veins running through the membranous skin. Varanus had also told her during the training for her staff construction that they would be using more than one type of metal. The process of melting would be tedious. The different metals had different melting temperatures, so her magiq would be getting a true workout. Varanus would also be assisting in the melting down of certain metals. Together they would fold them together to produce an incredibly strong headpiece, not just physically but magiqally too. When the mold was completed, she set it near the big heater to dry. During the night sometime, Rævii must have gone to check it out because when Tÿr awoke in the morning, there was a perfect fox-paw print in the center of the left wing. Tÿr was going to smooth it out, but during the nighttime, the clay had hardened sitting near the heater. The more she looked at it, the more she realized how much Rævii had become a part of her life. The paw print would stay. Tÿr did draw energy from the fox as well. Varanus had come to stand by the heater to warm himself, and he glanced down at the mold.

"You did fine work, Tÿr. The wings are very realistic, and… what have we here?"

Tÿr smiled up at him. "You noticed, I see."

"I see your friend wanted a say in the design. You can always soak the clay in water to soften it again and remove the print if you wish."

"I considered it," she told the tall wyvern towering over her. "Rævii has become a huge part of my life, and I think it only fitting that she has a part of the staff."

"Quite fitting," the large creature agreed. "If you are up to the task today, I'd like to go out and collect the presents and metals we will use to produce your headpiece. What we can't find in nature we will be able to locate in Yelliton. I believe your old friend Kuired might even have some of what we need."

Tÿr was excited at the prospect of seeing her old friend. Since his move, he had not taken on an apprentice nor anyone to keep him company. She was worried that he was lonely by himself since Aaxtagara's death.

"I'm up for anything. I slept well and have been since we moved into this mine. I never slept in the dark before this."

"Wyverns have used caves and tunnels for many millennia," Varanus told her. "Although we have excellent sight out in the open, our eyes are at their best in the dimly lit caverns of the mountains. As you move forward in your studies, you will find spells and charms that can aide you in darker places. This really helps when you are in a situation where you are forced to hide from an enemy during a battle." He went on. "It will be imperative that you be able to heal in dark places. If you ever are ever required to travel the seas of Peyda Noirin, it is generally dark all hours of the day on some places."

As the wyvern continued to tell her about healing in low-light places, she went and got the bags to store everything they procured on the trip today. She wasn't sure how much they would be gathering. She wasn't even exactly sure where the trip would take them. Because of frequent trips that could last all day or even longer, Tÿr had designed a harness to allow the little fox to join them on the journeys. It consisted of a bag where she could hide if she got nervous from the height and speed that they traveled. Generally, the fox wore a body harness made of a fiber webbing that allowed her to sit in front of Tÿr should she choose to ride in the open. Tÿr also grabbed some dried meat for her and the little brown fox to eat should they become hungry before they arrived home.

The trip did end up taking well into the evening, and everyone was exhausted when they finally landed on the plateau. The bags were loaded with different ores and also several pieces of lachtrys that they had found on the Anbry Mountains. The trek included hiking up part of Piral Volcano to collect the rare, diamond-like stone. She needed several pieces to cut into proper gem shapes to infuse its magiq.

Tÿr, although tired and hungry, was anxious to move on to the next part of the construction. Varanus, on the other hand, wished that she would at least put it off until the next day. He explained to her that the heating and folding of the metal would take all day before they could pour it into the molds. Then it would require a further day in the oven to fuse the two halves together. He told her that the only thing that could possibly be done was the careful cutting of the lachtrys. He warned her that this part could be dangerous as well, but Tÿr couldn't sit still. She was this close to having her own magiqal staff, and her patience was not winning.

"How hard can it be to cut three stones? We got the tools in Yelliton today. The merchant showed me everything I would need to know to use them. All I need is to sit down and start cutting!"

"Oh, for that to be true." Varanus chuckled. "This isn't just cutting, my young apprentice. There are many aspects to faceting a stone."

"Varanus, I've read those scrolls countless times. I know I can do this. I am sure the danger level is exaggerated tremendously. I'll be fine!" Tÿr tried to keep the pleading out of her voice without much success.

"I can see that your mind is set. I will allow this, but I did warn you. Remember, you may choose to go as far as you wish or stop at any time, but the stones must be perfect!"

Tÿr brought a short table from the cave to sit near the firepit. Though the planets were opening the gap between them and the Trë Suns, it was still very light outside. The dim period was still many days away. The girl rolled a small boulder from near the mouth of the mine to over where the table was sitting with a different thick book atop it: *A Compendium of Crystals and Stones with Magiqal Properties.*

It stood over five inches thick and was about eighteen inches by twenty-six. According to Varanus, every single stone, fossil, or granitized tree sap was in the book. It was an impressive tome with authentic gold lettering. Tÿr didn't even know where she could have gotten more than a few flakes of the stuff, let alone enough to gold leaf an old, leather-bound book like this one.

The apprentice flipped through page after page until she found what she was looking for—exact instructions on how to cut stones for magiqal use. She found the shape Varanus had said would be best for her needs. The large-winged lizard had moved outside to watch her. Even Rævii could tell that something important was going on, so she trotted over and sat right next to the girl, putting her small, shaggy head on her lap.

Tÿr was suddenly nervous. Her master was watching her every move to make sure the stone would be perfect. Suddenly she felt too warm. Sweat had broken out over her brow.

"Choose the exact spot for your first hit," Varanus instructed.

She raised the sharp little chisel and let the hammer fall. There was a tiny crack as a line formed on top of the gem. She struck it again with enough force to make it snap, but to no avail. On the third try, the small piece of lachtrys cracked down the middle and broke in half. She held her breath and chanced a look at Varanus. He wasn't upset.

"I did tell you this was very advanced magiq. Now, so we don't waste the precious lachtrys, you will grind it into a fine powder, please!"

Tÿr used the little hammer she had to grind the two pieces into dust. She checked to make sure there were no large pieces in it. The powder felt silky beneath her finger.

Varanus stopped her before she continued to try the next piece. "This might be the part you don't particularly care for," he told his apprentice. His pulled out a bottle of his dragon fruit wine and a small cup. He poured a small amount of the wine into the cup and instructed her to place the fine powder she had made into the little cup with the wine. He then stirred it by using some magiq and passed the cup over to the girl, who accepted it apprehensively. "Please drink this!" he told her flatly.

"Drink it?"

"That is correct."

Without hesitation, Tÿr tipped the small cup up to her mouth and swallowed everything in the cup. Tÿr's face turned into a grimace. The liquid was horrid. It was bitter and gritty, and the feel of the powdered rock in her teeth almost caused her to vomit.

"Gaunt shit!" She spat. "Whatever is the reasoning behind consuming that!"

"It is something that every apprentice goes through as they create their magiq piece. It is partially to ensure that the cuts of the stone are more exact. The biggest part is to amuse the masters, I think," Varanus said, and there definitely was a bit of humor underlying the statement.

Tÿr had to physically talk herself out of retching.

"Are you going to continue, or would you like to stop for the evening?" he gently asked.

"I'm going to get this right if it kills me. I'm pretty sure that's what you're trying to do with that stuff!"

Varanus wore an amused smile and nodded for the girl to continue. She stared at the images on the page much longer this time, the drink still fresh in her mind. She tapped gently, and little slivers began to fall away from the body of the stone. Each facet presented itself to be perfect on top. The apprentice took her time with each cut. The stone was perfect thus far and was only one facet away when she hit the chisel a bit too hard. It shot out of her fingers and struck a rock ten feet away. Her heart sunk immediately. The strike had missed, and she could feel her stomach tighten at the thought of her next cup of gritty bitterness. She reached for the stone, and lo and behold, the face was still perfect. Relief flooded throughout her body. Tÿr moved the small stone back over to the rock she had been working at. When she flipped the stone, her stomach dropped. There on the backside, where the gem had hit the other rock, a chip had cracked off the stone.

"Did it…" Varanus started to ask.

"Just pour me another one," she said, completely disgusted with herself.

When she thought that she had created the perfect gem, she rushed the last cut and subsequently ruined another. She finished the second small drink with as much disgust as the first. She didn't dare say anything because she had asked to do this. The third piece of lachtrys was cut much slower. It took her two hours to finish the front side. She stopped to grab a couple of pears to eat while she took a break. When she had rested enough, she began on the obverse side at the same careful yet slow pace.

Three times turned out to be a charm because when she finally put down her tools, she was holding the perfect of the gem on the pages of the huge book. She decided that one was enough for this day. She would work on the other two necessary stones the following day. Varanus had poured her a larger mug of the strong wine to help her celebrate the completion of the first gem for her staff. She drank it straight down. Even the strong wine and the pears she had eaten earlier didn't completely rid her of the horrid taste. With a light head, she collected the cut stone and book and went into the cavern. She was slightly disheartened that she hadn't gotten her three stones cut, but Varanus had told her that there was nothing to be disappointed about. She had only been studying for months, not years, and other apprentices usually didn't try what she had for years into their training. The wyvern admitted that he had advanced the classes that she was taking because of her ability with magiq. This helped to make her feel a little better.

"I will finish the other two stones tomorrow no matter what!" she told her mentor. "And I don't anticipate having to drink that muck again either."

"I believe you just may do it!" he told her with pride in his voice.

Tÿr walked back to the tunnels to grab a strip of dried meat. She hoped the seasoning on the smoked meat would take the horrid taste from her mouth. She thought about how the events had played out to get her where she was. One year ago, she would have never dreamt of being a healer. She loved helping Kuired in his shop, but the chances for a girl to become a healer before her were I feared of. *Now*, she thought to herself, *other girls have just as good of a chance as anyone*. The look on her uncle's face still bothered her. Was he so concerned that his son become a healer he felt he could bribe his way in? Tÿr knew Kuired and the chances of him accepting anything from her uncle were nonexistent. Kuired was an honorable man—everything, she was learning, the exact opposite of her pompous uncle. What would he do if he ended up needing her someday? Would his pride keep him from accepting treatment? She truly hoped that some of the man he had once been was still inside him.

Chapter 9

It was a day about five months later that Tÿr'Ynyn learned a deep, dark secret about her large mentor. Something woke the girl early on an overcast morning. It was a high, screechy shriek that was loud enough to wake her out of a deep sleep.

Tÿr had grabbed her newly constructed staff and sprinted toward the front of the cave. There in front of the cavern opening was her mentor, Varanus, with a large cyclopean owl in his mouth, shrieking loudly as the wyvern closed its powerful teeth around the large, feathery bird. The screeching stopped immediately. And in one swallow, it disappeared down the gullet. The girl who was still trying to wake up breathed easier for a moment. Then out of the sky, without a sound of a beating wing, came another startling scream. Tÿr looked up in time to see another even-larger owl diving at her mentor. The large eye was dilated in fury as it raced at the wyvern's head. Varanus wasn't quite fast enough to duck out of the way, and the owl slashed at his head with its sharpened talons.

"What the hell…"

The large creature was distracted by his apprentice's voice for only a moment. He followed the owl as it rose back into the air to make another pass at him. Unfortunately for the owl, Varanus was expecting the attack this time, and although he missed the initial dive, he snagged the owl from the air as it began to rise for another pass. The powerful bite came down in the bird's hind end and severed the back from the front just below the wings. The front continued to fly forward a few feet before crashing on the blue, leaf-covered plateau, causing a cloud of blue dust to rise up where the wings continued to flap. Varanus lunged forward enough to snatch the remaining bit of bird off the ground. He didn't even need to crunch back down on the remaining bit of owl corpse, and it, too, vanished down the awaiting maw. Tÿr was left standing in amazement. She had never seen her mentor feed on anything living. He was an amazing hunter—fast and deadly.

"I apologize for waking you, miss!"

Tÿr's face must have been full of shock to get her master to apologize like this. "There is no reason to apologize, Varanus! You may feel free to eat whenever you wish."

The wyvern almost hung his head with what could only be called shame.

Tÿr was confused. "What is it?" she probed.

"I wasn't just eating. I was indulging in one of my favorite snacks," he told her shamefully. "I had hoped to grab them without all of the noise."

"Please, there is no reason to be upset. I have things that I binge on as well. They just don't make a racket when I indulge. Please do think on it again!"

The wyvern relaxed a bit. It was clear that he was still embarrassed. "The cyclopean owl is my weakness, and when the pair followed me home to the plateau this morning, I couldn't help but to turn it to my advantage."

Tÿr could see that despite the shame he was trying to convey, there was the beginning of a smile all across his angular face. Tÿr smiled back at him to reassure him that it was all right. The apprentice was glad to have the owls removed from the area. A large owl could make small business out of the little fox that resided on the mountain with her and her mentor. The fact that the owls had made him lose his composure was terribly amusing to her. He was always so calm and together, and then to see him go after a mere snack that way was grounds for laughter, but only when she was alone. She didn't wish to make him feel any more discomfort than he already felt. It would also give her ammunition to tease him at a later time.

Tÿr extinguished her staff and decided to go back into the cavern to try and wake up more thoroughly. Her staff had become a constant companion to her. Whenever she was away from it, she felt as though a part of herself was missing. Varanus had explained why this was. During the crafting process, she had literally added parts of her physical self to the staff: her energy, blood, and hair. Not to mention that part of it had remained with her. At the time, Tÿr had thought that her mentor was making her partake of the ruined crystals of the lachtrys as a cruel joke. In reality, it was in order for it to fuse with her permanently. The powder, though soft to the touch, was comprised of extremely sharp, microscopic pieces of the stone.

As it worked its way through her system, some were flushed out, but much of it embedded itself in her system to stay permanently. Varanus had warned her of the danger, but at the time, she didn't want to hear it and powered through the process. For two days following the faceting of the three lachtrys gems, Tÿr had issues of coughing up bloody sputum. Varanus had been there to care for her and assure her that she would be fine. The bitterness she had experienced in the mixture of ground stone and wine was an anesthetic derived from a bitter herb called *kÿrrÿho*. It was used to numb the throat and innards in case of microscopic cuts. Her staff still fascinated her. The quartz crystal floated above the wings, which wrapped partially to protect it. The lachtrys gems had been fused using extreme heat. Both Tÿr and Varanus had needed to employ magiqal fire to raise the temperature of the stone and metals to bond together. The quartz was then placed in a magiqal force area over the gems, and Tÿr had been required to perform the most incredibly difficult and exhausting magiq that had ever been asked of her.

Even though the spell only lasted less than five minutes, she had needed to rest in her bed for over three days, only leaving bed to answer nature's call. Varanus had served as her nursemaid, seeing to her every need. She had eaten very little during this time. She didn't feel like she even had the strength to lift her hands to her mouth. With Varanus's care, and tinctures of different herbs and broths, the apprentice regained her strength. With her returning strength came extraordinary power. Her staff provided insights into most ailments she came across.

Varanus and her traveled to Vennex three times a week. She was a welcome sight for the ailing villagers. Varanus was always near should she come across an issue that wasn't easily solved, but those were few and far between. The villagers paid what they could afford. Sometimes there were small sacks of silver, and sometimes there were animals. The brothers were always there to greet the pair when they landed outside of the village.

In the months that followed, Tÿr had gained a great following and treated everything from the minor fever to much more serious issues that required surgery. The need soon arose for Tÿr to procure a place to treat the people. She had worked out of her cottage, but it was small and didn't have everything she required.

After performing a rather complicated surgery on a young village girl, Varanus brought up the need to seek larger quarters. Tÿr had been tossing the idea around in her mind for a short time, and there was no real need for discussion. The two healers set out to find suitable buildings to house their medical practice. The village was growing, and there weren't many buildings that would suit their needs, so Tÿr broached the subject of having a new shop built. Varanus was onboard from the beginning, and he went to speak with his paragon immediately. Ghra'zhenn agreed that a new building was the best course of action. This way, the healers could have exactly what they needed.

No place that they had looked at had everything to accommodate them. Ghra'zhenn got in touch with a builder's guild in a town close to Vennex and conscripted a crew to construct a surgery center and healer shop all combined. It would include a wall that could be opened to allow Varanus to observe operations that Tÿr wasn't completely confident with. The ceilings were made of large sheets of quartz bonded magiqally to huge posts of oak. This way, the entire place would have light enough to see in every situation. The tools that were gathered were the best that money could buy and came at a steep price. The surgery center needed to be large enough to accommodate Vennex residents, but also those from surrounding villages and towns who didn't have access to this level of care.

It took several months to complete construction of the new building, but at Varanus's insistence, the actual clinic was completed first so they would have a larger place to treat the ill and have a local place to store items like the ointments and medicines the people required. It was about this time that Tÿr had an idea. She knew that the brothers were getting older and that they would appreciate a place of their very own. She approached her mentor and asked his opinion on how he would feel about building living quarters on the site. The brothers could stay there and help with the cleaning and upkeep of the property and shop and attached building. She hadn't asked the boys about this yet, but she figured that they would jump at the chance to move into a place of their own. Even with the completion months away, people lined up outside the shop to be seen by Tÿr. She was popular with everyone she came in contact with. They loved her gentle ways and the concern over the issues they faced. She always tried to make them feel like they were the only persons on the planet when they were with her.

She still accepted payment with whatever the people could afford. She knew most of the folks that came to see her and also knew whether they could pay. If they tried to get away with paying nothing when she knew they had money, she had come up with a remedy to alleviate future issues. With Varanus's help, she had concocted a potion that was a placebo. She would order them back daily for a week or even two to be served a dose of the vile-tasting liquid. The liquid was brewed to be disgusting and to numb the throat and give the user extreme gas cramps. Only two people ever returned for more than two doses. In the end, she figured if they could tolerate the foul-tasting tincture, they could receive their care free of charge this time. She never had an issue again.

To make extra money for the shop, Tÿr not only sold medicines and salves. She also had the idea to make bësoms. There was a tree whose branches were incredible for making *bësoms*, medium-sized brooms made from the branches of the *taipuva tree*. The branches of this tree never grew brittle with age, remaining flexible enough to serve as sweeping instruments. The trees grew on Varanus's home island and were brought to Tÿr to construct by many of the dynasty. Ghra'zhenn had asked for volunteers to bring loads of the bendable sticks, and the response was overwhelming.

Many of the wyverns from the dynasty had wanted to get the chance to meet the new healer. Rumors of her abilities had spread throughout the Kirin-Noirin shift and beyond. Many healers from faraway towns and villages had brought patients to be treated because they did not know how to proceed. Tÿr was kept busy. Between traveling to Vennex three times a week, making bësoms to sell, and keeping up with mixtures of ointments and potions needed to treat the sick, she had no issues falling quickly to sleep at the end of each day. It had still not been a year, and she was treating cases that healers with over thirty years of experience had trouble with.

Varanus, too, grew—both in size and as a mentor. There were few things he could teach his apprentice. She devoured information in between the rest of the work she did. At one point, she had even asked her master if there was a way, magiqally, to enhance her learning and knowledge absorption. Varanus had heard of things that could be tried but had persuaded his apprentice against using magiq to aide in her learning. There were stories of people and wyverns both who had tried to do this, and in all cases, they had suffered severe mental issues.

The most famous case was of a magiq user called *Kaistam-Laq*. He was feared all over both planets because he had gathered a sect of assassins to him. *Murtair Amagii* was the name they had taken. They were assassins who also employed magiq in their practice. They remained hidden from everyone seeking them yet were always available to kill for the right price. They, above all other assassin sects, were the most feared. No one really knew how to get in touch with the mysterious sect, yet when their services were required, one of their numbers always found the individual in need. Using them was obviously strictly forbidden and always came with a high price. Tÿr had only heard stories, but the rumor said that after the job was completed by the deadly, magiqal assassin sect, unfortunate incidents always happened to those who employed them. There was literally no one, as far as Tÿr knew, that could identify any member of the organization.

Though highly illegal and definitely frowned upon, other sects of assassins could be found if one knew where to search. The Murtair

Amagii had been tracked and searched by trackers and other assassins trying to deal out their forms of justice, and most never came back. The problem with the most-feared sect was that no one knew who they were. They had no identifying marks, left no clues behind, and could literally be living next door to anyone without them knowing it. Even their name was only spoken in whispers in pubs and meeting places. At one point, Tÿr had even heard a rumor that the infamous Kaistam-Laq was taking an interest in her and wished to recruit her into his ranks. She would definitely be a great asset to him, considering his line of work.

As the medical shop neared completion, Tÿr's patient list was enormous. Luckily, most didn't require return visits after their initial trip to the shop. The modest cottage had been added to the rear of the shop, leaving the surgery center to remain available to open for Varanus to observe or assist should the need arise.

One thing Tÿr discovered in her studies was that one of the many properties of wyvern blood was an anesthetizer. If burned in a diffuser with a combination of other herbs and a powered stone called dragon's blood, ironically enough, it induced a deep sleep that allowed her to perform many procedures that she couldn't under other conditions. The one thing she also read was that the surgeon would have to develop a tolerance to the smoking mixture. If they didn't, they would literally fall under its effects and end up asleep where they stood. To combat this problem, Tÿr was required to slowly develop her low tolerance. She began at night by burning what, by all rights, was a small block of incense. She would inhale the thick black smoke that didn't rise through the air like most other smoke. It would drop down over the edge after rising only inches. This did help the surgeon, but there was still a certain amount that they would breathe in. Within a minute, she would be unconscious. She would inhale more, and more her tolerance grew.

It took several months before she could be around the potent incense without succumbing to its effects. By the time her surgery center was completed, she had grown an immunity to it completely. Varanus still warned that direct, long-term inhalation would render her useless. Luckily, the wyvern was unaffected by the anesthesia, as were all wyverns. Should treatment require an operation for any large lizard, they would need to find something else, preferably something that humans wouldn't respond to.

Everywhere that Tÿr traveled with Varanus and Rævii, people came to see what the big deal was all about. Young kids would ask the most outrageous questions of her, and she would patiently answer them. Most of the time, it amused her. She enjoyed that fact that little children were so interested in the life of a healer. She would have certain answers already prepared before any of the village children even asked. She was a big hit with the young people. Little girls now had a positive role model of their own gender. This was a big deal to Tÿr. She had never set out to be a role model, but she had decided to accept the position with grace and dignity. Women on the planet still were looked at as possessions, and if she could do something to change that way of thinking, she would be delighted.

It was upon the completion of her new surgery facility and healing shop that the first whispers of the infamous sorcerer and magiq user, Kaistam-Laq, surfaced. The village had gotten together to throw the healer apprentice a celebration for the opening of her new shop. She was rather surprised to see that her uncle and aunt had turned up. She figured that he wouldn't miss the chance to be seen by the people of the village. Tÿr'Ynyn heard the name twice as she moved through the celebration with her best friends and her parents. The first time she wasn't sure that she had even heard it, but later, as she walked past a group of men talking in hushed voices, the name definitely popped up again. Just the sound of the name raised gooseflesh on her arms and neck despite the fact that it was still quite warm.

Tÿr would remember to mention this to Varanus later. Why the leader of the deadliest sect of assassins' name was popping up in her small village was a complete mystery to her, but it was something she felt her mentor would want to hear about. She looked around the village square to locate Varanus. She didn't see him anywhere, so she decided to go back toward the clinic. If she stayed in the square, she would end up being completely drunk. The ale was flowing freely, and people she didn't even know were handing her mugs to drink. At one point, she had three at a time. She saw, as she neared the new building, that her mentor was speaking to her uncle and her parents. Her uncle, as usual, was gesticulating wildly as he talked. She was sure that if someone tied his hands to his sides, he wouldn't be able to speak. Tÿr'Ynyn was almost to her family when, once again, she heard the name floating on the air.

"From Murtair Amagii, he is definitely trying to…"

She stopped dead. Cocking an ear up to try to catch more, she listened closely, but it had stopped. Tÿr picked up her pace, all the while trying not to slop her ale down her tunic. Her uncle turned as she walked up. The smile disappeared from his face.

"Ah, and here she is," Siolad Tÿr said. There was no fondness in his voice now. No semblance of the young uncle she remembered from her childhood.

Tÿr was quite aware he had been talking about her before she walked up. And from the sour look on his face, she was willing to bet it wasn't anything nice.

"Hello, all," she said, putting on her best smile.

"Well, if it isn't our new *female* healer. Is your job everything you hoped it would be? I trust you are managing this very important job," he said with ice in every word.

Tÿr gripped her staff like she would die if it fell. She truly felt bad for the man in front of her. That horrid witch that he was married to must have done something truly awful to make him act this way.

"I love my job. I have an incredible mentor, and I am learning everything I can. Your town is in good hands!" She fought to keep her voice even without sounding too disrespectful. Her father wouldn't appreciate it if she fueled the situation with ugly words, no matter how much the pompous ass deserved it.

"That position should have gone to a man! Women have absolutely no business trying to—"

"That will be enough, Magistrate!" Varanus's voice sliced through the diatribe like a searing blade through butter. "If you choose to continue spitting that bile, our presence in your town can easily be removed. Perhaps you chose to put your care in the hands of your son? How long will you remain in your position without a healer? I believe your son may not be up to the task, unless, of course, your woman is standing close to whisper the solution in his ear. So what say you, Magistrate, do you wish our service to continue?"

If Tÿr's face showed surprise at the defense her mentor had shown toward her, it was nothing compared to the look on her uncle's face. Deep red began at the top of his balding head and continued to spread downward. The man looked like he had a thousand things to say, but they all got cluttered on his tongue. The best he managed was a slight grunt. He glanced quickly at Tÿr's father as if to say, "This is all your fault!" And then he spun around and stomped off, causing the ground to shake and he went. Tÿr wanted to thank Varanus for his defense of her and her character but decided against it for the time being.

"I apologize for my outburst!" Varanus told Tÿr's parents and anyone else in earshot.

Her father reached out a hand and cautiously patted Varanus on his folded wing. "There is no need for any apology. You told him what he needed to hear. Everyone in town has wanted to say that lately." Seryth Tÿr looked over the mug of ale as he took a long pull. "He has truly changed over the past few years."

Tÿr saw the remorse in her father's face. "This town would be in serious trouble if we had to deal with that toad of a son as a healer."

"Your town is lucky to have the one they have gotten. Your daughter is an incredible person, and you should be extremely proud!" Varanus told her parents.

Tÿr was watching her uncle as he skulked through the village. Surely, he knew his son wasn't a good choice. He was mainly mad because everyone else knew it as well. Siolad Tÿr walked up to his wife, who was talking animatedly to a small group of women. When he whispered in her ear, the smile instantly disappeared, and she left the group she had been entertaining. Siolad was holding her elbow, guiding her back to the village square. Neither was pleased to be seen right now.

People watched the magistrate walk away from the festivities, but no one seemed bothered. It was clear that the villagers' apathy toward their leader was at a dangerous level. The conversation between the healer, and her parents carefully steered clear from any mention of the earlier occurrence. There wasn't any real new news to share.

Tÿr made sure that she stopped by the cottage every time her and Varanus were in the village. They made small talk about the celebration and the new clinic, and then, before long, Seryth Tÿr looked at Tÿr's mother and told her that he was going to head back to the cottage. He wasn't really one to be out in large crowds like this. Her mom nodded and agreed that she'd had enough as well. They hugged their daughter and thanked Varanus again for everything and then walked off in the direction of their cottage. Other people made their way up to the healers to congratulate them or thank them for the new surgery. The celebration continued for many hours according to the brothers, but the healers left shortly after Tÿr's parents.

Halfway back to the mountain cavern, Tÿr suddenly remembered the reason she had gone back to see the wyvern. She put her hand on the fox strapped safely in her little cloth bag. She was harnessed to Tÿr and then strapped in the bag. There was no way she could fall off as long as her master stayed on. The girl was glad that the trip took almost no time to complete. They didn't travel that high on their way to and from Vennex. Varanus flew just a few hundred feet above the trees, and the air wasn't too rough at this height. Still the wind rushed past her head as they sped on their way. Tÿr could see the Ajenti River from above. The river flowed silvery through the trees of the forest. It never turned muddy or discolored. The sacred river held secrets that had never been discovered. It gave life to the towering trees along its banks and cleansed anything that came in contact with its waters. The mysterious waters could flow in different directions, depending on the needs of the lands surrounding it.

Tÿr didn't mind flying as much when they stayed low. The winds could be a bit stronger near the ground, but she hadn't yet gotten used to the heights. Flying high did lead to greater amounts of time spent gliding. They just didn't glide very large distances at lower altitudes. Despite being so high, the times when Varanus just spread his wings out as far as he could and glided for miles at a time were the favorite times in the air for the girl. When the wings stopped flapping and the only sound was the air flowing around her, Tÿr loved those moments. She felt so free. There were no troubles up there, no bouncing up and down, just silent racing air that whipped through her hair. It was freedom.

It only took them thirty minutes to touch down on the plateau. Her legs were still a little wobbly when she dismounted, but that was getting better each trip they made. The girl unhooked the carrier that the fox was in, and she set her down near the cavern entrance. She quickly went back to help Varanus unhook now. She grabbed the harness from around his body and put it on the wall near the back of the mine. Varanus came into the abandoned cave, and he checked to make sure that Tÿr was okay. He told her that he was completely disgusted by the behavior of her uncle at the celebration. Tÿr explained to him how things had grown worse since that woman had taken over his life. They both agreed that the demeanor of the people of Vennex was growing more dissatisfied with the leadership. If her uncle didn't do something to strengthen the bond between himself and the people, he might not have a position at all. Tÿr hated to think what would happen to him if his wife thought that he was losing his control over the villagers. She craved his power more than him. That's when Tÿr remembered what she had to tell the wyvern.

"Varanus, are you familiar with the assassin sect of Murtair Amagii?"

"Of course."

"Well, I heard that name more than once tonight. Actually, I heard that and the name Kaistam-Laq. Why would the people of Vennex be talking about him?"

"I have no idea. Are you sure you heard them mention the Murtair Amagii? Who was it?" he questioned.

"I'm not sure. I was moving through the crowd, and more than once I heard the name mentioned. I thought it might be important, so I wanted to tell you."

"You were right to think it. Rarely does anything good come from that name. It's been the experience of the wyverns, according to my paragon, that if someone is bandying that name about, a member or more is nearby." Varanus's voice was as serious as she had ever heard him get.

"What do we do?" she asked in earnest, trying not to panic. Her friends and her parents were still in Vennex, and she didn't want them anywhere near that kind of trouble.

"We wait and listen. We need more information. When we are in the village, listen for any whisper of the sect. And anything, anything at all for Kaistam-Laq." Varanus practically spat the name. There was hate dripping from each syllable.

"So I take it from your tone that you know more about him than you're letting on. I've never heard you speak of someone in that manner." She pushed a little harder than she had originally meant to.

"The person who calls himself Kaistam-Laq is one of the most vile people known to wyverns."

There it was again. The way Varanus said that name was with nothing but heated contempt.

"Why, what has he done?"

Tỹr didn't care if she was out of line. She had to know what had happened. The man whose name sent chills down her arms had also harmed the wyvern's. She had only heard his name whispered around fires at night, never about any injustice to the wyverns.

"Kaistam-Laq is a cold-blooded murderer who uses magiq to aid him on his quest for power. He kills whoever and whatever get in his way to stop him and his band of killers. They hide under the guise of bounty hunters and paid assassins, but they need no contract to kill anyone. If anyone of the sect Murtair Amagii are in the vicinity of Vennex, people will begin to disappear. Absolutely no one is safe. They begin by killing to prove that they can get away with anything. Then, one by one, the contracts come. People use the sect to exact revenge on their enemies. The victims never see them coming. No one has ever had one defensive-type wound on them. They never got the chance to fight, and with Laq in control, he has recruited users of magiq. People go out into their yard and are never seen again. They die in their sleep under the ruse of a natural death because some magiq doesn't leave any sign. It appears that the person just simply ceased to be.

"Wyverns have been teachers of magiq and healing for as many ages as man has used our wisdom. Over seventy deaths have been blamed on mysterious circumstances in the past twenty years. Many of them were trainers such as myself. The apprentices would wake to find the mentors dead, many of their parts missing to include heads, tails, blood, and hearts. All valuable magiqal ingredients that are usually harvested upon the natural death of the wyvern. The Murtair Amagii have become convinced that if the parts are taken from a live wyvern, the magiq is more potent. This is simply ridiculous."

Tÿr listened carefully, the horror openly showing all over her face. "Can't they be punished, I mean, if they're caught?"

"No one dares!" Varanus explained to the girl. "Even if they were caught, do you think any of the people would dare to try to do it? Everyone is terrified of the sect. They think their whole family might go missing, or worse. The problem remains that nothing is known about the sect, other than its leader. They recruit from everywhere, so anyone is a potential member. The only person known to be a member for sure is the leader, a sorcerer, a murderer, a person so filled with hate and greed and the desire for unlimited power."

"Kaistam-Laq," Tÿr said the name again. She was beginning to understand why it left such an unpleasant taste in her mentor's mouth.

"The very same."

"So how are we going to proceed? If this assassin master sorcerer or whatever he calls himself is now around Vennex, do we go to my uncle?" Tÿr asked.

"I'm afraid that would be an effort of futility. What do you suppose he could do? Even if we could convince him that the threat is truthful, I don't honestly believe that he has any power or resources to do what needs to be done. I'm afraid your uncle is barely holding on to his position even now," Varanus said gravely.

"How do you know this? Did anyone tell you this during the celebration?" She wanted to know.

Varanus looked more somber than she had ever seen him before.

"There has to be something we can do, Varanus! We can't let this assassin take control!"

"Before we proceed any farther, I must travel to see my paragon. He will know what we must do, if anything. We are healers. I am sworn to protect the village, but I am afraid it would become too dangerous to involve you. Your purpose is to heal, not get involved in a dispute with an entire sect of assassins. Especially the Murtair Amagii!"

"I will go where you go. It is my choice. I cannot stand to sit back and watch the people I love get involved in a dispute with these people."

"I appreciate the sentiment, but I am afraid that I cannot let you risk your life like this. The people of that village need you! You must remain with them and be their healer. Please do this thing for me." Varanus was almost pleading. "Will you at least wait until I have spoken with Ghra'zhenn?" Varanus stopped her from speaking as he saw she was about to continue her argument.

Tÿr wanted to plead, but the finality in her mentor's voice was such that she could tell that the subject was closed, at least until his return. She would wait. She would get to Vennex to stay until Varanus returned from his meeting with the paragon. She wasn't sure what she would do should she be allowed to join the effort. Right now, she and the wyvern were probably the only ones that even knew of the implications. Even though it was dark in the cave, and despite her weariness, Tÿr'Ynyn slept poorly that night. The name kept running through her mind. It had been a name she knew from childhood; a name used to scare children at their classes by their classmates. Until this night, she hadn't known the malice behind it. When sleep finally came, it was interrupted and shallow, dreams of whispers and horrors that were threatening to break through at a moment's notice. She woke in the morning feeling less rested than when she had gone to bed.

Rævii must have felt her emotions because the shift fox was moving slowly as well. It seemed as if she had joined her master in the restless night. The small, shaggy creature didn't move with her usual energy.

"We need to get moving, my little friend. We have another trip to make."

Tÿr went out of the cavern, with the shift fox walking slowly behind her. Varanus was sitting on the ground, staring in the direction of Vennex. He didn't move as she approached.

"I should come with you to see Ghra'zhenn. I need to know what is happening."

The wyvern didn't say anything for a moment. He seemed to be thinking of what to say. "The people of the village need you. I won't be gone long. We need to have a presence there to hear if anything else arises. I need you to find out if there are any more whisperings of that maniac and his cult of killers. We also need to find out what the magistrate knows of this. I must ask you to do something you may find unpleasant. If your uncle is aware of any assassin movement in the village, we need to know."

This all made sense, but Varanus was right, this was going to be unpleasant at best. Her uncle had not even looked at her since her appointment. How was she going to get him to speak to her about village business and security? What if he did know something about the assassin leader? The implication to himself would probably lead to his final undoing.

"I will do as you ask, Master. I only ask that you hurry back so we can begin to do something for the villagers."

Tÿr'Ynyn would never forgive herself if something happened to her parents or her friends back in the village, especially if there would have been something she could have done. The girl quickly packed a pack to bring along. She didn't know how long she would be there, but she also wanted to pack light. She could get food in the village, so there was no need to pack any. It only took her a few minutes, and she was back next to Varanus, helping him once again put the harness on.

They were back on their way to Vennex before most of the town had even awakened. The boys opened the door and were heading out to greet them as they descended to the field outside the surgery.

"How did you even know I was coming?" Tÿr questioned the brothers as they helped carry the pack into the shop.

"That would be my brother," Gordian told her.

"You might not realize this, Tỹr, but the wyvern's wings are especially loud on a quiet morning!" Dani explained. "There aren't many trees or anything to block the noise on your approach here."

Tỹr led Danior back to the shop as Gordian dealt with her large pack. Danior carried a smaller sack, and she carried Rævii. Tỹr tried to make sure that the little fox stayed near her at all times. The sentiment was generally unfavorable toward foxes in the village as many were responsible for small livestock deaths around farms.

"So, Tỹr beer, why are you back so soon? I'm not complaining, but you just left last night."

Tỹr was trying to decide what to say. The reason for her visit this time was of utmost importance. She always told the boys everything that was going on in her life, and she didn't know how she would feel keeping something like this from them now. On the other hand, Gordi had an issue when he visited the pubs. The more ale or wine he consumed, the looser his lips became. This was not something that could be spread around the village. If word got back to the leader of the assassin sect, the village and its inhabitants would be in serious trouble. Tỹr also knew that Varanus trusted her and would trust her with her decision on whether to tell the brothers or not. In the end, she decided to keep the information to herself. The less people involved, the safer the village. If anything happened to her friends, she would never forgive herself. The risk was just too great at this point.

Tỹr enlisted the brothers' help over the next few days. Both had a gift for being extremely caring toward people. Gordian was so gentle, and it amused Tỹr because she had known him her whole life. He wasn't what she would have described as a gentle soul, but he was amazing with the villagers, especially the children. Danior surprised her in other ways. He knew where everything was in the clinic and could identify almost every product by smelling the jars. The brothers kept the people moving in and out of the healer's shop at such a quick pace they had seen everyone seeking treatment by the early afternoon of the first day. Tỹr knew that they would do a good job, and she was so happy that she had given them the chance to show her. Not only were they efficient in the shop, they also tended the grounds of the place as well.

Even though Tÿr had only been healing for a short time, she had built up a large supply of animals that people had used as payments when money was scarce. The number of eggs and milk was astounding. She sold many in her shop but mainly gave them to her mother to sell or to the boys. She was able to pay them well for the jobs they did, and she also walked away with more than she knew what to do with. Work kept the trio busy for four days straight. She usually only spent three days a week in the clinic, treating people, but decided to open as long as she was in Vennex. The thoughts of Kaistam-Laq and his assassin sect never entered her mind as long as she kept busy.

It was one evening while her and the brothers were eating a huge evening meal with her parents that the thought of any of it came back.

"How long are you going to be in the village, dear?" her mum asked.

"Yes," her father chimed in. "Where is our defender while you are here all alone?"

"I'm not alone," she corrected him. "I've got Gordi and Danior with me. Since they came to work for me, things are running so smoothly that with a little training, they could be healing with me, or even in my absence."

"Don't let your uncle hear that. If he thought he could remove a *woman* from an important post like that, he would in a heartbeat," her mother said with disgust.

Tÿr knew that her mum had not gotten along with her uncle since that evil woman had slithered into his life. The slight from the previous evening was still fresh in her mind, as well as the whole episode at the tournament.

"Well, a woman does have the position, and I promise you, I'm not going anywhere. No one else seems to have a problem with it. My aunt is obviously involved in his thought process."

"She is a vile woman!" Her dad agreed. "The best thing for him to do is take her to the middle of the Qelibar Sea and toss rocks to her."

Both boys snorted at this. Tÿr knew her dad said this to get a laugh, though he didn't like the woman at all. She had alienated his brother from the family and made him think that he was better than everyone else. Her dad seemed to think that her aunt was the power-hungry one, but her uncle did very little to dispel the idea of him being quite the same as well. This seemed especially true as he had tried to bully his son's way into the apprenticeship.

"To answer your question," Tÿr said, looking at her father and trying to change the subject, "Varanus had some business to tend to with his paragon. There are issues happening that I can't yet discuss, and Varanus must see how we are to proceed."

"What issues could those be?" her dad quizzed her. "Are they anything that could be of danger to you or the village? Why the secrecy?"

"I must honor my mentor's wishes for now," Tÿr said, trying not to get defensive.

Her father just stared, unmoving, for a bit. The girl felt as if he was searching her soul. He'd always made her feel like this her whole life. He never said anything, but she felt like she was letting him down by not saying anything.

"I promise I will tell you as soon as I know more. Right now, I'm just waiting for more information myself."

Seryth Tÿr looked skeptical but let the matter drop. Tÿr could tell he would be asking more questions later. He did not like being the last person to know something important. The girl and her fox ate with her parents every day she was in Vennex. The boys usually joined them in the evening, but they liked seeing their mother for the morning meal. That way, they could help her with anything she needed before they went off to take care of the shop.

A couple of days turned into six. Tÿr had begun to tell Danior about her concerns for her mentor when he sat back on the chair he was in and told her that he thought she was probably worrying for no reason.

"How can you be so certain, Dani?"

"Well," he started, cocking his head slightly, "if I'm not terribly wrong, your friend is on his way now. Listen!" He pointed out toward the field.

Tỹr listened carefully. At first, she heard absolutely nothing, but then she heard what he was talking about. The faintest sound of flapping. Wings!

"I'll be right back!" she said as she ran out the door. "Go. I'll... uh, I'll be there in a minute."

Danior slowly got up from the chair he had been sitting in and made his way to the door. Despite the lack of vision, he managed to get around the shop as well as his brother. Varanus was landing on the field as Tỹr made it out to meet him. Danior was following close behind.

Varanus spoke quietly to his apprentice as Danior walked up. "I see your team is here helping you."

"They are the absolute best I could ever ask for," she told the lizard, patting Danior on the arm.

He reached out and gave her a one-armed hug. The wyvern moved in closer. "Have you filled him in? I know I didn't leave instructions for you, so I left it to your judgment."

"I haven't said anything yet. I was waiting to hear from you first."

"Said what?" asked Danior. "What's going on, Tỹr?"

"We'll wait until Gordi is around, and then I'll fill you in," she explained.

"I believe they should know," Varanus continued. "Besides, it might be good to have a pair of extra eyes and ears in Vennex while we aren't here."

Tỹr thought about it and told her mentor that she was concerned for the brothers' safety.

"I spoke with my paragon, and he and I both agree that the threat level is not at a high degree yet. It may change shortly, but if we can prepare a few citizens, we believe that it will prove to be to our advantage if we know what to look for. I think Danior and Gordian are excellent candidates to enlist. They will blend in with the population, and I believe we can trust them with discretion."

"Dani, do you think we can trust Gordi not to go spouting of at the pub once he gets a few pints in him?" Tÿr asked the elder of the brothers.

Danior shrugged his shoulders. "I'm not sure what you're even talking about. It sounds serious, and I know Gordian. He wouldn't purposefully say anything to bring harm to you, Tÿr. He loves you like you're our sister. We both do! If you ask to keep something confidential, I bet my life he wouldn't risk losing your trust. You mean too much to both of us. Both you and Varanus. Besides, I think he's still scared of him!" Danior said, smiling as he pointed in Varanus's direction.

"Very well. We will fill you both in when we all get together. There's no real need to repeat the details more than once. Let's locate your brother."

Gordian was out at the side of the clinic building, tending to the animals in an area that they kept the animals they had received as payments. There was quite a few egg-laying birds and some other larger animals that were used for milk or eventually for meat. The clinic was empty of any patients needing care, so the four went out back to make sure that they wouldn't be overheard.

Varanus began the clandestine meeting by telling the boys of the dire situation. He asked them both if they wished to proceed with something that had the potential to be dangerous one day. Both boys never hesitated. They both agreed to the strict need for silence, and when those formalities were agreed upon, the wyvern explained the situation. Both boys were grateful for being entrusted with such an important task. Varanus had given them an allowance to use at the pubs with stringent instructions to not overindulge. They were glad to have drinking money, and they quickly agreed to the terms set forth by the wyvern.

Both Tÿr and Varanus were anxious to get back to their mountainside home. Rævii, too, was ready to go. She hadn't been allowed to run free in the village. It was too dangerous. If one of the farmers' animals came up missing, Tÿr was concerned her fox might receive the blame, even as small as the creature was. Before leaving, Tÿr made a quick trip to her parents' cottage to bid them farewell. Her mother, always concerned that Tÿr wasn't eating enough, sent food back with her to eat. The girl knew there was enough for a week at least. There were several loaves of crispy, crusted bread and cheese and oils to eat with the bread. Despite the fact that Tÿr argued that she had enough meat in the tunnels keeping cool, her mum handed her some dried beef to take as well. Tÿr mentioned that she would drop some of the food off to the boys, and her mum told her not to be ridiculous. She had made bundles for them as well. She made Tÿr promise to send them over for dinner that night, and then they parted. Tÿr told her parents that she'd be back in a few days.

Finally, the two were ready to leave, and they were underway. Tÿr watched as the brothers grew smaller, standing outside of the clinic and shop. She had a good feeling about telling them. Both boys were very disciplined and would make sure to listen for any news of the assassins anywhere near the area. Rævii seemed to be more comfortable on this particular flight back to the mountain. She even dared longer glances out of her pouch, often licking the hand Tÿr used to hold the pouch close to her body.

Chapter 10

Tÿr and Varanus spent the entire rest of the day and into the night discussing his trip to see Ghra'zhenn. Varanus learned from the paragon that there were rumors of the Murtair Amagii assassins growing restless. Usually, there weren't a huge list of targets that the sect worked on. The price they charged for their services was steep, and so they were very choosy about the jobs they took on. From what Tÿr learned, the sect didn't take more than one job every two or three months during the year. This allowed the period of insanity that followed a hit to die down in between targets.

Tÿr began to feel weary and decided to call it an evening. It had been a few days since she had slept in her own bed. Rævii was tired as well and seemed ready to go to her cushion. The little fox was following at the girl's heels when it stopped dead in its tracks. The white tail was fluffed out as large as it could get, and its hackles had raised. Tÿr had never seen her little friend behave like this before.

"What's wrong, little one?" Tÿr stopped too. She watched as the fox's ears stood straight on end, and it didn't move a muscle. "Rævii?"

That's when Tÿr heard it too. It was a rustling sound coming from back in the cavern near the wall with the tunnels cut in it.

"Tÿr!" Varanus's voice shot through the cavern, echoing against the back.

Tÿr was sure that her heart had stopped. "Varanus? I think there is someone or something in the mine with us!"

"Ah, yes," he said from the entrance. "I had gotten busy telling you about my meeting with Ghra'zhenn and forgot to mention that we have a visitor with us. Actually, it will be staying here with us from now on."

Tÿr breathed easier, but the fox was still on high alert. "It? What it? What are you talking about, Varanus?"

"The paragon suggested that we include the brothers on our new mission. He was concerned that they might not be able to get in touch with us in a timely manner if we only continue to visit the village every few days or so. If there is an emergency, we won't know it until we visit again. He told me it might be advantageous to acquire a *Säqyr Wyvern*."

Tÿr had never seen one before, only in texts or drawings. She knew the danger that Rævii could be in, so she bent down to pick up her pet. The little fox jumped at her touch. "It's okay, little one. I'm right here."

With her staff in one hand and the fox in the other, Tÿr walked toward the sound of the scratching. There, in the back, was a large box with what looked like a nest of sticks inside. She intensified the light on the end of the staff. The circle of illumination grew enough to engulf the box with a jet-black head with deep midnight-colored eyes staring directly at her precious package. The little fox began to tremble in her arm.

"Oh my, Varanus, is it safe to approach it?"

"Slowly, child. It will need to be imprinted with you and the fox and the brothers. He won't harm you, I should think. You just woke him, but unless you try to pick him up or try to introduce him to the little girl in your arms, I believe he is quite harmless."

Tÿr walked even closer, and now Rævii was beginning to pitch a small fit. Scratching and trying to claw herself away from the tiny, feathered wyvern. Tÿr let her go, and Rævii scampered over to sit next to Varanus.

"I'm not sure if you know this, but the shift fox is a sworn enemy of the säqyr wyvern. It's going to take some time before the two of them get on very well."

The creature emerged from the nesting box. Some of the twigs fell out around it as it stretched its wings. Tÿr was surprised to see that, unlike a true wyvern, this smaller cousin had feathered wings instead of the thin, membranous skin. It also had a feathered tail. The feathers shone a deep orange-red, even in the darkened part of the cavern. It never took its eyes off the fox. Varanus made a shriek that the little wyvern stopped and listened to. It chittered back to the larger wyvern in a language that they both seemed to understand.

"I have instructed the creature to remain there while you bring the fox up to meet him. No harm will come to her."

Varanus then explained in great detail about how these creatures were gifted with incredible senses of direction and location. They were often used by larger wyverns as messengers because of their incredible speed. They could cover distances often ten times faster than that of a wyvern traveling at its quickest. Tÿr had never known it, but Kuired had often used a säqyr wyvern to deliver messages to the dynasty on Gelbryn Island, according to Varanus. The little wyverns were very rarely intercepted because they flew so fast and at extremely high altitudes. Tÿr walked over and picked up Rævii to bring her over to the smaller wyvern. It fidgeted in place but showed no aggression. The two smaller creatures sniffed each other curiously, watching the other without missing a beat. The shift fox had finally settled down enough that she wasn't trembling anymore.

"I'd like you to get a good night's rest tonight, Tÿr," Varanus said flatly. "There is something I need to discuss with you, and I want you at your best before you make a decision. It is something that will require you to decide whether you wish to delve deeper into my dynasty and the world of magiq."

Tÿr was intrigued. What could her mentor be referring to?

The girl went closer and observed the smaller wyvern. She wanted to be closer should there be problems. She could snatch the fox away from the other creature. She was surprised at how well they were getting along. The säqyr was as enthralled with the fox, and vice versa. Although Tÿr wasn't sure if it was for the same reason, introducing the animals seemed the best thing for them because the shift fox calmed down after this. Tÿr was sure that they would not be fast friends, but at least she wasn't so worried for her safety.

The apprentice tried asking Varanus about his cryptic statement, but he only said that they would discuss it in the morning. The girl decided then that she would get some rest. She went to bed without eating because she had so much weighing on her mind.

Sleep came fast, and with it dreams of frightening chases—chases of people with nameless faces and shaggy hair. They were familiar, yet Tÿr didn't know them. She was always just at the end of their long arms with jagged nails, and when she tried to scream, the breath wasn't there. These dreams plagued her every night. What was the reason? She wondered if she was being shown a glimpse of her future, or maybe of the past. Not hers, but she was growing concerned. Sleep was not restful.

Chapter 11

The sound of a shrill, piercing call woke Tÿr the next morning. She was so tired from the lack of peaceful sleep it took her several moments to remember where she was. The shriek happened again. Tÿr panicked for a moment. Her head darted around to find the shift fox. It was still curled up on its cushion, fast asleep. She could hear her mentor in the cavern, moving around. Finally, she awoke well enough to see the large wyvern standing over the nesting box in the darker part of the cavern near the entrance to the tunnels.

"That wasn't him, was it?"

Varanus chuckled a bit. "I'm afraid it was. Our new addition isn't used to being restrained in a cavern. Usually, säqyr wyverns are up much earlier than this, hunting for their morning meal. Once we know he won't fly off, he will be allowed to do this, but until I can trust him, he must be held captive. It should only take a day or two before we imprint, and he will be trustworthy enough to release."

"For starters, we must quit calling him *he* all the time. I've always named the animals that have chosen to spend time with me," Tÿr said. "He needs a proper name!"

"What do you propose then?" Varanus questioned his apprentice.

"Well, he's noisy and full of dangerous teeth. Do you have any words in your language that would fit that?"

"None that you could pronounce, I'm afraid. You should probably stick to a name in your tongue," Varanus told her.

Tÿr thought about it for a minute and then said with confidence, "Sëvyq! I believe it means hunter or seeker or something in one of the older languages."

"An aptly choice for such a magnificent creature," Varanus said, approving wholeheartedly.

Tÿr smiled. The little *family* of the cavern was beginning to grow. "Varanus, you said you wanted to discuss something important with me this morning. You were very cryptic last evening. Can we discuss it now?" Tÿr asked as she got out of her bed.

She grabbed her tunic and pulled it on as she waited for her mentor's reply. Varanus seemed to think this over for several moments before responding. It almost appeared that he had to talk himself into this. Tÿr simply stood near her bed and waited for Varanus to begin. The longer it took her master to speak, the more concerned she felt. The wyvern never thought something through this long. This just added to her feelings of unease and also to the seriousness of the matter.

"Before I tell you what was discussed with Ghra'zhenn, I want you to know that everything I do tell you is your choice alone. You must not feel pressured to do any of this, nor will anything be held against you should you decide against it. The situation has grown more serious, and we feel that measures must be taken to protect our species and also yours. What I am about to tell you is something that hasn't been done for over two hundred years. The closest we came was your friend Kuired, and in the end, he decided not to go forward."

Tÿr felt her stomach grow tight. The shroud of mystery was making her crazy. "Please, Varanus, just tell me."

"Very well, but remember, this is just a possible choice. If you should opt to not go through with it, my paragon and the dynasty will find another way."

"I understand. Now please continue!" The tone in her voice was a bit more demanding than she would have liked, but the suspense was thick enough to cut.

"I must begin with a short history lesson before I ask of you something that could risk your very life."

Tÿr understood but wanted to know, so she simply nodded.

"Many centuries ago," the giant lizard started, "wyverns were the keepers of the knowledge on these planets. We kept the knowledge locked away in the tomes and scrolls and other objects that you now use for your studies. We have histories of many of the peoples that have lived here from the beginning.

"In the first millennia or two, humans had no issues with us overseeing the information. But as the humans lusted for more knowledge and, as a result, power, they grew to resent the wyverns for keeping this knowledge to themselves. Wyverns are not known for seeking absolute power or rule over everything. We have ruled benevolently for as long as we have been on the planets. Humans grew, and with them grew the need for power. Some humans think that all of this knowledge belongs to them and have gone through great lengths to try to get it for themselves. At first, they simply asked. But as the years wore on, they were not happy to continue asking. Peace gave way to violence. Soon humans began to attack the wyverns. They didn't care if the wyverns possessed any of the information that they sought or not. The wyvern became the enemy in many peoples' eyes, and from that grew the Human-Wyvern Contention."

"But what does this have to do with me today?" Týr asked.

"Patience! I beg your patience for only a few moments more. Many of the human leaders formed groups and sects to injure or kill the wyvern populace. Even some wyverns chose to see the humans' reasons as logical. To this day, there are some wyverns that prefer to kill than keep the peace. I know you have heard some of these famous monsters. I call them that because they chose to kill for the belief and not for what matters."

"The protection of the information," Týr finished his statement.

"Precisely!"

"How did you ever keep the information in all of those tomes and other things?" Týr questioned.

"Sadly, we didn't keep most of it. The remaining volumes we have in our possession are just a fraction of what was. Most was destroyed by the human uprising."

Týr suddenly felt a hundred emotions rush over her in unison. They came through the surface as two large tears trickled down her cheeks. She felt anger, pity, disgust, embarrassment, and rage at the people who came before her.

"But these people said that they wanted the knowledge. Why would they destroy such items? It makes no sense."

"Alas, we will probably never know. It stands to reason that they felt that if they could not possess the information, no one would."

"Oh Varanus, I am so sorry. I never knew all of this. I'm afraid the schooling I received didn't tell quite the same story. I never knew the evil that men could do in the name of learning. Even keep themselves from doing the thing they were so desperate to do."

"I am not telling you this to garner an apology. I have learned to leave the past in just that, the past. I did harbor feelings of hate toward these people at one time, but now that I have learned the entire history, I've grown to pity them. The issue now is that a malodorous group of people is attempting another uprising, although I have hopes that we can quell the issue before it fully forms again. Ghra'zhenn, my paragon, believes that if we move quickly, we may be able to sever the head before it can create an entire body of people bent on our destruction and also the remaining bit of information left in the care of the wyverns."

Tÿr only needed a second before deciding to help. "I will do whatever it takes to keep this from repeating, Varanus!" She had fire in her veins right now. The anger and shame she felt because of her ancestors burned hot and passionately.

"Well, now comes the part where I ask for your sacrifice. This is something that can be dangerous, Tÿr. People have died doing what we are proposing. It is something that may give us an advantage and win."

"I don't care about the risk. I will do it," Tÿr stayed defiantly. "Too many people have suffered and died, and this must be important, or I know you wouldn't ask me."

"We believe it is," the wyvern said. "Now, do you wish to know what it is before you actually agree to it?"

"There is no need. If you and Ghra'zhenn think it is important, then I must do it. But please, continue."

The lizard bowed his head slightly before continuing. "There is a process known to the wyverns in which we would be able to communicate with ease. You would be able to speak to the entire dynasty and them to you. It will also help your magiq grow immensely. Magiq that has not been seen in many, many years. The process is called intercalation. In the wyvern tongue, it is a sacred process that only happens to ones we trust beyond all others. You have earned our trust, and with your knowledge of magiq and the speed in which you learn it, we feel you are the perfect candidate for this process. It has many risks, so please, think this over carefully!"

"I have already made up my mind," Tÿr said with confidence.

Varanus knew better than to warn any more. When the girl had decided something, she was unlikely to change her mind.

"Have you given me any texts to read about this?" Tÿr asked. She was hoping that she hadn't forgotten something she had read earlier.

The wyvern shook his head. "We as a society have never committed this process to word. It is sacred, and only six people in the history of our training have ever attempted to do this. We do not allow the process to be recorded. It is a very secretive type of magiq, and if the process ever became known to people like the Murtair Amagii or others like them, the consequences could be devastating."

"Why is this so secretive? Surely, all wyverns know about it. There has to be someone on the planet with this knowledge."

Varanus grew somber. "I am afraid the trust is not just against your people. There are also wyverns who would exploit this magiq should it be made known to them. Tÿr, not all wyverns wish to see the humans prosper. There are some who would exploit this because along with the process comes a form of control over the subject should the master deem it necessary."

"Control?" Now Tÿr sounded apprehensive. This was the first time she'd heard of this.

"When this process takes place, the knowledge of one becomes available to both parties. If something were to ever happen that would compromise the mission, the wyvern could basically force the person to do what needs to be done. It isn't harmful and has never been used, but I feel that I must disclose this to you before you decide. I want you to understand everything."

"'What would you do if you were in my place, Varanus? Would you be able to allow someone to get inside of your mind to keep you from doing something incorrect."

"Knowing what I now know, I believe I could do it. I believe that it would be my duty. That being said, I will also lose a piece of me when I permanently bond to you. I will give you one last chance to change your mind before we proceed. If your mind remains unchanged, you will be the first human to do this in over two centuries. Many have been given the chance but have usually decided against it when the time came. The treatment is brutally painful, but if you survive, the rewards more than make up for a day or two of pain."

The wyvern's eyes never left the girls as he spoke. He was trying to let her know the seriousness of this and could not just begin the process and then stop at the first hint of discomfort.

"My decision stands, Master. If you feel I can do this, and it will assist our cause, I must do it." Her voice didn't waver as she stared directly back into the obsidian black orbs of her mentor.

"Very well. You have been given the opportunity to walk away from this with no fear of penalty. The ceremony called *Ætulu Qoyulmasi* will begin in five days. You will be given this time to make your preparations and your peace. You may explain to your people that you are going to be undertaking a severely difficult mission, which will push you to the limits of your body and mind. In five days, when your affairs have been seen to, you will meet Ghra'zhenn and myself on this plateau.

"For one day and night, you will meditate. Your body must reach a state of perfect harmony with your mind. You will not eat nor drink. You will receive no visitors. At the end of your meditation, the two-day process of intercalation will begin. Ghra'zhenn and myself will perform the process. At the end of the two days, you will have a great feast with the wyvern dynasty to celebrate your birth into our fold. From then until you pass, you will speak with the authority of the wyverns."

"Can you tell me what to expect? What will happen?" Tÿr was not going to change her mind, but she felt like she knew absolutely nothing about the pending ceremony, and she was not used to being unprepared.

"I am afraid I can say nothing more until the morning we begin. You may not tell anyone what is going to happen or anything we have discussed. There are those who would seek to end you for even considering to attempt this. Not all wyverns enjoy the peace we, of my dynasty, have struggled to achieve. There are those that would cut down any who would dare to think themselves worthy enough of this great honor."

Varanus seemed like he wished to tell her more. Týr felt that he truly cared about her and her safety, but it was so difficult he couldn't tell her anything more than the name.

"I will prepare as many potions and ointments that my materials and time allow me to," she told the larger wyvern.

Even though she portrayed a brave healer, she was terrified beneath her calm exterior. Death wasn't the thing that terrified her either. She had made peace with the fact that it must happen to everyone at some point. What bothered her was the lack of information on anything she had just been told. Fear of the unknown had always proven scarier to her than the inevitable.

"Týr'Ynyn, it is okay to feel fear, especially of that which is not known to you. Fear is what ends up protecting us in the end."

"Thank you, Varanus. I'm not really scared of any of this. I just worry for my family and my friends. I don't want them to worry about me."

"Will you share this with them? I know there isn't much to tell them, but I mean this when I tell you, it is really better for them if they have no information. Should the wrong people or wyverns learn of this, the situation will become all the more problematic."

"I understand. It will remain my knowledge alone." There was a certain finality when she said this. Everything became so much more real.

Týr spent the remainder of that day and the next mixing tinctures and salves and other things the village might need in her absence. She didn't want the shop to run low on anything while she was away. She knew that the brothers would do well. They didn't need to be supervised. Things got done like they were supposed to, and everything was always in order when she went in to the clinic. The plan was to bring the säqyr wyvern back to Vennex the next trip they made. Varanus wanted him to be familiar with the area so if the boys ever needed to get a message back to Tÿr or her mentor, they would have a way to do it.

Varanus had already seen to the smaller wyvern's needs when she awoke that morning. Despite the shriek he had made, Sëvyq was calm and had gotten down from his nesting box to explore the cavern. Rævii wasn't exactly sure what to do with the intruder. He seemed amiable enough. The two smaller residents of the cavern were very interested in getting to know each other. The little wyvern might have had the upper hand strength wise, but the little fox pup knew the layout of the cavern and the plateau as well. Tÿr smiled as the two smaller creatures chittered to each other. From there, time seemed to speed up.

The trip back to the village was faster than Tÿr would have liked. They stayed overnight that day, and after a quick afternoon of checking on the clinic and seeing a few of the people who truly needed attention, the four travelers were back at camp on the plateau. Tÿr was physically exhausted. She had decided to take the last little bit of time to relax and prepare for her ordeal. Varanus was acting completely out of character for himself as well. Tÿr knew that once the ceremony was underway, she wouldn't be allowed to stop or rest until it was completed. Tÿr played with the smaller creatures, getting them to do tricks for pieces of meat she had left over from their morning meal. The little orange-winged wyvern hopped and played along with the shift fox like they had been raised together. Tÿr's reservations about the little wyvern's aggressive tendencies melted as the three played. To her surprise, the säqyr wyvern would do small tricks for pieces of sliced pear the way Rævii did. The girl had never expected the little wyvern to even try fruit, let alone enjoy it. Playtime ended with the arrival of the wyvern paragon.

Ghra'zhenn had decided to fly in for the night. That way, the intercalation could begin as soon as Tÿr's period of meditation was over. Ghra'zhenn teased Tÿr about spoiling the messenger wyvern but didn't seem upset. The paragon had brought some fermented dragon fruit with him for him and Varanus to enjoy. The two large creatures sat out on the plateau long after Týr went to her bed. They sat and discussed the upcoming procedure. Týr had tried to listen in on their conversation, but they had seemed to expect it and spoke quieter and quieter until it was just a deep, soothing noise that the girl fell asleep to.

The two older wyverns sat and talked about the rumors flying around the village of Vennex, both hoping that things were not as bad as they were beginning to appear. The name of Kaistam-Laq was not one that got bandied about without reason. They also talked about the hate that flowed close behind, another human called *Xyrfed Mai*.

Xyrfed Mai was as infamous as Kaistam-Laq in his own right. He had been taken in by the evil man as a trainer of assassins. It was rumored that Xyrfed came from a cluster of islands called the *Open Hand Archipelago*. This grouping of islands resembled an open hand and was thusly named by the leader of a family group native to the islands.

The leader, though no one remembered his original name, was called *Ekaj Joonts Laynn Imbröttiös*. Ekaj founded a colony on the islands back before anyone could remember and had only brought his family members along to colonize the island nation. No one thought anything about it for the longest time. Ekaj Joonts was a trouble-maker from his earliest known dealings, so when he disappeared, no one really cared. Ekaj and his children ran the island like a strict dictatorship. Inbreeding occurred, and soon the few became many. When the gene pool became too muddy, the sons of Ekaj would sail off the island in ships they had constructed. They would kidnap boys and girls to integrate into the family. Rule-breaking was met with strict punishment, or in most cases, death. Still the family grew, and over the generations came a huge empire of inbred maniacs.

Over two centuries of extremely long life, the family had become a menace to the ways of life all over the planets. Kidnappings occurred with regularity, and hopes of retrieval were dashed as any interlopers were met with extreme force by the family. The number of missing persons on the planets was unknown, but it was said that once a person was taken, they would never be seen again. Torture, blackmail, and brainwashing were just some techniques that were rumored to make sure no one attempts an escape from the archipelago. Militias and other forces had been called to retrieve missing or kidnapped people, and death was what met every one of them. The only person said to ever be able to come and go from the islands at will was Xyrfed Mai. There were some who believed that he was actually a direct descendant of the island group's founder.

Whatever the story behind Xyrfed Mai, he was now the right-hand man to the infamous sorcerer. From all that was known of him, he was skilled in almost every weapon on the planets, and he was a strict taskmaster. All assassins that learned from him went on to be the best. Unfortunately for those trying to capture them, they were usually met with a quick, untidy end.

The wyverns sat out, discussing the procedure that they would be following the next day. The dragon fruits had long since disappeared. Now they talked about how the apprentice would need to be the one to assist them in wiping out the menace that Kaistam-Laq had become. They hoped that she would have the strength to face his assassins and possibly others as the intercalation became known among the inhabitants of the planets. This was sure to be big news if word got out. The two massive wyverns sat out all night, talking about the apprentice. Their concern for her was very real, and she monopolized the conversations throughout the entire night. The pair were still talking when Tÿr awoke in the morning. Tÿr was rather surprised to see her mentor and the paragon sitting in about the exact same location she had left them the night before.

"Have you both been sitting there this whole night?"

Varanus smiled as best he could and told her that they, too, had to prepare for the undertaking she was to embark on. He instructed her to eat a small meal, and then her meditation could begin. The wyvern directed her to use the time to study and meditate on a more-complicated bit of magiq than she had yet learned, magiq that could be used to hide and misdirect a foe in case of an attack. He also instructed her to begin the learning of Cmok, the wyvern tongue.

It was a complicated language made up of deep, guttural noises and rasping sounds. These were things she would use to focus her mind on during her upcoming ordeal. He told her that he didn't expect her to learn the language in a single night, but he urged her to seek phrases and words she could repeat as a type of mantra. Tÿr collected the suggested works and went back into the caverns to begin. The little fox had already awakened and wanted her attention. She was petting the shaggy coat and carried her over to the wyverns for safe-keeping as she would be unable to help the creature once she began.

Tÿr began her meditation by lighting her staff with a bright light that filled her area of the cavern. She heard the säqyr wyvern stirring in his nesting box but realized that she would have to enter a deep, trancelike state in order to lock out the distractions of the day. The headpiece on her staff was truly amazing to her. It funneled the energy through her and made the light she would have produced with an ordinary crystal at least ten times brighter. The way the quartz piece seemed to float over the other three jewel-like gems cut perfectly always amazed her. She had never dreamed in her wildest imagination that she would have been able to do minor magiq, let alone craft a magnificent piece such as this.

There was one last bit of magiq that Ghra'zhenn had instructed her to look through during her day of meditation. It was a type of magiq known only to wyvern history recorders. It involved an ancient type of magiq, which employed a type of large crystal to hold and store information of wyvern history. The crystals could be "opened" by the magiq user and employed a technique by which the wyvern, or in her case, person, could lock away information for future generations. Ghra'zhenn had only touched briefly on the fact that the archives entrusted to his dynasty might be in danger of being lost forever to greedy, power-hungry sorcerers, such as Kaistam-Laq and a few others still terrorizing the planets. If the information could be stored in the crystals for later use, Tÿr thought, the need to keep huge books would become obsolete, and the crystals could be kept in a single place instead of being spread all over the country.

This suddenly gave Tÿr unlimited ideas for how to use and employ the crystals. Storing histories was just one possibility. Spells, recipes, and language could be entrusted to the crystals. Tÿr was so anxious to get at the manuscripts. She hadn't read anything about this type of magiq and was dying to get started, though both wyverns had instructed her to be calm and try to shut off parts of her body for the upcoming ordeal that she would face. Though they still hadn't told her anything about it, she planned on looking for any information that she could find about intercalation as well. Suddenly a day's worth of meditation didn't seem like very long to her, especially if she was to train her body to slow its responses.

The day went by faster than Tÿr imagined it could have. She searched the large volumes for any of the information she was seeking, but the mention of any of it was glaringly absent. She thought she was getting close once or twice, but it led nowhere. The only things she found were things she already knew or had briefly touched on. So instead of spending time searching in vain, she reread the text and continued to memorize what she already had read before. By doing this exercise, her mind began to sharpen. She felt that she could, in fact, command her body to lessen senses in areas or sharpen in others. She tried this particular discipline with her sight in the dimness of the mine. She dimmed the light from her staff, and even with the effects still lingering in her eyes, she looked over to the nesting box at the säqyr wyvern. Within her mind, Tÿr sharpened her vision for both distance and dark vision. Sëvyq sat in his nesting box, dozing, as night approached. His arrow-shaped head was laying on his wing as he slumbered. Tÿr then let her sight return to normal. She realized how useful this could be in everyday life.

According to the texts, many magiq users required a magiq item to be on their person at all times in order to perform even the smallest amount of magiq, but Tÿr found out early on that she was not one of these people. The magiq was a natural gift that flowed strongly throughout her body, and she could do most anything with just the slightest suggestion from her mind. Tÿr also realized that this was probably the reason that she had been invited to go through the ordeal, yet honor, of intercalation. From the way it was explained, hardly anyone was ever offered this esteemed honor, and even fewer had ever been able to endure it. The girl now understood why she had been given the task of meditation by her mentor and the paragon. Her paragon.

She was now becoming nervous at the prospect of this tribulation. It had finally sunk in that very few had ever survived the process. Her heart sped up. The fear of the unknown was becoming overwhelming, so her meditation needed to improve quickly. She did not want to disappoint her mentor nor his. She read for hours, sleep threatening at every corner. Each time she felt a yawn beginning to surface, she thought about the process the she would be going through, and a jolt would shoot through her stomach, waking her again. Tÿr must have actually fallen asleep at some point because when she opened her eyes, the two giant wyverns were walking in through the entrance of the mine. Neither said anything about the fact that she was sleeping. In fact, it was almost as if they had expected it. She stood as the wyverns approached her position.

"It is time," Ghra'zhenn said quietly.

"Are you still completely sure you'd like to do this, Tÿr?" Varanus asked the girl. "I am now offering you one last chance to change your mind. Once you've agreed to do this, I will explain the process to you, and then we will get underway."

"I am ready now. I have accepted that this is more important than everything that I have done so far. I realize that there is so much I do not understand yet, but this must be."

"I believe you have chosen wisely, young apprentice," Ghra'zhenn told her. "Your mentor will assist me in this the entire operation. You will be in our capable hands, and we will care for you should any issues arise. You need not worry about anything except this. You must focus your mind to block out what is bad. The pain you will endure is said to push a human to the breaking point. I wish there was another way. I will now let Varanus explain how the procedure will work and what will happen if we succeed. I have only ever performed this practice four times, and I am the only being alive that has done it on the planets today."

Varanus took a step forward. "I'm sure you have many questions. I will try to answer them all as I go through what will happen here over the next several hours. The time it takes depends mainly on you and how well you tolerate the process. To begin, we will be using hundreds of slender crystals, which will be inserted in your skin."

If Tÿr had not been awake before, she was now. She listened intently as her mentor continued to explain.

"Each of these crystals will be heated until they glow. When they have reached the proper temperature, Ghra'zhenn will begin to insert each crystal individually under your skin, starting at your left wrist and working up to your shoulder. When the first arm is complete, he will begin on the right arm with the same procedure. With the crystals at the proper temperature, they will slide fairly easily under the skin and then stay in place. The hole will then cauterize itself. It is a fairly straightforward operation. When the arms are complete, the paragon will begin at your neck and down across the shoulders and down farther until it ends in a point near your tailbone. There will be minimum scarring with this procedure. However, the flesh will go through a slight transformation. It is a process known as receiving reptile skin, or *Kÿrkÿll Tÿgymyst* in Cmok, our tongue, soon to be yours as well. With the skin will come the ability for you to speak and understand our language. A great honor for a human!"

Tÿr's head was spinning, not just from all the information flying at her but from the fear of the pain that was to come. Varanus continued to explain how the process would be aided by a mild, natural sedative and anesthetic. She would be given leaves of a shrub native to the dynasty's mountain in the Qelibar Sea. The salt from the sea of the only salt water on the planet mixed with the enzymes of the leaves created a strong anesthetizer. Varanus did warn that this would help only a small amount, but it was the best he could offer. The apprentice let the information sink in. It was so much to digest in a short period. She still had many questions, but she felt that it would be best to get it over. Two days was going to be a long time, especially if the entire time was spent in agony.

"I am ready to begin," Tÿr told the wyverns.

"Have you already told your family and friends that you were going to be embarking on this journey?" Ghra'zhenn asked her.

"I told them that I had to do something important, that I needed to go on an assignment from which I may not be able to return," she responded. "They know nothing more. I left them a letter explaining only minor details."

"Very good. Now, I will ask you to keep your staff near you the entire time of the procedure. It will help to serve as an indicator of your condition. You will command it to light and remain that way as long as you remain in good health. The magiq will subside if your own energy begins to fade. We will then cease the operation for the time to attend to you. Once you are able to rekindle the fire, we will recommence. It will continue in this manner until the process is complete."

Tÿr nodded in ascent and was ready to begin. This seemed to satisfy the elder wyvern. "Then I would like to commence. Perhaps we could bring one of the portable beds that you have outside. It would be best for this procedure if it could be done with as much light as possible."

Tÿr nodded and went to retrieve a cot. The wyverns were standing at a box containing thousands of thin quartz crystals. They sparkled in the light of the three suns. Tÿr place the cot with the head facing the box. The staff was put down into the blue earth near the head so she could control it with ease. She stood next to it, her stomach tied in knots at the anticipation.

"We need you to remove your tunic and everything else above your waist," Varanus said. There was no emotion in his voice.

Tÿr felt self-conscious as she began to loosen her tunic and undo the ties of her shirt. She slipped the tunic off first and then turned around to face away from the wyverns. The wyverns hadn't turned to face away, not realizing that there would be discomfort on the apprentice's part. Tÿr covered herself as she moved to the cot. The wyverns didn't think about her nudity. She realized this and relaxed as much as she would allow it.

"Please begin to chew on these leaves."

Tÿr used one hand to take a small bunch of leaves from the paragon and placed several of them in her mouth. She expected something bitter but was pleasantly surprised to find that they had very little flavor. If anything, they were salty. The bitterness she had expected was replaced by something that quickly made her tongue and cheeks begin to tingle. In a minute's time, her mouth and throat were overcome with numbness, and it was quickly spreading throughout her body.

"You should begin to feel the effects move through your body," Varanus began.

Tÿr could. Her head began to swim slightly, and her hand lost some feeling. It was hard for her to even feel the remaining leaves left in her hand. Her inhibitions no longer mattered. The drugs had taken over, and now she wanted to lie down. The two wyverns helped to position her on the cot, with her arms over her head. The girl was barely awake, but a rude awakening was right around the corner. Each wyvern took an arm and restrained it to the top of the cot with a width of cloth. They then tied strips around her body at her chest and waist and her thighs. Varanus tried to explain to her that this was for her safety. Tÿr nodded incoherently, but no words were making it through to her. She laid her head back down between her arms. Ghra'zhenn brought up a large rock bowl. It was large enough to hold all the slender quartz crystals. He dumped them from the box into the bowl, his throat already beginning to glow. The paragon let a stream of well-controlled white flame spew into the bowl and blast the crystals. In just moments, the crystals were glowing white hot.

"Varanus, I need you to turn her arm a bit so I can place the first crystal."

The younger wyvern took the girl's arm and twisted it slightly, exposing the skin on the back of her arm. Ghra'zhenn picked up a white-hot crystal with his claw and nodded to Varanus.

"And now it begins! Hold her tightly. She is going to jump. Whatever you do, do not let her go! She will only harm herself."

The older wyvern used his claw to push the crystal into the skin below the outside edge of Tÿr's hand. Varanus felt the girl stiffen as the heated crystal touched her skin and slid under it to find its place. It bubbled for a few seconds, and the blood stopped almost immediately as the white-hot crystal seared the wound closed. The smell of charred flesh hung in the air above the girl. The second and third crystal were not as simple as they were closer to the bone. Tÿr shrieked in pain. The leaves, with all their anesthetizing qualities, helped only a little. The pain was very intense and didn't end once the crystal was in place. It continued to smoke and burn under the skin. It damaged nerves, numbing it eventually, but until then, Tÿr writhed in excruciating pain. The process was terribly slow.

Eventually Tÿr could tolerate the pain no longer. As the tiny shards made their way to the back of her arm, a final incredibly long scream gave way to eerie silence. Ghra'zhenn stopped the process to glance at Tÿr's staff. The light has dimmed but still burned bright enough to suggest she was in good health. She had passed out. The paragon attempted to speed up the process of placing the crystals. If the girl was unconscious, she wouldn't feel any of it. He would take advantage of her silence to continue. In between placement of each shard, the wyvern would continue to heat the inch-and-a-half crystals to make sure they were hot enough to cauterize and also hot enough to kill any germ that would attempt to sicken the girl. Ghra'zhenn had studied the human anatomy for many hundreds of years, so he knew that the placement was of utmost importance. If they were too deep, they could burn bone and cause permanent damage. Too shallow, and they could ignite the fat layer, or just burn back through the skin.

It took over four hours to complete the first arm properly. Even though Tÿr had been unconscious for most of the operation, Ghra'zhenn had to make very sure that the crystals went in the right way on the first attempt. While Ghra'zhenn was working on completing other rows on the upper arm, Varanus concocted a brew of other herbs and ground roots and other items that he could wipe over the burnt flesh. It acted as a coolant and a topical anesthetizer.

Tÿr began to stir again. Sweat was pouring down her face from the ordeal. Tÿr was trapped in her mind, and she couldn't move. Her arm was on fire. Each little piece of crystal was more excruciating than the last, and she felt she would go insane. The plant was making things hazy to her, but she knew what was going on, and she wanted it to stop. She kept her eyes shut as tight as she could in between bouts of searing pain. Her stomach began to wretch, and just when she felt that she would vomit from the extreme pain, blackness would begin to creep across her already-darkened eyes. Mercy came in the form of unconsciousness, but that, too, was only temporary. She screamed when she became aware that she couldn't move to escape the fire in her arm, now reaching her shoulder.

The wyvern continued the slow, torturous process. He did his best to ignore the screams coming from the young girl strapped to the cot before him. One small crystal at a time, the ordeal continued. When the first arm was completed, Ghra'zhenn moved on to the other. Tÿr was barely conscious anymore. The pain was more than she could bear. Varanus was generously mopping the cooling liquid down her arm gently to keep from peeling the layers of burnt skin away. He was glad that the girl was under. He hated hearing her pleas. She was stronger than a human could be, but she had her breaking point and begged for it to stop when she was lucid enough to do so. Still the paragon continued through the wails of desperation. He wanted to stop this procedure more than once. He had never heard a human make such noises, but he knew that this was something that was absolutely necessary.

It took over eight hours to complete the arms. Ghra'zhenn made sure each crystal was in its precise place, all the while Varanus followed behind with the cooling elixir. Steam rose as it hit the still-glowing crystals beneath the skin. The smell was atrocious but had attracted both the smaller creatures. They wanted to know what they were smelling and if it was their dinner. Varanus had to shoo them away on more than one occasion. If the arms were bad, they were nothing compared to the flesh on the back. Even though Tÿr had awakened again as it started and had chewed on more leaves, she couldn't stay unconscious. The pain was too great.

"You're doing so well!" Ghra'zhenn told her. "We just have the back left to complete. I know how painful this is. Just remember how much this is going to help and do for you." His voice was soothing, and Tÿr quit writhing as much as she had been but soon began again as the crystals started their unique pattern on her back.

Varanus continued through the night. He mopped without stopping as Ghra'zhenn placed the quartz crystals. They stopped for nothing. Halfway down Tÿr's back, as the crystals came closer together, forming an upside-down triangle, she passed out for good.

The pain was so intense and complete she could no longer tolerate it, not even with her meditation exercises. Tÿr felt ever stab, every burn. She could feel her flesh bubble as it sizzled above the tiny glowing crystals. The burns were more than second degree, and nerve damage was going to be an issue for a long while. She chanted the mantras from the tomes that Ghra'zhenn had given her to prepare from, but her mind could not ignore the pain. It burned, even with the mopping; she just couldn't take it any longer. She was clenching her jaw so tightly she feared she was in danger of losing teeth. Pain in her face, as the muscles were so tight, was the last thing she remembered before she felt no more. There was nothing.

It was dark, and she could hear the procedure as it was going on, but it was so far away. The cloth with the icy water dropped over her side and down on the cot. She was in no position to try to change it though. She simply tried to turn to get away from the excruciating, torturous agony but could not make her body move. Ghra'zhenn relaxed when the final piece was placed under the girl's now-blistered skin. It truly looked like that of a lizard. It was charred in some spots, but most of those came off as Varanus gently mopped the skin with the herbed water.

"If you will continue to wipe the back with that liquid, I will make a salve to put on the burned areas. It will help to alleviate her pain and aid in the healing," Ghra'zhenn told his former student.

He moved off to the mine slowly to gather the ingredients, clearly stiff from standing in one place for so long. Varanus continued to wipe Tÿr's back until the older wyvern returned with a thick green ointment. He started on her arms and applied a thick layer all the way up to her shoulders and across to her neck and the down her back. Tÿr began to stir. Her eyes fluttered, and she moaned in misery.

"Welcome back!" Varanus said to her, breathing a sigh of relief.

The fact that the girl was awake so soon was a very good omen, telling the pair of wyverns that the operation was successful and that their patient would recover. They released the girl and woke her gently. She was still in horrific pain, but it wasn't as intense as it was while the paragon was executing the intercalation. Tÿr's arms ached from being over her head for over a day and a half. She reached up to rub them, but stopped when she noticed the poultice of green salve covering the backs of them. Varanus gave her more of the green leaves to chew. Her mouth was so dry she had trouble. The wyvern offered her a mug of sweet wine to drink, which she readily accepted. In minutes, her head was spinning, and the pain was in the back of her mind for the time being. Her staff still glowed at the head of her cot. She thought of telling the two wyverns how she had almost dimmed to light to stop the procedure. The only reason she hadn't this was because it would have begun again, and she wanted to be done as soon as it was possible. She felt weak from the lack of food, and she couldn't concentrate from the waves of pain still pulsing through her back.

"Is it over?" she asked weakly.

"It is. You did wonderfully, even through the incredible pain you must have felt," Varanus told her.

"I feel it still. I have never felt closer to death than I feel now."

"I understand. You have been through more than most any human has, and you did it of your own free will. Many injured in war don't have the pain sustained by intercalation."

"I knew it was important. I had no choice. If we are to keep the lands around Vennex and its people safe, there was no other choice. I'm am glad despite my grumbling right now."

Varanus dipped his head. "You have every right to your pain, and I would expect no less. You have endured something that the body shouldn't have to deal with. Reticence is not what I expect. Please feel free to continue screaming if you must!"

"I was screaming?" she asked, shocked by this revelation.

"I don't believe any being could sit quietly during intercalation. It is meant to be earned, not given easily."

"My body is on fire still. How long will this last?" She was almost pleading as she asked her mentor.

"It is different for each person. Ghra'zhenn is mixing a poultice to put on your back and arms. It will help to dull the pain. You will also be given more of the leaves you chewed at the beginning of your procedure. They are special and will help to keep your mind from concentrating on the pain. These are *doffyna* leaves, and when soaked in wyvern's blood, they make a powerful anesthetic."

Ghra'zhenn appeared at the entrance of the cavern, carrying a bowl. Tÿr breathed a sigh of relief. Her body craved release from the burn of the intercalation she had just undergone. The girl had raised up and was sitting up on the cot. At first, she still felt a bit self-conscious about being partially unclothed, but her arms ached so much she realized that this was no time for inhibitions. Ghra'zhenn gave the bowl to Varanus and instructed him to put the salve on his apprentice's back. Tÿr felt the burn subside almost immediately. She sat patiently as the wyvern gave her the relief she so desperately needed. The larger wyvern gave her another bunch of leaves to chew, and in just moments, the hazy feeling flowed down from the top of her head and gave her another level of comfort. Rævii had now come to check on her master. She jumped up on the cot next to Tÿr. The fox sensed that there was something wrong, so she didn't do her usual cuddling and nuzzling, for which Tÿr was eternally grateful.

"I would like to take a moment," Ghra'zhenn redirected the girl's attention back to himself. "On behalf of myself and my entire dynasty, welcome to our fold! My sincere appreciation on your completion of the most gruesome and painful of our traditions. Your name will soon be known around all the lands!"

Tÿr felt another surge of great pride. She had wished that she'd endured the process with more dignity, but Ghra'zhenn didn't appear to mind. She also felt a twinge of concern as well. What would happen to her once the wrong people learned of her new power? There were some people on the planets that didn't appreciate people gaining any type of power, be it magiq or political or wealth. Quite often these people who had become powerful would lose their power in mysterious circumstances. Or worse, their lives in circumstances even more perplexing. Luckily for Tÿr, she had training on her side, albeit less than she would like, but both wyverns would never have exposed her to the danger without being certain that she would be able to overcome the obstacles ahead.

"Tÿr, I understand the pain that you are going through at this moment. I know it must be more than anything I have ever faced in my entire life, and you chose to do it willingly. I'm afraid I need to find out if the process actually worked though," Ghra'zhenn tried to tell her as gently as his gruff voice would allow. "I'm going to ask you to try to give me a few different signs or indications that you still can perform basic magiq, and any deviation from the spell or enchantment will be thought of as a failure. I believe that you may have been rushed toward the end, so I have to make sure for your sake. I realize you have been through more than I had a right to ask, and to ask more is truly pressing my advantage, but I sincerely must ask this of you."

Tÿr thought she heard pleading in the paragon's voice. Varanus had completed covering the apprentice's back and arms with the thick green paste. She was feeling the relief from it but was dreading the upcoming tests needed to prove that the intercalation had worked. She didn't know all that she would be asked, but she could guess that she would have to light the crystals that were now under her skin, and she guessed that it would once again bring pain that she was just now feeling relief from. Still, she wanted to be done with it as soon as she could so she could get some much-needed rest.

"May we proceed then?" she asked the paragon. Her paragon. She was now a member of his dynasty, and she had never been a part of something so important.

"If you believe you are ready, we may begin immediately. You may have as much time as you require, my dear," Ghra'zhenn advised her. His voice was so gentle despite the gruffness of it.

Tÿr drew from reserves she didn't even know she possessed and nodded to her paragon.

Chapter 12

At a hidden base camp that bordered the Kirin-Noirin shift and the deserts of Peyda Kirin, the magiq user and sorcerer, Kaistam-Laq, was suddenly distracted from his conversation with his aides as he sat in his luxurious tent. No expense was spared when it came to the comfort of the powerful sorcerer. He got what he wanted. What he couldn't afford, his people acquired for him. They, too, were well paid for their missions as paid assassins. Immediately Laq's second-in-command asked what was happening. Xyrfed Mai did not like surprises and wanted to be kept informed of any issues he might be facing. If there was anything threatening the Murtair Amagii, he needed to know to keep the sect safe from any enemies.

"It appears there has been an old magiq of some type employed. One that I am not familiar with. Observe my staff."

The sorcerer held out the staff for his second and the other four in the tent to observe. The normally stark-white, wooden staff now had raised pale-blue-green veining running the length of it from the headpiece to the ground. They looked like human veins, almost pulsing with life.

"What does this mean?" a thin, dark-skinned lady with a shaved head asked.

"I am unsure at the moment, *Owonnyn*. I may need to consult some of the old manuscripts. This is old magiq. I am unsure if I even possess anything old enough to explain what I have just felt. There is one other place I may consult. I would prefer not to, but it might be necessary."

Those gathered in the meeting knew of the other source, and all present preferred their leader not have to go either. The other alternative was seeking out an old wyvern who was not only ill-tempered and hateful but was greedy and generally only helped if there was something in it for itself. The wyvern in question—*Nagarr Zmaj*. The name itself sounded evil, and it instilled fear in all that heard it anywhere on the dual planets.

Xyrfed Mai spoke first, "We will have to recruit more into our number and train them before you can consider doing that!"

"How can you even consider dealing with that piece of excrement?" Owonnyn spat with deep venom.

"Control yourselves," Kaistam-Laq oozed with caution. "This is my concern, not yours! You both with remain here should I need to hold an audience with that foul snake. Should I need to take anyone, I will choose them at that time. Have I made myself clear?"

His gaze moved between Xyrfed Mai and Owonnyn and then to the others. All present knew the subject was now closed, and to bring it up again would surely mean a possibility of incurring their master's wrath. They all had seen it too many times before to wish a repeat. It often meant having to recruit a new member to keep their seventeen members at a constant. Kaistam-Laq believed the number seventeen was highly magiqal and wove his spells and incantations around this number.

"There will be no recruitment! We will deal with this situation if it arises. I alone will handle any issues with Nagarr Zmaj." Laq's voice always sounded like it was on the verge of pronouncing a death sentence.

The others present for this council of Kaistam-Laq's most-trusted advisors were *Mynnÿ Sï*, a young desert lady of unknown origin, whose knowledge of the staff boline earned her a spot in the infamous sect and also seat on the council. *Kkyllum Jannyk* occupied the fourth seat on the council. He was a tall, pale, thin man whose hardworking and cruel ways were a perfect compliment to land him as a confidant to Kaistam-Laq. Finally, the youngest member, he was small and quiet and able to get into places that the others often couldn't. *Gaerrod* specialized in close-quarters, up-close-and-personal-type killings, choosing to use blades of lachtrys to great advantage. It was rumored that he could separate a person from their skeletal structure in under five minutes, leaving a mass of flesh behind and a piled of charred bones in the firepit. These were the types of assassins that were recruited by the head of the Murtair Amagii.

Along with Xyrfed and Owonnyn, they composed the *Ÿffymÿ*, a word from the old language, meaning *the five*. They were in charge of the rest of the sect and kept things running smoothly so Kaistam-Laq didn't have to become involved in the day-to-day dreary stuff. In fact, Laq didn't even know most of the seventeen assassins in the sect, which helped keep him out of the usual day-to-day functions of his organization. It also kept him from becoming so mad at his people he needed to continually replace them. What he did know about Murtair Amagii was that the mere mention of the name put fear in the hearts of everyone with half a brain. His people were well-trained and could walk in and out of places without being noticed. The jobs they did were efficient and thorough.

When people needed a job to be done correctly without any mistakes, they called his crew. It wasn't just a regular person who wanted revenge that called them either. The price required was astronomical, so usually the clientele had money, and lots of it. Royalty often sought out the services of the Amagii. There were many other sects that could be called on for the more-menial tasks and lesser jobs. The Vrasës sects had several different branches, and most of them were more reasonably priced with skilled assassins, but they didn't take on the big jobs of Murtair Amagii. They just didn't have the resources nor the wherewithal to attack during the day or in the open as their rivals.

"What we must do right now is listen!" Kaistam-Law told his advisors. "How this magiq has gotten past me is unnerving. We are going out into towns and villages. This is something that cannot continue!"

The aides looked at each other. They knew that when their master got this way, there was no talking him out of anything.

"You will gather everyone and send them out into the countryside of the shift. They are to go in to each and every magistracy and look for signs of any type of new or very old magiq. Not knowing what is going on is very dangerous to all of us. It could mean our very safety. Report back to me immediately in the normal way. Leave no village unsearched, no stone unturned!"

The council took this as a definitive sign that the meeting was at its completion. They would be packing their packs to go out into the Kirin-Noirin shift, and farther if necessary. This also meant that the entire sect would be employed to go among the general population of both the Peyda planets to enlist the help of the citizens. Only the citizens would never know. The assassins were gifted at lifting information from people without them ever realizing that they had ever said anything wrong. The pubs and taverns always had folks who loved to share information for the price of another drink or two. Strong drinks loosened lips better than any interrogator could.

Kaistam-Laq adjourned to his personal quarters at the very back of the tent. His actual quarters were essentially a smaller tent set up in a much-larger tent. There were alarm systems set up all the way around the tent to keep out unwanted visitors. There were magiqal traps and alarms set up by Kaistam and all the sect. If anyone ever got through, the person whose trap failed was punished most severely. Usually, they were removed from the sect, and no one was allowed to know who was in the sect. This meant that the search for a new sect member would begin in earnest. Kaistam-Laq was adamant about keeping his number at seventeen.

The "inner sanctuary" where Kaistam lived was lavish and contained powerful pieces of magiqal antiques and books and scrolls. There were comfortable chairs and sofas around one room, and the other room was divided by a wall of crystals hanging like beads on long strands of string. Many of the items in the open room lit up as the sorcerer approached them with his powerful staff. The tomes and scrolls glowed eerily with a sickly, greenish light. They appeared to be daring anyone to touch them. The sorcerer had so many protection spells placed on his relics and spell books anyone who even touched them would be permanently damaged or outright killed.

The sect also paid to have their leader's tent guarded by elite militia forces as well. There were six guards posted around the outer tent and another six around the inner sanctum. Security was tight, and trespassing was punished severely. Anyone who managed to make it in to the private chambers of Kaistam-Laq himself was actually given careful consideration for possible induction into the Amagii. They were given one chance to agree, and if they refused, they were parted from their head quickly and without ceremony. No one left Murtair Amagii willingly, or any other way. There was no retirement. When you were too old for missions, you remained in the camp and trained the new members. This was how it had always been!

The head of the Amagii went to a huge obsidian mirror used for scrying and divining the truth. He drew his first finger across the glasslike surface. And then again. He continued to form a glyph with the long, pointed fingernail. All his nails had been artfully painted a deep blood red that faded to black at the base of each nail. The first glyph he had drawn glowed like lava. An orange fire from deep down pulsed in the ancient letter. He drew another over the first, and at first, it was hard to see what it was. As the seconds passed, the second glyph glowed with the intensity of a sun. The sorcerer placed his hand on top of the glowing symbols, and immediately it began to smoke. Despite the pain it was causing him, he kept his hand firmly in place. His face was drawn into a horrid grimace. His golden eyes faded in and out at the pain that seared his hand. And then as quickly as it had come, it retreated. Kaistam looked down at his hand. There was no mark or anything to show that there had been searing heat there just moments before.

The sorcerer seemed satisfied with the magiq that had just taken place. He left the mirror and went to sit in his chair, an elaborately carved chair that could have been argued was a throne. It was actually nicer than that of some of the emperors, but Kaistam liked that. He loved the lavish things in life. He could afford them, or at least acquire them, so why not enjoy them? The throne was carved from a single piece of teakwood of the highest quality. It stood over twelve feet tall at the center and was covered with carvings of angels and demons fighting a massive battle over heaven and earth. The throne was very gothic in appearance, with spikes rising austerely from the peaks of the chair to point up into the heights of the huge tent. Draped between the spikes were long deep-red scarves of silk that hung down to the black satin cushion with golden tassels. As elaborate as the throne was, the sorcerer didn't really have it out in a great place of prominence. He kept it off to the side, among his other magiqal tools and items. No one in the sect had ever dared to sit in it, even as a joke. Kaistam-Laq wasn't known for his quick party jokes. In fact, no one had tried telling him a joke in over a decade.

Kaistam walked around the tent. He adjusted one item or made sure another was working. He walked over to a large bookshelf and took out two old leather-bound tomes. The leather on the spines was beginning to crack, and the gold leafing of the title was faded so badly the sorcerer had to have known which book it was. He placed both books at a table near a smaller chair; this one was designed for comfort. The tall man also took down several parchment scrolls wrapped in leather sheaths to protect the delicate manuscripts.

Kaistam-Laq had just about settled into his comfortable reading chair when the scrying mirror began to sizzle. Sparks flashed and crackled on the surface as a glowing figure rose out of the fiery sparks. The sorcerer glided over to the obsidian mirror and waited as the figure on the surface turned into a glowing hand. It was holding another scroll, which also had sparks of fire falling from it, onto the flat, shiny black surface to die out almost immediately. Kaistam-Laq reached out and took the leather rolled scroll. The hand sank back below the surface of the mirror in a mass of shimmering orange sparks.

"Thank you, my friend!" Laq said after the hand disappeared.

He brought the new scroll back to his table with the other manuscripts. The new magiq that Kaistam-Laq had experienced was troubling him for many reasons. First and foremost was that he thought he was the expert on all types of magiq in the immediate area. The second thing that troubled him was that this magiq was old, and if he didn't know it, there was a possibility that the snake and enemy of the Amagii, Nagarr Zmaj, had this magiq and could employ it against Kaistam and his sect of assassins. If the magiq was as powerful as he thought it to be, he was in danger.

Kaistam-Laq settled into his comfortable green chair to begin to study the volumes of magiq before him. He reached over to a shelf next to the chair, not even looking up from the huge book as he read. He took down a crystal decanter and small cordial glass and poured himself a small glassful. Without missing a beat, he downed the amber liquid in one and poured another. With the stopper back in place, the sorcerer put the clear crystal bottle back on the little table and set his glass of some type of liqueur next to the bottle and continued reading.

He read for almost nine hours straight and was surprised to find out the time when one of his aides came in to ask him a question later in the night. Kaistam was disappointed by his lack of progress regarding any magiq of the magnitude he had encountered earlier in the day. He was certain that the scroll he had requested would have some information to explain magiq of that power. This was no new magiq that had just been thrown together. This was old magiq, since the creation of the planets, or so he was almost positive. The leader of the Murtair Amagii gave the final order to send the sect out into the villages. They were to report back in two weeks' time if they had any information. He himself had vowed not to leave his quarters until he could discover the source of the new magiq. This meant long days and nights sitting in this chair pouring over volumes and scrolls for even one little mention of power. He wasn't sure what it was that he was searching, but he was sure he would know it when he saw it. And so began the hunt.

Chapter 13

Tӱr healed quicker than she had expected to. Ghra'zhenn had stayed in the mine with her and Varanus to help tend to her back and arms with the salves and other things he had provided to her. They helped with the pain and also the actual healing. The redness had gone away after just three days.

Luckily for Tӱr, the worst of the pain had subsided by the end of the second day, and she could actually bear to have a light shirt on. She had long since lost her inhibitions around her mentor and paragon. They treated her very professionally and as a healer treated a patient. Not being the same species also helped. Had they been human, she probably wouldn't have gone around so long without her top no matter how much pain she was in. Had the brothers shown up, she didn't know what she would have done. Now was not the time for modesty however.

The intercalation had worked, and it had worked better than the trio could have ever hoped. The wyverns had been testing her abilities every day and were excited by everything they saw. Tӱr got out of her bed, having had slept the entire night without a single bad dream. She had been put through tests of all types to see what her new powers would allow her to do.

Today the wyverns would be showing her a way to compose information and save it in ways known only to wyverns of their dynasty for millennia. Rævii was there to greet her as she pulled on a light chemise. Ever since the intercalation, Tӱr was certain that she could almost understand the little shift fox. Varanus had told her to expect things like this to happen. She might be able to talk to or understand several animals before all was said and done. The apprentice could now fully understand and cognize the wyvern tongue, Cmok. It wasn't just a few words either. She perfectly grasped the vocabulary and the unique rhythm in which the native speakers spoke. She still hadn't tried to speak back any words yet, but she was sure that she would be able to if the need actually arose, but her mentor had given her several texts to use while studying. So far, the wyverns had only spoken to her in their own tongue. Immersing her into the language would help.

Tÿr'Ynyn made her way out to the firepit and the two wyverns sitting on either side of it. If Ghra'zhenn had been fond of Tÿr before her intercalation, he absolutely oozed pleasure around her now. Varanus just smiled. He treated his apprentice like a younger, more-human sister.

Today, once the testing of the intercalation was done, Tÿr would begin the process of learning to store information. The wyverns were very enthusiastic to teach Tÿr this process. There were many things that needed to be stored, and the wyverns have used this system for many centuries if not longer. Tÿr would be the first human to learn the wyvern way. Others had been through intercalation in the past but had not proven trustworthy enough, or had not lived long enough to go through the "record-keeping" system. Though the wyverns had literally thousands of tomes and scrolls and papers, with letters advising how to heal every creature on the planet, they also had thousands of stacked crystals that carried information on magiq and plants and other crystals that were used in ceremonies and just about everything Tÿr could think of.

Rævii followed Tÿr out of the cavern and sat next to Ghra'zhenn. Ghra'zhenn always had some little treat to give the little fox. Her bushy blond tail was straight out behind her in anticipation of the delectation from her large, winged friend. Tÿr knew Ghra'zhenn had taken a liking to both of the camp's newest additions. Rævii and Sëvyq both benefitted from being favorites of the wyvern paragon. Ghra'zhenn was always slipping them bits of meat. He said it helped to train them, but Tÿr often caught him passing them little snacks just for coming near him and snuggling up to him. It was really quite a sight to see.

Tÿr had her staff with her and was ready to be put through her paces. Some of the healing she had learned she was actually able to use on herself. One of the techniques for lessening burns and healing scars she was able to employ on her back and arms, and instant relief flooded her. Most of the searing, biting pain had subsided substantially since the first day, but each day that she treated it, the lingering effects melted away. She was sure she would be back in her usual tunic in a day or so.

One of the new things that she had to get used to when tapping into her magiq was that fact that the crystals that were now healing under her skin glowed each time she called upon them. Neither Ghra'zhenn nor Varanus had told her to expect this, and immediately following the intercalation, the wyverns had asked her to experiment with her implants to make sure the process had not been done for nothing. The technique for employing the crystals was almost the same as it was for lighting her piece of quartz she had been given by her mentor. Once it glowed at her command, she began to give it simple instructions. That was the way her embedded crystals worked as well. Just on a larger scale. She was so surprised to see her arms glowing she almost yelped out in fright. She expected burning heat to come from the shards in her arms and back but was extremely grateful to find that there was no extra pain at all. Once the concern of added pain was removed from the equation, Tÿr was concentrating on her magiq with her whole mind. She performed much more effectively than either wyvern could have imagined that day.

The days since her intercalation had been filled with exercises, things like moving objects and stacking them carefully, doing two or more at a time; choosing three, four, or even five targets to attack at once, using a large ball of fire or something new that Varanus had taught her, a concatenation of lightning that struck out and could attack numerous things in a nonlinear path. Tÿr could also call out fireballs at the same time. She was told that she would be able to do even more once she had fully healed and had time to train. Each time she exercised her magiq, the crystals in her glowed brightly. Her arms and back lit up eerily, making her appear almost alien. The wings shone brightly as the crystals glowed. All the metals of the wings appeared to undulate and flow into each other. As her magiq concentrated, the whole headpiece glowed with white fire, too bright to stare at without hurting your eyes. With a deafening screech, she yelled out and shot a beam of pure energy into the air. The mountain actually rumbled from down deep inside. Tÿr'Ynyn had never felt power like this before.

Energy crackled in the air around her and seemed to absorb into her and reemerge more powerful yet. The power was amazing, but it frightened her. She was only beginning to grasp the use of magiq. If someone chose to use this power against people, the damage they could do would be devastating. If Tÿr could mend things in the body of a being by touching on her newfound magiqal energy, she felt sick at the thought of what could be done by a person who wanted to harm. Both Ghra'zhenn and Varanus had been teaching her that it was much more difficult to harm with magiq than it was to heal. They had explained that it went against nature to want to harm, and so to force the magiq to obey a command to destroy a living thing was much more complicated and required more concentration, leaving the magiq user vulnerable for a moment while they were attempting the spell. They also expounded that magiq was as natural as trees and creatures and crystals. To go against nature required a great deal of willpower and determination.

Tÿr and the wyverns practiced all her magiq that she had learned thus far. The giants were more than pleased at the incredible progress the apprentice had made. She not only could make elixirs now but, using magiq, she could increase the potency tenfold. Ghra'zhenn had told her in a very serious conversation that he anticipated that she would finish with her training several years before schedule. The way she was retaining the magiq and the knowledge that he and Varanus were teaching her was continuing to astound the paragon. She literally knew more now than healer apprentices that had been training for over twelve years. She had only been studying for three months to the day.

Varanus had said that he felt comfortable enough to let her stay at the healer's shop for long periods of time without him being present. She already knew as much as her predecessor had. Kuired was an excellent healer, and he had taught Tÿr a lot as he worked. He did not, however, choose to teach her magiq. He felt that magiq was best left to him and other healers. He was a cautious man when it came to the use of any magiq at all. Tÿr had only seen him use it a handful of times, and he usually asked her to leave unless he needed her to stay and hold the patient's hand or to help restrain them. Tÿr also felt she would be cautious with whom she would share the magiq. She was sure this was the type of thing that Kaistam-Laq would want to know. She was also sure that it could put her friends and family in danger if he should find out about her newfound abilities.

Ghra'zhenn stopped Tÿr for a moment to ask her what was troubling her. He told her that the aura of her magiq had suddenly changed, and he was wanting to know the cause. Tÿr told him of her concerns, not just of the worries for herself but mainly for those left back in Vennex. If Murtair Amagii was to find out about Tÿr, her friends, family, and the people that she saw every day could be in danger. She wasn't sure what that madman would try, but everything she had heard about Kaistam-Laq suggested that he didn't deal well with competition. All it would take was one drunken villager with a loose tongue at the pub. Things could turn ugly quickly for Tÿr and the wyverns, and not just them. Ghra'zhenn reminded Tÿr that the boys were also out at the pubs, listening for anything out of the ordinary. They were given instructions to send message back to the cavern immediately.

Tÿr was taking a short break to heal up, so the boys looked after the shop until she could get back. They had a cover story and had not had to use it yet.

When Tÿr had completed her exercises and had enhanced some of the salves and potions she had made the day before, she went over and dropped to the ground in front of the firepit in between the two large wyverns. It was now time to learn record-keeping. The ancient art learned and taught of the wyverns.

"I am ready to learn," Tÿr said to her teachers. "I'm still not exactly sure how this works. How can you store information on a crystal? You did say we would be using crystals…"

"That is correct," Ghra'zhenn said, tilting his large, viperlike head.

"Since you seem to learn at an accelerated rate," Varanus picked up where the paragon had stopped, "we will first teach you to identify the proper crystals to use. We have gathered some large pieces of quartz from different places. Some are acceptable, and some are just quartz. You can use any crystal for this provided that it is correct type. We choose to use the largest ones that we can find to suit our purposes. The larger the crystal, the more information we can layer in it. You can tell the proper crystals by small triangles etched on the facets of the terminations. In other words, look for little triangles etched on the pointed ends of the crystals. Pieces without the markings are not useful to us. We can use them for talismans or elixirs or other things, such as decoys. We will touch on that later!"

Týr noticed two large sacks sitting behind the wyverns. She hadn't been paying attention at first, but now she couldn't understand how she missed them. They were large cloth bags made out of some type of strong, canvaslike material.

Varanus reached behind himself and hoisted one of the bags over to where Týr was now sitting on the ground, near the cooking pit. He made it seem as if it was filled with feathers. Týr got up and went over to open the large bag. It had the normal, wooden-toggle fastenings that the wyverns seemed to prefer. She was going to move the bag closer to her, but found that it was extremely heavy. It was completely filled to almost bursting with large, clear quartz crystals. Some were double terminated while others only had one point.

"I will go through a few of these with you to make sure you understand what you are looking for," Ghra'zhenn explained to Týr.

She reached down and picked up a few of the glass-clear crystals. Some were so clear, with hardly any defects in the crystal, while others had shadowy, ghostlike figures. There were even some that had inclusions that caused incredible rainbows. Týr could have stared at the crystals for hours, but Ghra'zhenn was ready for her to begin her lesson.

"Varanus, do you have an example to show our student?"

Varanus had a couple of the large quartz crystals in his hands and passed one to Týr. "See if you can spot what we are talking about. There are quite a few on several of the faces. You may have to look carefully, but they are quite visible."

Tÿr'Ynyn took one of the foot-long quartz pieces from her mentor and looked carefully on the pointed ends. The first facet was plain, but as she turned the crystal to the next side, etched quite clearly were about fifteen tiny triangles spread around the face. She turned the crystal to the next facet, and sure enough, there were several more.

"I see them!" she exclaimed excitedly.

"Very good," Ghra'zhenn told her. "You are now of my dynasty and will know what they are and what they will mean. When you begin to store information on them, you will be shown a mark that is used by our dynasty alone. That is how you will recognize our record keepers."

"Do other dynasties use different symbols on theirs?" Tÿr asked.

"As far as I am aware, our dynasty is the only one on the planet that knows how to utilize crystals in this way. I have never heard of any other wyvern, nor human, tribe using them for this. It is a secret that we guard jealously. In fact, there are only five wyverns alive that know of this. They are all on the council of elders, and we store ancient history and magiq this way for future generations. You are the first human to have this honor bestowed to you!"

Tÿr again felt pride beyond any that she had in the past. These wyverns had seen something in her and had chosen to trust her enough with their ancient secrets. The girl made a silent vow that no matter what happened in the future, she would never let her mentor or paragon down. They had trusted her, and she had trusted them enough to let them make her one of them. She had never felt the pride that she did at this moment.

"What do I do now?" she asked, ready to learn.

"The very first thing you will need to learn is the symbol of my dynasty," Ghra'zhenn began. "Each time we use a crystal to hold information, we mark it with our dynasty glyph. That way, we know that the crystal is our record keeper. Then, even if only one word is put into it, or one memory, we mark it with another, directly below the dynasty glyph. That tells us that there is information stored on the crystal. Both Varanus and I will open several crystals and store a word or a short phrase. We will explain how to retrieve the word or phrase, and you will tell us what we stored on each crystal."

"Okay, let's start. I'm ready!"

Varanus produced three crystals and handed them to his apprentice. She studied them, taking in each imperfection and mark. She could see the tiny, triangular markings on the facets, signifying the crystal as a record keeper. She could also see a mark on the bottom quarter of one of the long sides. It looked like a letter Y at first glance, but the left side of the Y almost looked like a head, and the tail of the letter appeared to be a wyvern tail. The right branch of the letter had four lines coming off it and rounded out the appearance of the wyvern. There was a mark under it that resembled a comma, signifying that there was indeed something stored in the crystal. Tÿr ran her fingers over the markings on the smooth quartz. She could barely feel them as they seemed to be etched into the quartz itself.

"What you will need to do to open the crystal is to raise the triangles by heating them. Use your magiq to warm the triangles only. Cause them to glow. You will cause them to change their physical location. From there, I will instruct you on the extraction of the information."

Tÿr concentrated on the large crystal in her hand. Light began to shine from its depths, and in seconds, the whole thing flowed brightly with searing white light.

"Concentrate on the triangles. Heat them as hot as you can. Don't heat anything else!" Ghra'zhenn coached.

The light dimmed slightly in the crystal, and in no time, the little triangles began to glow as well. Red and angry. The hotter they got, Tÿr noticed that they began to rise out of the surface of the facets on the quartz like tiny little buttons. They began on the face with the wyvern glyph and rose on each of the other facets that contained the tiny triangles, moving anticlockwise.

"The crystal is now open!" Ghra'zhenn told her.

"It spoke to me," Tÿr told the ancient one. "I'm not sure if I'm correct, but I think it spoke in Cmok. I believe it told me that Ÿkkynnÿk was my home if I choose it to be!"

Though a wyvern could smile, it was a rather-bizarre look. It appeared as more of a grimace of pain, but when it lingered, Tӱr learned to guess that it was, in fact, the closest thing to a smile she could get. She chose never to bring up the point, so she didn't hurt either of her superiors' feelings.

"You are correct about the message that was stored in the quartz. I chose something extremely easy, yet not so simple that you could easily guess it."

Ghra'zhenn looked extremely tired from all the training he had done, but he still managed to radiate pride to the apprentice. He could not have been prouder of the apprentice.

"Now I want you to try to store something by concentrating the way you would to light the crystal. It will take more energy, and when you have the energy in place, instead of making the crystal glow, I want you to will your words into the quartz. This will take some practice. It is much more difficult to do than to open and retrieve the information," Varanus explained.

He and Ghra'zhenn were taking turns with Tӱr's training. "When you believe that you have stored the information in the record keeper, press down on the triangles in the same direction that they rose, anticlockwise! That will store them permanently, and they can only be removed by the person who stored the data."

Tӱr thought for a minute about what she wanted to say. When she had a short phrase, she quickly energized the large quartz point; and when she felt that she was prepared, she willed the short phrase into the windowpane-like stone.

"Now, just press down the tiny, triangle-like buttons."

She pushed them in the correct fashion, and the stone sealed itself.

Varanus took the quartz from his apprentice. Immediately it began to heat up, and a warm glow spread almost as fast. The raised record keepers were barely noticeable in his hands. He took several seconds trying to find to message Tӱr had left in the quartz crystal but was unable to find it. He tried several more times, all with the same results.

"What is it?" Tӱr asked.

"I am unable to find your message."

Týr was instantly disappointed. Things had been moving along so well, and it seemed she couldn't fail, until now. "May I have it back?" Týr asked.

She wanted to try again. Failure was not an option for her nor was letting her boss or his boss down. Varanus handed the quartz piece back to Týr, who snatched it rather more forcefully than she intended.

"It is okay to fail at something your first time, Týr'Ynyn! You have been progressing faster than you could possibly know. For you to not do something on your first attempt, it is not a problem. It took me several tries to even save one word. Please do not become discouraged!" Varanus tried to inspirit her with positive reinforcement.

Týr appreciated this but was still disappointed in herself. She tried again, concentrating harder this time. She passed the crystal back and waited. The look on Varanus's face gave her her answer without saying a word. Disappointed again, she didn't understand what she was doing wrong.

"Why? What is causing me so much trouble?"

"Please do get down on yourself. You have only had two chances. Some wyverns can take weeks to learn it! Just give yourself some time."

Týr wanted to snatch the crystal back again, but she controlled the impulse. It wasn't her mentor's fault that she couldn't do this. "Is there anything either of you could suggest?" she almost pleaded.

Ghra'zhenn began to explain that instead of trying to make the data appear inside the quartz crystal, she should try to pour it into it. "Let it fill the stone. Like you would fill a cup with wine. Don't try to make it appear from the inside. You are storing the information inside by adding it little by little. I think you have practiced lighting the stones, causing them to glow by calling the magiq out from deep inside. This is almost the exact opposite. Try this the next time you attempt it."

Surprisingly, this made a lot of sense to Týr, and she would definitely try it the next time. She had not been doing anything like it when she had attempted it before. She had just sort of crammed the information in. Magiq sometimes required finesse, and this was one of those times, it seemed. The apprentice took the crystal again and began to prepare it to receive information. The tiny triangles glowed almost immediately and began to rise. It was open, and Tÿr tried to remember everything she had been told. She watched as she concentrated on the point at the top of the crystal. In her mind, she imagined one of the facets opening like a door on a hinge, and she let the information enter the opening. Of course, the opening was only imaginary, but it helped her to move her short phrase into the crystal and then press the buttons to close the record keeper. A dim, orangey light endured in the heart of the crystal. Tÿr felt hopeful as she passed the stone back to her mentor. Varanus held out the stone and opened it. His eyes widened.

"Well? Did I do it?" Tÿr pressed him.

Varanus didn't speak for a moment. He knew that Tÿr was anxious to hear how she did, but he wanted to tell her exactly what she needed to hear. "There was something on it," he began. "I could not understand everything that you had put in it, but I did get some words. I believe you will have this mastered very soon."

The younger wyvern gave the record keeper to his paragon. After a moment, Ghra'zhenn also agreed. He understood a couple of the words and was very pleased to be able to. He told the apprentice that they would continue this for the next several hours until she could send a complete message. Tÿr was worried that she was coming down with a massive headache but made herself a quick tincture of herbs and ground stones. She mixed it with a small amount of wine and drank it quickly. She wanted to perfect this technique today. It was something she was going to force herself to learn even if it drove her mad. Varanus knew that Tÿr was determined to make this work. He also knew that it was taking a great strain on her mentally. Magiq could really put a burden on certain parts of the brain and could lead to crippling headaches when performed over and over.

"How do you erase the information that is stored on the crystal?" Tÿr asked. Her headache was threatening burst through at any time. Ghra'zhenn shook his head very imperceptibly. "I'm afraid that we have not found a way to remove any of the information yet. Once we have filled them up, we usually do not have a need to erase them!"

Tÿr thought to herself how she would like to figure out how to be the first to remove the information on the crystal. Throwing away a crystal seemed like such a waste if it wasn't completely full. With crystal in hand, Tÿr'Ynyn began to prepare once again. She took deep breaths as she prepared the crystals to accept her information. An idea came to her as she prepared to store the phrase. Instead of using the common tongue, she chose to command the information in her new language. She wasn't very familiar with it, but so far, she had been doing well with the rhythm and basic vocabulary. The magiq flowed into Tÿr, and she felt ready to let it course out of her and through her staff and into anything that stood in her way. She let the information pour into the quartz tower. She didn't force it. She didn't plead to make it go where she wanted it to. She simply let it fall where it wanted to. For the first time, she sensed that there were sections in the crystals; and when one was filled, it could no longer be used until it had been emptied.

Tÿr made a quick trip around the inside of the clear gem and found where the previous information was stored. She tried, and as far as she could tell, she removed all the previous information on it. The parts and sections of the gems made perfect sense to the apprentice now, and she was not about to pass up this opportunity to show off a bit. Whenever she did, the wyverns fawned over her; and truth be known, she did like it. This time, when she handed the crystal back to Varanus, she was not only sure that she had been able to put information on the record keeper, but she was also sure that she would be surprising her mentors with a piece of crystal that had been erased. Varanus took the record keeper first, and after opening it, he handed it to his paragon. If Varanus was surprised, he showed no sign of it. Ghra'zhenn also showed no sign other than glimpsing at the other wyvern for the merest second. Had Tÿr not been watching, she would have missed the subtle glance.

"You are very welcome. We are very glad to have you in our dynasty," Ghra'zhenn told her in Cmok.

He had gotten the message! Tÿr's heart leapt! She had left a message thanking the wyverns for accepting her into their fold and trusting her with their knowledge and secrets.

"I have a question for you though," Varanus stated simply. "How did you erase the other information that we stored on there? You should not have been able to do that!"

Tÿr got a sly grin on her face. "You like that, do you?" she asked.

"No one has ever been able to do this before. What is the technique you used? You just only figured out how to store information. Erasing is something Ghra'zhenn and myself cannot do."

Ghra'zhenn spoke up now, "Can you teach us? This is a magnificent breakthrough if it can be done consistently. It is also a potential problem if someone else can figure out how to do it. They could erase all of our histories and our methods on healing and magiq. This is definitely something that cannot ever be made known!"

Tÿr hadn't realized the implications at first. She was just excited to have been able to do something completely new for her mentor. Now she almost wished she hadn't. The paragon must have seen the conflict in her eyes and on her face because he tried to reassure her that what she had done was amazing and would be very useful. The number of crystals that had been thrown out or destroyed because of incorrect information being mistakenly put into them was staggering. Now, if the information could simply be removed and replaced, the waste would be cut significantly. Rævii and decided to come over and sit by her friend as Tÿr tried to explain the method she had used both for writing into the crystal and for removing the excess information. The giant lizards were completely flabbergasted by the simplicity of the procedure.

The next hour was spent practicing Tÿr's new technique. She, along with the wyverns, added and removed messages and information to and from the crystals. Rævii seemed fascinated by the whole process. The crystals seemed to keep her entertained as they glowed and faded again and again. By the end of the hour, Varanus had found he could do erasures as easy as recordings. He was satisfied, and Ghra'zhenn had made sure Tÿr could consistently do it as well. It was getting late in the afternoon by now, and the wyvern knew that the girl and her fox would begin to need sustenance.

"I think now would be a good time to a break. You and your little friend must be getting hungry," Ghra'zhenn told Tÿr.

"This little one is always hungry!" she said, ruffling the fur on the shift fox's belly. The bushy white tail was splayed straight out behind her, and she practically purred with delight.

"Ghra'zhenn and I will be going to hunt this evening. You should be fine until we return. If there is something you would prefer to eat that isn't in the cooling tunnel, just let us know, and we will try to bring it back for you!" Varanus told her.

Tÿr couldn't really think of anything. She would grab a couple of pears for her and the fox. She was pretty sure that there was a bird or two that they could share as well. The wyverns took off to hunt while Tÿr prepared the birds and put them on a roasting spit. In just a few minutes, the smells coming from firepit were making both girls' mouths water. Tÿr was hungrier than she had originally thought. Rævii kept walking up to her and licking her fingers. The birds weren't very big, so they cooked quickly. They were exactly how the apprentice liked them. She had put a generous sprinkling of salt and some of her favorite herbs, and while basting it with generous amounts of pig fat. The skin was crispy, and the meat was delightfully moist and juicy. She really had grown to enjoy eating outside in this wilderness with a cup or two of wine and a great-tasting meal. She had just removed the first drumstick from the second bird. Rævii was still eating on the second breast that Tÿr had offered her before.

The silence was breached by a screaming, shrill screech. A shadow circled overhead and descended to land next to Tÿr where her and the fox sat eating. Sëvyq, the säqyr wyvern, walked up to Tÿr. She realized that he probably carried a message for her mentor or Ghra'zhenn. Sure enough, the little tube on the collar he wore contained a rolled-up piece of parchment. The girl removed the parchment and unrolled it to read:

To the Healers Three,

Interesting visitor in the village for the past two days. Nothing special about him, but he is asking questions about our new healer and her mentor. They are also asking about anyone who has been through

*the village that has performed any type of magiq. No
one has been talking to our knowledge. Just thought
you should know. Will continue to watch for anything unusual.*

Tÿr didn't know what to think. She hadn't done much healing
since her intercalation, so no one in the village could possibly know
of the new addition to Tÿr. The only people that had any ideas were
her mother and father and her two friends. Even they weren't exactly
clear what it all meant. Tÿr took another couple of bites of her dinner and then got up and hurried into the mine to write a message
to Varanus. It was hard to say how long the wyverns would be out
hunting. They could be gone for as little as an hour or two or up to
a day or longer. It just depended on where they chose to feed and
what else they needed to do. Tÿr was pretty sure that eating was only
a small part of the reason for their departure.

She got in to the mine and went to a small writing table she had
made. There was a bit of parchment laying on the desk. She took it
and quickly scribbled a message to the wyverns. She also included the
note from the brothers. Within less than five minutes of his arrival,
Sëvyq was back in the air with instructions to go find the wyverns.
Tÿr had also given him a bit of the food she had given the fox. The
tiny wyvern had appeared extremely happy with his mouth full of
meat as he sped toward his next target.

Chapter 14

It had been nearly three weeks since Tÿr had been back in Vennex healing. She had missed it so much. It was now part of her life, and she was truly happy when she was helping people feel better. Now that she was fully healed, she would wear a heavy tunic and shirt, complete with bracers. There was no way that they could let strangers in town know about Tÿr's new powers. Nor could anyone know about her induction into the wyvern dynasty. Tÿr had been allowed to share that information with the brothers and her parents, but literally no one else. Even those few people were at great risk should the wrong person or people find out what they knew!

Tÿr and Rævii prepared to leave for Vennex. This would be her first full day of healing at the shop since undergoing the intercalation. She was now back at her full strength and felt great. She couldn't wait to get back to the village and help the people who needed her. Varanus would be staying close to the clinic with her for the next few sessions in case anything out of the ordinary were to happen. Ghra'zhenn thought about going too but didn't want to raise suspicion. The säqyr wyvern was already at the village. The boys had built him a nesting box behind the clinic, and he spent time there when he wasn't at the cave with Tÿr. The boys had taken an instant liking to Sëvyq, and they spoiled him rotten. If they had a chance, they would slip off into the woods and go fishing and bring him back fish, which were turning out to be a favorite treat of his.

The flight into Vennex was uneventful, and Tÿr and her passenger arrived with Varanus after just a short, low flight. Sometimes Varanus liked to dip down low and practically skim the treetops. It made Tÿr very nervous, but she never said anything. She trusted her mentor completely, and he had never given her any reason to feel otherwise. Once on the ground outside the shop, Rævii ran over to find Sëvyq. She was missing her buddy. He hadn't been at the cavern for a couple of weeks. The boys had been keeping him with them so they could send messages back to Varanus or Ghra'zhenn should the situation warrant it. The two small animals romped and played around the back of the clinic while Tÿr got her gear settled in the office. Then she called to Rævii to come in. She knew that the fox would probably not get up to any trouble, but one angry farmer, and that could spell trouble for the blond-tailed creature.

Naturally, the brothers had everything ready to go when the doors were open for patients. Tÿr walked in to cheers from the patients standing in the line to be seen. The large doors were opened so Varanus could observe. This was more for show than anything else. Tÿr could handle most anything that came into the clinic, but her mentor wanted to be there on the off chance that one of the new visitors to Vennex came calling. He doubted that anything would happen here in the presence of so many people, but if they were dealing with the Murtair Amagii, all bets were off.

Everyone standing in line as the clinic opened, Tÿr knew personally or at least knew of them. Tÿr worked halfway through the morning without one problem. The people were so pleased to have her back. Even people who were somewhat reticent about having a lady healer seemed pleased with her work. They paid with without complaint and promised to return again when the need arose. It was turning into a wonderful day.

As lunchtime neared, Tÿr was looking forward to going to her parents' cottage for a quick meal. Her dad had mentioned that he had wanted to talk to her about something, and curiosity had gotten the best of her. As she finished up the last patient before lunch, she had the boys get everything ready for the afternoon crowd. She had decided to stay in town for a few days to make sure everyone that needed treatment got it.

Varanus didn't like the plan at first and had tried to talk her out of it. After all, it didn't take effort to fly back and forth from the mountain to treat the people. Tÿr decided she could get more work done and have a chance to see more people each day. In the end, Varanus told her it was her decision to make and that he would respect whatever she decided to do. Varanus, on the other hand, decided to return each night to the cavern on the mountain. It would be more comfortable and less dangerous for him should the assassins sneak up on him as he slept.

Tÿr finished up at the clinic, leaving the boys to replenish the supplies that had been used and the medicine and salve tinctures that had been sold. When she was sure that Danior and Gordi were set, she left the clinic and headed over to her parents' cottage. She could smell her mother's cooking while she was still a hundred yards away.

"It's good to be home!" she told the little shift fox that she was carrying.

Rævii beamed at her. The fox, too, could smell the aromas coming from the cottage ahead. Her little nose was twitching as the smells of cooking food assaulted her. Tÿr walked through the front door of the cottage. The smells of roast hog and some type of vegetables permeated the room. Tÿr's mouth immediately began to water. She hadn't realized that she was hungry until she smelled this incredible meal, complete with gravy!

"Hi, Mum!" Tÿr said cheerfully.

"Hello, love! And what have we here? You thought you'd bring your wee beastie for a free meal too, did you?" she asked, winking at Tÿr.

"She's heard all about your cooking and wanted to try it for herself!" Tÿr teased.

"I just hope there's enough for everyone." Elmky worried.

"Why, who's all coming over?" Tÿr asked, puzzled.

Her mother hadn't mentioned any extra guests when she told Tÿr to come by.

"Oh, it's just us, dear, but I thought I would take the boys a plate down at the clinic. I just want to make sure everyone gets enough!"

Tÿr turned her head away from her mother so she wouldn't see her rolling her eyes. Nothing had changed. There was enough food sitting around in the kitchen of the cottage to feed most of the people that had come to the clinic that morning. Her mother would always worry about not having enough, whether she was feeding one or ten.

Seryth Tỹr was already sitting in the kitchen when Tỹr arrived. She was surprised to see him just sitting there. He had a small tankard of ale with him at the table, and he was puffing slowly on his old pipe. The pipe was antique, given to him by his great-grandfather. He only smoked the pipe when her parents had a row or when he had something important on his mind. Tỹr was sure that they hadn't been rowing, so now she would have to pry out of him what was wrong. She pulled up a stool next to her father and sat down, impatiently waiting him to give some sign that he was ready to talk.

Her mother called them to get ready to eat, despite the fact that they were sitting at the table where they would soon be eating. Elmky had already served up a dish of meat, and pieces of chopped vegetables for Rævii. The little shift fox was struggling to get out of Tỹr's arms and down to the bowl waiting on the floor. Tỹr sat and ate until she couldn't fit one more bite. She was beyond comfortable, and into the realm of stuffed. Her father, too, seemed to have eaten way too much. He pushed his chair back from the table which, was still overloaded with food, and brought out his pipe again.

Tỹr liked when he puffed on the pipe. The combination of herb that he smoked brought her back to her childhood. Her grandfather had smoked the same type, and it reminded her of the nights that her dad and he had sat up talking with numerous pints of ale. Her uncle had often come by to join the debates too. Tỹr would sit near her grandfather and listen to the conversations of when he was a child, or of when he was part of the militia. He had wonderful stories that Tỹr would stay up later than she was supposed to so she could hear of his heroics on the battlefield or of his romantic conquests. Only much later, when her grandfather had passed, did she learn that the stories might have been embellished. She didn't care. She chose to remember the stories the way he had told them.

Once her father had his pipe burning well, he settled back into his chair again. "Would you care for a pipe, lass?"

The question caught her by surprise. He had never asked her this before. She thought of refusing outright, but then she decided this was a special occasion.

"Tÿr'Ynyn doesn't want one of your filthy pipes, Da!" her mum spat. She didn't like smoking as a general rule but tolerated it because she did like the smell of the herb.

"No, Mum, it's okay. I'd actually like to have one. Yeah, Da, go ahead then."

If Seryth Tÿr was surprised by his daughter's choice to have a pipe with him, he didn't show it. He went to the mantle where he kept his smoking apparatus and extra pipes and brought his daughter back a carved, smoky quartz pipe that had belonged to his father's father. The bowl was round and polished highly. Below the bowl were many rough quartz crystals, making it look like they were a handle for the bowl. The bowl itself was stained dark brown from many years of use. The stem was a long piece of qyrry, carved for the bowl perfectly. The pipe would have been expensive when it was purchased originally. Tÿr's father filled the bowl with his favorite mix of herbs and then shook a small amount of a cordial he liked with his pipe. It gave it an extra dimension in flavor and scent.

Tÿr took the beautiful pipe carefully and picked up a narrow piece of wood. Her father always used these little wooden pieces to light his pipe. She placed the tip in a candle that was burning on the table, and when it was lit, she moved it to the bowl and puffed in a mouthful of the aromatic smoke. The taste was as delightful as the scent.

"Try not to inhale an entire mouthful at first," her father instructed. She let a little of the thick smoke find its way down her throat and immediately began to cough. "Not so much!" Her father told her.

"I told you she shouldn't smoke that wicked thing!" Tÿr's mum spat at her father. "It is a filthy habit!"

Tÿr finally quit her coughing fit. "I'm okay, Mum. I just did too much. I'm fine!"

"Bah! You shouldn't even be trying that cursed pipe. Who ever heard of a lady smoking a pipe? It's just not proper!"

Tÿr's dad gave her a quick wink and then told her to give it another try. It took her a few tries until she wasn't gagging and choking from the smoke.

"So," her mother asked sarcastically, "is it everything that you wanted it to be? Do you enjoy choking?"

Tÿr giggled. "It's actually not that bad once you get used to it, Mum. You should give it a try!"

"What? Me give it a try? Young lady, a woman does not smoke a pipe. It is not ladylike!" Her mother smoothed her frock as she sat down on a rocking chair, putting on an air that she had just been insulted.

"Don't let her fool you! She's smoked a pipe more than once in her day, Tÿr. And she said she liked it, but she refuses to do it because she thinks it makes her look like a man."

Tÿr choked on another mouthful of smoke as her father made her laugh. When the coughing fit subsided, she turned back to her mother. "You could smoke in here with Da and me," Tÿr told her.

"With you and your father? Does this mean you're going to smoke a pipe, young lady?"

"Yeah, I'm seriously thinking about it. This is really nice. It would give me and Da time to sit and talk after a meal or in the evening. I seriously like the taste. It reminds me of my grandfather."

"And mine," her father agreed. "If you seriously would like to have a pipe, I'd like you to keep that one. It's one that should stay in the family. I think your great-granddad would love that his granddaughter wants to smoke a pipe!"

"And I think you are all nuts!" her mother interjected.

Her dad just rolled his eyes and got up to retrieve something from the mantle. He got the box that the pipe was stored in and a small container. He filled it with some of the leaf that he and Tÿr were smoking.

"Here," he said, handing the two boxes to her. "Your smoker's starter kit. It's the box that the pipe came in and enough herb to get you by for a few days. You can come back if you need more, or I can take you with me next time I buy some."

Tÿr knew it wasn't the healthiest of habits to be starting, but it made her feel closer to her father, and it also made her think of her grandfather and his dad as well. It might not be healthy, but the nostalgic value was priceless. Rævii climbed up by Tÿr to see what she was doing. Tÿr showed her the pipe. The fox sniffed at it for a moment and turned away quickly.

"What's wrong, little girl? Don't you like my pipe?"

The fox jumped back down and ran back into the kitchen.

"See, your pet doesn't like you smoking either! You should quit while you're ahead. Your father knows how much I hate it when he brings that pipe out."

Her father just smiled and continued to puff away lazily on his pipe.

"Okay, Da, what do you need to discuss? You don't have Mum prepare a huge meal like that and then offer me this old heirloom pipe if there wasn't something on your mind."

"Am I that transparent, lassie?"

"Well…" she teased.

Her father turned serious. He got quiet and moved in closer to his daughter. "Tÿr, I don't want your mum to hear this, so let's keep this down."

Tÿr moved in closer. Her dad was hard to hear now. She glanced toward the kitchen to see where her mother was. They appeared to have a little time as she had busied herself in the kitchen, tidying up after the meal. Tÿr heard her talking to Rævii as she bustled through the room, collecting the dishes.

"I need to speak to you about your uncle," her father continued.

Tÿr almost rolled her eyes at the sound of her uncle. The very thought of him left a bad taste in her mouth. "What about Uncle Siolad?" she asked. Quite frankly, she didn't really care, but if her father thought it was important, then she would at least hear him out.

"Well, you know he has been acting peculiar as of late."

Tÿr nodded. She knew peculiar was an understatement.

"I think there is something going on between him and that wife of his. He was talking to me the other day, and it was just the way he was saying things. It almost seemed as if he was worried. He didn't say it in so many words, but his tone made him seem like he felt threatened."

"What did he tell you?" Týr asked.

"It wasn't so much what he told me that bothered me. It's just how he was talking about his home life now. His popularity in the village is dropping fast, especially after the contest. Your aunt is not taking it well."

"But that was her fault!" Týr pleaded. "She was the one who cheated. She was the one gave that brat the answers!" Týr was livid now.

Despite the horrid treatment from her uncle, the girl knew that 90 percent of the problem was the rotten woman she called aunt. Her cousin was walking the same path too if he continued to follow his mother. Týr wished above anything that there was still hope for her Uncle Siolad. He had once been a kind man, and she prayed that there was still some of that left in him.

"It's true that your aunt is not helping my brother. She has made him more unpopular with each year. She is the one who tries to get laws passed. She is the one who tries to raise taxes so they become richer. Siolad has told me this in the past, and he literally doesn't know how to stop her. He told me that he hoped that he would lose the next election, but also said that she practically went into a rage at the suggestion. She wants the power. I am almost positive that she has been influenced by an outside source, but I have no proof, and I don't dare to ask my brother for fear of his safety."

Týr listened to these words. She was stunned to hear her father so helpless to do anything. "Has Aunt Ellysse ever threatened him?" she asked her father.

"He would never admit it if she had, lass. He is a proud man, and if a woman was running him like a slave, it would be a huge source of embarrassment."

"Something has to be done! I don't trust her at all," Týr told her father. "I will speak to the paragon and see if he can think of something. He and Varanus are sworn to protect Vennex, and I believe they need to know this. Give me a little time to work on this!"

Her father drew deeply on his pipe and nodded. "Okay, I will wait before I talk to him again. But only for a short time. I feel something bad is about to happen, and I don't want him harmed, no matter how poorly he has treated us!"

Tÿr went on to fill her father in about the possibility of assassins lurking around villages in the area. Her father didn't seem to think Vennex was in danger of being overrun by rogue assassins, but he told her that he would keep his eyes and ears open. Tÿr knew that her father wasn't a big pubgoer, but she knew that he sometimes popped down for a glass or two of ale. It got him out of the house with his pipe and her mum off his back.

Tÿr finished smoking the bowl of herbs with her father and then told him she had to get back to the clinic. She put the pipe back in its box and took the container of herbal smoke her father had given her. She gave him a quick hug and kiss on the cheek and went out to join her mum in the kitchen. Her mother had already cleared away the dishes, with the exception of the two she had prepared for the brothers. They were both stacked high with food. She kissed her mum on the cheek as well.

"You better run along and get those plates to the boys before they cool off. Just tell them to drop the plates off later!"

Tÿr grabbed the stack of things, and Rævii followed close at her feet. She tried to wave as she walked out the door. "Thanks for dinner, Mum!"

"Of course, lass. Now run along!"

Her mother closed the door behind her, and Tÿr hurried back to the clinic. The walk went quickly enough as she balanced the food and other things the whole way back. Danior and Gordian were happy to get a meal from Tÿr's mother. They took it out back of the clinic to eat. Tÿr went inside and prepared to open up again. The line of people had already begun to form at the front door, so Tÿr opened up the clinic to begin seeing the patients. Varanus was sitting outside the large doors that opened into the exam rooms and surgery bays.

As the people filed in the clinic, Tÿr went out to talk to her mentor. She wanted to fill him in on the conversation she had with her father. She wasn't sure if it meant anything, but she wanted to alert him of anything out of the ordinary. This was the way they would catch any assassins in Vennex or any other village—little bits of information brought to them by villagers who found things to be a bit out of the ordinary.

Tÿr returned to the waiting area and called back the first person. They had a simple rash that Tÿr knew exactly how to treat. Most all the cases were easy. A tonic or salve or a tincture, and they would be better. One mother had brought in a small girl who had fallen down a ravine on the other side of town and had fractured her arm. Tÿr was cautious as she brought the young girl into the treatment room. She would need a towel cut into strips and a piece of wood for a brace to place on the arm. The girl's mother left the girl in Tÿr's care while Gordi cut strips for the splint, and Danior prepared a tonic to help ease the youngster's discomfort. Dani then helped the little girl drink the bitter liquid and after went out to talk to the mother. He knew that there would probably be a little yelling going on from the room as Tÿr set the arm and then mended it. Healing was a wonderful thing, but it wasn't exactly painless.

When the tonic had been given enough time to work effectively, Tÿr took the little girl's hand and told her to squeeze her fingers. As the girl did this, Tÿr called on the magiq of her staff to begin to mend the broken bones. The little girl whimpered a tiny bit as the arms of the healer began to glow. Luckily, Tÿr was covered by many layers of clothing, so when she used her magiq, the glowing was covered. Tÿr made sure the arm was well before she let the girl back with her mother. The mother was so grateful she was in tears. She hugged the healer and promised her anything she needed in the future. The lady didn't have much money, so Tÿr was happy to take her promise as payment. She gave the young girl a paper straw filled with honey as a treat for being so good during the visit. Tÿr kept a cup of the honey-filled straws for all children who came in. They were a favored treat among the youngsters.

The brothers had finished eating by the time Tÿr had completed with the first patient. They came in to assist those who just needed medicine or ointments or tonics. They also got Tÿr's next patients to their rooms. It helped to move things along quickly. It only took three hours to see all the patients that had come that afternoon. The boys were going through the rooms and cleaning them for the next day. Tÿr was recording everyone she had seen into a ledger that she kept for her records in case someone needed a follow-up appointment.

The large doors to the surgery and clinic had been shut and bolted. The rest of the clinic had been closed up, and Tÿr was just about to close for the day when Gordian came back and told her that there were more people there to see here. It was technically too early to close, so she walked out front to greet the next patient and was completely shocked to see her uncle, aunt, and cousin standing in the waiting room. Her uncle looked most uncomfortable, standing there with his hands behind his back, rocking back and forth from one foot to the other. Her aunt never looked up nor even acknowledged that she had come into the room.

"Um, Tÿr'Ynyn, I need to see you. In a professional manner, I mean."

"Okay," she told him. "What is wrong, Uncle Si?"

"He isn't feeling well, of course!" her snotty aunt bit at her. "He is sick to his stomach, and he is—"

"I'd like to hear it from him, if it's all the same to you," Tÿr said, forcing politeness with every word. "Why don't you come back to an exam room, and we will see what can be done."

"Which room do you want us in?" her aunt questioned as she took a step forward.

"I just need to see Uncle Si. The rest of you can wait out here. If I need you, I'll will send for you."

"I don't think you understand, missy. I go where the magistrate goes. I am his personal assistant, and I take care of all of his personal business."

"Well, if you would like my uncle to be seen in *my* clinic, you will abide by my rules. He will be seen alone. It is for his privacy, as well as everyone else's. It applies to an emperor, a magistrate, and even someone like you, Aunt."

"How dare you speak to me this way? You will treat me with—"

"I will treat you exactly like everyone else that walks through my doors, seeking help. If there is any problem with these policies that I have put in place, you may talk to my partner and mentor who helped to draft them. He's the twenty-five-foot wyvern sitting outside. I'm sure he would love to assist you with your complaint."

Her aunt looked like someone who had just been smacked across the head with mallet. She looked like she wanted to continue her tantrum, but maybe her good sense had stopped her.

"If you'll come with me, Uncle, we can see what is bothering you today."

Tÿr thought it a bit strange that her aunt was so adamant about staying with her uncle. There definitely was something going on; she thought her father was correct about that. Her uncle followed her into one of the large rooms. The doors had already been closed, so Varanus was outside and not sitting in on the consultation.

"Don't you need to have your master in here with you for this?" her uncle asked. There was still a hint of superiority in his voice. It was almost like he felt he had to put on this face in front of his niece.

"I'm sure I can handle any issues you might have. If I run into a problem I can't solve, I can always consult him. According to him and his paragon, I am more than ready to run my clinic on my own." He looked like he wanted to say something but bit back anything that he was about to. "Now, what brings you in, Uncle Si?"

Tÿr kept her voice as friendly as she would for any other patient. If he wouldn't make an effort to be pleasant, she would. It would make her father happy if she didn't cause any waves. Her uncle looked at her uncomfortably for a minute and then glanced at the door.

"You're sure we're alone?"

"Yes, of course. It's just you and me. What is wrong? Are you ill? What is bothering you, Uncle Siolad?"

Tÿr suddenly felt a little stab of fear for the man sitting in front of her. He seemed genuinely upset by something.

"I'm not exactly sure, Tÿr. But I have been feeling bad for the past few weeks. At first, I put it down to my campaigning all over the village and the outlying areas. I thought it might be because I was missing some meals. Now I have been getting sick every day almost. It's worst after I eat. Do you think I could be coming down with the flu or something similar?

Tÿr reached out and touched his forehead. It seemed to her that he was warmer than he should be. She got in her physician's bag and removed a thermometer for an accurate reading. He had not been holding it for close to the proper amount of time needed, and the needle was already three degrees above normal.

"For starters, you have a fever! Have you been getting enough sleep?"

"I try to, but sometimes I just don't get as much as I'd like to."

"What about water? Are you drinking enough water? I mean more than just a glass or two."

"Not every day, I guess. I have qafi most all day. It is made with water. Does that count?"

"I would prefer that you drink a glass of water for every two cups of qafi you drink. You must maintain hydration. How long have you been feeling poorly?" Tÿr asked him. She had a hunch she might know the answer.

"I'm not sure of the exact time, but it was sometime shortly after you became a healer. Some coincidence, isn't it. You become a healer, and I begin to get sick at the same time. Your aunt seems to think…" There was a strange tone in her uncle's voice. It almost sounded accusatory.

"Just what are you trying to say, Uncle?" Her tone changed from sweet to hard in a second. She didn't like the way the conversation was heading.

"Your aunt told me that I was awfully rough with you about getting that apprenticeship. She thinks it wouldn't be too far-fetched for you or someone you know to get back at me by making me sick."

Tÿr was furious. "And just how am I supposed to have done this? I haven't even been here most of the time since I began. I definitely don't need to justify my actions to you. You came to see me, if I remember correctly."

"Tÿr, I'm not accusing you of anything. At the moment, your aunt just seems to think that you would have the most reason to get back at me, that's all!" He was almost pleading.

"I took an oath to heal people and save their lives!" Tÿr was almost screaming now. Her face a blotched color of puce. "I don't need to explain anything of my actions to you nor that witch of a woman you call my aunt. If this is how you plan to treat me when I'm trying to help you, you can get the hell out of my home! And take those other miserable beings with you. When you would like to treat me like an equal or at least like a professional, you may come back! Until then, take that harpy of a wife, along with my cheating cousin, and get out! You are no longer welcome!"

The blood had drained out of her uncle's face. He hadn't been spoken to like that in over four years. Tÿr had walked to the door and opened it for her uncle. He just stood there, gaping at his niece.

"Wait! Please! That came out wrong! I'm sorry. I was just saying that it began about the same time as you and, and I just…"

Tÿr was still beyond mad. Her uncle and his bitch of a wife were trying to besmirch her good name. All it would take was a rumor spread to the wrong person, and half the town would be talking about it.

"Uncle, I know that you and your stick-thin watchdog in lipstick have never forgiven me for winning the apprenticeship. I didn't try to. I was chosen! I beat out the two boys that were trying, and I was chosen. Not because I entered, Uncle! Because they saw my potential! Now, if you would like my help, I will give it freely to you, but if you ever accuse me of this again, I will let you rot where you sit. Do *not* think I won't. It is in my power, and it will happen. Now, do you wish my help?"

Siolad Tÿr was suffering from a huge inner turmoil. He needed to be seen. He needed to get better, but he needed to save face as well.

"I'll help you, Uncle. The next word out of your mouth will be either yes or no! Anything else, and I will open the door, and you can go to another village and seeker their services, *if* they will even take you."

She could see he had to physically contain himself from saying anything more than yes. But in the end, he managed a quiet and very restrained, "Yes."

"Good. Now that we have that out of the way, let's get to the bottom of this, shall we?"

Her uncle managed a faint nod, and she began a thorough examination. As she was looking at his arms, she noticed that the veins on both arms appeared to be red lines running from his hands up to his shoulders. That was unusual. It was a sure sign of poisoning. But of what? She would have to consult the guides that she had on her shelves. Several poisons and toxins could cause these symptoms, and unless someone was paying attention, they might have missed it.

"Who has had access to your food, Uncle?" Tӱr asked. She tried to make it sound casual so his hackles didn't rise again. She needed him calm for this.

"Um, the servants and my family. Some of my workers bring me cups of qafi at work. Why, what is this about, Tӱr'Ynyn?" Her uncle was immediately suspicious.

"I can't say for sure just yet," she lied. "I need to do a bit of research."

"But you have an idea, don't you? I know I have been feeling sick for a while now, and I don't seem to be getting better. My stomach is getting worse if anything. My stomach aches constantly. I'm coming to my wit's end. Your aunt thought I should come to see you before I got any worse."

Hm, thought Tӱr, *why is she wanting me to look at him? Does she trust me?*

Tӱr was sure that her aunt was behind this in some way. She moved over to her research shelf and chose a book on toxins and poisons that were prevalent in the midlands. There were so many it would be hard to narrow it down quickly. She looked up symptoms first, and there were several that matched. She was able to rule some out by questioning her uncle. As the list of toxins shrank, she decided she would consult Varanus. He would possibly be able to help. She asked her uncle to follow her outside to talk with her mentor.

Varanus was sitting out in the back, talking to the brothers. The boys were polite and moved away as the magistrate came forward. There was no love lost between them, but for the sake of their friend, they backed off quietly to allow her some privacy. Tӱr explained her theory to her mentor and then brought her uncle forward to show the wyvern his red-striped arms.

"May I feel your arms, Magistrate?" the wyvern asked.

Siolad Tÿr stretched out his arm, and the wyvern took a gentle hold of it. They stood together for several moments. No one said anything for a time, and then the wyvern turned to his apprentice.

"I want you to feel his arms. This is definitely a toxin, and you can tell by feeling the red veins what we are dealing with."

Tÿr took her uncle's other arm and was surprised to find that the veins were not only warm. They were hot.

"Uncle, do you feel this?" she asked him. "Your arms are literally burning up! Do they hurt? Are you having any discomfort right now?"

Her uncle felt his arm with his other hand. He seemed as surprised as she by the heat it was radiating. "I never really gave it any thought," he told her. "It's mainly my head and stomach that are bothering me."

"You have been poisoned, Uncle Si. It's a toxin that has to be processed to be used."

"Toxin! What are you talking about. What toxin?"

"It's an oil called *bÿchymme oil*. It comes from a small clam that lives in the waters off Berdæra Island."

"How in all hell did a toxic oil find its way in my body?" her uncle asked.

It was Varanus that answered this time. "You ingested it," he said simply. "It doesn't have the potency to be absorbed through the skin. It must be taken orally."

"Who could have done this? I'm around my family all the time and my staff when I'm not home. I trust all of these people. Who could do this to me?" he asked incredulously.

"Who indeed?" asked Varanus.

Tÿr had an idea but would wait to share it with Varanus after her uncle had gone.

"Let us return to the clinic and discuss this further. Boys!" Varanus called to Gordi and his older brother. "Please open the door to surgery bay one."

If the boys thought the request was odd, they didn't say so. They got up and completed the request without any questions even though they had just closed it shortly before. The trio moved inside, and voices lowered.

"I brought you inside, Magistrate, because I need to tell you something about your new healer. This can help to clear the air once and for all. The other reason I need you in here is to advise you, from now on, you need to get your own food and drink. No exceptions!"

"How am I supposed to do this? I have a full-time staff to do this for me. My wife gets my meals at home. I trust all of them," the magistrate said.

"That may be true, but you are the one who has come to see us. You obviously think highly enough to come and see what we might recommend to you. This is what I believe you must at least do to keep yourself out of any danger of poisoning."

"What do I do now? Is there something I can take to neutralize the poison in my body?" the magistrate asked with concern in his voice.

"There is something that we will do," Varanus told him. "There is something that you need to see, and it must be kept in the strictest of confidence for now. Tÿr'Ynyn, please remove your bracers and roll up your sleeves."

Tÿr obeyed at once. She sat her bracers on the table next to her uncle who watched curiously. His eyes stopped on her arms with the rough texture that the crystals had caused.

"Good gaunts, child, what has happened to your arms? You look like you have been to war and scarred terribly!"

"Please keep your voice down, Lord Magistrate! This is something she has done of her own free will. You are the only one in the village to know about it. As magistrate, it is your responsibility to know what the healing capabilities of your healer are. She has undergone an ancient procedure known as intercalation."

Tÿr walked over to where her uncle was sitting, and with her staff in hand, she called on her power of healing. Her uncle watched in amazement as her staff glowed with a blinding light and then was even more shocked to see the crystals under her arms take on a similar glow.

"What in all levels of hades?"

Tÿr's hand took on the glow, and she reached out for her uncle's arms. They immediately felt like they were beginning to go to sleep. They tingled and had a sensation that they were growing lighter. Her uncle gasped at the unique feeling. The red lines on his arms were being absorbed into his niece's hands, where it disappeared into the light coming from them. The color returned to Siolad's face, and his respirations even seemed to come easier. It was obvious to Tÿr that her uncle hadn't realized how ill he actually was.

The healer girl removed her hand when they quit glowing. Her uncle took a deep breath as she took her hand back.

"What just happened, Tÿr?" He seemed very concerned yet grateful at the same time.

"I've just healed you, Uncle!"

"I don't understand. How did you do that! What has happened to you?"

Tÿr looked to her mentor. She would let him answer these questions.

Varanus looked at the magistrate, and his voice lowered, "You must not repeat what you have seen here. Since you are the magistrate, you have the right to know the capabilities of your healer. This is why we are not only telling you but now showing you what your niece can do."

"But why is this such a secret? Why can't we tell everyone about her? All villages will want to use her power!"

"This is probably true, Magistrate, but there are also others who will want to exploit her powers. Others that are best kept away from your village!"

"Surely, I can tell my wife. She will want to—"

"You are to tell no one!" Varanus raised his voice a bit. "If anyone learns of her talents, she will have to be moved from here. It will become too dangerous for everyone, and your town will be without a healer again."

"I can't even tell my family?" he asked.

"Again, and for the last time, Magistrate, *no one!* I trust the young woman standing in front of you and no one else! You, as I told you, are the head of this village and have the right to know about your healer. The citizens need only know that she is an excellent healer and she will tend to all of their needs quickly and professionally. If any news of her intercalation is leaked to the public, Your Honor, we will know right where to come to discuss the matter. Are we clear on this?"

Clearly Tÿr's uncle was not used to being threatened and did not respond well. He began to puff up like an angry water bird, but one look from the wyvern caused him to settle back.

"Yes, we're clear. I still am not sure why my family couldn't be back here with me for this. I trust them implicitly!"

"But I do not!" Tÿr stated.

A cloud covered the magistrate's face. His mood darkened almost instantly. "And just who did you not trust?" he hissed through clenched teeth.

"This is not the time!" The wyvern cut across the man. "If you have any more symptoms, I need you to come back here immediately! Will you do this, Magistrate?"

Tÿr could tell that her uncle wanted to say so much more. He was a man who was used to getting his own way and getting the last word.

"If you have no more questions, Uncle, you may go. Please gather your family and go. Remember what we've told you, and if you begin to feel ill at all, please come back here immediately!"

Tÿr opened the door for her uncle and signified that the appointment was complete. The magistrate looked as if he still had something to say, but as he glanced back at the wyvern sitting in the opened doorway, he appeared to change his mind. Varanus called Gordian up to help close the large bay door, and Tÿr went through with her uncle to close the door behind him and his family. She could see the shock on her aunt's face when she saw that her husband was no longer pale and looking ill, the way he had when she had brought him in to be seen.

"What on earth did they do to you? Are you all right?"

"They figured what was wrong and gave me something to help! I feel worlds better now!"

Tÿr watched her aunt. She could see that the woman seemed less than pleased at this turn of events—one more reason that Tÿr'Ynyn was sure that her aunt was to blame for the sudden ailments that had begun to plague her uncle. When the magistrate reached his family, his wife started in, and she didn't bother to keep her voice down.

"Why have we been kept out here this whole time? I bet she loved keeping us out. She had no right, the little witch. Her father will be hearing about this, you can bet on that!" She kept up her rant even as she walked out the door.

Tÿr just smiled as big as she could and yelled to her uncle. "Remember to come back immediately if you begin to feel poorly again!" she said as she waved to the family.

Her aunt turned and glared a most-venomous face to behold indeed. Once the relatives had left, Tÿr's burst of adrenaline vanished. It was gone as fast it as it came. She went out to meet with her mentor.

Varanus and the brothers were waiting for her outside.

"What in the hubs of hades was that about?" Gordian asked her. "Your aunt was yelling at your uncle all the way back to the village square!"

"I don't think she appreciated being left out," Tÿr said with a sly grin. "Most people don't talk to her like that," she said. She was trying not to laugh. "Varanus," she began again. "I can't prove anything, but I believe that whatever is happening to my uncle is being caused by my aunt."

"That is a very big accusation. What grounds do you have for such an accusation?" Varanus questioned his apprentice.

"My uncle told me he began feeling poorly right after I was chosen for the apprenticeship. He practically accused me of poisoning him. He suggested that my aunt may have told him that. I feel that she is trying to put the blame on anyone else to keep them from accusing her."

"That isn't proof, Tÿr, but it does give us a person of interest. From everything I have heard about this woman, she wouldn't surprise me at all if she has been poisoning the magistrate. He is losing popularity quickly, and if the trend continues, he may no longer hold his position. I believe that would be a tremendous blow to her ego, and she might resort to some sort of revenge on him."

"I believe you are right, Varanus! That woman is evil," Danior spoke up. "She has never been nice to Tÿr nor my brother nor me!"

"Being a rotten person doesn't automatically make a them a poisoner. If that were the case, there would be thousands of dead people all over Vennex and other villages on the planets," Varanus said.

Tÿr disappeared into the clinic and reappeared with her pipe. She knew that this was likely to be a lengthy conversation and figured it would be a nice distraction to have a bowl of herb. Gordian gaped as Tÿr pulled out her pipe. He had never seen her smoke a pipe before. If Varanus was surprised, he didn't say anything.

Danior was the only one that said anything. "What's burning?"

"Tÿr's smoking a pipe!" Gordi told him.

"Really? Do you have another pipe with you? I'd like a bowl too."

"No, my dad just gave me this one today. Don't you have one at home?"

Gordian asked if he wanted him to run home and grab it. Dani asked if he would mind, and so Gordi ran home for a minute while the conversation continued about Tÿr's aunt and her uncle's poisoning.

Tÿr and Dani sat and smoked a bowl of the herbal mix that her father had given her while the conversation continued about her uppity relatives. In the end, Varanus was convinced that there was definitely something going on in the magistrate's house. There was a long list of suspects as well. Tÿr felt that it was her aunt still, and both boys tended to agree. Varanus didn't want to jump to any conclusions. He wanted hard facts, and there just weren't any.

"If you're uncle shows back up in the clinic, we will investigate a bit more aggressively, but for now, we will keep an eye out for any strange occurrences from the magistrate's manor. If you get wind of anything, let Tÿr or myself know immediately. You have the säqyr wyvern, and he can reach us in just minutes."

The meeting broke up, and Tÿr went back into the clinic for the night. Rævii was waiting for her when she walked in. The little fox wanted some attention. Varanus flew back to the mountain home, where he would consult with Ghra'zhenn. The boys had filled him in about the rumors floating around the pubs. So far, that was all they had, rumors. Varanus was pleased with their subtle spy work as they drank their way through the pubs of Vennex. He told them to keep their eyes open for repeat customers who were asking the odd questions, especially ones of the magistrate. Now that he seemed to be a possible target, Varanus wanted to make extra sure that he was watched as much as possible.

Chapter 15

Kaistam-Laq was in a foul mood yet again. The new magiq that had been showing itself in the area of the midlands was not sticking around long enough for him to locate it. It was infuriating because he knew neither how to figure out when this magiq was going to be used nor where. It appeared to be employed during the day at almost-regular intervals, but just when he thought he had a pattern, it changed. He sat at his piece of polished obsidian for hours during the day, scrying to find this magiq, all to no avail. As the days moved on, his mood soured even more. It got so bad his staff were nervous about even approaching him.

The council was called together after days of absolutely no new information. Kaistam wanted any information from his assassins in the villages and towns around the shift. Surely, they had heard something about this new magiq, but the council had no information of worth for him either. None of this did anything to improve the mood of the leader of Murtair Amagii.

"I don't understand!" he almost shrieked. "How can we not find anything? This magiq is unique, and no one can decipher it, including myself. It is old, old magiq, and I should have found something by now! I will ask again, has anyone learned anything?" Kaistam's voice was satin smooth now. Dangerous for the council. "Is there any business I need to hear?"

"There are possible jobs all over the shift. Some not worth our time, but others might need to be looked into. Maybe we should gather the entire sect together and let them all speak."

Kaistam-Laq considered this for a moment and then nodded. He would hear from everyone why there was no advancement on the job at hand. Eventually someone would have seen or heard something that they didn't know was useful.

"Yes," he told his council, "we will meet tomorrow at the same time. Have everyone here. No one is excused from this meeting! Now leave me!"

With that, the meeting was over, and he went back to the scrying mirror to study it and to figure out why this magiq continued to elude him. His inner sanctum was elegant and ornate, with flowing satin hanging from the walls. Candles lit the medium-sized space. He had several chairs, all expertly crafted by the finest craftsman throughout the shift. There were bookshelves and tables made of heavy oak and stained dark. All the wood in his chambers was highly polished by servants that he kept on staff. He never saw any of them though; the rule of the house was that if he was in a room, they were not. He also had several safes in his room. Some sat on the earthen floor, some were buried in it, and some hovered in the air at the top near the ceiling. None of the safes had the traditional numerical dials. They all worked with his magiq and were impossible to break into.

The sorcerer was at his black mirror. He had several little bags of different powders sitting on his lap. With one hand, he drew a glyph, which glowed before sinking into the shining obsidian. With the other hand, he sprinkled a glittering powder over the now-invisible symbol. Smoke rose instantly, thick black smoke which curled up to the vent at the top of the tent. He took another powder and threw it across the scrying mirror. More smoke burned and disappeared as before. The sorcerer watched the smoke intently as it raised to the vent. *Interesting*, he thought to himself. *This might not even be human magiq.* Could this be his rival? Was this new magiq coming from the deplorable Nagarr Zmaj? What was he up to? Kaistam preferred not to go to war with the wyvern if he could help it. He was foul and very cunning. More than likely, the evil beast already had people near the town where the Murtair Amagii were located. This would need to be thoroughly discussed at the meeting of the sect tomorrow.

Kaistam sat at his mirror the whole night. His mood had not improved by the morning, and when the sect filed in, he had an incredible headache.

The sect was sitting in the large tent when their leader emerged from his sanctuary. They knew from the beginning that they needed answers soon. He was no mood for failure, and they were not wanting to have to replace any members at this time.

Kaistam-Laq was actually using his staff to hold himself up as he walked to the head of the table. He had taken a solution made from ground dragon heart and other rare herbs from the planet. It was used to treat pain of all types. The heart was very valuable and was usually reserved for those who could afford it—emperors and other wealthy people. Dragons were nearly extinct, and their healing properties were well known to all healers. The heart was the most valuable item on the planets for use in potions and other healing medications. Hearts were rarely found as dragons lived for centuries. Wyvern hearts were almost as valuable and just as rare. In order for the heart to be of any use, it had to be harvested and prepared within just a few days of death. Any longer, and the caustic blood would eat away at it until there were no useful parts remaining.

The entire sect was gathered as ordered, and the chattering died down the second their leader appeared. No one wanted to draw his wrath today.

"We are here today," Kaistam-Laq began without vacillation, "because no one in this assembly can seem to find a sign or even a hint of a magiq user who is using magiq so powerful it rivals even my own! I find this impossible to believe." The words were soft and oozed venom with every syllable.

With the sixteen sitting in rapt attention, the sorcerer continued. "So far as I can figure out, the entire lot of you has been drinking your way from pub to pub and gathering absolutely no information. This is money that is completely wasted if you ask me, and since I am the one financing this operation, I am the one that matters. So I'd like each of you to step forward and let me know the number of villages you've visited since I've sent you out. I'd like to know the approximate number of public houses that you've visited in the towns and villages that you've traveled to as well. Consider that no information that you have is beneath mentioning. Now let's begin with you." He pointed at a pale thin woman sitting in front of him.

She was dressed in dark-blue, tight-fitting clothes of the forest people. Slung from one shoulder to her waist was a black leather belt with several lachtrys blades in sheaths down its length. It attached to another belt. She held her long staff boline at her side. The female assassin, though already pale, seemed to blanch even more as she stood to give her report to the leader of the sect. She tried to avoid his eyes, but she felt he might have a mesmerizing spell or something similar on her because each time she looked up, Laq's piercing gaze was staring into her soul. She wasn't sure what to say that would keep her out of the hot seat with her boss.

Unluckily for this girl, the boss was ready for some explanations regarding the shabby handling of the searches for the new magiq and its user. She had no answers for her master, and she knew that it could spell disaster for her. The one fortunate thing that she had going for her was that she has been sequestered to a tiny town in the middle of absolutely nowhere. The town consisted of only a few straw huts, and the pub was a tent that only sold a few types of ale. Information was hard to find about anything. She had been sitting at the pub for the better parts of two days, with next to no results. The leader of Murtair Amagii was never pleased with a member who was lacking with information.

"I trust that our next meeting will prove more fruitful. You may find yourself looking for new employment if not."

The words chilled the female assassin to the bone. People did not locate new employment when let go from Murtair Amagii. They generally found a casket, if they were the lucky ones. The leader's words also sent barely audible whispers through the others gathered for the meeting. He stood in front and let his words settle in to the sect. They knew they were on the cusp of their master's rage right now, and so they tried to say only what they thought he wanted to hear. When Kaistam-Laq was in this mood, there was almost nothing to pull him out of it. One after the other, the assassins told similar stories of frequenting the pubs with no unusual information. With each report, Laq's mood darkened still farther.

"Let me see if I've got this now," the magiq user said. "You have all been sitting at pubs around the Kirin-Noirin shift, drinking ale and who knows what, with my money, and not one single person has one thing to share with me? How can this be?"

The room of assassins looked around at each other, none of them daring to answer yet each wanting to explain.

"If that is everything, I will say I am extremely disappointed with all of you. I have asked you to do a simple job, and you haven't been able to come through with that…"

At that time, a young, dark-skinned assassin in black robes stood. "Sir, I do have some business that needs to be dealt with. A possible contract. I have been in the town of Vennex and have heard about a woman who is interested in a contract on her husband. She is wealthy, and everything she has tried to eliminate her husband has been unsuccessful to this point."

"How do you mean unsuccessful? What woman?"

"As I mentioned, it's only a rumor, but she has attempted to poison her spouse, and it has failed. He was apparently healed by the new healer of the village, according to the wife."

"And I'm just hearing about this now?" Kaistam-Laq roared. "You didn't think this was pertinent information to bring to me?"

The assassin cringed as Laq stormed around the table, blowing his priceless objects off their shelves with blasts from his staff. The assassins ducked as he continued to rage, shattering objects, with glass and stone flying all around the room. The assassins were getting cuts and scratches from the flying debris, and still the leader raged on.

"Why! Why was I not told? This is the exact thing I sent you out to find!"

The sorcerer's eyes took on a red gleam, and the staff continued to burn brightly, ready to shoot out on command. The young, dark-skinned assassin who had spoken had taken a defensive stance, his lachtrys dagger in one hand and his fingers glowed on the other. Kaistam-Laq saw this as an attempt to attack. His eyes dilated with fury so intense the others in the tent pulled back in fear. With one hand on his staff of power and the other outstretched in the direction of the lone, black-garbed assassin, invisible hands grasped the man and lifted him off the ground. Laq rounded with his staff, and a red beam of light shot from the headpiece and hit the man in the chest, killing him instantly. The power was overwhelming, yet the sorcerer didn't stop there. Balls of energy shot down the shaft of light, hitting the limp man suspended by invisible hands, each time causing his body to tense up with the energy generated by the staff. Kaistam-Laq held the man twelve feet above the ground in a gory, burning display for the others to witness should they, too, disappoint him like this. When he was sure his point had been made, he dropped his arms and the man in black, still smoking, fell back to the blue earthen floor of the tent. His bones shattered in his legs as he hit, making a sickly, squelching sound.

"We are now down one person! No missions will happen until that spot is filled. In other words, we bring on a new assassin quickly. Need I repeat myself?"

He glanced around at the scattered assassins. Many were still staring at their fallen brother's body. Kaistam refused to acknowledge that it was still in the room. No one in the room dared speak.

"Now, where was this…" He strode forward and poked the dead man with his staff. "Where was his area?"

He looked around at his council for an answer. It was Kkyllum Jannyk who finally spoke. "I believe, Your Grace, he was near Yelliton, or a village called Vennex, or another small town in that area near the Ajenti River. I can't be positive, but I believe he monitored those small towns around that area."

"Then as soon as we number seventeen again, we will send more to find out what is going on. I suggest we recruit from the usual place. Make it fast. I want us back at full strength in two days' time!"

The usual recruitment place was from the sect of assassins called Galdram Vrasës. They were the elite of the Vrasës sects, and they were easily trained in the art of sorcery-assassin skills. It was an honor to be accepted into Murtair Amagii. Kaistam was very superstitious and believed that seventeen was his lucky number for the group. He always had seventeen people and would refuse to go anywhere on trips if he had one more or one less person to mess up the count. The sect knew what had to be done and the speed with which it needed to happen.

"Kkyllum, you're in charge of finding our new assassin. I expect them ready to go by tomorrow evening. I trust I won't have to tell you or anyone else these issues again."

There were quick mentions to the negative, and the matter of the meeting was closed.

Chapter 16

The first night back at the cavern was extremely restful for Týr. She didn't have to wake for the clinic the next morning, and she decided to sleep in for a change. Varanus didn't have her training for anything, so she fully intended to enjoy an entire day with nothing to do. Rævii figured that was a good idea as well and came to sit next to her friend. She nudged her with her head and tried to get Týr to pet her. The two sat, snuggling for several minutes. Rævii was eating it up as Týr rubbed her shaggy belly. Varanus was outside and waiting for the paragon to return.

Ghra'zhenn had been back on Gelbryn Island to address the dynasty regarding their newest member. There had not been a human inducted into a wyvern dynasty in several eras, and this was huge news. Ghra'zhenn was also going to harvest some *taipuva* branches for Týr. She used these branches to make bësoms, which she sold in her clinic. They were the finest small, personal brooms that money could buy. The people of Vennex were always in need of new, good-quality bësoms as they were so good they would use them until they literally fell apart. Others that people sold used sticks made of inferior wood, which would split or fray. Taipuva bent just enough to keep it from breaking, which made it perfect for making bësoms.

At some point in the near future, Ghra'zhenn had told Týr that he wanted her to accompany him back to Ÿkkynnÿk Mountain to introduce her to the whole dynasty. She would present herself to them as the newest member and then give a demonstration of her new powers. This was not only for Týr's benefit but to prove to the dynasty that she belonged with them.

The thought of the long flight gave Tӱr some anxiety as she had never flown so high or so far. The flight would be extremely high, so Ghra'zhenn could catch an air stream situated above the mountain range where they were and ride it all the way to the Keltainyn Sea and Gelbryn Island itself. She was already told to dress for the ride. It would take them two days even at the tremendous speeds allotted them by the air stream. Rævii would come with her, of course, and they would camp overnight along the way. Varanus was going to go with them but thought it better if he stayed behind and helped the boys at the clinic. He would do the healing, and they would run the shop and everyday duties, which had really begun to grow. Many people still had not been able to pay with money, so Tӱr told them to continue to accept whatever they could give, and most often that was livestock. The area behind the clinic had grown into a large area of pens and fenced in areas for birds and hogs and sheep.

Tӱr was still in bed, snuggling with the shift fox. She could feel herself beginning to drop off to sleep again. The fox was cuddling hard against her chest, and she was almost purring. From a distance, Tӱr picked up a high-pitched shriek. It grew louder with every second. Rævii's ears perked up instantly. She knew the sound immediately. It was that of Sëvyq, and it was coming in fast.

As the small wyvern neared, the shrieking got louder and more frequent. Tӱr jumped up, almost knocking Rævii off her lap. She hurried out to join Varanus outside so she could be there when the säqyr wyvern arrived. She had only been back for a day when the messenger had come to deliver his news from Vennex. This left Tӱr wondering what was so important that had to be delivered immediately. What could have happened in just a day's time? A black dot in the sky got larger as it grew closer to the plateau. The little wyvern's wings were beating nonstop as it dove to meet up with the three assembled on the ground, waiting for him. The säqyr wyvern hit the ground and almost flipped as he skidded to a stop. Rævii ran forward to make sure her friend was okay. It immediately turned around and walked to Tӱr, who bent down and opened to tube on his collar, containing a rolled piece of parchment. She knew it was from Gordian as she could tell his semilegible handwriting on the paper. She quickly unrolled the note and read:

> *Two strangers in the pub. Asking strange questions.*
> *They carry lachtrys blades. Am sure they are assas-*
> *sins, possible magiq users as well. Will observe at*
> *distance until we receive any other news.*

> *G and D*

Týr reread the letter out loud to Varanus. He was immediately concerned, and as soon as he heard what it contained, he asked Týr to take another note to send straight back to the brothers. The apprentice ran and grabbed a piece of parchment and waited for her master to begin. His low, raspy voice dictated a short but succinct letter:

> *Boys, use extreme caution. If these people are part of*
> *an assassin sect, they are very dangerous! If you can*
> *find out which sect without getting near, that would*
> *be useful. Do not take unnecessary risks! Report back*
> *with any information.*

> *V*

Týr rolled up the small bit of parchment and slid it back into the tube on the collar of the small wyvern. Before sending the creature off again, she got him to drink some fresh water. When he had rested for several minutes, Varanus commanded him to go back to Vennex. With a short squawk, the little wyvern leapt from the ground and began its flight back to the village. Where it could take Varanus over a half hour to reach Vennex, the little säqyr wyvern could navigate the trip in about fifteen minutes, less if he did not become distracted. Already Týr was having doubts about not taking back the message in person. But after hearing her mentor's reasoning, she understood why she needed to stay. He explained that by now, one or more sects could be looking for the new magiq user. If they came across her without any protection, things could sour instantly. One or more magiqal assassins against Tÿr on her own could prove disastrous.

The thought of assassins running through Vennex made Tÿr nervous. Her parents should be fine. They usually stayed at home, or if her dad did go to the pub, he went for an ale and came straight home. It was the boys that she was concerned about. Danior tended to be the reserved one of the two, but if Gordian got a few pints in him, he had been known to raise a little hell. Against the regular pub patronage, he could hold his own in a scrap; but against a professional killer, Tÿr had so many doubts, especially if magiq was involved. However, *if* magiq was involved, that would narrow the list of sects tremendously.

"Tÿr'Ynyn," Varanus began after making sure the little wyvern had gotten off all right. "I believe it is time for us to make the trip to Ÿkkynnÿk Island. There are too many things going on to suggest that you are going to be safe even here! I will talk to Ghra'zhenn when he returns, but I believe that he will agree with me on this. I am not sure right now, but we may have to close the clinic for a while. We will see as time progresses. I also have an idea that I must discuss with the paragon. It is something that is unconventional and also quite dangerous if we are dealing with the sect that I have speculated that we are. If we are allowed though, the information we could gather would be invaluable."

Tÿr's interest grew. She wanted to know what her master was talking about but also knew that without permission from their paragon, he wouldn't be able to tell her anything. She had read of ways to spy from some of the older scrolls. There were ways to eavesdrop on people from across a room. There were other things she didn't remember as well. She hadn't read them in depth as she didn't figure that she would need some of the more-secretive arts. Tÿr decided to go back and reread some of the older passages from an ancient tome she had found very interesting regarding subterfuge and hiding. It was magiq that was rarely used anymore, and definitely not for healing. It could, however, come in useful for what she was going to need.

The apprentice sat under the three suns, reading for several hours, before she heard the flapping of large wings descending from above. Part of the light was blocked as the huge wyvern slowly made his way down to the plateau where she sat with Rævii at her feet. Varanus was laying in the suns, absorbing the heat from them to gather the energy they would need for the long trip to the wyvern's island if that was what the paragon decided was for the best. Tÿr's stomach jolted again as she thought about the long flight they would be taking and the heights that it required. Despite the fact she had flown all over the shift, she still hadn't gotten over her basic fear of flying. Gordi and Danior still teased her about it every time she got back to Vennex. Her face was always a bit pale, and her hands and neck were clammy.

Ghra'zhenn landed with a thud. He was loaded on both sides with taipuva branches for Tÿr. She ran over and began to help him unload them. Rævii followed her because she knew that there was probably a treat for her, and sure enough, the large wyvern tossed the little white-tailed fox a slab of meat. Rævii ran over and snatched it up and then took off into the cavern to eat it in privacy.

While she was unloading the large bundles of sticks, Tÿr filled in the paragon regarding the note from the brothers back in Vennex. He, too, showed similar concern as Varanus had. Tÿr was certain that both wyverns already knew which sect was responsible for staking out Vennex, but it seemed that they wanted to be completely sure.

The two wyverns sat and discussed what was to be done while Tÿr continued to move the branches into the cavern, where she would make the sought-out bësoms. The wyverns talked for over an hour as Tÿr organized the branches for her bësoms. When she was finished, she went back to her reading to try to find out anything she could about the art of spying with magiq and making yourself appear to be unseen. Varanus walked over to Tÿr and asked her to join him and the paragon. She got up and walked over to where the wyverns had been talking. Both looked very serious as she walked up to join them.

"Young apprentice, both Varanus and I believe it is time for you to leave this place for a while. We can't be sure from the missive dispatched by your friends back in Vennex, but we both feel that Kaistam-Laq, leader of Murtair Amagii, has begun to take an interest in your work at the clinic. Especially now that you have treated the magistrate there. The sorcerer cannot have any idea as to your identity yet, but we feel it is only a matter of time." Ghra'zhenn looked graver than she had ever seen him before.

"There are other things to consider as well. Your friends will not be safe if news gets back to the assassin sect that they know you. They will be brought in for questioning and tortured until they give up your location. The Amagii have ways to break even the strongest men. I do not want your friends subjected to any of this! I think in the interest of everyone, you will have to close down the clinic until the threat has passed."

Tÿr wanted to object, but she knew in her heart that Ghra'zhenn was correct. How had they found out about her uncle so quickly though? She was puzzled by this. The boys would not have said anything to anyone about it. They weren't even fully aware of all that had taken place that day in the clinic. Only her uncle and her were present. She didn't think he would say anything either.

"What will we do with the boys?" she asked. "Can they come here to stay?"

"Ghra'zhenn and I had discussed that very thing, but in the end, we both feel that this cavern is too close to the village. What we will plan to do is to take you and the brothers to Ÿkkynnÿk Mountain. There you will remain safe. The entire sect of assassins could not get through our dynasty to you. We will charm this mine, and it will remain under enchantment until we can return. No one will be able to enter."

"What about my patients at the clinic?" Tÿr asked. "Who will tend to them while I am away? I don't feel right leaving them without a healer."

"I will talk with the town's previous healer, Kuired Gÿann. I will arrange for him to attend to the sick for one day a week," Ghra'zhenn interjected. "It is just how things will have to be for now. I will also arrange to have an elder wyvern accompany him to Vennex every week for added protection."

Tÿr really disliked the fact of leaving her village so soon after building up a good clientele base, but if it helped to protect the people, she would go. Then her thoughts shifted to her parents. "What is to happen to my parents?" she quickly asked the two wyverns. "They can't be expected to come with us to the mountain as well. My father will have jobs to complete, and I know my mother will not want to have to just pull up and move for as long as this could take!"

"Is there family that they could visit in another town?" Varanus asked.

"Not really." Tÿr shook her head. "My father's only relative is his brother, and my mother has a couple cousins that live down near the sea. She rarely speaks to them, so staying with them would be out of the question."

"We will have to increase a protective presence in Vennex then," Ghra'zhenn stated. "I will request another one or two brothers to come and stay in the forests outside Vennex should anything happen."

Tÿr wasn't pleased to have to leave her family behind, but she knew that the more that remained "normal" around the village, the less likely any stranger or spy would realize that anything was amiss.

"When would you like to move to Ÿkkynnÿk?" Tÿr asked Ghra'zhenn.

"I believe if we do it within the next few days, you and those involved will remain out of danger. The one thing that troubles me is if the Murtair Amagii find out that you healed your uncle, they will descend on the village in force. He does not strike me as a man with a great constitution. I'm concerned he would lead them straight to you. Of course, I hope I am incorrect, but we must plan as if we are not."

Tÿr was inclined to agree with the paragon. Her uncle was exactly the type of person who would take the easiest way out of any situation even if it meant giving up his own family. Thanks to the snake of a wife he had taken, he held no loyalties to anyone.

"The first thing we intend to do is have Varanus fly to Vennex to let your friends know what is happening. They will be given a choice, but hopefully, they will see that this is the best alternative. Varanus will also speak to your parents while he is in the village. We will let everyone know the situation. It is better for them to know it now than before matters elevate to an emergency situation. When he has informed everyone in Vennex of the plans, he will fly to Kuired's place in Yelliton and let him know of the events as they have begun. That should give the brothers enough time to close up the clinic and pack for the trip. We plan to meet back here this evening. If everything goes according to the plan, we will fly to the home of my dynasty tomorrow. It will take us two days of hard flying to reach the mountain, so I suggest plenty of rest because it will be very tiring for everyone involved. I will carry the brothers on my back, and you will travel with your mentor on his."

Ghra'zhenn finished the briefing and then motioned for Varanus to be off. The younger wyvern wasted no time. He bid Tÿr and the paragon goodbye and immediately rose into the air and toward the village of Vennex.

"Paragon, I want to be a part of this too. I have been reading about using magiq to blend into the background to spy on people. I'm trying to find something so I can assist on the assignment in Vennex. I *need* to know who these people are that are causing trouble in my home. It feels like I'm the one responsible for it, so it's only right that I should find a way to help get us out of the situation." Tÿr was adamant about assisting.

"Ah, young one, your desire to take responsibility for your actions and those that are beyond your control is admirable. There is a magiq that is usually reserved for the most advanced magiq users. Your mentor and I foresaw this scenario and have decided to teach you our ancient and most sacred of magiqs. I say this is most sacred because it is performed with the most sacred parts of a wyvern. They are always reserved for master healers or those willing to pay the highest prices for them.

"In wyvern history and lore, the two most important parts of a wyvern are the heart and the eyes. They are always harvested by the master healer at the time of death of the current wyvern. If the healer does not use them in his or her lifetime, they either pass them down to the next master if they are deserving or they return them to the dynasty. As you can probably tell, we have many of these organs that we have stored deep in the mountain of Ÿkkynnÿk."

"How does this magiq work?" Tÿr asked. She had been through many volumes and scrolls and had no idea what the paragon could mean. She had always come up short on information regarding the very subject Ghra'zhenn was discussing now. Her heart was in her throat. Was he about to teach her one of the wyvern's most sacred spells?

"Varanus and I agree that you are already at a level with your healing that usually takes a regular apprentice over ten years to learn. You appear to absorb information, and you can recite it as well. This is a skill enjoyed by very few people over centuries. It is an amazing gift, but unfortunately, it is going to be drawing unwanted attention. Not because of the healing you can do but because of the magiq that you can use to enhance the healing. From all the signs I have read, the sorcerer Kaistam-Laq is going mad trying to figure out who is using ancient magiq."

"But don't wyverns use ancient magiq all the time?" she questioned the paragon.

"We do. Well, not all the time but often enough to let him know that we are still around. From what I have come to understand though, he was able to tell when you used the magiq, and he also was able to tell that you were no wyvern. What is giving him fits is that he can't figure out where the magiq came from nor who or what performed it."

Tÿr gave a devilish grin. "So we have the advantage right now!"

"It would appear so," Ghra'zhenn agreed. "Unfortunately, the only thing standing between us and him is your uncle. A man that I believe could be bought or threatened into giving up information too easily."

Tÿr nodded in agreement with his last statement. Her uncle was exactly that type of person. He liked to seem important and had in the past pretended to have information for sale for another town. It turned out to be a lie and had almost caused a war between the two small places. Luckily, her uncle's militia had been able to quell the uprising before it had begun. There would have been a useless loss of lives otherwise just because the man liked to play God and appear more important than he actually was.

"So," Tÿr asked, "what is this magiq you will be teaching me? How will I be able to use it to spy? Will I blend into the surroundings or become a blur?"

Ghra'zhenn's lips pulled back from his teeth in a devious sneer. The effect was almost scary. "When you utilize this magiq, you will not blend or fade into surroundings. You will actually disappear. You will be able to stand nose to nose with a person, and they will have no clue that you are not there. Now, with magiq users, they will instantly know that there is magiq being employed, but they will not be able to locate you. This magiq is one of the strongest that we teach, and no other dynasty or sect knows of it. This is why we have our healers harvest the eyes of the Wyvern's immediately upon death. The fresher they are upon harvesting, the more magiqal properties they will extoll."

Tÿr sat, fascinated by the knowledge that Ghra'zhenn was sharing. She meant to get up and pack her belongings, but the paragon was so interesting and such a wealth of educational facts she sat and asked him question after question. He patiently answered everything she asked him, and when the questions began to slow, the wyvern suggested that she gather her belongings and get ready to leave. Even though they weren't leaving until the morning, he wanted to be ready as soon as he woke.

Tÿr knew that was early and that the day would be extremely long. The alternative, though, was less appealing. It was still another two hours before Varanus returned with Danior and Gordian. The boys were very happy to see their friend, and they were also concerned about the situation back in Vennex.

"So we have to leave because of that useless, piece-of-dung uncle of yours?" Gordi asked.

"That is just one of many reasons, Young Gordian," Ghra'zhenn told him. "There are many things going on in Vennex."

The boys got their belongings unloaded, and they decided to join Tÿr in making the evening meal. They all decided to have roast hog steaks with herbed salt and pears. Rævii was right there with them to eat as well. Tÿr gathered extra food for the flight tomorrow. They would be flying over land, so the wyverns would be able to hunt when they got hungry. The meal lasted well into the night as everyone sat around and talked about what would happen at the mountain of the wyverns. Rævii made her rounds to everyone to sneak bites of wild hog and bits of pear.

Varanus explained to Tÿr that the säqyr wyvern was staying with her parents in Vennex. That way, if anything happened, they would be able to send news quickly. Both wyverns had considered leaving magiq devices with Tÿr's parents to allow them to contact the dynasty quicker, but they risked the assassins being able to detect the magiq. Things would go badly for her parents if they had to explain the presence of magiq items in their home. Magiq was not forbidden in the land, but many people didn't trust those who used it. Healers were the only ones who were not shunned for using it. If any common folk had magiqal items, they kept them hidden away from view. There was a stigma placed on things that the people couldn't explain, and magiq was the biggest.

Eventually Tÿr decided that she was ready to go to bed. The boys had agreed to have one more glass of the dragon fruit wine that Varanus had introduced them to. It had become a treat to them. Varanus had even talked his paragon into bringing back some of the fermented fruit so they could all enjoy a nice, relaxing evening before the long journey the next day. The season was beginning to change as the planet started to tilt, going into its cooler season as it began its journey away from the Trë Suns. The journey past the largest sun, Prymÿÿ, was the hottest time on the planets; but as the gravity shifted when the planets flew past, the planet tilted, and the Kirin-Noirin shift became more shaded by the smaller planet, cooling it tremendously. The shift had only just begun a hundred days ago, but the days were beginning to cool. It would make for a chilly flight as they would be much higher than any of the riders had ever been before. Tÿr had gotten to her bed and was surprised to see the paragon walking up behind her.

"Tÿr'Ynyn, I would like to discuss the magiq that you will be learning. It will require something of you that might require you to step out of your zone of comfort. We have discussed a bit of the magiq and what it can do."

225

Týr nodded. "You said that it can help me to actually disappear."

"That is correct. I wanted to prepare you for the procedural part of the operation. We will have you go over this many times to learn how to move when you are unseen. It can be a…unique experience, and your two friends will be there as well."

Týr sensed that the paragon was feeling uncomfortable about this subject. Usually, he plowed straight through the subject at hand, but now he was almost unsure of what he wanted to say.

"I understand. It may be unique, but I might also be freeing to be invisible."

"It is correct that *you* will disappear from sight. Only you!"

It was then that Týr picked up on what he was getting at. "You're saying that I will need to be undressed while I am doing this?"

If a wyvern could have blushed, Týr knew he would be doing it at this moment. "I am afraid that is what I am telling you. You will have a good amount of time to do what needs to be done, but I am sorry to be the one to tell you that the magiq is relegated to your body alone. Clothing does not accept the magiq. Even hair is difficult to vanish, but with your magiqal prowess, I believe you will have no trouble calling on the magiq when you require it."

If the situation wasn't so serious, Týr would have burst into fits of laughter. She had never seen a wyvern so uncomfortable. "So what you are trying to tell me? Am I to walk around Vennex without clothing? I believe that may draw some undesired attention from people."

"Just remember, young one, you will be invisible the entire time. You won't be working on a time restraint, so that should help to ease your mind some, I hope. When you go under the spell, you will only come out, when you—and only you—bring yourself out of it. I cannot do it. This is also part of the danger as well. If something were to happen to you, no one would be able to locate you to assist you."

Týr hadn't even thought about this. She was still being modest and worrying about being nude and wandering the village. She hadn't even given the idea of her getting hurt while she was under a curtain of invisibility.

"As always, when danger is on the line, you have the final choice, Týr," Ghra'zhenn told her.

"I realize that. It's the thought of being unclothed that is making me uncomfortable. Is there any way to get around it?" Tÿr felt like she was pleading with Ghra'zhenn, which she hated doing. She knew that she was being silly, that no one would be able to see. She had never even been swimming naked!

The paragon told her that he would allow her to sleep on the whole situation. He didn't want to push the issue with the apprentice. He had always found that asking and explaining ideas produced much better results than demanding and giving ultimatums. Ghra'zhenn left the apprentice to sleep on the choice she would have to make. He knew that having her friends with her would make the decision harder. Having to appear unclothed even if she was indiscernible was probably very daunting to her.

Tÿr lay in her bed, worried about not being able to fall asleep. She had so many things going through her mind, and every time she thought she was ready to fall asleep, another thought would catch her attention and draw her mind back into another racing cacophony of images. Finally, she got back out of her bed and went back out to see if the boys were still up. At the mine entrance, she could hear Varanus telling one of his famous tales while the boys sat in rapt attention. She smiled. Maybe a cup of wine would settle her mind and send her off to the sleep that she so desperately needed.

"Is there room for one more?" she asked as she took a cup and filled it half full with the deep-red, velvet liquid.

"Tÿr beer! Join us! Varanus was just telling us about the time when he began his healing lessons and lit the tail of his mentor on fire!"

"Really, Varanus? How come I've never heard this story?" she asked, mockingly scolding him.

Without missing a beat, Varanus looked her straight with cool green eyes and told her that he didn't want to give her any ideas. Gordian about choked on the sip he was taking. He imagined what Varanus would look like, hopping around, trying to douse a fire on the end of his tail. Danior joined in the laughter as well. Before long, even Varanus was chuckling appreciatively. Story time didn't last much longer. Varanus declared that he had probably eaten a couple too many dragon fruits, and so he went into the cavern to lay down next to the warming stove. The boys opted to stay out under the partly cloudy sky. They enjoyed any time they could sleep under the stars.

Týr went back into the cavern and got back into bed. The wine had calmed her thoughts enough to let her sleep in a short time. Before long, she was sleeping deeply, dreaming again of distant islands and their inhabitants. It wasn't until just before she had to wake that she began to have the usual dreams. She was on an island that she had never seen before. There were primitive huts lining a long, sandy beach. She had chosen one to hide in. There were shouts and screams from those seeking her. Wild people.

Týr dared a glance out of a window that she was hiding beneath. She could see the mob of wild people a few hundred yards down the beach. They ran in all different directions as the main body of them slowly proceeded toward the cabin she had sought shelter in. The huts were being destroyed by the mob as they moved closer. They literally ripped them apart with their bare hands, not caring that they were their own or not. As frightened as Týr was, she could not bring herself to duck back down. She continued to watch the angry people frenzy each time they reached another hut. Both men and women grabbed the stick and leaf-built huts and tore them apart like they were nothing.

Týr had to make a decision soon. The crazed mass of people were getting closer each minute. She figured she should abandon the shanty that she was hiding in for better cover. If the swarm reached her, there was no doubt in her mind that she would be torn limb from limb. Týr decided that she would rather die trying to save her own life than to be killed by a bunch of psychotic, inbred crazies who would find her hiding like a coward.

When the mob ripped into the next shack, Týr sprinted from the hut she had been hiding in and ran away from the beach and toward the wooded area that led into a densely forested area. She was nearly there when she heard a shriek from one of the people at the demolished hut down the beach from where she had been. Týr dared a quick glance over her shoulder in time to see several of the mob screaming in her direction and pointing. Some had already begun running after her. The girl's breathing increased as she dreamed, breaths coming in short gasps as she sprinted in her nightmare. The dirty, crazed-eye people gained on her quickly. They could run faster than humanly possible, their filthy, knotted hair blowing back as they sprinted toward the apprentice.

She had just reached the woods when a searing pain shot up her leg. She tripped and went down, reaching for the agony coming from her calf. Her hand came back bloodied from a gash left by a crude blade that was still stuck in the back of her lower leg. Trying to pull the blade caused even more pain, so she left it there for the time being. Tÿr tried to stand and realized that she was already being surrounded by the group of wild-eyed people. She had never been so afraid. How was she going to get out of this?

As the barely human crowd moved in, something happened to Tÿr. She felt her arms and back pulse with electricity. She looked at her arms and could see the crystals were glowing brightly under the skin. The pulsing grew more rapidly as it traveled up her back and down her arms to her hands and back again. What was happening? She could smell cloth burning and looked around to find where it was coming from. Her tunic was beginning to smoke on her back, and the light shone through from the crystals embedded in her skin. The maddened crowd slowed its approach. They had never seen anything like this and had no idea what to do or how to advance safely. Tÿr's tunic continued to smolder and fall off her. She would have been self-conscious had she not been so afraid. She covered her chest with her arm. This seemed to enrage the women of the maddened crowd and to urge the wild men forward.

One of the younger men made a move to rush forward and grab the defenseless girl. It was the last thing he ever did. She held out her other hand that was not covering herself, to push him away, and a blinding bolt of energy shot from her palm and slammed into the boy, lifting him into the air and instantly blackening his skin. The energy then shot from him to four others standing nearby. They, too, were blasted off their feet and fell dead, smoking from their heads, blackened areas on their bodies where the energy had entered them and lightning-like markings where the energy had traveled through their bodies to ground itself again to the nearest thing it could find.

No one else in the crowd dared move for a moment. Then what seemed to be the leader of the grungy crew grabbed a blade from his belt and, with incredible speed, threw it at the girl's head. He had every intention to keep her from ever doing that again. But the blade had hardly left his hand when another jet of energy shot it out of the air. Tÿr lost all modesty, and both hands came out. She began to arc large lines of deadly blue energy through the crowd, where it hit one person and shot two more. In less than five seconds, her attackers lay dead at her feet. There were over fifty of them.

It was then that she realized that she still wasn't alone. She heard a rustling sound behind her and turned, ready to fight again if she had to. Suddenly Tÿr was wide awake. She was sweating profusely and still breathing hard. It had been a very intense dream and so realistic. Unfortunately, she never got to see who had snuck up behind her. She was sure it had not been one of the inbred family members, but she had to know who it was. She turned over on her bed and would try to go back to sleep, but it was going to be difficult. That had been such an insane dream. Tÿr could hear Danior snoring a bit as she closed her eyes and tried to get ready for the trip in the morning. It took a while, but sleep did finally come.

Chapter 17

The travelers were in the air later than planned, but still by an acceptable time according to Ghra'zhenn. The paragon took the lead with the boys onboard. They enjoyed flying much more than Tÿr did. She knew how much Danior wished he could see the view from the heights they were flying, but his younger brother described everything in breathtaking detail. Dani had a huge smile as the air whipped past his face. The trio of humans had dressed in warm clothing, including thick traveling cloaks. The air this high was thin and cool, and the wyverns could only stay up for short periods because of their cold-blooded nature.

After about two hours of high-altitude flight, they would drop closer to the face of the planet to warm. Tÿr grew a little more comfortable as the flight progressed. The long dives toward the planet surface and the tireless way the wyvern's wings flapped to climb back to the stronger air currents were her least favorite times. She always seemed to feel like she was slipping off, even though she had fitted the rig on Varanus's back with a safety harness in case she did fall. She knew that she was perfectly safe. Rævii, too, was in a pouch attached to her.

The wyverns flew side by side the entire day. They were tireless. Tÿr was surprised by the stamina Ghra'zhenn showed. She didn't know his true age, but she did know he was many centuries old, and for him to fly effortlessly the way he was, was amazing to her. It made her want to complain less when she felt tired during her training.

The flight went on for six hours before Tÿr began to hunger. She knew the fox would need to eat, and so she yelled over the rushing air to her mentor. He, in turn, discussed a short respite with his paragon, and the two began a long descent to the ground below. From extreme heights, Tÿr was amazed at how beautiful the planets looked at the shift, the blue-tinted ground surrounded by the greenish-brown water of the sea, the mountains stretching their highest to meet them in the sky, but to no avail. The wyverns had them so high even the mountains looked like small insect mounds. The thought gave Tÿr chills that ran up and down her arms like a thousand little insects.

As luck would have it, the group landed in a clearing of a densely wooded area. Tÿr had never been this far away from Vennex. She didn't know where they were, but the trees were unfamiliar to her. They were tall and had silvery-white bark with golden leaves, incredibly beautiful with some smaller, red-leafed trees scattered in among them. The blue ground was rocky here, and there were many pieces of quartz sticking out of the soil. Boulders of lapis lazuli and kyanite dotted the clearing and wound their way between the trees into the forest depths. Tÿr began to gather pieces of quartz to take back to the cavern whenever it was safe to return. She knew there would be no unwanted visitors while she and Varanus were away. Ghra'zhenn had worked a charm on the front door of the mine, and no one would be able to just walk in. He had used what he termed an "oldie but goodie" enchantment, which, in essence, flipped the door. If one walked into the doorway, it would instantly rotate to have them walk right back out. Tÿr had wondered about the validity of the door and tried to get past the enchantment several times without an ounce of success. She tried sneaking in, running as fast as she could. Nothing worked! She didn't understand why she didn't just trust the paragon. He'd never led her astray in the past.

Each time she tried to enter, she would come walking right back out the way she went in. The enchantment worked well! She was finally satisfied with the magiq that guarded the cavern. Ghra'zhenn just chuckled at her. He enjoyed watching her test his work.

Shortly after the enchantments had been put in place, the traveling group took to the air for the two-day flight. Everyone was in the process of stretching their legs around the clearing. Tÿr stayed on the one side closest to where they touched down as the boys both said they had the need to visit the woods for nature's call. They had only been gone a couple of minutes when Tÿr heard Danior yell louder than she thought possible.

"Tÿr! Varanus!" His voice was high and extremely panicked. He never managed to get out Ghra'zhenn's name.

The ancient wyvern was already moving before the blind man could call his name. Tÿr and Varanus were right on his tail.

"Dani, what's wrong?" Tÿr screamed as she continued to sprint toward the sound of his voice.

The shift fox darted ahead of her master and then stopped suddenly in its tracks. The white tail bristled out. Gordian yelled for Tÿr to stay back.

"What is going on, Gordi?" she screamed at her friend. "What is it?"

Ghra'zhenn and Varanus had also stopped dead in their tracks.

"Tÿr, do not approach any farther!" Ghra'zhenn said with caution in every word. "The boys are being stalked by a huge *shift panther*."

The apprentice stopped dead in her tracks. She did not want to jeopardize either of her friends. Shift panthers rarely killed humans, but that was because humans rarely saw the panthers in the wild. They were opportunistic feeders and would eat about anything that crossed their paths, provided they could fit it in their mouth and that it was palatable. Tÿr looked into the woods to find the boys. She squinted to see into the darkening forest and spotted her friend Danior, but where was Gordian? She continued to scan the area, all the while keeping the panther in sight. It was hard to spot in the trees, and only when it moved could she make it out. It appeared as if a shadow had come to life and was moving closer to Danior.

"Gordi? Where are you?" Tÿr yelled.

"Shh, over here," came his reply.

He was about fifty feet from his brother. His eyes were fixed on a completely different spot. It was then that Tÿr realized with horror that Gordian had a panther of his own, quietly stalking him.

"Varanus, there are two of them!" she screamed.

Her mentor was closer to Danior, along with Ghra'zhenn. She would let them deal with the panther on him. She didn't know what she would do, but she had to help Gordi, or he would be dead. With her staff in hand, she started for the panther; and to her horror, Rævii jumped ahead of her. The fox, defending her master, put herself between the panther and Tÿr. It was enough of a distraction that Gordian was able to move farther away from the panther. The black-velvet animal hissed in frustration as its quarry had gotten farther away. It turned to the little fox, its anger unmistakable. Tÿr tried to move between Rævii and the huge cat, but every time she got close, the little fox put up her defenses and hissed back at the cat. It bounced at the cat and then leapt back, causing as much of a distraction as it could. It was trying to save Tÿr, not understanding that Tÿr was doing the same for her.

Gordian had managed to escape the cat, pulling his trousers back up as he ran. He ran at the one that was hell-bent on attacking his brother. Gordian grabbed a large blue rock off the ground and hurled it at the cat, who shook off the blow. This did the trick though. Its attention was now drawn off the blind brother and onto the one which the cat perceived as the bigger threat. In a second, the huge beast lunged at Gordian. Unfortunately for the cat, it hadn't seen Ghra'zhenn, who was climbing through the trees above them. As the cat flew, the wyvern dropped down on it, grabbing its neck in his powerful jaws. The panther shrieked its last as the paragon severed its head from its body, both parts landing just feet from Gordian, who took one look and vomited. Varanus had changed direction and was moving quickly to his apprentice.

She was frozen now, not moving as the panther slowly advanced. The fox was making a racket, doing anything it could to draw the cat away from her master. Varanus was approaching quickly, and that had distracted the panther enough for Tÿr to think. She held out her staff and attacked. Blue searing fire shot from the head of the staff in crooked, electrical bolts. They hit the panther broadside and completely blew him off his feet. The fox jumped at the charge that slammed into the black cat. The shock was evident on the panther's face. It had never come up against such a formidable nor mysterious foe. It did not deter it from swinging back around and coming at Tÿr again, this time much faster. It was determined to put an end to that thing that caused such pain. Its coat was still smoking and singed from where the bolt had struck it. Tÿr was ready for the attack this time. She was glowing as she sent a second bolt at the cat.

Varanus had just reached the cat and had swung his massive tail to catch it right in the chest at the same time Tÿr's lightning hit. The giant cat flew back and hit a tree with a sickening crunch. It did not get up. Varanus went over to where the creature lay. Its back legs were twisted into a position that they shouldn't be. Tÿr could see from where she was that the creature's back was broken. Varanus made sure the creature didn't suffer. He grabbed it by the head, and with one quick, powerful shake, he snapped its neck as well. The light went out of its eyes with a final hiss as the breath left its lungs. That's when a surprise no one saw coming happened.

Another black streak shot from the shadows of the forest and another. Two more panthers that no one had seen leapt through the air and onto the wyvern's neck. Tÿr screamed as she saw them biting the back of her mentor. Varanus stumbled, and as he did, yet another much-larger cat came shooting in from another direction to attack. This cat knew exactly what it was doing. It went for the softer flesh under Varanus's neck. The wyvern was still too fast for the attacking cat and knocked him easily away with a huge wing. This movement cause one of the other cats on his back to try to attack the thinner, skin-like membrane of the wing, but again, Varanus was too quick and had folded it back up.

By this time, Ghra'zhenn had checked on Danior, who said his was just fine and told the paragon to go help Varanus. Tÿr, too, had gotten better footing and was preparing to attack again. The head of her staff shone brightly in the dusky afternoon. She let fly another burst of pure energy. It shot between the three cats. Smoke poured off their backs, yet they clung to the wyvern. Varanus thrashed in rage, trying to shake the cats, but they had dug in with their huge teeth and enormous black razor-sharp claws.

Ghra'zhenn made it to Varanus and ripped the first cat off his neck. Bones in the cat crunched and shattered under the force of the ancient wyvern's bite. The other cat let go of Varanus and turned to face the new attacker. Tÿr ran up to Gordian and pulled him back to Danior. They tried their best to stay hidden behind some trees while the battle between the last cat and the wyverns continued. Instead of more fighting, Tÿr heard hissing and what sounded like spitting. She chanced a glance to see the paragon doing what appeared to be talking to the large black cat. The cat had stopped in its tracks and was listening. It, too, began what could only be talking back to Ghra'zhenn. The two circled each other as the conversation continued, each taking turns speaking and then listening.

"Tÿr," Ghra'zhenn said in a loud voice. "He is still prepared to fight and is looking for a meal. Prepare yourself to attack should it get past myself or Varanus!"

Immediately Tÿr brought her power up to her staff, her arms and back glowing brightly, as well as the winged head of her staff. In a last-ditch effort to escape the wyverns, the panther seemed as if it would vault over Varanus; but at the last moment, it threw itself flat on the ground and slid under the younger wyvern. A cloud of blue dust exploded, hiding the panther for one brief second. Tÿr had not been fooled and had anticipated its move. As the panther emerged from the dust cloud, Tÿr struck. She held nothing back. Instead of a stream of energy, an immense ball of lightning shot from the magiqal weapon. It burst out, growing to fifteen feet across, and consumed the large black wildcat. It was lifted off its feet and traveled with the ball of fury one hundred feet back. The ball finally hit a huge tree trunk and exploded in a mass of electrical energy. There was nothing left of the cat, only bits of smoldering fur to send it to oblivion.

Gordian stared at Tÿr. "Holy shit, Tÿr beer! Where did that come from?"

"What happened?" Danior asked.

Gordian was explaining to his brother what had just happened to the panther when the wyverns came walking over.

"Well done, young one!" Ghra'zhenn told Tÿr. "That was some bit of conjuring!"

Tÿr smiled up at the paragon. "I believe I know what I need to boost my magiq," she told Ghra'zhenn. "Just put me under attack, and I can take down anything you put me up against."

Ghra'zhenn chuckled at this.

Varanus also joined in the sharing of praise to his apprentice. "Does the magiq flow more naturally?" he asked Tÿr.

"Well," she began, trying to think of the best way to say it, "it was as if the magiq knew that we needed protection. I did as well, but I wasn't the one that determined the size of blast to use. It was almost as if the magiq knew what to do once I called on it."

"It will do that the more you use it and the more comfortable you become using it," Ghra'zhenn told her. "Once you become more accustomed to conjuring, you will be able to summon what you need without the magiq stepping in. It will just take time, but you are well on your way. You will learn to control the intensity of your blasts without even thinking about it. For instance, you wouldn't have used an energy ball of that size to take down a small creature the size of a wild hog. It would be overkill."

Tÿr thought she understood.

"My gods, Tÿr beer!" Gordian started. "That was amazing. I told Dani about what you did, and he didn't believe me at first until he heard the loud pop that happened when you vaporized that panther!"

Everyone took a moment to catch their breath while Tÿr went to check on Varanus's wounds. The panthers had left several puncture and claw marks on his neck and back. She made him sit still so she could heal it. Varanus told her that it was perfectly fine and would heal on his own and he didn't require her services.

"Don't be ridiculous," Tÿr told the younger wyvern, and she called up her healing magiq.

Blue light hovered over the wyvern's wounds and began to knit the deep punctures in his neck and back. It took a couple of minutes, and there was no evidence of a scar when Tÿr had finished.

Gordian was impressed by this. "How long have you been able to do this kind of magiq, Tÿr? Is this from that inter-whatever it is?"

"Intercalation," Tÿr said patiently. "Yes, that is when my magiq really began to grow."

"Could you teach me any of that magiq?" Gordian asked.

"I'm not sure if I'd be the best teacher." She turned to Ghra'zhenn. "Would you be able to teach either of the boys any magiq?"

Ghra'zhenn took a moment to answer, and when he did, the answer completely surprised Tÿr. "First, we would have to discover your aptitude for magiq. If you have no natural ability, there is nothing I can teach you. If, however, you show some potential, we could definitely begin some training. It would be good for you to have some magiqal training for protection back in Vennex when Tÿr isn't there."

This seemed to please Gordian as he had always wanted to be able to do magiq. Tÿr could remember that when they were kids, he had always wanted to be a magiq user of some sort. He would even pretend to be an evil sorcerer some of those times. News that he could possibly be trained in magiq had brought Gordian's spirits through the roof. He was excited to find out when they could start. Ghra'zhenn told him again that it was only *if* he had the propensity for magiq. Gordian had already accepted this as a forgone conclusion. He knew in his heart that he would be able to do what would be required.

"And does that go the same for my brother?" Gordi asked.

"If he chooses to try, I will personally take him under my wing and take the time to teach you both magiq that will help you protect yourselves and the ones you care about back in Vennex," Ghra'zhenn told him.

"You truly mean that?" Danior asked.

"I truly do, young master. We will do some testing when we get you to Ÿkkynnÿk Mountain."

Both boys could hardly contain their smiles.

Even Ghra'zhenn gave a large, toothy grin. "If you three will excuse Varanus and myself, we are going to clean up the mess that we have left. Why don't you have something to eat while we take this rest."

At first, Tÿr didn't understand what Ghra'zhenn meant, but then it was all too apparent when she heard the crunching of the bones in the forest where the fight had taken place. She was used to the big lizards eating, so it didn't bother her in the least. She knew they would need the energy for the flight. There was still a long journey ahead of them. The humans and the fox fed on leftover roast hog and pears while the wyverns consumed what was left of the panthers. When Tÿr and the boys were done eating, they sat and replayed the events of the panther attack in gory detail.

Gordian was still amazed by Tÿr's magiqal abilities. "And then you just shot that huge ball of energy, and that thing, it literally disintegrated! What were you feeling when that happened?"

Tÿr wasn't sure how to answer the question. She was proud of the magiq that she had conjured, but she wasn't sure how to answer the other part of the question. "I'm not exactly sure, Gordi. I was mainly scared and thought if the magiq didn't work, we would be in big trouble. Luckily, the magiq sort of took over and did what it needed to without needing to be told. It was kind of bizarre!"

Danior sat and listened to the play-by-play from his brother as they ate. They all fed until they were full and sat back to wait on the wyverns. It wasn't long, and everyone was together again. Both wyverns had gore smeared on their faces from where they had eaten. Tÿr mentioned this to them, and immediately they used their long tongues to attempt to clean their blood-covered faces.

"Did you have enough to eat?" Gordian joked as the two wyverns returned to the group.

"Ah, yes, Master Gordian," Ghra'zhenn replied, "more than enough."

After that, the group of them made small talk and got their belongings together so they could be back on their way. They still had a long way to go. The boys mounted first, and Tÿr jumped back up on her mentor's back to round out the trio. Rævii was tucked away nicely in her pouch on Tÿr's chest. Both wyverns lifted off at the same time and shot straight up. Tÿr held on tightly as they flapped up noisily, gaining height with each wing flap.

Before long, the land was just a painting from a surreal artist's print book. Everything was so beautiful from so high up above it was hard to believe that on the land below them, someone was trying to find them to cause troubles because of her new magiq power.

Chapter 18

Kaistam-Laq was furious. More magiq had been used. Powerful magiq. Magiq that he wasn't sure that he himself could conjure. He knew all this, yet he still couldn't figure out exactly the where or who of this equation. The Murtair Amagii had replaced the missing assassin and were back at full strength. The assassin teams were split up in the central part of the Kirin-Noirin shift, and still there was not one word about a magic user who was as powerful as he himself was. Either this new sorcerer was hiding himself for fear of detection or for fear of his life. Whatever the case, Kaistam-Laq's assassins should not be having such a difficult time locating him. Being masters in the magiqal arts themselves, they should be able to pick up the signs. The magiq coming from this man was immense. Detection should not be a problem!

The more Kaistam thought about this issue, the madder he became. Luckily for his entire sect, they were out in the field, trying to find signs of the "new magiq user," as he was referred to by Laq. There was no doubt in the leader of Murtair Amagii that this powerful new magiq user was a great and powerful man. In his heart, he knew it was the only way it could be. No woman could generate the power this person could. They were rumored to be a healer too, and a woman couldn't be a healer. She would never have the aptitude for such an important job.

It was while he was fuming about not finding anything, it happened. A massive amount of energy was used. He could see it plainly in his scrying mirror. It was as a blast bigger than he thought possible by one person. For a moment, he calmed and began to think this wasn't a person. A wyvern maybe. Or a wyvern and sorcerer together.

This was no mere human, and it wasn't the one he was looking for. The one he was searching for was much closer, and they had no way to travel as far as they had in such a short time. Again, things began not to make sense. Who was this person? Why had he, Kaistam-Laq, never heard of him? If this sorcerer was so powerful, surely, word would have gotten around the planets and the shift especially. Aggravation was beginning to rear its ugly head. What was stumping him so badly was that the magiq was so big, so it should be showing up close to where the other magiq had shown up. It just wasn't making any sense.

He decided that the mirror was no longer reliable for what he needed. At one point, he almost smashed it; but it was his favorite mirror, so he calmed down and went to look for other means of detection. He went to the shelves and began to throw things, looking for something in particular. Eventually he came back with a golden box. He sat it down and moved over to the side of the room and brought out a structure that was a large brass circle on a stand. It was a type of candelabra. On the circle, there was a place for seventeen candles spaced out evenly around the circumference.

Kaistam went back to the box he had set down and opened it to reveal a box full of candles. He took out the blood-red candles and arranged them around the hoop candle holder. At the bottom of the hoop was an empty spot that held incense. Once the candles were in place, he began the process of choosing the incense. He chose ones not for their scent but for their seeing properties, ones that would help him divine who and where this huge blast of magiq was coming from. He chose exactly seventeen sticks. When the incense was in the holder, Kaistam-Laq waved his hand over the hoop, and the candles lit instantly. The incense caught fire, and he let it burn for a few seconds before blowing out the flames to let the smoke fill the hoop, which would act like a window. The sorcerer dimmed the rest of the lights in his tent so that this circular candelabra was the only light in his lavish tent. The seventeen candles threw bizarre shadows around Laq's sanctuary. Light flickered and shone off the metal instruments and other items he had sitting on numerous shelves around the room. When the smoke had filled the round window, Kaistam raised his staff and shouted in an old tongue.

"Sÿall Dhomh Ÿodænn Anke Kkecht Dræoidhækdd Zÿnë!"

The space between the window filled with dark, billowing smoke, which was lit by the candles surrounding it. The smoke just stayed confined by the hoop. Figures began to appear, hazy at first. They began to take form, but there seemed to be stronger magiq working against the sorcerer's because the forms immediately began to dissolve back into smoke. Kaistam-Laq was able to see the forms of what he believed were wyverns and another of a human, but the forms had shifted so quickly he wasn't sure if he had seen correctly. He screamed in rage and used his staff again to yell the magiqal incantation to the window. A beam of energy shot from his staff and through the smoke and into the other side of the tent, burning a hole there immediately, but the figures formed in the smoke again.

He watched more carefully this time, even though the figures dissipated as quickly again. Yes, he was sure there were wyverns involved. He couldn't tell how many, but he could see that the wyverns were with at least two humans. It had to be the wyvern magiq protecting the humans against his magiq. Now he had an idea of what to look for and what to have his assassins looking for while they were scouring the shift for this magiq that had been eluding him for the past little while. If there was magiq that was more powerful than Kaistam-Laq's, he would see that his sect recruit this magiq and use it to remain the most powerful killers on the planets.

Kaistam extinguished the candles and incense with a wave of his hand. He would be using his whole sect to go after this sorcerer he had discovered. He was sure he had seen wyverns, which the sect could dispose of easily, but this sorcerer that they were protecting would be another matter. He didn't want him destroyed. He wanted him next to him, showing him this magiq that he used. They would have to use care when bringing him in, and anyone who harmed this powerful man would pay dearly. Kaistam did not deal well with failures, and the harming of whoever this was would definitely be considered a huge failure. The thought of one of his assassins killing or wounding this unknown person was making him upset just thinking about it.

He turned to his staff and performed a fancy wave over the headpiece. It glowed blue in the darkness of the tent. He brought it to his mouth and began to speak. He told all the sect to return immediately to his headquarters, to stop their search, for he knew who and where the target was. There was a great deal of pride in his voice as he recalled the assassins back to his tent. He gave them two days to assemble before him and then stopped the message. The headpiece went dark, and Kaistam-Laq walked to his favorite chair to sit and think of his next move.

He really wished he had seen the magiq user's face, but he felt there was enough to go on now that they would be able to apprehend this person and bring him before the leader of the most-feared group of assassins on the face of both planets. He was sure that with a little coaxing and perhaps some persuading, he would have a new partner for the first time ever. If it was true that this person was a healer too, it might take a good deal of persuasion and maybe a bit of threatening as well, but Kaistam would not pass up this opportunity!

Chapter 19

The trip to Ÿkkynnÿk Mountain was quicker than the travelers had planned. The wyverns had gotten into an airstream and were flung forward faster than anticipated. Instead of the two to two and one half days, it took only a day and a half. As they neared the island, Ghra'zhenn let out a huge ear-shattering shriek that broke the silence and almost made Tÿr jump off Varanus's back. From above, Tÿr had watched as they followed the Ajenti River into Peyda Kirin. The river originated from the Keltainyn Sea and flowed down through the shift and into Peyda Noirin. Depending on the tilt of the planet and the placement in its orbit of the suns, the river could flow either way.

Up ahead, the island could be seen in the middle of the Keltainyn Sea. The smell of the fresh water was incredible from even this height. Tÿr could see seabirds circling below them above the water. Her stomach began to drop a bit as her ride did the same. This was her favorite part of flying to be sure—the descent. Even though she was still over a mile above the planet, she began to relax as Varanus and Ghra'zhenn slowly started to lower their flight toward the island.

Ghra'zhenn opened his mouth again for another ear-splitting roar, but she was ready for it this time. Tÿr realized that he must be signaling the dynasty on the ground to his return. She even noticed that she had let the death grip on her reins ease up a bit. In her mind, she was closer to the ground now, even though they were still a mile up. She felt that if she fell, somehow, she could save herself with magiq if she kept her cool. She grinned at this thought, and it occurred to her that she probably could.

The rest of the flight only lasted about fifteen minutes, and they were circling over the island in ten. It was so nice to have the ground that close underfoot. Despite the fact that they were still several hundred feet up, Tÿr felt as if she could touch the ground. It had been a long flight, and she was hoping that it would be a long while before they had to make the return trip. This island looked as if it was going to be a little sliver of paradise to Tÿr. She could hear Gordian telling his brother all about it while they sped to their final destination. Danior had a big smile on his face as he imagined the sight from above. Ghra'zhenn promised them that they were just a couple of minutes away, and both Danior and Tÿr were planning on holding him to that.

Tÿr could finally see the top of the mountain as they circled in on the island. There were many figures moving below, and suddenly it clicked in Tÿr's head that the reason Ghra'zhenn had bellowed was to signal their arrival. He was letting the wyverns know to gather and meet them upon their landing. There were openings on the mountainside that could only be caves where the wyverns lived. Some were coming out as the travelers neared the top of the mountain.

Both Varanus and Ghra'zhenn began to flap their wings more and more as they neared. They had left the strong flow of the airstream above, and so they had to flap harder to stay in flight, especially with their loads of passengers and their belongings. Rævii even dared a quick peek out of her pouch before settling back at the bottom. She preferred the safety and warmth that it provided next to her master's body. Finally—and as promised—a few minutes later, after circling one final time, Ghra'zhenn and Varanus turned onto the peak of the mountain and came to rest among the other wyverns, who had gathered to greet them and the newest member of their dynasty.

Tÿr was a bit nervous to meet the dynasty. She had never been around such a gathering of wyverns before, except at the funeral of Aaxtagara. Even then, the entire dynasty had not come. There were some who had stayed back to tend the home and protect the area from danger. Tÿr dismounted as soon as they landed and steadied herself on her feet. She had been sitting for a long time on Varanus's back, so her legs had gotten a bit wobbly. She walked over to Ghra'zhenn and helped Danior down, who was having the same issue with his legs. Gordian didn't show any signs of having leg issues, but Tÿr believed that he was doing his best to hide it in front of the others. Even if his legs weren't bothering him, she knew his backside had to be. Riding for a few hours gave her "saddle" issues, so she knew that he was miserable at the very least as well.

An olive-green wyvern who was almost as large as Ghra'zhenn walked up to greet the travelers. Tÿr could tell immediately that this was a female. Though the voices were almost identical, females were just a bit different. That was the best way to describe it. They didn't sound male and female like a human; there was a bit of vibration in the female voice. Tÿr found it completely enthralling.

"Greetings, humans. I am *Glædi'Lann*, and I serve as deputy paragon in the absence of our leader. It is my greatest pleasure to welcome you here to Ÿkkynnÿk. It is especially thrilling to welcome you, Tÿr, a sister to the dynasty. I know you have just now arrived, but I have been anxious to ask you this."

"Please, by all means, feel free to ask anything," Tÿr told the deputy.

Glædi'Lann didn't say anything for a moment, as if she was talking herself into something. "It's just that we haven't had a human join the dynasty for so long that I have forgotten many things. I was wondering if I could see the intercalation? Would you mind?"

Tÿr was taken aback by this question. She hadn't expected this in the first minute of her arrival. She had been warned by Ghra'zhenn that some of the dynasty would be fascinated by it and possibly ask to see it, but not the moment she arrived. "Um, yeah, I suppose," she said.

"Glædi'Lann! She has only now arrived. Give her some time!" Ghra'zhenn admonished.

The deputy hung her head a bit, but Tÿr told her it was okay. She smiled at Ghra'zhenn. "You warned me that they would ask. I guess I better get used to it."

The paragon chuckled, and Tÿr took off her cloak. She offered any of the other wyverns who would like to see a chance as well.

Gordian, too, was curious to see it. He had never seen the whole of the procedure. She undid the sides of her tunic so she could lift the back and hold the front closed.

"Can you help me, Gordi?"

Gordi blushed. He had never been this close to an unclothed lady before, but she told him it was okay. Tÿr still clutched Rævii to her chest in the pouch and then had Gordian lift up the back of her tunic. There was immediate murmuring throughout the gathered wyverns. Many had never seen the "wyvern skin" on a human before. It was a beautiful thing to behold indeed. Gordian just stared; he couldn't take his eyes off her back. After a minute of letting them look, Tÿr instructed Gordian to lower the tunic again, and she cinched it back at each side.

"That was amazing, Tÿr beer! Did it hurt?"

"Very much! I don't remember a lot of it, thank goodness, but what I do remember, I know it was the worst pain I've ever experienced."

"I couldn't look away," Gordian said. "It was mesmerizing."

Tÿr nodded to her friend and walked back over to help unload her belongings from Varanus. The boys did the same.

When they had gotten everything down, Ghra'zhenn spoke up to those assembled, "These are my friends and, as such, are friends of this dynasty. They will be treated with respect. Also, the girl is Tÿr'Ynyn, our newest member, so please welcome her to our dynasty and treat her as you treat each other. These are my wishes and my orders. They will be followed!"

All the wyverns that had gathered genuflected in unison to show their respect. When Ghra'zhenn was satisfied with the response, he turned to the humans and told them to collect their belongings and follow him to his living quarters. They would be sharing his place with him while they were on Ÿkkynnÿk. The travelers followed the paragon to the topmost cave, and when they entered, they all had the same expression on their face.

The cavern was filled with glowing crystals, not the little ones that Tÿr had used to craft the headpiece of her staff but huge ones, some two and three feet long sitting on shelves carved into the mountain. They glowed with what could only be magiqal fire, and the cavern sparkled with the light. There were many gold-and-silver candlesticks and other stands and objects that Tÿr had no idea what they did.

Gordian stood, gaping at the magnificence, all the while describing it to his brother, who was impressed in his own way. "This place is amazing, Ghra'zhenn!"

The paragon beamed. "Being as old as I am does allow for some creature comforts." He chuckled.

Gordian looked around and saw benches of the finest woods and chairs and even some artwork on the walls of the cavern.

"Of course, I can't use most of it," continued the leader of the dynasty, "but it doesn't mean that I can't appreciate it. Please feel free to use any of the furniture that is in here. It should be used for more than just observing. I'm glad I can finally have visitors who will appreciate it all!"

Gordian led his brother over to a chair piled high with velvet cushions.

Danior felt them all before taking a seat on top of them. "Is there anything you would like me to do while we are here, Ghra'zhenn? As long as you don't have me matching colors, I can help with many things."

"I believe you can. Once you have settled in your new temporary housing, I will find you something you can do. Besides, I believe you mentioned something about learning some magiq. If that is something you still wish to do, I will make sure you have the basic spells you need to know to begin. This will prove to us whether you have the aptitude to continue studying. If you do, I will make damn sure you are trained in the proper arts."

This made Danior and his brother extremely happy. They were ready to begin right then, but Ghra'zhenn had business to tend to. He hadn't been at the dynasty for a long while, and there was a lot of business that needed tending. Tÿr, too, was amazed by the living space of Ghra'zhenn, not only by the furniture and golden fixtures but more by the enormous crystals. She could feel the energy that came from them. She walked up to a giant, three-foot piece of quartz, which was glowing from within.

"May I touch this, Paragon?"

"Of course. You can do it no harm! Unless, of course, you drop it, but fear not, I have hundreds more where that came from in my stores."

Tÿr walked over and picked up the huge gem. It was nearly as tall as she was. The vibrations that came from it seemed to pulse deep into her, beginning in her hands and growing stronger as they traveled into her body. She loved this feeling. Had she needed to conjure anything, she could right now. While she was on this mountain hideaway, she would ask Ghra'zhenn for the location of possible spots to locate her own crystals. She was sure he would gladly give her any amount she wished, but she felt the power would be more controlled and available to her if she found it herself. Tÿr also wanted to craft a weapon—a crystal dagger. If she could make a dagger out of quartz and use it the way the Murtair Amagii used lachtrys, she would have a formidable, close-quarters weapon too. She didn't like the fact that she needed to arm herself, but the sad truth was that nowadays, it was no longer safe for her nor the brothers. If she needed to defend them, she wanted to be prepared. She would ask Ghra'zhenn to appoint a wyvern to teach her self-defense courses, or at least a type of protection for her and the boys. She got them into this, and if anything happened to them, she would never forgive herself.

The three humans spent hours going through the cavern, looking at the treasures that Ghra'zhenn had collected over the many, many years of his long lifetime. Finally, Gordian mentioned that he was getting hungry.

"I will send one of the dynasty out to hunt, and you can eat shortly then," Ghra'zhenn told Gordian. "There are usually mountain goats or deer on the peaks. Does that sound good to anyone?"

"I could eat a whole deer by myself!" Gordian said, and his brother agreed with him.

They had only been able to bring a small amount of meat with them on the journey, so they mainly lived on fruit. Tÿr, too, said that she was hungry, so Ghra'zhenn went to prepare for one of his subjects to hunt for some meat. Tÿr said she would like to walk around through the trees and see what she could find to add to the meal. She and Rævii went out of the cave and left the boys to do whatever they wanted.

The boys went out where there was a large fire burning near the entrance to the cavern. Several of the wyverns were gathered around, talking in Cmok, but they quickly changed to the common tongue out of courtesy for the boys. The boys seemed pleased to be the center of attention as the wyverns asked them of their backgrounds and what they did back in the village. The boys explained how they were very interested in learning magiq and that Ghra'zhenn had promised to see if they showed any promise while they were living on the mountain with the dynasty. Many of the wyverns found this to be of great interest. Most had never been around humans before, so this was just as interesting for them as it was for the boys.

The boys grilled the wyverns about everyday life on the mountain and of the magiq that they could do. Before they knew it, the meal was cooking on a spit over the fire. One of the younger wyverns volunteered to stay and turn the meat while the others went to hunt or do other things that needed to be done. Because of the tilting of the planet, it began to get darker in the evening. The mountain sat on the outer edge of the planet, so it never got truly dark; but back in Vennex, it had gotten darker with each passing day.

On the other planet, Peyda Noirin, it was dark most of the time now, and the waters were becoming rougher and more agitated. Within a month or two, there would be massive waves that traveled the whole planet, devastating smaller islands in their paths. The blue mountaintop was still warm from the three suns that warmed it during the day, and the wyverns continued to absorb the heat from the ground.

There were other fires burning at other cave entrances as well, where wyverns had curled up to enjoy the added warmth. Most had fed within the past day or two, so they didn't need to eat. The wyvern, who had taken charge of cooking their food, had cleaned the deer and had laid leaves from a tree that none of the humans recognized. He folded the deer together and weaved it onto a large spit. While the boys talked to a couple of the wyverns who had stayed at the fire to talk, Tÿr came back with a bowl full of different berries she had found on her walk through the trees. Everyone ate until they couldn't eat another bite. Whatever the leaves were that the wyvern who had cooked—now named *Krÿ'zhed*—had put on the meat, it was fantastic. It was like nothing the humans had ever tasted before. It had a bit of spice and a lot of herbal quality, and it kind of made their mouth go numb. All the same, it was delicious.

After the dinner was gone and the meat stored in Ghra'zhenn's cave, Varanus showed up with a box of dragon fruit for the wyverns sitting around the fire and a couple of bottles of wine for the humans. Tÿr went to fetch some cups. She thought they could all use a drink after the long flight. The dragon fruit disappeared quickly, and Varanus went for more. Many of the wyverns gathered became a bit goofy and asked silly questions of the humans. The boys took no notice because they themselves were imbibing a good deal of the wine Varanus had brought with him. Tÿr drank cautiously. She had already suffered a hangover from the potent wine before and wasn't about to be miserable from it when she knew she'd also be sore from the long trip as well.

On one trip back to the cavern, she had already fished out a headache remedy for the boys in the morning because she saw the way they were getting through the deep-red wine. She shook her head as she sat out the herbs for the morning-hangover fix but smiled. With everything they had been through in the last few days, she figured that they deserved a nice drink. She, on the other hand, would err on the side of caution and sip her cup slowly. She also got out a pain-relief remedy for herself. She would wait until the morning to take it. She hoped the wine would help to dull it a bit this evening.

Ghra'zhenn retired to his cave fairly early. Tÿr knew he had to be exhausted from the long, two-day flight. It wasn't long, and the boys and her followed behind the giant lizard. She figured the boys would have stayed much later than they did, but Danior was having trouble keeping his eyes open. Soon Gordi was doing the same. She suggested they go to sleep and half expected an argument, but the boys said their good nights and staggered to bed right behind her.

Chapter 20

Morning came earlier than Tÿr expected. She hadn't realized how late it was when she had finally crawled into bed. What surprised her, though, was the fact that Gordian was already outside, talking to Ghra'zhenn. He was truly interested in learning magiq.

Tÿr was getting up and around when Danior came walking past him and out of the cave. He walked right out and over to his brother. It always amazed Tÿr to see Danior get around as well as a sighted person. She had no idea how he did it, but he managed to deal with his disability like he didn't have it. It never really stopped him at all.

When Tÿr got out to the firepit, the boys were discussing how they would be tested on their magiqal acuity. Ghra'zhenn explained how he would ask them to do simple tasks, many that had nothing to do with magiq at all. Gordian told the paragon that he was ready to begin that afternoon. Dani also said that he would like to try as well. So Ghra'zhenn said he would prepare the tests for the magiq aptitude to be given in three hours' time.

Gordian and Danior both went to sit by Tÿr. They had many questions to ask before they tried their tests. Mainly they wanted to know what the magiq felt like. They grilled her for over an hour about every little thing they could think of regarding magiq—from feelings to how she got things to happen—anything that they thought would give them an edge for their trials. Tÿr tried as best as she could to explain how the magiq worked for her. She was able to tap into it with very little resistance. She tried to explain resistance to the boys and how a tragedy or an attack could help her bypass that resistance. She was sure that she had completely bored them to tears by the time the paragon walked back out of his cave. They fidgeted and kicked the blue dirt, and the paragon approached.

"Boys, you may come with me now."

Gordian took his brother by the hand and led him back to the cave with the paragon. There was a table in the central part of the cavern with crystals and other things setting on it.

"Go to the table and chose one of the crystals that calls to you. Danior, you can choose one by touch. Chose the one that feels best in your hand. This is what you are going to use as your conduit to assist the magiq to move through you. I would suggest you choose a piece of amethyst or a piece of quartz. Size doesn't matter for your test. You are only trying to get a reaction—not a huge, spectacular piece of magnificent magiq—for your first attempt. You are going to try something like a faint light in the crystal. Something simple, something easy."

Gordian led Dani up to the table. There were over fifty different crystals and stones set on one side of it. On the other were about twenty thin pieces of wand-like, wooden branches. There was an incense holder with three different types of incense and some candles burning in certain spots along the edges. There were also some metal weapons that Ghra'zhenn hadn't mentioned, so Gordian just left them alone. Despite what the paragon had advised, Gordian took a six-inch piece of yellow citrine. He liked the way the faces were arranged near the point. Anyway, he knew it was in the quartz family.

Danior felt around the table for several minutes. He tried many different pieces of quartz and amethyst. Eventually he settled on a piece of lachtrys. It was a medium-sized, oval-shaped piece the color of midnight. There were even pieces of a sparkly type of crystal in it that made it look like the night sky. Of course, this made no difference to Danior as he couldn't see it. He simply liked how it felt in his hand.

"Which of you would like to begin first?" Ghra'zhenn asked.

Gordian was nervous and didn't even know why. There wasn't anything riding on this. There was nothing to be gained, except lessons from the paragon. He just didn't like to fail at anything. He knew his brother was the same way, but Danior seemed calmer at the moment, so he suggested that his brother try first.

"Okay, Master Danior, just relax and try to let the energy flow through you into the stone. Just let it do what it will."

"What do I want it to do?" Dani asked. He had no clue what he was supposed to be doing, only that he would love to be able to do *any* type of magiq, even the smallest bit.

"From what I understand, your friend, Tÿr'Ynyn, conjured a light inside her crystal. You may try that. You have chosen lachtrys, and it has hundreds of uses, so feel free to try anything. We are looking for any sign. It need not be large. The merest flicker will suffice. Now, please, go ahead!"

Danior stood there for a few moments, still not sure what he was supposed to be feeling. He did know of assassins that could mold lachtrys into blades by the use of magiq. First, he would attempt to light the stone and then cause it the form into a blade. That was all he knew at the moment. He concentrated. Nothing. He thought how he wanted this to work and how disappointed he would be if it didn't, and still, he heard nothing from the others observing him. It hit him then. *I'm overthinking this. Tÿr doesn't sit and think about it forever. She just makes it happen.* He began to imagine the stone getting warm and pliable. And then it was beginning to glow, in his mind anyway. He couldn't see light very well, so he had to imagine what it was. The lachtrys suddenly grew heavy in his hand.

Gordi gasped. "Look!"

The stone that Danior was holding was beginning to twist in his hand. Light from the depths of the stone grew to a faint glow. The oval stone began to lengthen and thin itself on one end. He was so shocked he stopped the process. But the stone continued to glow in the depths of the dark-blue stone, though it gave off no heat. The stone had taken the rough shape of a crude blade, long and thinner on one end, with a perfectly molded handle in his hand.

Danior reached out with his other hand to feel the stone. A huge smile split his face. "*Holy smokes*, Gordi! I did it!"

"How?" His brother wanted to know. "How did you do it?"

"I'm not exactly sure. I know you can't force it. You have to let it happen. When I was trying to make the magiq happen, nothing would, but then I kinda let it do what it wanted to, and it just sort of took over. My arm felt like it was almost tingling when it happened."

Danior held the crude dagger up to his eyes at a strange angle, but that was where his only sliver of sight was. He admired it and how it had changed shape.

"Now, Master Danior, can you extinguish the light?"

Danior held the blade to his chest, and in less than a second, the light blinked out.

Gordian stood next to the paragon, with his mouth gaping wide. "My brother can do magiq, Ghra'zhenn!"

"And so, perhaps, can you, young master. We are going to be finding out in just a couple moments."

Gordian's heart skipped a beat. He did not want to fail. His friend and now his brother could both perform magiq. What if he couldn't? He would feel so inept.

"Danior," Ghra'zhenn continued, "I wish for you to keep your piece of lachtrys. It will serve as a reminder throughout your upcoming lessons. I wish for you to try to complete your dagger with the passing of each day. Gordian, it is time. Please step forward and try to do anything. Remember what your brother said. Don't force it. Let it move through you."

Gordian closed his eyes and held his crystal tight against his chest. He tried to make anything happen. He began to strain, and his head began to hurt. The wine from the night before was not helping.

"Do not think about it so much!" Ghra'zhenn told him after five minutes with no results.

Gordi kept stealing peeks at the stone to see if anything had happened, but he already knew in his heart that it hadn't.

"Either it will come to you or it won't. You can't rush it, Master Gordian!"

"I just need a little more time!" Gordian said desperately.

"Please continue," Ghra'zhenn told him patiently. "There is no rush. We have plenty of time!"

Gordi continued to try for over a half hour. His head was pounding, and he was no closer to doing anything. Still, Ghra'zhenn sat and watched patiently. Gordian squeezed the gem harder. It was making an indentation in his hand, and his head felt like it would split. He was beginning to see spots in front of his eyes despite the fact that they were closed. Ghra'zhenn let Gordian go on for over an hour before he asked him to take a break. Gordi was disheartened with his lack of any sign of magiq.

"Do not let this disappoint you, young master! Remember that your friend did not get it on her first attempt either. Now look at her. She is one of the most powerful magiq users in the shortest time that I have ever seen in over seven hundred years. Now, the fact that your brother has shown the aptitude to produce magiq also gives me reason to believe that you, too, might just be able to as well. So don't give up hope just yet! We will have another session after you have eaten in two hours. Please meet me back here then."

Gordian was disappointed, but after hearing Ghra'zhenn speak to him, he felt a bit better. He was going to go and grab a handful of berries and then come back to practice. He didn't care what it took, no matter how hard he had to work at it. Today he would perform some type of magiq, even if it was a tiny wisp of smoke. On his way out, he ran into Tÿr and Varanus.

"How'd it go?" Tÿr asked cheerily.

"It didn't," Gordi responded, but after his talk with Ghra'zhenn, he wasn't as upset.

"I'm sorry. Just don't give up. It took me a while too. I was beginning to get frustrated, and then it happened! Magiq can be a funny thing. Keep at it!"

"Oh, I plan on it. I'm not going to stop until something happens. I don't care how long it takes. I'm stubborn like that," he replied.

"That is very true." Tÿr chuckled. "Are you coming to eat something? You should keep your strength up!"

"Uh, I was going to get a few berries. I'm not sure how much more I could eat. After last night, my stomach isn't too pleased with me."

Tÿr nodded, knowing exactly what he meant. She, too, had fallen prey to the dragon fruit wine before. "Well, follow me. I'll get you some berries. We have plenty left over. They will help your stomach once you get a few in you."

Tÿr led Gordian off to get a small bowl of fruit, and the two sat and talked for a bit while he ate. She tried to explain how she felt when she used the magiq so he might know what to look for when he was trying again later. When he was done, Tÿr gave him a hug and a kiss on the cheek for good luck.

"Now, go and show us how it's done!" she told him as he walked off to the cave.

He felt better prepared this time. At least he hoped he was. Ghra'zhenn was waiting near the table when Gordi walked in, ready for the boy to attempt the magiq once more.

"If it is okay with you, young master, I have invited two of my offspring to watch you. I would like them to see and understand what it takes to begin magiqal learning."

"Your offspring? You have children?" Gordian had only seen Ghra'zhenn as a leader of the wyvern dynasty and had never thought that he could be a father.

"I do have progeny, young master. I have several hundred offspring. Being over seven hundred years old gives me many years to amass such a large family. Many have moved on to different places on the planet. Sadly, many have passed into shadow. Still, many remain here on the mountain with me and my partner, and these two—which I have invited today—are very young and wish to pursue similar paths as you wish, I believe. Being paragon, it is part of my duty to help train my subjects in those arts. So I've asked them here today, and if you agree to allow them to observe, I think it will help them see that it doesn't just happen. That they will actually have to work for it."

"But doesn't a wyvern already know magiq?" Gordian questioned the paragon.

Ghra'zhenn chuckled. "I wish that were so. It is true that we do learn magiq easier than other creatures, humans for example, but we have to work for it as well. We are not born with the innate ability for magiq, my friend."

"Other creatures? There are others that can use magiq too? More than wyverns and humans? Like what?"

"Dragons can use magiq. They have very powerful magiq that rivals any magiq user to include myself. There are others that we can discuss at a later date when you begin your training."

"You mean if," Gordian corrected the paragon.

"I spoke correctly. I will be training you whether or not you can perform any magiq at this time because I see potential in both you and your brother. Something that I do not wish to waste. I fear that if I do not train you in the proper use, no matter how much or little you can perform, someone else will try to envelope you into their web, and you do not need that kind of darkness in your lives."

Gordian didn't know what the paragon was referring to, but he wasn't bothered by it at the moment. It didn't matter if he was able to do anything today; he would be taking magiq courses with a very powerful being. His heart soared at the thought. He couldn't wait to tell the others.

"Thank you so much, Ghra'zhenn, I mean Master...I mean, what do I call you now?"

The paragon gave a toothy grin and said in his usual raspy voice, "You may address me as Master or by my name or as Paragon. All three are proper and suitable. My other students will probably just address me as great-grandfather."

Gordian's face broke into the biggest smile he had ever remembered having. He would have never had this chance back in Vennex. This made his thoughts drift back to his mother, and he hoped she was okay. He and Danior had convinced her to go and stay with her cousin in a village several miles away just to be safe. They would send for her when this insanity was over. There was some scraping from the cavern entrance, and Gordi turned to see two small wyverns coming in toward them. Both were very light blue in color and about ten feet long. Their undersides were pale-cream-colored, and their wings were a translucent-amber hue. Gordian was impressed at how beautiful they were.

"Gordian, I would like to introduce you to two of my offspring. Their father is one of my great, great-grandchildren. Their names are Trækka Paa and Srätir qä."

Trækka Paa raised himself up to his full height and spread his small but magnificent wings. His voice was almost melodic. "I am very pleased to meet you!"

Gordian offered his hand, and the wyvern took it with his wing hand. The wyvern's sister dipped her head in respect.

"I'm pleased to meet you both!" Gordi told them. "Thank you for coming to watch me do my tests."

The wyverns expressed their delight and went to stand near the paragon. Gordian moved back to the table again and took the same piece of crystal he had used that morning.

"At your pleasure, Master Gordian."

Gordian held the piece of citrine tight in his hand. He was aware of the audience but tried not to let it bother him. He remembered what Tÿr and the paragon had said, but he really wished that he had spoken to his brother. He wished he had asked what he had felt, the feelings in his head and body, but now was too late. He concentrated on the crystal, imagining he was inside. He tried to figure out a way for him to light it from where he was inside the multisided structure. In his mind, he could see the light reflecting back and forth from the glass-clear surfaces, and all he wanted to do was brighten the glow. Gordian couldn't decide if the command should come from his head or from his chest and heart. It was as if there was a wall that blocked the ability to allow him to do it. As he began, his head began to ache—not just a nagging pain but a sharp, stabbing headache. He put one hand to his temple as he concentrated on the crystal in his hand. Gordian's head began to throb. The pain was beginning to get unbearable. Again, there were little objects floating in front of his eyes. He must have been moaning because Ghra'zhenn stopped him for a moment.

"Are you all right, Master Gordian?"

"Huh, what's wrong? What do you mean?" He snapped out of his trance.

"You are moaning. Are you all right? Is everything okay with you?"

"It's my head. It feels like it is going to split open."

"Do you need a break?" the paragon asked.

"No, I just began. I'll be fine. I need to do this!"

"Just don't overdo it!" Ghra'zhenn told him.

Gordian closed his eyes again. He began back inside the crystal. In his mind, he reached out and touched the smooth walls. They were cool to touch. He felt that in order to light the crystal, he should heat it, so he ordered the crystal to increase its temperature. Immediately the sides of the crystal began to heat. As the heat rose, his headache increased. Gordian brought his empty hand back up to his temple and began to rub it where the pain was the worst. The pressure had increased tenfold, but in his hand, he noticed that the crystal too was warm, almost too hot to hold. Ignoring the headache, Gordian was sure he was on the right track. He ordered the crystal to cool back down. In his hand, he felt the citrine turn cold. A shock of excitement ran through him despite the pain in his head. He was doing it, but he couldn't stop now. In his mind, he put both hands on the glassy walls of the yellow citrine crystal. As bad as it hurt him, he commanded the walls to produce light around him. Searing light shot around him, and at the same time, his head felt like someone had hit him with a heavy sword. It was the worse pain he had ever experienced. It brought him to his knees, and he almost dropped the citrine.

Ghra'zhenn rushed forward to catch him before he fell. "Gordian!"

Gordian's eyes snapped open despite the excruciating pain coming from behind them. He looked surprised to see that he was kneeling on the floor, with the paragon standing over him. He was even more surprised to see the crystal in his hand blazing brightly. He held his hand out to show the wyverns.

"I did it," he croaked.

Just talking made his head ache more. Ghra'zhenn took the boy by the shoulders and attempted to lift him back to his feet, but the pain was too great. Gordi just sat where he was. The pain burned as bright as the crystal. It was then that something else caught his eye. The table seemed to be glowing as well. Even though the pain was great, the curiosity got the better of him, and he let the paragon assist him to his feet. He had to see what was going on. Upon rising, he saw that every crystal on the table was also glowing, causing the incandescent shimmer that he had seen from the floor.

"You have done incredibly well, young master. You may extinguish the light."

Gordian dreaded having to perform more magiq at this time. He felt like he was going to be sick from the pain. Despite this, he did as he was instructed and doused the glow. Instantly the crushing ache in his head went away. The color returned to his cheeks, and he breathed a sigh of relief.

"Great gaunts! What just happened?"

"I believe you may tell your friends that you have just performed your first bit of magiq."

Gordian couldn't believe it. "Truly?" he asked, flabbergasted. "I just did magiq?"

"You definitely did, and it was more than just a little bit. You lit the entire table!"

"What does that mean?" Gordian asked.

"I am not sure. I can only speculate right now. Can you describe these pains you were experiencing?"

Gordian told the wyvern how the pain grew worse each time he got closer to actually performing the magiq; how when he was able to finally light the crystal, he felt as if he might seriously die. The pain was actually that intense.

"I believe what you are experiencing is quite rare. I also believe that this may happen every time you attempt to perform any type of magiq. There are some people who are at odds with themselves, and when they attempt any type of magiq, their own bodies rebel and cause a situation similar to what you experienced just now."

"So are you saying that my body doesn't want me to do magiq?"

"I'm saying that it could take a while before your body becomes accustomed to you during the use of magiq. Some people never adjust. You may always experience discomfort each time you try to conjure. It will all depend on how you adapt to the magiq over time."

Gordian was torn. If continued his magiqal studies, he could be facing some horrific pain, but if he gave up, he would be giving up on a dream. Now that he had a taste of it, he wanted more. He could never go back to the village knowing what was possible. The two young wyverns next to Ghra'zhenn had questions too.

"Grandfather, does this happen to wyverns as well?" Trækka Paa asked with concern in his voice.

"I have never recorded any incident of a wyvern having a reaction like this, child, but there are always firsts. You will just have to try, and if it happens, we will go from there. I believe you have already done some magiq, and so the chance of it happening is far less," the elder wyvern replied.

The two younger wyverns came up to congratulate the boy on his success at performing not only a bit of magiq but a tableful. They were very impressed. This was the first time they had been around a human, and they wanted to practice their social skills. Ghra'zhenn beamed at them as they showed grace, interacting with Gordian. Gordian, too, enjoyed being around the young wyverns, but what he wanted more than anything was to try his magiq again. Whether or not Ghra'zhenn would agree was another thing altogether.

"Ghra'zhenn, can I try again? I'd really like to have another go!"

"Are you sure you are up for it, Master Gordi?"

"No, I'm not really, but I figured that I better try again while I remember how I did it the first time."

"This may be going against my better judgment, but if you are sure that you wish to try again, I shall allow it."

From the door of the cave, two more voices came through, followed by their owners, Tÿr and Danior. "Has he already gone? We've come for moral support."

"Actually, he has already gone, and wishes to attempt another try," Ghra'zhenn told the pair walking up to observe.

"I did it, Dani! I did it!" Gordian shouted.

"Really? Well done, you! You can show us. We came to watch if we won't bother you."

"No, I'll be just fine."

The boys beamed. Without preamble, Gordian closed his eyes and held the citrine close to his chest. In his mind, he went over everything he had done the time before. This time, he was able to skip a few steps because he knew exactly what and where he needed to be mentally and physically. As soon as he asked the crystal to light, his headache was back with a vengeance. Again, he dropped to the floor, but this time he didn't quite fall. He knelt, with one hand on the stone and the other rubbing his forehead. With a death grip on the crystal, he commanded it to light. He opened his eyes the second he did. The yellow crystal in his hand sprung to life, beaming as brightly as the sun. The table lit the crystals as well. The dim cavern was bathed in the warm glow of crystal light. Gordian could only tolerate the pain for a couple of minutes. He didn't say anything nor did he move. He just looked around in awe of the power he had used. He knew would be able to go rest in a moment once he relinquished the power over the stones. The look on his friend Tÿr's face was sheer amazement. She was pointing at the table. Gordian turned slowly to look. His head ached so badly; anything faster, and he was afraid he would pass out. The wooden wands on the table were smoking as well. Had this happened before?

Immediately he doused the light. It went away, along with the crippling pain in his head.

"Did I do that too?"

Tÿr nodded excitedly. "Yes. I'm surprised that they didn't catch fire!"

The smoke continued for a minute after Gordi had shut the crystal down. He was amazed. How had he done that? He would need to be more careful. If not, he might set anything close on fire!

"Again, I congratulate you, Master Gordian. You definitely have shown the ability to conjure. I expect great things from you as well. From all of you." Ghra'zhenn gestured to all of them gathered in the cave.

Chapter 21

Xyrfed Mai sat at the bar of a run-down, grimy pub off the main street in Vennex. At first, he didn't even think it had a name; there was no sign above the entrance, but as he pulled on the door to go in, he saw a sign on the ground laying in some bushes. The Hooded Boar. It had a picture of a wild boar in an executioner's black hood over a large, bloody axe. Xyrfed was sure that this was the type of establishment he could buy the information that he needed. He was here to figure out a way to get close to the magistrate. Someone had put up a lot of cash to have him removed from his position. Xyrfed neither knew nor cared who the person was. He was here to find a way to remove this person without causing a huge panic. There was to be a silent execution without going near the home or the family of the man in question.

Xyrfed was here in this run-down shithole to find a way to do that without attracting any undue attention. Of course, once he got his information, the informant would have to be removed from the equation as well. Kaistam-Laq never wanted anything pointing back to Murtair Amagii, even if they claimed responsibility. No loose ends. So Xyrfed sat at the bar, drinking ale from a dirty glass and watching the door to see which unsavory patron would be his lucky victim.

Despite sitting in the middle of the bar, Xyrfed Mai sat with the hood of his traveling cloak pulled up over his head to keep his unique features hidden. He came from a place called the *Open Hand Archipelago* on Peyda Noirin, a group of islands with the resemblance of an open hand. He was part of a notorious family feared by most on the planets, the Imbröttiös family. He was careful to keep his hood as high around his features as possible.

Imbröttiös family members had unique features that were immediately recognizable. Firstly, they had no earlobes. Years of inbreeding had seen to that and had also given them a wispy layer of hair that grew most everywhere on their bodies—from the face to the bottom of their feet. Local people might recognize him personally as a drifter, but if word got out that an Imbröttiös family member was poking around this village, panic would definitely spread, and his job would immediately become twice as difficult. And he needed this job to be simple and easy as possible.

The barkeeper was an older lady who was in no fear of recognizing Xyrfed. Every time she wiped a counter or a bar glass, she reached under her skirt and pulled out a flask from which she took a pull. It fascinated the assassin that this short lady didn't fall over. He had seen her refill the flask at least two times. No wonder she was such a cheery old lass. About this time, three grungy-looking men walked in the pub and walked to a table in the back of the pub. Xyrfed kept an eye on the men from under his hood. They obviously had some shady dealings and looked like they could use a drink. He got up from his stool and walked back to the table. The men were watching him suspiciously as he came to join them.

"Would you mind if I bought you gentlemen a drink?"

This was not what the three men had been expecting, and they looked around at each other before agreeing. "Sure, stranger. Three ales."

Xyrfed went back to the little lady barkeep and ordered two ales each for the men at the table and a cane rum for himself. He went back to join the men while they waited for their drinks to arrive.

"You're new to this town, stranger. What brings you to Vennex?"

"I'm here to put an end to the magistrate's rule." Xyrfed looked from one face to the next. None of them seemed to care nor did they seem surprised.

"Good," one of the men said. "Worst magistrate we've ever had. Doesn't care about this town at all. He likes his position and the money that goes with it."

The two other men nodded in agreement. Another man held out his hand, but Xyrfed didn't take it. Eventually the man let it drop back to the table awkwardly.

"My name is Jellis Ÿlk. How can we help you?"

Xyrfed began to explain that apparently someone needed to remove to present magistrate from power, and he needed a way to get close to the man to do this. He asked Jellis if had any ideas. The three men all began to talk as the barkeep walked up with their ale on a tray.

"Is this all you need for now?" she asked.

"This will do for the moment," Xyrfed answered her. "If we need anything else, one of us will come up and get it," Xyrfed said the last part a bit more churlish than he had meant to, but she had been a bit drunk. He imagined that she would have stayed and tried to worm her way into the conversation, and she definitely was not invited.

The barkeep didn't notice. She took her tray and left.

Jellis began again, "I have no way to get to the magistrate, or the problem might not be as bad as it is now. There are people going hungry and others without work while he sits in his mansion and gets fatter and richer and—"

"His wealth is no concern of mine nor is his girth. I have been tasked to remove him from his position permanently. I'm not concerned with the whys nor the wherefores. I'm an end-result kind of guy, and I need to get up close and personal with him. Do you have any suggestions?"

Jerris blanched at the cold words of the stranger but thought quickly. "Mÿlo here has a brother in the magistrate's militia. He may be able to get you in close. I must warn you though that someone has already tried and failed to poison the bastard."

"How do you mean, failed?" Xyrfed asked.

"There is a rumor that he was being poisoned by someone close to him, and he was taken to the new healer. His niece. She completely healed him, which had to be a kick in the seat of his pants."

"Why is that?" Xyrfed pressed.

"He openly opposed the placement of her as healer. He had tried to get his son the position, but it was found out that he was cheating, and he lost the spot. The magistrate's niece got the position instead, and he was furious. Then after making such a huge fuss about it, he had to swallow his obnoxiously huge pride and go ask her to heal him. Nobody knows what happened in the healer's shop, but when the magistrate came out, all of the poisons and toxins had left his body. It's thought that maybe his wife had tried to do it. She's just as afraid to lose the power as her stuffed-shirt husband."

"Is that so?" Xyrfed inquired.

"Oh, sure," one of the other men piped in. "I think she's the one with the real power anyway. He's just a puppet, and she's pulling the strings!"

"And you are?" Xyrfed asked, turning to the man.

"Everyone just calls me Potts," he said.

"Okay, Potts. You wouldn't happen to know how to get at the magistrate, would you?"

Potts shook his head. "Your best bet is with Mÿlo here. His brother is usually on the detail that protects that toad magistrate and his family. If anyone could get you near to them, it would be him."

Xyrfed thought for a moment.

"You were saying something about a healer that helped this magistrate heal. How is that possible if he was so ill? Who is this healer, his niece, you said?"

"Yes, a young girl called Tÿr'Ynyn. I believe it's his niece. I don't know how she did it, but I do know he was fine when he left the healer's shop."

"You enjoy telling a story, my friend. I trust you will show discretion when remembering our conversation. If I have to look you up because I hear stories of our talk this evening, you won't be pleased to see me again."

None of the three men said anything, but there was a silent understanding that passed between all four men. Xyrfed Mai was excited to relay the message back to his master. As soon as he was back in his room, he would contact Kaistam-Laq and let him know of the situation in Vennex. Perhaps this healer girl was who they were looking for all along.

He bought the three men at the table one round of drinks, with a shot of rum this time. He figured that they might as well enjoy their last night on the planet. He bid them farewell and went to sit back at the bar. He would wait for them to leave before tying up these three loose ends. If they were good and drunk, they would put up less of a fight, and he didn't want a huge, noisy fight because he still had business in Vennex.

It was when the three men began to stir and appear to be getting ready to leave that another person walked into the pub. This person had a cloak pulled down over themselves and did not wish to be recognized either. The cloak was edged in fur, making Mai think that it could be a female traveler; but they were extremely tall, so it was very difficult to say for sure. Despite the fact that there were several open barstools at the bar, the stranger took a seat next to Xyrfed Mai. The assassin felt uncomfortable being so close to a stranger. He enjoyed his space and was not comfortable with people who encroached in it. To break the awkward silence, he offered the stranger a drink.

The voice that came from beneath the lowered hood surprised him. It was cultured and very proper. "I will have what you are drinking, stranger," said the melodious, female voice. "Are you Murtair Amagii?" she asked quickly, lowering her voice so the barkeeper couldn't hear.

Xyrfed began to nod, but caught himself mid-nod and asked, "Whom do I have the pleasure of speaking to this evening?" Xyrfed asked in his best syrupy voice.

"For now, let's just keep this informal. I've heard that Murtair Amagii was sending someone to deal with the situation in the village, and I was hoping it might be you. I know everyone here, and I don't recognize you, stranger." It was a woman's voice, strong, with no fear. She was not the typical person who spoke to an Amagii like this, or even someone who she expected to be an assassin. "Are you here to take care of this issue?"

"Which issue are you talking of, good lady?"

With this question, the lady dropped her hood to reveal a stunningly beautiful woman. She was tall and thin, with an elegant neckline, wearing a string of intensely pink pearls around her neck. Xyrfed recognized the pearls as Berdæra Island pearls, the only place on the planet that could produce such colored pearls because of the island's unique red coloring. Each of the pink marble-sized pearls could have easily fetched three thousand credits or more, depending on the quality.

"As you may or may not know, I want my husband gone. My son and myself would be in a far better position without that bumbling fool in our lives," she continued.

"So I am to deduce that you are the spouse of the Vennex magistrate?"

The proud lady nodded slightly.

"What reason for you have for removing your husband?"

"Let's just say, for now, that if removed by law, I will take power as new magistrate. I will be a powerful leader and make sure that the people here are taken care of and get them the food that they have needed for so long."

There was something in her voice that Xyrfed didn't believe, but that was not his concern at the moment. His concern was how he would finish his mission and then find the new healer. Bringing the healer back to Kaistam-Laq would be rewarded well.

"I assume you can get me in close to your husband. I'll need access to do my job, and with all of his guards and all of the people around him all of the time, I have not been successful as of this moment."

"I will make sure you have access. You will be invited to a party that I am throwing on the weekend. You may walk freely into the mansion and do what you need to. If you can carry out your task," she said, moving her hand to her necklace, "you may have this as a reward. The old bastard gave it to me as a present on year ago to show his undying love to me, yet he hasn't touched me in over three years. Some love, huh?"

There was bitterness in her voice and a hatred that Xyrfed had rarely heard between two people. The assassin reached up and lowered his cowl. He heard a slight gasp from the lady sitting next to him. "You…you are an…Imbröttiös!"

The woman was prepared for many things, but this definitely was not one of them.

She took in the features of the man. His hairy face. He hadn't even shaved his face. It was covered by thin, wispy black hair. She could also see that the rumors were perfectly true; they had deformed ears with no earlobes.

Ellysse Týr decided that she needed that drink after all. "Madam Barkeep, I'll have a cane rum, please."

She went to pay, but Xyrfed put his hand over hers. He laid down the coins to cover the drink. "It's on me," he said, smiling.

If she thought the smile would help to calm her down, she was wrong. Instead, it made her cringe; and when the assassin had touched her hand, she felt his palm on the back of her hand, and it went a long way to make her skin crawl.

"Thank you," she told him, trying to sound calm.

Xyrfed noticed that the three men that he had been drinking with earlier were getting up from their table, about ready to leave. "I'm afraid I must be leaving, m'lady. I will see you this weekend. I will have to see if I can find something in the line of fancy dress so I'll fit in at your party."

"You may come as you are, Mister…"

"You may call me Mai if you would like. I have to go and prepare myself for the event on the weekend. It was a pleasure to have met you, Madam Týr."

Xyrfed pulled his hood back over his head and went out the door to wait for the three men when they left. Luckily, he was ready when the men walked out the front door. He had walked around the corner of the little pub and was crouching when he saw them leave and walk toward the woods. They were heading away from the heart of the village. Xyrfed followed into the woods. The drunken trio had begun singing pub songs loudly as they walked. The assassin assumed that there weren't too many people that lived out this far, or these men wouldn't be caterwauling so loudly.

When they got deeper into the woods, Xyrfed took off his traveling cloak and placed it on the ground to keep from messing it up. Beneath the cloak, he wore all black and had a large pouch from which he removed a large piece of lachtrys. As soon as the gemlike stone touched his hand, it morphed into a razor-sharp, dark-blue-black knife with a handle that seemed like it had been molded especially for him.

Xyrfed waited for the right moment when one of the men straggled behind. Without making a sound, the assassin moved up behind the unsuspecting man and spun him around. The man's eyes grew wide with surprise as the lachtrys knife slashed his throat. Once, and then again. Blood spray arced across the path, but the assassin was too quick to be hit. Potts raised his hands to his neck and tried to scream, but the cuts had severed his voice box and ensured that no sound would escape. Even if it had, Xyrfed Mai doubted if the other two men would have even heard him with all the racket they were making. The assassin let Potts fall where he lay and continued after the other two men, who had no idea of the demise of their friend.

Xyrfed caught up with the others quickly, and it wasn't until their friend was supposed to sing a certain line in one of their favorite songs that they even realized he was missing. They were so bombed out of their minds even their attacker had to smile. This was going to be easy. He lunged forward in a fluid movement and stuck his knife into the throat of Jerris. There was a slight gagging noise, and then the assassin ripped the knife out the side of the neck, cutting the head half off. Jerris took one step before collapsing on top of himself. Mÿlo decided that he wasn't going to go down without a fight. He could barely stand straight, but he grabbed the hunting dagger from his belt and started to circle with Xyrfed.

"Why are you doing this?" he slurred to the other. "Assassins aren't supposed to kill just for the hell of it!" There was definite fear in his voice now.

The assassin smiled as he circled with Mÿlo. He wasn't about to play this stupid game. In one fell swoop, he jumped across the invisible line and stabbed straight into Mÿlo's chest. The man gasped as the air evacuated as a long, terrible breath left his lungs through the gaping hole in his chest.

"Why? What did we ever…"

Mÿlo never finished the question. He dropped his dagger, and his hands came up to the wound in the middle of his chest over his heart. Fear was in his eyes as he couldn't feel the normal pumping of blood anymore. Xyrfed held his lachtrys blade, and as he commanded it in his mind, the blade elongated. It looked too long and narrow to do anything useful, but he swung it quickly before Mÿlo's body fell. The tiny blade lopped the head clean from the shoulders. Xyrfed kicked the body over, and the head dropped straight to the ground. The eyes were still wide with terror. The assassin had played with his quarry long enough. He went back down the long trail to collect his cloak. There was no way he wanted to be seen by anyone around the corpses. There would be awkward questions to answer, and he just wanted to go and get things for the party on the weekend and also report back to his master. He would want to know about this new healer with such incredible magiq powers, this girl called Tÿr'Ynyn.

Chapter 22

Xyrfed Mai had left town after the murders of the trio of drinkers from the pub. He had left the bodies where they fell as a warning to others. He wanted people to know that there was trouble brewing in Vennex, and it would help to keep the eyes off the magistrate's house for the time being. If he had to take out a couple more unfortunates from other pubs, he would do what had to be done to keep the eyes of the town off the magistrate. There were three more days until the party being given by the wife of the magistrate. He planned to buy some clothes befitting the event. He also wanted to scout the location and see what he was dealing with. He had the ability to blend into the background and remain unseen when he needed or wanted to, a useful bit of magiq his mentor and master had taught him many years ago.

Xyrfed was now in the forest about ten miles from Vennex, standing in his tent. He had used several different spells to camouflage it from wandering eyes should anyone happen upon it. It was getting late, and since the planets had tilted, the suns were hidden behind Peyda Kirin. Hunger began to gnaw at his stomach, and he decided to go out and hunt for his dinner. He had noticed fresh deer tracks in the area and decided that he would attempt to snag a deer for his dinner and meals for the next few days. Being from the islands originally, he had learned to hunt when he was young and also to prepare the food to eat. All the Imbröttiös knew how to prepare food from a young age. Not just the woman of the clan either. Boys were taught alongside the girls.

Xyrfed walked into the darkening forest and was able to locate fresh tracks immediately. He put a spell of absolute silence on himself so his footsteps would go unnoticed in the leaves. He walked lightly and soon located three deer. Two does and a fawn—way more meat than he would need for a couple of days in the woods. He knelt down to keep from spooking the animals, and instead of throwing a knife, which was his favored weapon, he reached out with invisible hands and took the larger doe's heart and began to squeeze. The animal cried out, warning its fawn and the other doe, causing both to sprint away. Xyrfed squeezed the heart until it stopped beating, and the animal fell over dead.

The assassin picked up the deer and walked the short distance back to his tent where he skinned the creature and cleaned it, dropping the innards onto the skin. He pulled out a piece of lachtrys and formed a blade to cut up the deer into manageable pieces. Once completed, Xyrfed sat down and began to eat from a section of the leg. Uncooked—the way all Imbröttiös ate their meat. The father, Ekaj Joonts Layne, taught them that cooked food lost the essential nutrients, and so they ate all food raw on the Open Hand Archipelago. It was a disgusting habit to non-natives. Xyrfed smiled as he chewed a large mouthful of the deer. He needed to hurry and finish his meal. Already insects were gathering on the rest of the carcass that he had left on the ground near the tent.

When Xyrfed had finished eating, he went into his tent and grabbed an herb from a pack on the floor near his sleeping roll. It was used to flavor the meat, and it also helped to keep the bugs off it. He sprinkled the meat generously with the herb and then hung it over spikes he had pounded in the ground to keep it up, away from insects and the dirt. It had been almost a day since he had relayed a message to Kaistam-Laq regarding the knowledge of the magiq user, Tÿr'Ynyn. He was still awaiting a response from the leader of the sect on how to proceed. He assumed that his master would want to be present when he captured the girl. Kaistam-Laq enjoyed questioning people that were considered unfriendly witnesses. He had a plethora of ways to make them talk.

As the evening progressed, Xyrfed changed out of the clothes he had been wearing the night before, lest there had been anyone who might have seen him at The Hooded Boar. He did away with his traveling cloak this evening and opted instead for his usual black attire: long black boots that laced up the side and velvet black pantaloons. He wore a loose black linen shirt that he kept tied all the way up to his throat. The less amount of body hair he chose to show, the better! People could still see his face and see that it was covered with the telltale, sparse layer of wispy brown hair—just like that of his mother and hers before her—an unfortunate effect of interbreeding that started centuries before he was born. When he was younger, he thought that the hair on the face of a girl was very attractive; but as he matured, it grew to be repulsive to him. He didn't mind the look on a man. Men were supposed to be hairy and masculine, but a woman with similar features to that of a male was not at all what Xyrfed found alluring anymore.

The assassin began his long trek into Vennex. He walked fairly quick and had a little magiq to assist him should he wish to use it. All the assassins in the sect Murtair Amagii could use magiq. Some could only make blades from lachtrys rocks, or maybe a bit more, but there were some that rivalled Kaistam-Laq. None of those assassins ever let it be known how much magiq they knew because then their life expectancies could be cut in half. Literally.

Xyrfed knew almost as much magiq as his mentor and leader, Kaistam-Laq, but he never let on that he knew it. Other users of magiq were quick to want to assimilate the power of the more-powerful sorcerers. They believed that the absorbed power would make them greater and that they would automatically gain the dead sorcerer's power and spells. It was ridiculous, of course, but it didn't keep some from trying it.

Xyrfed made it into Vennex in about an hour. He didn't need magiq. He enjoyed the walk. It was quiet and gave him time to think as he traveled. He decided that he would go into each pub and dispose of one person from each. This should keep the eyes off the magistrate. If people were dying in pubs, no one should suspect that the next place to be hit would be the magistrate's mansion in a few nights' time. He could not use poison or any type of toxin for the magistrate. If the healer had healed him before, there was always a chance that this girl could heal the pompous twit again no matter how fast the toxin was. No, he would use his lachtrys blade, the same way he killed the bar patrons. He liked to dirty his hands.

It was one thing to poison someone and leave. With that, you had too many variables. Would they drink it? Would it work? Would they get help? With a blade across the neck, there were no doubts. There was the quick intake of breath through the new opening in the throat and the bloody gasp, the look of pain on the face, and the two minutes of watching the person bleed out and asphyxiate on their own blood. It was a very good feeling for an assassin who liked to get his hands dirty on the job.

It was when Xyrfed was just getting ready to enter the busiest pub in Vennex, The Chained Dragon, that he felt the small, scrying mirror around his neck begin to vibrate. The pub was located on the high street, and so he backed away to shield the mirror, which glowed blue on the chain at his neck. When he was sure he was alone, between two buildings, he pulled out the mirror to look at it. In the reflection was the face of the leader of the Amagii, Kaistam-Laq.

"Have you found the girl?"

Xyrfed shook his head. "She is not in the village at the moment, but I am trying to locate her whereabouts. At the moment though, I am finishing up a contract. The high-profile case."

Laq nodded. "As soon as you are done with that contract, I wish for you to put all of your energy toward the location of the girl. I don't care what it takes. I want her, and I want her alive. No foul-ups! I will send a team to assist you. If the girl is harmed, the person who did it will pay with their life. Have I made myself clear?"

"You have! I will see to it personally!"

"Good! I will see you soon enough, Xyrfed Mai."

"You are coming out to this godforsaken part of the planet? There's really nothing here, Master. You might be better off by staying where you are!"

"Don't you worry about where I stay. I *will* be present for the questioning of this girl once she is located."

"Yes, Master." Xyrfed bowed his head as a sign of respect. He didn't fear the leader of the sect, but he did respect him. He could cast faster than anyone the assassin had ever known.

"What are your plans for Vennex, Xyrfed?" Kaistam asked.

"I plan on fulfilling our contract here in two days' time, and until then, I will be leaving false clues around the village. I began last evening by extracting the information I sent to you and then disposed of the witnesses. After that is when I found a way to get near the target. His own wife is the one who hired us. She will let me in during the party she has planned, and I will eliminate the target there and then disappear into the woods. I wasn't going to stay in the area, but if you are arriving here, I will wait for you in the woods just outside town."

"That will be best. The panic that will follow the killing of the town's magistrate will cause great alarm, and the militia will scour the town to find you. All paths leading in and out of the village will be sealed. You going into the woods as quickly as you can is the best idea, I believe. From there I will locate you, and we will seek out the girl healer who can perform this great magiq. Until then."

The image of the sorcerer disappeared from the small mirror that Xyrfed Mai was holding. He put it back under his shirt to keep it hidden in case the sorcerer should call again.

The assassin stepped back onto the high street and opened the door to The Chained Dragon. The atmosphere of this pub was completely different from the previous night's. It was crowded and filled with smoke from pipe herb. Xyrfed looked around the crowded hall and found a table with only two young men sitting and talking very loudly, a heated debate about the local government and the lack of support the people were feeling from the magistrate. Xyrfed Mai walked up and asked if he might join them at the table. They both seemed hesitant at first, until the assassin's coin purse came out.

"Perhaps I could buy us a round or two of drinks?"

The reticent behavior vanished, and soon Xyrfed was drawn into the conversation of the useless magistrate with the two young men. He didn't bother to find out their names; they would be dead in less than an hour. What the assassin needed to decide was if he was going to kill them here in the pub with everyone around, or would he lure them out into the streets and leave them there to be found later by those people traveling home after having a drink or two? In the end, he decided that it would be a bigger challenge to him and a larger thrill to do it in the pub around everyone. Of course, he would take them to a dark corner and make it as quiet as possible.

After listening to the young men argue for over an hour, and they didn't seem to say anything, Xyrfed decided it was time to start stirring the pot in Vennex some more. There were people playing a game of skill on the back wall of the pub, consisting of a target and small throwing knives. The assassin suggested that they walk back to watch the game. He told the young men that he had never seen the game before and that maybe they could explain it to him. After buying them each another tall glass of cane rum, they were putty in his hands. They would have walked into a volcano had he asked them.

There was a table in the corner where they would be able to watch, yet far enough away for people to see exactly what was getting ready to happen. He led the two young men to the table with their drinks, and before the first one could pull out his chair, Xyrfed had taken his lachtrys blade and cut through his neck. He had cut so hard the man's head had almost come off. It flopped back and was hanging on by just threads and a bit of the spine. The other young man didn't even realize what had happened until he saw his buddy drop. By then it was too late. Xyrfed plunged the knife silently deep into the boy's chest, ripping it up toward his head. Blood instantly spread over the shirt of the second young man. No one in the room paid any attention until he crashed through the table and onto the floor. Blood splashed all over the closest people to the table and walls. It was then that people took notice, and they began to look around. Xyrfed had used a bit of camouflage magiq to slip out the front door of the pub. Once he had killed the last young drunkard, he dropped the lachtrys, which transformed back into a piece of smooth rock. He wasn't worried about losing it. There were plenty more to be found. He waited by the front door until someone came in, and then Xyrfed slipped out past the couple who came in.

It took him about twenty minutes to walk back to the tent in the forest. On the way back, he passed a couple people in the forest, travelers, from the way they were dressed. He walked up to their fire where they sat eating.

"Greetings, strangers!" He hailed them. "Do you have enough to eat, friends?"

The travelers told him that they could always use food on their trips, so he told them that he would run over to his tent and fetch some fresh venison that he had gotten the night before. This gave him time to change out of his blood-splattered clothing. Xyrfed returned to the camp of the travelers with two legs of deer meat preserved with the herbs he had used. He had also brought his linen shirt, rolled up in some paper. He asked if they would mind if he burned his trash, and they obliged. It was best that he not be caught with it on the rare case that someone found him camped out in the forest. With the deaths of five people, Xyrfed was sure the militia was going to be stepping up security measures around the village. Luckily for him, he had a sure way in—the magistrate's own wife!

Chapter 23

The magiq lessons on Ÿkkynÿk Mountain were proceeding well. Gordian was still plagued by the intense headaches each time he was able to conjure even the smallest bit of magiq, but he was now able to control the power behind it. Danior was also doing phenomenally well. If Ghra'zhenn didn't have time to assist and train the boys, Tÿr helped them with the easier spells. Tÿr, too, was improving. Her control was so improved Ghra'zhenn had put her in charge of the boys' extra training with the two young wyverns.

It was on one of these days of training that Tÿr was brought aside by Varanus to let her know that her training with him and Ghra'zhenn would begin. Tÿr was both excited and a little anxious to be beginning her invisibility training. Not considering herself particularly modest, she wasn't worried about being nude in front of the wyverns—if, in fact, she would be completely invisible. She had never shown any part of herself to the brothers, though, and never intended to. Ghra'zhenn explained that she would be making the potion that she would be using. It would be made using the eyes of a wyvern, along with other rare ingredients. And she found out that it wasn't so much a potion as it was a salve to be rubbed on the body. It worked with the eyes to make the user completely unseeable to any living being for hours. Unfortunately, it only lasted a couple of hours, so Tÿr would have to collect the information she needed quickly and get away from the area. She was very excited to learn this magiq. It was extremely advanced, and she was so grateful that the wyverns felt that she was worthy and ready to begin already. She did get the feeling that the necessity of her needing to spy had something to do with it as well.

It was during an instruction session that the necessity grew more crucial. Tÿr had been working with herbs and grinding crystals she had never heard of until now. The salve had to be especially smooth and velvety, or it could cause her to be scratched when applying it. There were ingredients such as rainbow obsidian. It had to contain the entire spectrum of colors, or the potion would be useless. There were herbs that had to be prepared in a special sequence, herbs that had to be of certain ages, and many that Tÿr had never heard of. Luckily, the wyvern's storeroom was well-stocked and immense. The catalyst for the ointment was the eyes of Aaxtagara and the sap of a tree found at the top of Peyda Kirin. The tree was particularly hard to find because of its location on the desert planet. Only about one in one hundred contained any of the sap needed because rainfall was so scarce.

Varanus watched as Tÿr carefully prepared the potion. When she was finally finished, it was well into the night. She had worked straight through, and in the cave, she had no idea what time it was. She only knew now because the boys had come to see where she was and what she was doing. She was surprised to learn that they were about to turn in for the night. Varanus had fetched a large crock for her to put the ointment in.

"I'm not sure if this will work, Var. I've been stirring it for an hour like you told me, but the spoon isn't invisible."

"Ah, well, it wouldn't be." He secretly liked when she shortened his name. It was a term of endearment that he had taken to and had allowed as long as it was just the two of them alone. "You see," he continued, "the potion only works on organic, living tissue. If you feel you are up for it yet, rub a small amount on your hand. You will see how it works. The effects only last a couple of hours, which will seem like no time at all when you go in to spy in Vennex."

Tÿr was both tired and hungry, but she was anxious to see her potion in action. She opened the crock and dipped a rag she had been using into the potion. With her other hand held out, Tÿr'Ynyn rubbed a thin layer of the thick, silky, ointment-like potion on her hand. For the first few moments, she felt nothing at all, but that was short-lived. There was a sensation of squeezing, not a tight, painful squeezing but as if someone was shaking her hand. And then, before her eyes, her hand began to fade away. It was the most interesting feeling.

"Oh gaunts, Varanus!" she exclaimed.

"I understand." He smiled.

Tÿr held her hand up to look closer at her missing limb. There was no sign of it. She could look straight through it as if it were missing completely, and there was no shadow or any sign that it had ever been there just minutes before. She picked up different things at the table. How bizarre to see things float through the air with no visible means of support. She touched her other hand and got the strangest feeling when she did it.

"Have you ever done this, Var? It is the most unique feeling! I can't see it, but I still feel it!"

"I have not ever used this potion before. It is way too valuable and generally reserved for paying clients. A small jar, one tenth of the size that you made, usually costs one hundred thousand credits. By the way, it is called *ÿsynllÿkk potion* in Cmok."

"One hundred thousand credits?" Tÿr repeated with a whistle. "That's more than my uncle's house costs!"

Tÿr loved when the wyverns spoke in Cmok. It was an elegant language for such a huge creature. She was learning Cmok as quickly as one could be expected, but she just didn't have the tongue to make it sound as beautiful as Varanus and Ghra'zhenn did when they spoke.

It was while Tÿr was exploring the possibilities of the potion and talking to Varanus that a sudden shriek broke the night silence. Tÿr recognized the noise instantly. It was Sëvyq. She hadn't even thought of him in the previous days because of being so busy, but her heart skipped a beat when she heard the säqyr wyvern approach the camp. He had been in Vennex with her parents, so if he was here now, that meant something was happening back in the village.

Tÿr approached the small wyvern and saw the tube around his neck contained a note. The säqyr wyvern let her retrieve the note and then went to find the other wyverns.

"Varanus, here, the note from Vennex!"

"You may read it," he told her with confidence. "You are part of this dynasty, and your wyvern brought it to you! I hope you learn to feel a part of this dynasty."

"I, well, it's just that, well, I thought it could lead to something important that maybe you would like to know."

Varanus nodded. "It is important. It is also true that you, too, are very important. I want you to read this and decide what to about the it."

Tÿr pulled the letter open and began to read the scrawled hand of her father.

> *To Tÿr, Varanus, and Ghra'zhenn*
>
> *Trouble here in Vennex. There have been five murders here in just two days. All people we knew, and they were killed in town. We will be leaving before anyone can put two and two together and bring us in. You stay where you are, and we'll give you information on Vennex as we get it. Please stay safe. I included something for Tÿr.*
>
> *ST*

Tÿr looked at the säqyr wyvern's collar and saw a small leather pouch. It was from her father, and she could smell it immediately. More pipe herb. She smiled at the thought of him taking the time to send her this before evacuating the village. Tÿr wasn't exactly sure where her parents had gone, and it was probably better that she didn't for the time being.

"Varanus, I think we need to make a trip back to Vennex. It's time I use the potion."

Sëvyq, the säqyr wyvern, sat patiently, as if waiting for a response to the message. Tÿr went quickly to her belongings and got out a feathered pen and parchment to write a quick message to her parents. She told them that she would be returning in a day or two to do a bit of spying. She also told them to remain where they were and to never mention where they were lest the message become intercepted. Then she thanked them for the pipe weed and sent the little wyvern on his way.

"I believe we should now go and speak with the paragon," Varanus told her. "He is going to need to hear this!"

Tÿr nodded her agreement, and the two left the cavern to locate Ghra'zhenn. The wyvern paragon was out on the mountainside, speaking to several of his offspring, including the two young ones who were now taking the magiq courses with Dani and Gordian. He was speaking in Cmok as they arrived. Tÿr tried to translate what he was saying, but he was speaking too quickly for her understand.

"*Zhÿ dÿynykkÿ rrÿjak gÿtty!*" Ghra'zhenn was saying to the two young wyverns as Tÿr walked up. "Rrÿjak gÿtty!"

Tÿr caught the last bit and thought it meant very good or very well. "Master Ghra'zhenn, I'm sorry for the need to interrupt, but I believe you will want to know this!" Tÿr told the paragon.

Ghra'zhenn stopped talking for a few moments to see what Tÿr needed. She filled him in on the note from the säqyr wyvern. He told the young wyverns that he had to go and that he would return in a while. Ghra'zhenn had pressing matters to attend to at the moment.

Tÿr and Ghra'zhenn left to go back to join Varanus at the cavern. The boys had woken up to see what was happening as well. Varanus and Ghra'zhenn began to discuss the situation in Vennex, and both were of the opinion that Tÿr should get back as soon as possible. If Varanus had begun right then, even with a back breeze, it would take two days. Ghra'zhenn, on the other hand, had an idea that would be an insane risk, but it would pay off well. They would arrive in less than an hour.

"I will need to go and prepare," he told the assembled people. "Tÿr'Ynyn, could you please come with me?" Ghra'zhenn asked the apprentice.

Tÿr was now filled with curiosity. Never had the paragon asked her to follow him into the depths of his cave before.

Ghra'zhenn led the way far deeper into the caves than Tÿr had ever been before. They took twisting and turning tunnels that led deeper into the mountain. Eventually Tÿr and the paragon came to a large cavern. It was big enough for Ghra'zhenn to rear up on his hind legs to stand without hitting his head or wings. It was almost pitch dark in this place, but Tÿr had already lit her staff head for light. Even with the staff, which burned with the fury of a sun, it appeared that the cavern was trying to dampen the light.

"Ghra'zhenn, why doesn't my staff burn brighter? It should be almost green in here," she explained to Ghra'zhenn.

"It is the magiq. I have initiated a heavy amount of protective magiq around this area of the tunnels in the cavern. There is an area that, until now, no living soul has ever seen. I am going to show you because we are going to need to travel to Vennex quickly, and the only way I can think to do this is by employing magiq." Ghra'zhenn went to the back of the empty cavern, obviously looking for something. "Could you bring your staff over here please. I know it's back here. I just need a bit of light to help me find it."

"What are we looking for?" Tÿr asked. She walked back to join the paragon, light spreading in a small circle around her.

"Ah, here we are," the paragon said.

He pointed to an indentation in the wall. Above it was the wyvern rune that Tÿr had learned recently. Had it not been pointed out to her, she probably wouldn't have even noticed it. Ghra'zhenn put his hand into the indentation. It fit perfectly, and when it was in, the rune above it began to glow. Tÿr wasn't sure what she expected to happen next, but it wasn't this. The back of the cavern melted away to reveal a large room behind the rock. Inside the room were crystals on shelves. The crystals were the size of Tÿr's legs, huge and glowing: quartz, amethyst, citrine, and one Tÿr wasn't familiar with. Instead of a single huge crystal, they were huge clusters of water-clear crystals the size of dinner platters and standing over a foot high.

"What is this place, Ghra'zhenn?"

"This is my private sanctuary. It is where I gather my strength and power for long flights, or battles, or for what we are about to do." He looked very serious now, more so than Tÿr had ever seen him in the past.

"What we are going to be doing in here is absorbing as much energy from the stones as we can. You will join me in the center of the room, and then I will talk you through the process. We will be traveling in a somewhat-risky fashion. By using the energy stored in these crystals, we will have a great deal of protection when we move through the continuum to Vennex."

"Continuum?" Tÿr asked. "What exactly is that?"

"It is an array of doorways that I can open to make traveling shorter. It takes incredible energy and is very rough to travel through. I am bringing you here into my sanctuary to help prepare for the flight. You will need to absorb as much energy from these crystals as you can, and when I open the portal, you will protect yourself with your wyvern hide just as I will. The actual travel time through the doorway will last only seconds, but it is dangerous, and you will need to be protected. By using your intercalated skin, you will put up a barrier around yourself and will come out the other side unscathed!"

"So how do I begin to absorb the energy from these crystals?" she asked the paragon.

"It may work differently for different beings, but I imagine myself as an empty vessel. I simply pull the energy into myself. At first, I began slowly, but now it only takes a few seconds. You will just have to find what works for you."

"How will I know if it works?" she questioned.

"Once it happens," Ghra'zhenn began, "there will be no doubts. You will feel it immediately. You will not have to ask. It is a very unique feeling that you won't forget. Now, let's do this so we can get to Yelliton."

"Aren't we going to Vennex? There aren't any problems in Yelliton!"

"I don't want to give these people any warning that you are coming," Ghra'zhenn told her. "Surprise will be on our side for the moment."

Tÿr nodded her agreement and immediately began to fill her body with energy as instructed. She activated the intercalation and then, in her mind, imagined herself a pitcher of water. She began by going to each large crystal and pouring it into herself. At first, she didn't feel anything, but then she remembered Ghra'zhenn's words about her needing to absorb. Instead of pouring the next crystal into herself, she held it aloft. With both hands on the large, glassy stone, she pulled. There was an immediate difference. She felt energy flow through her hands and down her arms. It was a vibrant, tingling sensation, and Ghra'zhenn was correct, she was not going to forget this. She continued to fill herself, faster and faster, until she felt ready to burst. Then it stopped.

"What happened?" She turned to the paragon. "What's going on, Ghra'zhenn?"

"I stopped you. You were in danger of overloading yourself. It goes very quickly, and you could have had issues had you not unplugged."

Normally, Tÿr would have bugged the paragon for an explanation, but she trusted him and knew that he was busy right now, preparing himself to leave. Ghra'zhenn asked her to go and prepare a pack of clothes. She would be gone for just a day or two. That was the plan anyhow. He also said that he would try to find information about her parents. He knew this would help to set her mind at ease. She hadn't said anything, but Ghra'zhenn knew she was worried about them.

Tÿr left the cavern and was worried that she might have trouble finding her way back to the entrance, but a second sense had taken over and led her straight out. The brothers were awake and wanted to know what was happening. Tÿr gave them a quick overview and asked them to keep an eye on Rævii. She couldn't make this trip, not without protection. The boys were glad to help out. They wanted to go and help but understood why they couldn't make this trip. Gordian helped her throw things into her pack. She wanted to be ready when Ghra'zhenn came out. She was nervous about the new mode of transportation. Ghra'zhenn hadn't really told her too much about it, other than it allowed them to travel quickly through dimensions that would normally take them days.

The paragon came out from the tunnel in a matter of minutes. Tÿr had to do a second glance. He was actual glowing from the energy he had taken in. His head and neck had an eerie blue haze that clung to him.

"Tÿr'Ynyn, if you are ready, I wish you to do one more thing. I need you to assist me in getting my harness on. You will need it for your belongings and also to hold on to when we dive."

"Dive?"

"Correct. What we are going to do to open the portal to take us to the village of Yelliton is, I will climb quite high, and then I will dive and expel most of my energy to open the portal that will transport us in an instant to the village. You will need to be strapped on and tethered to the harness. The sensation of the dive is quite extraordinary and unparalleled. I need you strapped in place should you lose consciousness or accidentally let go."

"Agreed," Tÿr said and went to locate the harness hanging on the far wall.

She had never really looked at it before. It was quite beautiful. The leatherwork was flawless and depicted vines of flowers curling along the lengths of it. It had taken the artist many hours to make such a gorgeous piece. All the metalwork was made of *dyr* a metal indigenous to the Peyda planets. It was extremely strong and didn't tarnish. A perfect choice for weapons too, as it never lost its edge. The only downfall to it was that even though it could be somewhat light, it was extremely dense and tricky to form. It took master-craftsmen hours to work with dyr.

Tÿr and Ghra'zhenn managed to get the harness on fairly fast, and she bid farewell to her friends, old and new. Many of the wyverns had turned out at the cave to see what was happening. They knew something big was going on as Ghra'zhenn was full of energy, and he didn't just do that every day. Ghra'zhenn did end up giving a short speech about the happenings in Vennex and what they were going to attempt.

The wyverns were all behind this course of action and wanted to join them, but the paragon told them to stay there and prepare themselves. He didn't know what was happening, but he asked them to stay at the mountain and to remain vigilant. He didn't know what would happen once, or even if they were found out, but he felt that a war could be a possibility.

"Remain vigilant always. I will return in a few days' time to discuss further actions. Remain alert and guard our home against every foe. I do not believe that the enemy knows of our involvement yet, but that will soon change. Brothers and sisters! We must prepare for war, if that is what the Maker intends for us! I will return!"

With that, Tÿr stepped into a makeshift stirrup and mounted the wyvern's back as comfortably as she could. With two great flaps of his enormous wings, Ghra'zhenn had them aloft and moving almost straight up into the air above the mountain. Tÿr held on loosely for the time being. Ghra'zhenn's wings were much larger than Varanus's, so he didn't have to beat as often. Each flap raised them twenty feet or more into the air.

As Tÿr looked off to the side, her stomach lurched to see how high they were already. It was then that the wyvern began to move them away from Ÿkkynnÿk Mountain and out over the freshwater sea. With each flap forward, they climbed higher. Ghra'zhenn was beginning to pick up speed as he flew. The air up this high was cool. Tÿr's hands were beginning to hurt from the cold and from grasping the harness so tightly. Eventually Ghra'zhenn decided that they were high enough.

He turned his long neck to talk to Tÿr. "I am about to dive. When I do, I will expel my energy, and at the bottom of the dive, the portal will open."

Tÿr could feel her jaw tighten. And then the wyvern dove, not a gentle, sloping dive like Varanus did when landing but practically straight down. He roared as he did, and Tÿr wanted to plug her ears; the sound was deafening. Tÿr's stomach was in her throat, and still they dove. She could see the ground closing in. As they neared, Ghra'zhenn roared again; and this time, his neck and mouth exploded in an electrical storm, sending blue bolts of lightning toward the ground below them. The air crackled with the static electricity, raising Tÿr's hair on her head and the backs of her arms. She watched as the lightning swirled above the ground in a furious ball of energy.

They grew closer and closer, and she couldn't take her eyes from the seething mass of energy. As they dropped down, something was happening to the central part of the ball. A black circle was opening.

It grew and grew as they closed in. It was the doorway Ghra'zhenn had talked about—dark and ringed in lightning.

The crackling of the energy became deafening as they closed in on the door. Týr didn't know when she was supposed to use her energy—he hadn't said—so she called upon it then. Her arms and back glowed with the same ferocity, forming a bubble of protective dynamism that kept Ghra'zhenn's spraying energy off her as she lay flat against his neck. She was in awe of the power she was able to produce just by charging in the sanctuary of crystals.

From below, many of the wyverns watched as the lightning went streaking down at the ground. A tiny speck at its head shot toward a mass of roiling, electrical energy. Just before the two connected, the tiny speck shot forth another ball of energy, which slammed into the larger one, creating a huge explosion. A black void opened into the sky and swallowed everything in a matter of two seconds' time and then closed again. The twilight sky was silent once again. Týr remembered diving at the portal and a huge explosion, and then suddenly they were on the ground. There were a couple of seconds—or were they minutes?—she didn't know. She did know they were on the blue ground, standing outside the village of Yelliton. It took her every bit of self-control to keep from getting sick.

"Oh my." She looked at Ghra'zhenn. "I think my stomach is still back over the mountain."

"It will catch you up in a minute or two. It is a strange sensation, is it not?

"Very!"

"We have two choices right now," Ghra'zhenn told the apprentice. "You can go into the village and procure a room for yourself, and I can make do with sleeping in the forest. Or we could go to the mountainside cavern and sleep there. We would be in a central place, and it would allow us to go into Yelliton or Vennex easily. What do you wish to do?" he asked the girl.

"I think we would both be more comfortable if we were to go to our mountain home. It would be easier to kip down there. As long as no one knows about it, we will be fine there, don't you agree?"

"I do, and flying will be about the same distance from either place."

"I just figured that you would be able to sleep better on the mountain than in the woods. We can defend the mountain better if the need should ever arise."

"You think like a leader, Tÿr'Ynyn. Your skills are coming together nicely. I hope your relatives understand how much you have grown in such an abbreviated time. It has never been recorded in our histories that a healer has learned our customs and ways and healing as quickly as you."

Tÿr felt a little embarrassed by all the praise that the paragon had just given her. She hadn't really been used to getting such high accolades. Sure, she had done well, coming up in her regular classes as a young girl, but now things just seemed to make sense to her. It made her feel proud, but she didn't want it all to go to her head.

"Zhä kllywwÿzh zhÿ ghræzhyy nhav zhraaxxtyy," Tÿr said slowly, trying to pronounce every syllable correctly.

"You please me greatly with your hard work and your learning. You are working so hard to even pick up our language. Before long, you won't even have an accent. Your knowledge is growing so quickly, and I am very proud of you, Tÿr'Ynyn. Everyone that knows you should be proud. You have done your family and your species very proud. I have never once had a regret about asking you to join our dynasty. In time, the others won't even realize that you aren't a natural-born wyvern."

There was a look in Ghra'zhenn's eye that Tÿr didn't see often from others. Her parents, of course, were proud of her, but the pride that the paragon was showing now might have surpassed even that.

"All right, Master, let's get home and get some sleep. I know you must be exhausted after our flight."

Ghra'zhenn chuckled at this but gave no sign of his condition. He told her to climb aboard, and then they were off to the mountaintop cave. Tÿr, too, was exhausted, but if Ghra'zhenn didn't let on that he was tired, neither would she. The pair headed back and were at the mountain in about forty-five minutes. Despite her weariness, Tÿr still needed to build a fire in the warming stove to keep the paragon comfortable during the night; plus, she picked a couple of pears to eat while she worked. It took another hour to make the fire and unpack. She didn't even bother to put on a nightshirt. Tÿr smoked a bowl of pipe herb that her father had sent her and then went to bed in the clothes she was wearing. Ghra'zhenn was asleep before she was. And the two remained that way until early afternoon the following day.

Chapter 24

Kaistam-Laq was preparing for his long trip to the village of Vennex. There he would be joining his assassin, Xyrfed Mai, who was doing his best to cause chaos in the town. The sect had taken on a contract to eliminate the magistrate from the village of Vennex; and although it probably could have been done several times over, Xyrfed Mai had a particularly unique style when he killed, and he truly liked to challenge the authorities and the lawmen of a village to find him when he finally did commit the heinous act. Kaistam had to make sure that he had enough of his magiqal ingredients and tools in case he should need them on his way or once he arrived.

Xyrfed could handle himself, but Kaistam had learned his lesson long ago: never travel unprepared. Of course, he had his staff, which went everywhere with him. He also carried certain potions with him in case he or his assassin should become wounded. There had been too many close calls in the past that had come close to claiming his life, and he was not ready to die like that yet. He had several people, assassins, to help him load his carriage. He would be traveling with one other assassin for protection and the company. The trip would take nearly a week, and sitting in a carriage by himself for that long would drive him crazy.

He had chosen Owonnyn to travel with him. She was his most-trusted advisor and his best-trained assassin. Trained by Xyrfed Mai himself. She was fast and intimidating when people saw her. She was well over six feet tall and moved with such grace. Kaistam had to admit that he enjoyed watching her work when matters became necessary. She was skillful with the staff boline—better than anyone he had ever seen before—and she could mold lachtrys fast and use the weapons with surgical skill. She was busy loading the packs and trunks Kaistam couldn't live without on his trip, not to mention the huge marquee that he needed for sleeping in.

The first time Owonnyn saw the tent, she just rolled her eyes. She knew the man would find a use for every square inch of the place and would probably leave her sleeping under a lean-to or up against a tree trunk if she was lucky. More than likely, she would be patrolling the area for the enemy while her master slept peacefully in comfort. This was how it usually was. During the day was when Owonnyn found time to sleep. She knew there were protective charms and other things guarding the convoy as they moved south toward Vennex.

Xyrfed had been out spending money on new clothing at a shop in the village: black linen pants with a black linen shirt to go with it. The tailor had seen to the fitting and promised to have it ready in time for the party that evening. *You better have it ready*, Xyrfed thought as he sat in the leather-goods shop. He was trying on a new pair of expensive black boots. The leather was soft, and the soles were incredible. There would be no blisters from this pair of boots. They cost him over three hundred credits, but the calf's skin was so soft and pliable the boots just felt like a second skin. They were light, and when he employed his tracking magiq, there would be absolute silence from them. It was a pity that he would probably be a wanted man in Vennex for a long time after the evening's events.

Most people frowned on the murder of a prominent politician, but the money was incredible, and Kaistam told him to take the job. He had already figured out how to get the lachtrys into the magistrate's mansion. He had purchased a long silk sash, and it would need a clasp to hold it in place at his shoulder. He would mold the lachtrys into the clasp, and once he was alone or nearly alone, he would remold the lachtrys into a long, thin dagger and punch the magistrate several times in the heart. He would then use the sash to descend from the upper-floor window and escape into the woods using a magic charm to blend into the scenery. When a search was underway, he would simply walk away slowly and leave the chaos behind. The magistrate's wife would be the one to answer any awkward questions that the militia might have. Xyrfed would be miles away and awaiting the arrival of his master. With the job done, he would collect the fees, and that would be that. Another assassination without a hitch.

The party was still hours away, so Xyrfed went to a pub he had not frequented yet and decided to have a meal. He was getting hungry, and he didn't feel like hunting now that he was cleaned up. If people in the town recognized his features as belonging to the Imbröttiös clan, no one said anything. The people of Vennex usually kept to themselves where strangers were concerned. On occasion, he would get the odd, questioning look, but he would simply smile and nod or tip his cap, and they wouldn't give him a second glance. Even with the threat of a murderer or murderers in town, nobody really paid him any attention. The philosophy being that if they didn't notice anyone else, they were less likely to be singled out by a stranger.

The landlady came by his table in the pub and asked what he would like. She seemed pleased that he wanted to eat. There weren't many people drinking at a time the pub should be full. Apparently, the murders had taken a toll on the businesses in the village. Xyrfed ordered a carved dinner of freshly roasted venison slices with a half of roasted squirrel. It came with assorted, boiled vegetables and pan gravy. On the side was a plate of asparagus, which had just now come into season. There was a basket with different types of fresh bread and a bowl of freshly churned goat butter. It was a meal for a dignitary, to say the least, but Xyrfed could tell that there weren't many people eating; and everyone was being treated to the same huge feast.

When he had eaten as much as he could, the landlady returned and asked if he would like some fresh berries and cream for pudding, but his pants were already cutting into his sides. He declined the offer but did take one last glass of the house ale. He would nurse the glass until the party began in an hour's time. It was then that the perfect plan got its first hiccup. Xyrfed was sitting in his chair at the table, trying to digest the huge meal he had eaten, when a semi-drunken patron at the bar got up to presumably use the facilities. Xyrfed paid him little mind as he walked to the back of the pub.

However, the now talkative man decided he would introduce himself on the way back.

"Splendid evening to you, stranger!"

"And you," Xyrfed said, raising his glass of ale in a salute.

"I can't say that I've seen you in Vennex before. What business brings you to our village?" the man asked politely.

Xyrfed began to get uncomfortable. He didn't like to get chummy with people when he was on the job. It only led to trouble, and usually another funeral. "I have personal matters I must attend to. Then I'll be on my way."

"Are you a merchant?" the man asked.

Xyrfed could tell that the man had drunk more than he had first suspected. He had grabbed the edge of the table to steady himself. "As I said before, my business is personal. It's best I not get into it. I don't really know you."

"Oh my, where are my manners?" the man said, feigning embarrassment. "My name is *Sä'li Rïamm*. I come through here selling trinkets that people can't live without. Would you care to inspect my wares, fine sir?"

"I'm…no, thank you. I'm just trying to relax and finish this glass of ale before I leave. I have an appointment this evening."

The man looked a bit disappointed but didn't let the rejection stop him in any way. "Sounds important. Do you mind if I tag along with you? I'm rather alone here tonight and could use the company!"

Xyrfed shook his head. "I'm afraid not. I have personal business that I need to tend to, and I won't have time to talk and keep you company. It is mainly a one-person event."

"Ah, an event, sounds exciting. I think I just might tag along. You say you won't have time, but there's always time for good company."

Xyrfed was becoming frustrated with this man, who couldn't take a hint. In a minute or two, one of two things was going to happen. Either Xyrfed was going to have to get extremely rude and tell him to piss off—and with a drunk person, you never knew how that could end up—or he could do what he was going to end up doing in a few moments anyway. The entire time Xyrfed Mai had been figuring out what to do, the man had not stopped talking. He had yammered on, nonstop. Xyrfed was a man of few words, and he usually only spoke when he needed to. This man was not only a nuisance, he was becoming a risk by drawing attention to this table.

Finally, the assassin had taken as much as he could tolerate. He reached into his pouch and found a smooth piece of lachtrys. At the same time, he reached up with one hand and grabbed the man by his short beard. Shock registered in those eyes. With his other hand, he took the lachtrys—which had already transformed into a short, wide, triangular-bladed knife—and he drove it into the man's jugular. Bloody spit erupted from the chunky man's lips, and he began to sag.

Xyrfed helped the man into a chair across the table from him. Another plunging stab to the other side of the neck severed the other jugular. The lachtrys had already turned back into the smooth, oval stone, which Xyrfed wiped off with his cloth napkin. He quickly reached into his pouch and pulled out another crystal. It was a long, narrow piece of citrine. In his hands, one end of the crystal began to glow white hot. Xyrfed made sure no one was watching as he drew the crystal across the puncture wounds, which sizzled like bacon and were cauterized. The bleeding stopped pouring down the front of the man but continued running down his throat. The man gagged and choked, but no one seemed to notice.

The assassin did the final bit of torture to the man. He pulled the crystal across his mouth so it burned closed as well. Blisters formed, and the distinct smell of burning flesh rose at the table. There were now three lines of blistered flesh on the overweight man, one on either side of the neck and one across his mouth. Blood could only go down his throat or out his nose. The man would be dead shortly, but Xyrfed was not going to wait for the man's swan song. He reached into his coin purse and pulled out at least ten times more than what the meal cost.

As he reached the bar, he took the landlady's hand and dumped the coinage into it. She had a huge look of surprise and went to argue, but Xyrfed shook his head and told her that the meal was exceptional. She smiled a semi-toothless smile and waved to Xyrfed as he walked quickly out the door. He had reached the high street before the alarm was raised. It was time for him to get to the party anyway. He just hoped that the rest of the evening went smoother than his dinner had. Xyrfed went from the pub to collect the clothes he had fitted.

He decided to take a room at an out-of-the way inn and settled on The Branded Griffon, an inn just off the high street that was set back in among the trees. It was quiet here, and he doubted that he would have any troubles. He found the landlord in the kitchen, and he was offered the largest corner room on the third floor. So far, all the other people were on the first floor, so he would have complete privacy unless the inn filled up. Xyrfed was sure, with the scare of a murderer on the loose, people just didn't go out traveling in Vennex right now. They were scared. He had all his belongings in a traveling pack and the boxes from the seamstress. It was time for him to be heading over to the mansion. Hopefully, there would be no issues getting in.

The assassin undressed from his dirty clothes. He still had blood from the chunky man at dinner on them. Depending on his mood and the need for egress, he might just leave the old clothes behind and wear these new things. The pants and shirt were very comfortable. He liked to wear linen whenever he could. He liked the way the material breathed. The only thing to put on was his sash-belt combination. For that, he would need one of his lachtrys pieces. He took it in his hands and carefully molded it into the shape of a large, round buckle that he could thread the sash through at his waist.

He glanced at the mirror over the table at the wall and thought how well he had cleaned up. He wished now that he had showered. Luckily, he didn't smell himself yet, so he wasn't worried about it. With everything on but his boots, he grabbed them and sat on his bed to pull them on his sockless feet. He had never worn socks. When he was young, it drove his mother crazy—trying to keep his feet clean—but he just didn't like the feel of socks on his feet. Shoes and boots were constricting enough.

One last thing, he thought before walking out the door. He grabbed his money pouch and attached it to his belt. If anyone looked in his coin pouch, they would see enough coins to make him appear to be a wealthy supporter of the magistrate. What he didn't want them to see was the other piece of lachtrys that he kept hidden underneath the coins. He had magiq at his disposal if things got out of control, but the plan was to slit this pompous ass' throat and watch him try to figure out why before he hit the floor. Xyrfed smiled. Sometimes he loved his job. Tonight was one of those times. He always tried to stay and watch the target pass from this life to the next. That way, he could assure his clients that his mark was indeed dead when he left them.

Xyrfed left his room and walked down the stairs and out the door of the inn. To his knowledge, no one had paid any attention to him. From there he walked to the center of town to the magistrate's mansion. It was crawling with militia. They were checking invitations of everyone, turning those who didn't have them away. Xyrfed felt a minor stab of annoyance at the fact that the magistrate's wife had not given him one, but he guessed she figured he would find a way to get in. The assassin cloaked himself in a minor magiq spell that allowed him to blend in with his surroundings, and he walked the entire perimeter of the mansion.

There was no way he would be able to sneak through them. They were everywhere, and most had wolves sniffing around on chains. Xyrfed changed his strategy right then. If he couldn't sneak in the back, he would have to walk in the front. There was only one way this could happen. He would have to get permission from the lady of the house. He bet that she was not going to be pleased to see him waiting at the front door, but she had left him little choice. After slipping back to the front walkway, he smoothed his clothing and adjusted the sash and walked straight up to the guards posted at the front doors.

"Invitation please!" the guards asked in unison.

"Uh, I have seemed to have misplaced mine."

"Yeah, right, buddy. You and fifty percent of Vennex. No invitation, no entry!"

"If you could just ask the magistrate's wife, she will tell you that I'm supposed to be here!"

The other guard eyed Xyrfed warily. "The family is not to be disturbed by anyone, sir. If you don't have an invitation, you will have to leave!"

"Just wait a moment! I was seriously invited here tonight. If I'm not allowed, I'd hate to be the one who refused me entry just because he wouldn't ask the lady of the house!"

The two militia officers discussed the situation in hushed voices before one of them finally turned to go into the mansion. "You better be telling the truth, buddy. If she comes out and screams at me, you're going to have a rough night of it. With all of the things going on around Vennex these past few days, we will not go easy on you!"

The guard must have thought he was intimidating because Xyrfed took a step back. He had his hand on the lachtrys buckle. If he had to fight his way in and out, the plans were definitely not what he had in mind; but moments later, the assassin saw the other guard returning, followed closely by the wife of the magistrate.

"Now what is all this trouble?" she asked, annoyance seeping into each word.

"As I told you inside, ma'am, this gentleman says he was personally invited by you, but he can't produce his invitation."

Ellysse Tÿr looked at Xyrfed for a quick moment and then at the guard. Her voice rising. "And you still haven't let him in? How long do you plan on keeping him out there, knowing that I personally invited him?" Both guards began to stutter and try to speak, but she slammed through the both of them and took Xyrfed's arm, pulling him into the mansion. "If there is one more issue with either the two of you, I can promise my husband will have you both looking for new jobs by the morning. Do I make myself clear?"

Both men turned bright red, as if someone had poured hot water in their heads. Xyrfed didn't stand to watch. He took the lady's arm and followed her in. Ellysse took him into a back room and turned on him.

"Are you insane? Coming in the front door and drawing all of that attention to both of us?"

"My lady, there was no other way. I would have had to kill several guards, and I did not want to raise an alarm before I even got in here."

"You may be right, but we need to be careful. Siolad is upstairs, getting ready yet. When will you do this? Will you go up before he comes down? Will you do it in front of the guests?

"What is your preference, ma'am?"

"Right now, I don't care. I just want his disgusting body gone from my sight forever. I suppose the sooner you do this, the sooner I become magistrate."

"Do you wish to witness it?" Xyrfed asked.

"Does it make me a horrid person to want to see the bastard breathe his last? I can't take it. Give me ten minutes, and then I will go with you to introduce the two of you. Do it then. Make it painful and gruesome. I've been dreaming of this day for over ten years."

Xyrfed's only reaction was, *Damn, what a cold-hearted bitch!*

She left him in the room to wait for ten minutes. While he waited, he got his lachtrys out of his pouch. He meant to be prepared. With women like this, he felt he needed to be prepared for anything. He didn't trust her. She was a cool, calculating woman, who had a plan for everything, and he was sure if he didn't get his fee up front, he probably wouldn't see any money from her at all. Something just didn't feel right. Ellysse Tÿr returned in ten minutes as she had promised. To Xyrfed's dismay and horror, she was leading a young teenage boy by the hand with her. Surely, she couldn't mean to do what this was implying! Yet here the boy was.

"Uh-umm, what is this? What is going on, lady?" This was the first time he noticed that she also carried a pouch with her.

"This is my son, and I am going to show him what happens when power goes to your head. When you become such a grossly, overstated pariah, when you should be a leader of the people, and a father and husband. This," she said, holding up the pouch, "is your payment." She sat the money pouch down on a small, ornate table in the corner of the room. "I shall leave it here in the drawer, and you may claim it when you have completed the job. I will give you the key to this room, and you may come down and get your reward. I will give you five minutes. Then I will scream bloody murder. That will give you time enough to be gone. Is this acceptable?"

Xyrfed didn't have to think about it. "It is," he stated numbly.

The thought of him killing the boy's father in front of him still left a terrible feeling in the pit of his stomach. He'd been asked a plethora of strange requests in his time as an assassin. This would probably remain one of the most bizarre of his lifetime.

"Okay, if you have found this all acceptable, let us move into hallway."

Xyrfed held his hand out to the woman to take the key. He still didn't like the idea of having to come back down to collect his fee instead of being paid like normal. Once he had the key in his pouch, the three of them made their way upstairs to the room where the magistrate was still putting the final touches on his outfit. The magistrate preferred to look his very best when he was out in his constituency. He had gotten so good at looking down his nose at everyone.

Ellysse didn't even bother got knock when she got to his door. She and her son stormed in, followed closely by the assassin.

"Oh, hello, dear, Sämir, and I'm afraid I don't know you, friend."

There was something in the way he said *friend* that really made Xyrfed Mai cringe. *If he did this to me*, he thought to himself, *there must be many more that want his heart in their hands.* The man was a pompous ass, and despite Xyrfed's misgivings of killing the man in front of his young son, he was beginning to lose any sympathy for him. The magistrate had finally fastened his cloak around his neck with a faceted-lachtrys cloak pin and was ready to go down to greet the guests. To add the finishing touch to his ensemble, the magistrate put on his antique monocle. Finally, he turned to get a better look at the man his wife had brought in to meet him. As always, he began looking at him, taking in the man's clothing and footwear first. Siolad Tÿr didn't care who you were as long as you were dressed properly and didn't look like a pauper. When his eyes finally came to rest on Xyrfed's face, Siolad knew something was out of place.

"What is this person doing here?" he shouted to his wife.

Ellysse remained cool and collected. "He has come to give you something, my dear," she explained.

"But do you even know who he is?" There was now a little bit of panic in his voice. "This man is an Imbröttiös! One of those inbred lunatics from the islands. How could you bring this psychotic animal into my house?"

Ellysse turned to the assassin and asked, "Are you just going to let this pompous ass talk to you like this?"

She was right. Too many people had treated him this way, and this was the thing he needed to help raise his anger. Xyrfed tried to never be angry when he killed though. Anger could lead to fatal mistakes, so he took a deep breath first to calm himself. At the same time, he reached for the buckle on his sash. Instantly it morphed from a round buckle to a long, needle-thin, bladed dagger. He reached into his pouch and grabbed the other piece that was hiding under his coins. This he turned into a short, wide-bladed dagger. The lady stood with an evil grin. She had anticipation written all over her face. The boy still didn't seem to know what was going on. The magistrate, however, knew that he had just made a grave mistake.

"Magistrate, I am here to deliver you to death tonight. I am an assassin hired to end you, and I want you to know this. You have been horrid to many people, and you will pay now."

Still, the boy didn't say anything, though it had registered as to what was getting ready to happen. The magistrate started to shout out for his guards, but Xyrfed was so much quicker. The long dagger shot up under the jaw and slammed it closed as it pierced straight through the top of the head. The lady had a maniacal grin as Xyrfed went to work on her husband. The next dagger found its mark, slicing the voice box, causing a spray of bright red to paint the floor and wall. Xyrfed removed the dagger that had pinned the magistrate's mouth closed and formed it into a wider, shorter dagger, which he plunged into the magistrate's chest over and over again. Each time his hand came back bloodier and bloodier. He had punched a hole with the dagger so much there was literally just ground meat at the opening of his chest.

Xyrfed dared a glance at the boy, who had turned into his mother's chest. She, on the other hand, was laughing and laughing. The thought of her as magistrate of the village made Xyrfed's stomach turn. He didn't really enjoy involving himself in politics, but he felt he might be getting ready to do this. Yes, he was a paid assassin, but how could he, in good conscience, let this woman run the town of Vennex, who could literally take out anyone who annoyed her at any time?

Xyrfed's hand was in the chest cavity, making sure that the heart of the magistrate was stopped. It didn't even flutter. He pulled his bloodied hand free from the chest cavity and took hold of both pieces of lachtrys. The stone morphed again in an instant into two long, round-bladed daggers. In one quick movement, the assassin leapt at the woman, knocking the boy to the floor. At the same time, Xyrfed brought the daggers up and quickly dropped them both in a crossing motion into the woman's chest. He felt the thud as the daggers hit their mark, and the magistrate's wife gasped her last breath, dropping to the floor. Red bubbled around the daggers as her heart attempted to pump the last of its life-giving serum, but it stopped short. Both daggers had pierced it, and there was no way for it to continue on. Xyrfed pulled the daggers from the woman's chest and wiped them off on her now-blood-covered dress. He reformed one piece of lachtrys into a buckle and tied his sash back around himself. His hands were red from the blood of the magistrate and his wife.

On the floor, the boy turned to see his mother and father dead in two piles of bloodied savagery. He began to yell. First a little wail, and then he began to yell in earnest. Xyrfed turned and hit the boy on the jaw, hard, knocking him out and leaving him in a heap on the floor next to his parents. He was just about to reach for the door handle when blinding light filled the room. The outline of the top part of a person glowed from across the room, arms outstretched and burning with light. He couldn't tell what was happening. Balls of energy appeared at the end of the arms and shot at him. He felt the fiery blasts, but only for a moment. He only had a second to ask again, *What in the hell is happening?*

The last energy ball hit him, lifting him up off the floor and slamming him against the wall. The fire burned him, and he was dead before he fell back down to the floor.

Tÿr'Ynyn stepped out of the corner, where she had managed to hide after using the invisibility potion. She had waited to see what would happen to her uncle and his wife. The assassin had been so quick she hadn't been able to assist her uncle. By the time she had realized it was her aunt behind her uncle's death, she let the assassin finish off her aunt. She drew the line on her cousin though. He was still innocent enough to not deserve such a fate. Tÿr got her cousin under his shoulder and lifted him off the floor. She needed to work quickly. The mansion was already burning on the wall where she had blasted the assassin.

She half lifted, half dragged her cousin down the steps to get him out of the room and eventually out of the mansion. She would take him to her cottage, where he could stay for the time being. Tÿr hoped that the assassin was working alone and that it would take a while to get anyone else into Vennex. By then, she might be able to figure out what to do. As she passed the dead assassin, she froze. The face made her stop dead in her tracks. It was a face she was so familiar to her. She had seen one almost exactly like it in her dreams for the past year or two. Same hairy face, same earlobes. Her breath caught in her chest.

"Don't panic now, Tÿr'Ynyn!" she told herself. "He's dead."

She continued to move her cousin out of the house. Guards began to question what was going on and rushed up the stairs into a room now fully ablaze. Tÿr knew the passages that were less traveled in the mansion. She and her cousin had roamed freely when they were younger. She would know the way.

Chapter 25

While Tÿr's aunt was preparing to have her uncle executed, Tÿr and Ghra'zhenn were preparing her to go to the village. Ghra'zhenn was using a bundle of grasses tied into a makeshift paintbrush and was stirring the potion that Tÿr was to be using to spy with. She would be entering the village of Vennex unseen and would be spying on people in the pubs and other places throughout the village. There was definitely someone here in the village who was murdering innocent people.

As the wyvern dabbed the ointment on her body, Tÿr helped by rubbing it in. She started with her legs and arms. She wanted to prolong having to remove the rest of her clothing as long as she could, even though the paragon had never mentioned any type of interest in her at all. They were two completely different species, and she figured that he was as indifferent to her as she to him. Tÿr could feel her skin begin to tighten as the invisibility began to take effect.

Ghra'zhenn had finished covering her legs and the back of her arms and head and then had asked if she preferred that he left while she finished the rest. Modesty didn't really bother her as they were trying to work as quickly as they could. She wanted as much time as possible with the potion. Tÿr told him it was okay that he stayed and asked him to finish her back areas that she couldn't reach. She felt the brush paint her lower back and more-private areas, but finished up with her own hands. She thought matters would become a bit awkward if he used his hands to rub in the salve on her private bits.

The last thing they covered was her face. Here they had to be incredibly careful not to get any of the greasy ointment in her eyes. It had never happened before, so they didn't know what would happen if they did accidentally get a small bit in the eyeball. Best not to find out, Ghra'zhenn agreed. When Týr was completely covered, the paragon inspected her to make sure she was totally invisible. If there were any parts that were left "floating" in the air while she walked around the village, there was sure to be an alarm raised by someone.

When Ghra'zhenn was satisfied, he handed her a small bone carved into a whistle. "This is for you to use. Should you become trapped or in need of help, you can blow it, and no matter where you are, I'll will be able to hear it. It has been imbued with powerful wyvern magiq. It is tuned to my ears alone, and since it is bone, it can be made invisible." He rubbed the whistle with the ointment and watched as it disappeared. "Keep it in your mouth. That way you won't lose it."

Týr took the tiny whistle and blew on it. Immediately Ghra'zhenn perked up. She heard nothing. "Try to never use it that close to me. It is extremely loud and shrill. I know you don't hear it, but believe me, it is extremely loud."

Týr put it on the side of her teeth next to her cheek. And with Ghra'zhenn's blessing, letting her know that she was unseen, she headed into town. The walk into Vennex was most unusual for the apprentice as she had never walked around naked since she had been a toddler. The wind blew in places that were refreshing and yet made her self-conscious even though she was completely concealed. She passed the healer's shop on the way into the village and then later her parents' cottage. There was no smoke coming from the chimney, which was a first. She had never seen the house without a fire in the fireplace, cooking something.

Týr angled from the cottage to the closest pub, *The Landlocked Anchor*, her father's usual pub. Now was the true test of her potion. She waited for the door to open and slipped in between two patrons as they entered, making sure not to bump into either of them. The pub was not crowded as usual. Her father liked this place because it was quiet and usually only had about ten to twelve people in it at any given time. She chose a stool at the end of the bar. It was still pulled out from the last user. She wouldn't have to do anything but sit on it; that way, she wouldn't draw any unnecessary attention as she would if she had to pull out a stool or chair. She waved at the barkeep but forgot that he couldn't see her. She peered in the mirror behind the bar as she walked past. Sure enough, she was completely imperceptible. A thought went through her head, and she gave a little chuckle. Týr hoped that Ghra'zhenn had covered her backside well enough. She could imagine the stories that would spread through the pubs of a floating ass walking through the streets.

Týr settled on the barstool and tried to listen in to any conversations that were audible enough to hear. She wanted to find out anything she could about the murders that had taken place in the days prior to her and Ghra'zhenn's arrival back in Vennex. She hoped that someone, somewhere, knew something. After spending a short time in the *Anchor*, Týr decided it was time to move on to the next one. If anything had happened here, no one was talking about it. Týr had heard from someone passing her earlier that there was a large get-together at her uncle's mansion that evening. She thought that somebody there had to have *some* information about the murders. *The well-connected people always seemed to have the best gossip…and the tightest money pouches*, Týr thought. Ironic, they had no trouble buying art and other things to show their friends to impress them, but when it came time to pay the fee at the clinic, they suddenly had no cash for anything.

The apprentice decided to try a pub along the high street. There were three. For such a small village, there really were a lot of pubs. Seven in all. She could tell as she neared *The Golden Thistle* that this venture would require more stealth and cunning as there seemed to be many more people entering. Again, Týr fell in behind a couple of patrons, who were just getting ready to enter and sneak around them before they could close the heavy wooden door behind them. She entered the large common room and saw that practically every chair and stool was taken by the evening's regulars. Many were chatting loudly from the abundance of ale at the tables. Týr figured she would stand in a corner and try to catch bits of conversations taking place at different tables. At more than one table, the discussion focused on the party taking place at her uncle's mansion. From the snippets of conversations she could overhear, a lot of the drinking villagers felt snubbed by their lack of invites. It seemed that only those whose had money or influence were invited. The people in the pubs were neither, and they loved to tell anyone who would listen.

"Apparently, there is going to be big news coming from the mansion tonight!" one patron was telling the table. There were several other conversations that sounded very similar. "And that snooty witch made sure we couldn't get in. We aren't the *right* kind of people."

"She's got the whole bloody militia up there protecting them, but what happens to us if that damn murderer strikes again? We are totally unprotected! I've got my knife with me here!"

The mood was the same in the pub. People were angry about not being invited to the magistrate's mansion for some big news that he apparently was going to tell the elite of the town. Even for her uncle, something didn't seem right. He was much more uppity since his marriage to her aunt, but having a party and leaving most of the town out was not like him at all. Týr was ready to bet that this all revolved around her aunt. She doubted that her uncle even knew that the town was divided like it had been. When it came to his wife, he gave her free reign to do what she saw fit to do; and as long as she was happy, he didn't care. Týr felt that the mansion was a better place to be. The pub was not where she was going to find out anything useful. She needed to use her invaluable time to spy on the people in the magistrate's manor, where the elite would be way more likely to let their tongues slip tonight. Especially after they had a few drinks of her uncle's expensive, complimentary wine.

Týr decided that the patrons here had probably been drinking too long to be very useful. Besides, she recognized most everyone in the pub. There was no cause for alarm, from what she could tell. She truly believed that the murderer was from outside Vennex. She had grown up with these people, and although she didn't know each person enough to have a personal conversation, she did believe that none of them were capable of murder. Murder required a darkness that Týr didn't see in anyone that she knew in Vennex. Well, maybe her aunt; she put that thought out of her mind. Her aunt was too lazy to do anything as involved as murder would be. She would hire someone to do it. But why would she have some drunkards killed? The more questions Tÿr asked, the more questions popped up.

Tÿr walked carefully to the door and waited for someone to come in or go out, but no one did. When they didn't, she became impatient and just walked out the door herself. She was at the point that she didn't care what anyone said or saw. Most people were drinking and wouldn't remember it in the morning anyway. She passed a group of three young men walking up the footpath to the door as she quickly exited.

"Did you see that?" one of them asked.

"See what?"

"The door! It just opened!"

"Must have been the wind!"

"No, it was just—"

"Who cares? Let's just get some ale!"

"Uh, okay, but I could swear…"

"Forget it! Come on!"

Tÿr smiled as she jogged past the arguing trio. She moved her trajectory to intersect the mansion. The girl had to make sure that she wasn't chewing on the little whistle in her mouth. She had to make sure it worked in case she got stuck with her compliments down. Ghra'zhenn would be her only hope in case she was trapped or caught or worse. By her estimation, Tÿr had been out for about forty minutes. This still gave her over an hour. She would call it an hour in case she had estimated too short.

As she approached the mansion, she could see the militia spread around the grounds. She felt her shoulders slump. Even being invisible, it was a huge number of soldiers. Most were just standing around, doing nothing. To get to the front door, Tÿr would have to pass through eight soldiers, all carrying staff bolines or other pole arms or swords. Tÿr felt naked without her staff, or her clothes for that matter. The apprentice circled the building two times before she found a way she liked to get in. She would just use the front door.

While the front doors of the mansion doors stood wide open between two large men in personal militia uniforms, Tÿr decided it was now or never. The guard on the left side of the door looked bored as he stood, leaning on his boline. As Tÿr walked past him, moving quickly, she kicked out and knocked the weapon out of his hand with a loud clatter.

"What the he—" the guard blurted out. He was wide awake now.

Tÿr figured if he was supposed to be working on her uncle's security detail, he should at least be awake for it. She heard the other guard laughing as she pushed her way inside, taking care to keep from running into too many people. If she did, she made sure the place was crowded already so no one would notice.

More than once, to start an argument, she reached out to grab the bottom of a woman in a short skirt. Tÿr would duck as it always elicited the same response. The woman would slap the face of the closest man. Not only was it funny to Tÿr but it helped to cause a bit of chaos that she needed she needed to slip up the stairs past the four guards standing at the bottom. Luckily, she arrived at the top floor in time to see her aunt Ellysse entering a room with a strange man and her cousin. Immediately something felt off. Usually, her aunt would be downstairs, showing off to the guests. She never missed a time to entertain and rub elbows with the elite of Vennex.

Tÿr didn't see the man's face, but he was dressed in black and did not look like he belonged at the party. He was not the type of person that her aunt usually associated with. Plus, there was something about his face that was almost familiar. If only she could have gotten a better look. She had almost reached the door when she heard a click. Her aunt had locked the door. Tÿr stood and listened at the door for a few moments. She could hear her uncle Siolad's voice now too. Something bad was about to happen, and she didn't know what, but she wasn't about to stand around and let it take place.

There was a balcony that connected all the upper rooms of the mansion, so she needed to get to that. Tÿr tried the door next to the one occupied by her aunt and uncle, but it was locked. Then she remembered a bedroom that she had used as a child. It was farther down the hall. She ran down to check that door, and it, too, was locked. She knew there wasn't time to spare to check every single door. She would have to concentrate on the far one where she stood and hope no one came up.

Tÿr reached deep into herself and imagined the lock opening. The tumblers in the lock clicked softly as her skin glowed from the minor spell she used. The apprentice checked again to make sure no one had come up the stairs and was relieved to find herself alone still. The door was now opened, and Tÿr walked in quickly to avoid any eyes that might surprise her. She flew over to the window and threw it open. The girl still had no idea why she felt the need to be in the room with her uncle, but the urgency pressed in on her more and more with each second. Tÿr sprinted down the balcony and found the window.

She was horrified to see what was waiting for her. Siolad Tÿr was laying on the floor, covered in blood, and the man in black was attacking her aunt as she peered in the window. She managed to slide it open and step through into the corner of the room. Tÿr saw two daggers pierce her aunt's chest. Even though she despised the woman, she didn't feel like she deserved this death. Anger and rage unlike any before surged through her, and she drew upon her magiq. Despite the fact she was invisible, her arms and back glowed as bright as the sun as she conjured energy in the form of a huge, frothing ball that she shot at the man who had just killed her aunt. Her cousin was cowering on the floor when the ball of pure, plasmic energy blew from her spot in the corner and hit the assassin in the chest. And then another, picking him off his feet and slamming him into a wall behind him. The noise was like a thousand explosions of lightning crashing at once.

Yells of shock and panic came from the lower floors. Tÿr could hear what she only assumed were soldiers clambering up the stairs. Right now, her main concern was her cousin. She was sure that had she not acted when she did, he would probably be laying dead next to his parents right now. Tÿr bent down and picked him up over her shoulder. He weighed a thousand pounds. His feet did not want to work. She could tell that he was in shock. The sight of seeing both of his parents die in front of him had done terrible things to his brain, and he just didn't want to move.

Tÿr planned to take him out of the door and down the stairs, but she could hear the clamber of feet on the stairs coming up quickly. She chose to go out the window. She quickly dragged Sämir to the window and took the whistle from her mouth. If this was going to work, she needed to get her cousin out of the mansion now; and if she was found, there would be too many awkward questions to try to answer, most of which she couldn't until she had time to investigate what had happened here tonight. As soon as she reached the window with the lump of her cousin's body, she blew on the tiny whistle as hard as she could. There was no sound at all, but she hoped that Ghra'zhenn could hear it.

The soldiers would be through the doors in seconds, and she had no way to be out of the mansion. Before Tÿr could drag her cousin's body out of the window, she heard flapping from outside of the balcony. Ghra'zhenn was already there. On her way out of the room, Tÿr got a good look at the man who had attacked her uncle and aunt. It froze her insides. He had the face just like one of the people from her dreams. No earlobes. Crazy hair. His face was covered with hair, or it had been before she had hit him with the balls of energy. Tÿr made sure to remember this so she could discuss it with Ghra'zhenn. Maybe he would know who these people were.

The girl managed to get her cousin onto the flying wyvern and hold onto him all the while holding on to Ghra'zhenn at the same time. She knew they wouldn't be able to fly very far like this, but they needed to get away from here first. That was the main issue at this time. Ghra'zhenn lifted up and flew over the treetops. He meant to fly back to the clinic so Tÿr could strap her cousin on to his back better, and then they could head back to the mountain home. The boy's breathing was shallow, and he barely had enough strength to hold on to the wyvern, but they managed the short trip to the back side of the clinic. Tÿr could tell from the loosening of her skin that the invisibility would soon be gone, but that didn't matter. Her cousin was practically catatonic and would probably not remember nothing of this.

Tÿr dismounted the paragon when they landed at the healer's shop. She rushed in and grabbed to harness. She was able to secure it on the wyvern and get her cousin tethered into it. She would sit behind him; flying as much as she had recently had given her confidence to fly without a tether for a short distance like the mountain cavern.

"Okay, let's go before we have company!" she yelled to Ghra'zhenn as she mounted him.

Three huge wing flaps, and they were airborne. Ghra'zhenn didn't do any fancy flying this time; he shot like a bolt toward the mountain. Tÿr held on to her cousin as they sped off. There were many things going through her brain as the invisibility began to subside. Luckily, they were high enough that no one would be able to tell that she was naked from the ground. The trip that usually took twenty minutes on a good day took only fifteen today. She was grateful to the paragon for his quick flying. Ghra'zhenn was able to take Sämir and move him to a bed in the cavern. Tÿr would tend to him once she got dressed.

"Ghra'zhenn, is there something we can do for him?" she asked her paragon. "He is in shock!"

"What exactly happened back in Vennex? You didn't really take the time to tell me. I was more concerned about getting us out."

Tÿr sat and told the wyvern what she could piece together of the events. She explained that her aunt had let the killer into the room. This was troubling to Ghra'zhenn. He was trying to figure out why the magistrate's wife would bring a man into a room, only to have him kill her as well. There was something the two of them were missing, and he was sure that the boy on the bed might be able to give them some of the answers that they were looking for.

"I believe we may find some of the answers we seek when we can get your cousin to speak. He is having trouble processing what happened tonight. I'm not sure if there is anything that can be done for him."

"We have to try, Master." Tÿr's voice was practically pleading with the paragon. "What if there are more assassins in the village? What if they've found my parents? What if..." Her voice fell off at the thought of what might be.

"These are all things I am aware of, Tÿr," Ghra'zhenn told her. "We are going to have to give him a while to come out of this stupor."

"But how long could that take?" Tÿr was practically pleading with the paragon.

"There is a bit of magiq that I can try. Something to move his mind back a bit, but I can't guarantee that it will even work. This is extremely dangerous and can often result in baking his mind permanently. If you wish to try, I shall require your hands and mine."

"Yes, yes, let's do it. I'm the only family that he has left. It's what has to be done. Tell me what I need to do."

"I will guide you," the paragon told her, "but, Tÿr, beware. Anytime that you attempt to heal the mind, things can go badly very fast. The brain is a delicate instrument and can be destroyed without warning if great care is not used. If you feel that you are having any trouble with the healing or are feeling any resistance from the boy, you must back out. Damage can happen to both of you!"

At this point, Tÿr didn't care. It was true that her cousin was a prat most of the time, but he didn't deserve this. Besides, if someone else got to him, they could torture him more or try to get information that could possibly lead them to Tÿr or her parents.

Tÿr worked on her cousin throughout the night and into the next day, gently prodding his memories and his brain to heal itself. Ghra'zhenn sat vigil over the two the entire time, watching and guiding to make sure she didn't press too hard. She talked to the boy, coaxing him slowly back from the edge he had been throw against.

By afternoon, the boy said his first words. "Where am I? I'm thirsty!"

Tÿr left the boy with Ghra'zhenn on the bed and ran to grab a goatskin. She aided him as he took a drink. She could see his eyes focus on the cavern and then on the enormous wyvern next to the bed. Fear registered in the eyes, but Tÿr assured him that there was no need for concern. She explained how Ghra'zhenn had helped rescue Sämir from the burning manor house. Then the memories came back to him. His father and mother. The man dressed in black. Tÿr tried to quiet the boy as words came flooding out. She wanted to hear. She needed to hear, but now was not the time.

"There will be time for that, Sämir," she told the boy on the bed. "Try to rest now. We will talk when you have slept."

It was then that Tÿr realized how weary she was. She hadn't really had a chance to sleep since they had left Ÿkkynnÿk Mountain. Tÿr went over to the medical supplies that were stored on the shelves lining the side of the cavern and brought a bottle back for her cousin. She had a cup and poured three doses in it and then handed it to the boy.

"I want you to drink this," she said, handing him the cup.

"What is it?" he questioned her.

"It is a potion called *kyskÿzha*. It will help you get a restful sleep without bad dreams."

At first, the boy looked apprehensive but then drank the potion down in one. Tÿr poured another dose and drank it herself. They both needed uninterrupted sleep. Ghra'zhenn was there, and she knew he would see to it that they remained unbothered. Tÿr felt the effects of the potion almost immediately, and so she lay down. Her cousin seemed to fight it a bit more, but she saw him finally lay his head down too. Within minutes, both humans were asleep and would remain that way for six hours. Ghra'zhenn lay on the floor in front of their beds and watched the doorway. He was glad to be able to rest as well. The energy he had expelled to travel to Vennex had exhausted him, and he was ready for a rest.

Chapter 26

The soldiers broke through the door to the where the magistrate and his wife lay dead. They looked to see another unknown person in black, burned and lying on the floor. The priority was the magistrate though, and they rushed to his bloodied body on the floor. He had been slashed and had a gaping hole in his chest. His wife, too, had been stabbed to death. Pulses were searched, but only in vain. It was then that they turned their attention to the other man in the room. His face was scarred with burned flesh, along with seared clothing that went all the way down the front of him.

One soldier dared to feel the unknown man's pulse and drew back his hand in utter shock.

"Gaunts alive! This man lives. Get him a healer now!"

A low, rasping breath escaped the man's lips, grating from the difficulty he was having just drawing in the precious air.

Soldiers began to scatter to try and find the village healer but didn't realize at the time that she wasn't even in Vennex. She had taken a leave of absence to train with her mentor on the wyvern island.

It took ten minutes before anyone returned to give the bad news.

"The healer is away! We will have to go to the nearest village for their healer. How fast can anyone ride to Yelliton?"

The room was in chaos as people were running back and forth, trying to figure out what had happened to their leader and who could have done such a heinous act on the first family of Vennex. Each question someone answered caused two more to be asked. The biggest question on everyone's mind at the moment was, where was the son? Several of the guards had seen the boy and his mother with the man on the floor.

There were two soldiers that were tasked with trying to save the man in black. Four more were assigned to the door. No one was to come in or leave without the express permission of the captain in charge of the detail. People were scared and worried about what would happen next and if the killer was still out there. If he had been so bold as to attack them in the magistrate's mansion, would he try it again?

Moaning continued to grow louder and more frequently from the man on the floor.

Some of the soldiers had some type of medical training and began to treat the man on the floor.

"We must locate the boy!" the captain of the guards yelled frantically. "Has anyone seen him?"

Many of the troops began to spread out from the room to find the magistrate's son. There were some soldiers reporting to the captain that they had seen a large wyvern abduct the boy. Others reported seeing the wyvern outside the manor house too. The captain didn't know what or who to listen to. There were so many conflicting accounts of what happened, but the one thing that remained constant was the wyvern's appearance outside the balcony.

After working on the man for nearly an hour, the stranger was beginning to awaken. He wasn't happy to be awake. The pain that wracked his body must have been excruciating. He tried to talk but could barely manage a muffled moan.

"Try not to talk," one of the soldiers that was working on him said. "You need to save your strength." The man in black tried to sit up but was met with resistance as he came up on one elbow. "No! Just save your strength! Do you know what has happened?"

Xyrfed shook his head. He knew that he couldn't let on that he knew what had happened, or he would surely be taken into custody, or imprisoned, or worse. He felt like his whole body was on fire from the fireball that had caught him unaware by the shade of the magiq user that had almost done him in!

Xyrfed felt like his skin was burned off on many parts of his body, including his face. The good thing, if there was one, was that the burns and damage caused by the attack had helped to disguise his face somewhat. No one had mentioned the name of Imbröttiös, so he felt safe for the time being. Besides, he was so weak the only thing he could really do was lay there and let them tend to his wounds until a healer could be fetched. From what he could gather, that could take some time.

Xyrfed tried to glance around and see what had become of his two pieces of lachtrys. When the magiq user had hit him, they had gone flying, but for now the soldiers were assuming someone else had attacked the magistrate and his wife and that he wasn't even a suspect because of his injuries. That would all change when they found the son though. Right now, his best hope on getting out of this situation was Kaistam-Laq. The sooner the sorcerer arrived in Vennex, the better Xyrfed's chances of escaping the village were.

It was nearly four hours later, and Xyrfed Mai was in a bedroom in the magistrate's manor. He was put in a back room on the first floor, with two guards posted on his door. He was in terrible pain when he tried to move. His arms burned, but he had to locate his scrying mirror. It was the only link between him and his master, Kaistam-Laq. He needed to warn Kaistam about his situation and the reception that the sorcerer was likely to receive when he arrived. The guards were looking for a magiq user, and they wouldn't know the leader of the sect of Murtair Amagii. He would be an automatic suspect.

Xyrfed tried searching his chest area, but there was still a lot of damage where he had been blasted by the balls of lightning. He tried to lift up his shirt and realized that much of his skin was still stuck to it. The blisters had grown over much of the burnt edges, and to pull it out would have meant more pain and possibly reopening the wounds. He felt around and could tell that part of the mirror had been broken, but he needed to get to it not matter the cost. Speaking to his leader was imperative. He had to warn him about the situation and what he would be walking into. Xyrfed reached for the piece of scrying mirror still burned into his chest and began to pull slowly.

He heard hollering and felt a wave of agony so intense he lost consciousness for a few seconds. When he woke, he found two soldiers standing in front of him.

"Are you okay, sir?"

"I heard screaming!" Xyrfed said. The soldiers looked at each other, with the look of not wanting to tell someone something. "What? What is it?" the assassin asked.

"I'm afraid the screaming was you, sir!"

Xyrfed felt foolish, but he half expected that answer. He remembered trying to pull out the piece of obsidian. What had happened to it? He began to search frantically as the pain would allow. He had to find the shard. It was his only link to his master.

"I was trying to pull a piece of stone out of my chest and must have passed out. I can't seem to find it," Xyrfed told the guards.

"This thing?" One of the guards bent down and picked up the piece of bloodied black glass. "I was just going to throw it out."

"Please! Please don't do that. It is part of a medallion and is a treasured keepsake. Could I please have it?"

The guards looked at each other and then shrugged.

"Here," the guard said and handed him the piece of volcanic glass.

Xyrfed examined it to make sure it would be big enough to reach the sect's leader. It was still about the size of two large coins and covered in burnt flesh. The assassin rubbed it off on a part of his pants that wasn't covered in singed dermis and dross.

"If you won't be needing us for anything else," the higher-ranking guard told him, "we will be outside your door until the healer arrives from Yelliton."

"Actually, I am in a good deal of pain as you can imagine. Does anyone have anything to help with it? I would be grateful for any type of painkilling agent! I'd even be happy with a glass of strong rum or wine!"

The soldier in charge called out to another soldier and had him go and find a bottle of wine. When the soldiers had left the room, Xyrfed Mai pulled up the piece of obsidian and conjured the spell to activate his mirror.

Quietly he spoke to the sorcerer. "Master, there has been a set-back. The target has been eliminated. In the process, I was wounded by an unknown entity. I was attacked as I eliminated one of the witnesses. The other witness seems to have escaped. I was unable to collect our fee due to my injury. Be warned, all magiq users are under scrutiny. It is believed that I was attacked by the magiq user that we seek. They are stronger than anyone I have ever seen, and they have the power to become invisible and attack while they are cloaked. I have no description."

It was clear from Kaistam-Laq's face that he was not happy with the news. To have been so close to this powerful being and have no information about them did not please the leader of the Murtair Amagii. Xyrfed knew that if he were anyone else in the sect, he would be dead now. Kaistam-Laq didn't tolerate failure well and would have made sure a lesser assassin wouldn't talk. Xyrfed, however, was a trusted leader in the sect and had been training assassins for over twenty-five years.

Xyrfed talked as quietly and quickly as he could. On one occasion, he had to hide the stone as a soldier brought him half a bottle of cane rum and a stone tankard. Kaistam was speaking when Xyrfed had to put the stone away under the side of his bed. One of the two soldiers that came in with the rum was listening closely. He swore he could hear a voice, but Xyrfed convinced him that he was mistaken. Both the soldiers left, the one glancing back one last time to make sure there wasn't anything strange going on in the room.

The assassin could hear the soldiers talking to the two guards at the door, but didn't catch what they were saying. As soon as the talking died down, he pulled out the piece of broken black, glass-like stone and held it to his face. He had to explain to his master that there were visitors, and he needed to keep the piece of scrying mirror hidden lest he draw attention to himself. If the soldiers thought that he could do magiq, too many questions would arise, and none of them would care how badly he was wounded if they thought he had anything to do with the murders of their magistrate or his wife, though most people in the village had grown to loathe her in the past few months. It had become clear that the magistrate had proven to be a puppet for his wife's agenda, and she did nothing to hide the fact. Kaistam had let his assassin trainer explain what had happened before he spoke.

"I am still two days out from the village. Can you stay where you are until I arrive?" he asked Xyrfed.

"I believe that is their plan for me. I should be seen by a healer shortly. They had to fetch one from a neighboring town as their own healer is out training. I'm not exactly sure what is going on. They've only just gotten me some cane rum to help keep the pain away, but I really need a healer with their knowledge of pain potions."

Kaistam also told Xyrfed to ask to see if one of the soldiers could possibly run out to the woods and search for a specific leaf. When burned and mixed with the rum, it should offer some relief. Xyrfed also warned the sorcerer not to arrive in the village looking like a sorcerer.

"Use a disguise to hide your features," he told the sect leader. "The soldiers are all looking for a magiq user, and they have no idea who."

The two shared the information that they needed to and then were done. Xyrfed called to the guards again to see if he could entice or at least talk one of the soldiers in the manor to go out and get the leaves he needed. If not, he would spend the next couple of days suffering more than he needed to, with severe, burning pain shooting through his arms and chest. One of the guards was familiar with the plant that Xyrfed had called *Octyfoil majoris*. The soldier quickly called to his superior to see if he could be allowed to go into the surrounding wooded area and find the plant needed by the wounded man. Upon receiving permission, the soldier went out of the mansion and returned less than ten minutes later with a handful of the large, variegated leaves. Each leaf was deeply lobed into eight sections, from which it got its name.

Xyrfed explained how to prepare the plant, and the soldiers lit the leaves and burned them on a plate so that there were just ashes left. According to Kaistam, the plant was potent, so he needed to go sparingly. With some assistance, Xyrfed managed to mix in some of the bitter ash with his rum and drank it down immediately. The effects weren't instantaneous, but when the plant began to work, much of the pain was relieved. Xyrfed didn't know how long the elixir would last but knew he should try to get some rest.

From what he had heard from listening to the soldiers around the room, the healer from the other town was already en route and would be there soon. Hopefully, he would have something to help with the pain and the burns. As it stood right now, Xyrfed was in for some nasty scarring. The energy that hit him left markings all over the front of his body. His chest had taken the brunt of the attack, but his arms and legs, his neck, and his face, too, were affected. He hadn't seen himself in a looking glass other than the tiny piece of the scrying mirror. From what he could tell from that, he had taken some major damage. Of course, he had seen his chest and knew if that was a sign, he could be scarred for life.

The assassin let the elixir he had made take full effect. He was more comfortable than he had been since the attack. Slowly he let his mind shut down, and he drifted off into a dream-filled sleep. Over and over, he was in the room with the magistrate. His blades were taking the man's life, and then he turned to the laughing woman. She, too, dropped when he had run the blades of lachtrys through her. Now his brain kept trying to tell him two different things. The boy! Kill the boy! No witnesses! But at the same time, he *had* to see who had come through the window. Who was the invisible attacker? If he watched carefully, could he see them this time? All he had seen the first time were arms and possibly a back lit up like the sun, and then balls of energy slammed into him. Who could it have been? Another sect? Why would another sect be protecting the magistrate? Had he suspected an attack? Questions spun around his mind, making him dizzy.

Xyrfed slept until the healer arrived several hours later. He was awakened by a calming man's voice.

"Can you hear me?"

Xyrfed began to stir, leaving the dreams behind. He opened his eyes to see the face of a bearded man trying to talk to him. The man was bent over him. He wasn't shaking him or grabbing him; he was simply asking if he could hear him.

Xyrfed finally replied, "Yes. I hear you."

"What is your name? Can you tell me that?"

Xyrfed thought hard. He always used a false name when he was in the field. Xyrfed Mai was well known in certain areas and didn't dare give his true name. "I'm called Caryl," Xyrfed told him. "I was attacked while I was talking with the magistrate and his wife."

"That's of no importance to me right now. I am called Kuired Gÿann, and I am a healer from Yelliton. I will be working on you to see if I can get you feeling better."

Chapter 27

Tÿr'Ynyn was the first to wake from the effects of the potion. Ghra'zhenn was still in the spot he had taken before she had gone to bed. He laid there with his eyes closed, and Tÿr wondered if he was sleeping as well. She got up from her bed to walk out of the cavern. Fire still burned in the heating oven, which meant the wyvern had tended it throughout the night. Tÿr reached the entrance of the cave when the paragon spoke.

"I trust you slept well."

"As well as could be expected under the circumstances. I was worried about Sämir, but the potion wouldn't allow me to get up to check on him. I was just too weary."

"That is good. You needed uninterrupted rest. I have been tending to him, but there wasn't much to do. He tossed and turned in his sleep mostly. I just kept an eye on him."

"Thank you, Ghra'zhenn!"

"It is my pleasure, child. I am pleased to be able to help. When the boy awakens, I would like to see if he can explain to us what happened back in the village last night."

"Aren't you worried that it might put him into another fit? Is there something we can do to prevent that?"

"Actually, there is," the wyvern explained to her. "We will burn some herbs and some dried wyvern blood in a bowl, which will have a calming effect and keep him as tranquil as possible. That way, he won't go back into shock at the thought of last evening's events. I know they are going to be traumatic for him to relive, but we must hear what took place in the mansion so we can figure out our next move."

Tÿr was anxious to learn what had happened as well. She wanted to learn why the boy had been in the room with the assassin too. Had she not come in when she had, most likely, there would be three graves that would need to be dug. Tÿr was also trying to come to terms with something she never in her life thought she would need to deal with—a death caused at her hand. The anger she had felt had caused her to react and shoot the assassin dead. Over and over, she had played the scenario in her mind, trying to figure out if there could have been a way to simply stop the man from killing her cousin instead of killing him. Each time she felt the same hatred. Guilt made her ashamed that she had not disarmed the man. Would she have had time to get her cousin out? Each time she came to the same conclusion—she felt that she had acted properly—but then why did she feel so bad?

"Ghra'zhenn, I need to speak to you about last night."

Tÿr went over next to the wyvern's enormous head and sat on the blue stone floor nearby. "You are having feelings of guilt, are you not?" he asked plainly.

"Yes, I am." She was glad he had opened the conversation. "I have gone over everything that I did last night. Each move, every feeling. I was enraged to see my uncle dead on the floor, and so I attacked the man with the daggers. I didn't try to disarm him. I wanted him dead!"

"And you are feeling like you failed in some way?"

"I'm not sure how I feel. I never gave that man a chance to defend himself, to say what he was doing. He couldn't see me, and I attacked him to harm, to kill! I didn't want him to hurt anyone else. I was afraid that he would kill my cousin! The rage was unstoppable."

Ghra'zhenn thought about this for a couple of moments before he responded. "You are a healer, Tÿr'Ynyn, first and foremost. You protect life. I believe that is just what you were trying to do. Your cousin was in grave danger, and you felt your only choice was to remove the immediate threat. You did that! Please do not continue to second-guess that. You did what had to be done to save an innocent life."

Tÿr thought about it for a moment and began to feel a little better. It still didn't change the fact that she had taken a life, but the way that her paragon had explained it made her not feel so guilty about taking the life of a murderer. The man, after all, had killed both her uncle and her aunt. Despite their differences, Tÿr didn't feel that they deserved to die in this manner.

"Thank you so much, Paragon. This does help. I have never killed another human before, and my stomach has been in knots. You have truly helped."

The ancient wyvern dipped his head in acknowledgment. "I never want killing to be easy for you, Tÿr. It should always make you miserable. Taking the life of anything should be harder on you than the subject. But if it was justified, and you did this to save another innocent being, I believe you did the right thing. You are truly growing each day, both as a person and as a magiq user. I am proud to have you in my dynasty."

"Thank you for saying so."

Tÿr was overcome by emotions: pride, sadness, joy, and regret. It all manifested itself in a single tear that ran down her left cheek, which she quickly brushed away. From behind them on the bed, Tÿr could hear her cousin beginning to stir. It was late morning, and he was waking. Hopefully, the treatment she had done the night before had helped, and he would be able to answer some questions for her and Ghra'zhenn.

The healer went to prepare the calming incense that they would be burning for her cousin as they asked about the previous night's events. Ghra'zhenn greeted Sämir, who seemed to be in better condition than he was the night prior. The boy's color had partially returned, and he had gotten out of bed. Sämir looked around as Tÿr came back, carrying the incense. He appeared to be a little confused.

"What is this place, Cousin Tÿr?" He managed time get out.

"This is one of the homes that I use when I stay in Vennex," Tÿr explained to her cousin.

"Do you know why I am in this place? My parents will be worried if I don't return soon."

The look on his face was somewhat unfocused. He hadn't had the chance to look around much, but he appeared to be very intrigued by the cavern home of the wyverns and Tÿr. He took in the shelves filled with medication. He also could see the tunnels in the back that led to the cooling areas for the food and other medications. The boy was impressed by the size of the cave.

"Sämir, this is the leader of the wyvern dynasty from a place called Ÿkkynnÿk Mountain," Tÿr'Ynyn explained to the boy.

Sämir seemed to follow her so far. He also seemed to have some questions that Tÿr might be able to answer in a few moments when they began talking with the boy. The apprentice used a minor spell to light the bowl of incense.

Her cousin looked impressed. "You can do magiq? How?"

"Later!" she told him, smiling.

She seemed to have found an interest of his that she could exploit while talking with him. If she could keep his mind from dwelling on the horrid affairs of the previous night and keep him focused on anything else, she might be able to get more information out of him without him shutting down. It was worth a try anyway. Tÿr brought out her pipe.

"Do you mind if I smoke some herb weed?" she asked her cousin. He shook his head. "Are you allowed to smoke?"

"Doesn't matter now. They're dead, aren't they? There's no one to tell me no now," he said with no emotion in his voice.

Tÿr was surprised by the lack of sympathy he showed.

"Ghra'zhenn and I would like to ask you some questions about last night if you think that would be all right."

"Uh, yeah, sure. There isn't much to say. That witch had my father killed."

Tÿr glanced at her paragon. The two shared a knowing look.

"How do you mean, Sämir?" Ghra'zhenn questioned the boy.

"I mean, my mother brought that man in black into the room to kill my father. He pulled out some stones, and they turned into knives. He just killed him!" The boy was getting emotional for the first time.

"What did Ellysse do?" Tÿr asked him.

"She told my father that things would be different when she was in charge, and then she told that horrid man to kill him. She asked him what he was waiting for."

"And then what happened?" Ghra'zhenn pressed.

The incense was taking effect. The boy was almost dreamy. His words were strong though. "The man, that evil man, just killed him, and she stood there and laughed. She sounded like a madwoman. I don't think she was supposed to die, but I believe that the man was frightened by her. She was scary. She laughed and laughed, but he shut her up. She was still laughing when he stabbed her. It happened so fast that she didn't even scream. The next thing I knew, she fell down, dead."

The boy talked in a monotone voice. The emotion was gone. There was no emphasis on any word or phrase. The anesthetic quality of the burning herbs and wyvern blood was helping.

"This man, can you remember what he looked like? Was there anything unusual about him?" Ghra'zhenn pressed even more.

"I could tell he wasn't from here. He was strange-looking. He talked funny too. I can't say how. It was just a different way of speaking."

"Do you mean like an accent?" Tÿr asked quickly.

"Um, I think so. I just know he didn't come from the shift. He is definitely not a midlander. He had hair all over his face too."

"Like a beard?" Tÿr asked.

"No. It was all over his face. Long, straggly hair that grew on his face. On his nose and cheeks and just all over. He didn't have these either." Sämir pointed to his earlobes. "They were just missing."

"Imbröttiös!" Ghra'zhenn said quietly.

"Are you sure?" Tÿr asked.

"I am sure," the wyvern said. "Did you get a look at him when you were there?"

"Not as good as I wanted," Tÿr said. "I was too worried about getting him out of the room to look to closely," she said, nodding her head at her cousin. "Can you remember anything else, Sämir?" Tÿr asked him.

"I just remember the huge blasts of lightning that blew the dark man into the wall. They killed him immediately. He fell to the floor dead, but by then my head went blank, and my arms and legs didn't work."

Tÿr watched her cousin try to remember the rest of the events in the room. Tears ran down his cheeks as he sat there silently.

The healer was worried that he had gone back into his catatonic fit, but then he turned to her. "May I have a couple puffs on your pipe?

Tÿr was surprised by her cousin's request, but she handed the pipe to him and watched as he drew in the fragrant smoke and exhaled. He seemed to relax with each inhalation.

To her surprise, Sämir turned back to her and asked, "It was you last night, wasn't it? You saved my life. That was your magiq. No one else can do magiq like that, can they?"

Tÿr'Ynyn looked him straight in the eye and nodded. "It was me."

It was then that Sämir astonished her more than she had been in ages. He rushed up to her and threw his arms around her shoulders.

"Thank you, Tÿr!" he whispered in her ear, silent sobs coming as he held her.

Tÿr didn't know what to do, so she just held him. She was one of three family members that he had remaining in the world. Tÿr decided that she would take him with her and watch out for him. She could show him the love he had never gotten before. She also had to protect him because he was also, by default, the magistrate of Vennex, until other arrangements could be made.

Chapter 28

Kaistam-Laq and his entourage pitched camp in the forest outside Vennex near the Ajenti River. They took up a large area, with four large tents and one huge marquee reserved for the master sorcerer himself. There were trunks upon trunks of things that Kaistam needed to run his mobile headquarters. It took his servants over three hours to set up everything to Kaistam's satisfaction. Kaistam had traveled without his normal number of seventeen assassins. He needed to get here as quickly as he could to find out about the newest magiq user with the strength to almost kill one of his strongest assassins in a single shot. The sorcerer was sure that this was the source of the enormous power he had located. He brought ten of his assassins to help bring in this person or thing or being. Whatever he was dealing with, he would see them in his sect, or he would personally see to their death. The power that they wielded was too incredible to allow to roam free and potentially be used against the Murtair Amagii.

Right now, Kaistam was concerned about getting in to see his assassin trainer, Xyrfed Mai, who still lay in a room at the former magistrate's manor. The trick was going to be gaining access to his trainer. From the news Xyrfed had shared with him, he was guarded night and day; and the only person that was allowed to see him, other than the militia guards, was a healer from a nearby town.

Kaistam had a plan to get in. He was planning on using a disguise and an alias to convince the guards that he was Xyrfed's family member. Whether that worked was dependent on his ability to act. He planned on getting to the bottom of the attack on his assassin without letting any of the guards know his true identity. If that failed, there was sure to be a fight. The chance of wiping out most of an assassin sect couldn't be wasted by any militia. Kaistam-Laq figured that if a fight had to take place, ten of his highly trained assassins would be able to take out the militia of a small village like Vennex. As long as no other town was called in, an assassin could easily take out ten men who weren't trained in assassin skills. Assassins were trained with all weapons, as well as barehanded combat.

It was rumored that a Murtair Amagii assassin armed with nothing but his hand and magiq took out seventeen trained soldiers, leaving them all dead as a lesson for any who wished to try meddling in any further Amagii affairs. The assassin grew in status and in power, eventually removing any competition from the lead position. His name was Kaistam-Laq. Since that fight, the number seventeen had become an obsession with the sorcerer. Everything he did revolved around the sacred number—from the number of assassins in the sect to the number of magiq rings he wore on his fingers.

Kaistam planned on going into the village the next day. He still needed to figure out a way to get into the mansion. He would have to travel as mundane as possible. From what Xyrfed had told him, the soldiers were looking for a magiq user. They had not figured out that his trainer was an assassin, or he wouldn't have needed to make this trip. From everything he knew about small, rural villages like Vennex, their form of justice was swift and severe. The mystery of the magiq user who had practically killed Xyrfed was driving him mad. He knew almost every magiq user from the Kirin-Noirin shift and the few that lived in the islands. He was used to spying on them regularly. And he was sure that some of them had ways and the means to try to keep tabs on him and his sect.

Often the assassin sects didn't or couldn't use magiq, but it didn't imply by any means that they were not deleterious to any target marked by them. They were, after all, trained killers, and therefore a huge threat. Kaistam was proud and certain that his sect was better than the others because each assassin could employ magiq in one form or another to kill, an edge he found to be most advantageous when fighting or killing something larger or stronger than the assassin involved. It was simple, common sense like this that had helped him achieve success as a leader of his sect. The fact that he demanded respect from his team but also gave it when earned also made him a good leader. He wasn't liked; he was feared and respected enough that his people always performed to their best abilities.

Upon the completion of setting up the camp and fixing the evening meal, Kaistam retired to his marquee to continue figuring out the next day's plan. Some of the other assassins stayed up later to have a glass or two of wine that traveled with the convoy. Kaistam always had strong wine to accompany his team. He believed that if a crew worked hard, they should be rewarded. It was late into the night, and it was dark before the leader of the Murtair Amagii finally fell into deep, dreamless sleep.

When morning came, the leader of the most dangerous assassin sect on the planets arose and went to the tents of the rest of his assassins. He told them to dress in plain, unassuming clothing that would not draw attention to them. They needed to get in and out of the village with their trainer, Xyrfed, with as little commotion and detection as possible. It was rumored that there was at least one wyvern who stood guard over Xyrfed, but they didn't really know for sure; but if it was true, they would need and want every person in the sect for distractions and muscle should the need arise. Kaistam-Laq also knew that rumors were spread on purpose to keep undesirables away from areas of interest. He felt this might be the case now. Xyrfed had never mentioned anything about a wyvern presence prior to this, so it meant nothing until he actually saw one.

The clothing that the assassins had chosen was very provincial and plain. Kaistam hoped it would blend in with the locals' garb enough to keep them from standing out too much. Being from the desert region of Peyda Kirin, they usually dressed in much-lighter colors and in way fewer layers of clothing. Kaistam would have to remember to leave his jewelry behind. Jewelry was a sign of wealth, but it was also a dead giveaway that the wearer was a possible magiq user, at least it was up in the lands where Kaistam came from.

The leader of the assassin sect inspected his assassins. Any that appeared too exotic were sent back to change. Mundane was the look they were attempting. Kaistam made sure each assassin had their two pieces of lachtrys incorporated into their outfits somehow, whether they be buttons or buckles. He hoped that there was no need to use them, but preparedness was the key to this expedition.

The camp was approximately six miles from Vennex as the owl flew. Despite Kaistam's advanced age, he still moved as fast as the others. They didn't follow any path, but he forged their own through the light brush and brambles. The forest was fairly dense here, and the undergrowth was sparse compared with other places. Even without a compass to guide them, they arrived at Vennex in an hour's time.

Kaistam was glad to see that their garb was similar to the residents of the village, so they didn't stand out. It was easy to locate the magistrate's mansion along the high street. There were still militia soldiers posted all around it. Kaistam instructed his team to watch the building to see when would be the best time to get in. With all the soldiers, he was worried that a peaceful approach might not be possible. It was always a possibility that they would need to fight their way in to get their brother, Xyrfed, out. Hopefully, he wasn't in such bad condition he couldn't walk. Kaistam's plan was to approach the manor as a relative of the injured man. With any luck, that would get him in the building. From there, he would have to take matters as they came.

Earlier in the morning, he had contacted Xyrfed with the scrying mirror. The plan was set that he would be arriving as Xyrfed's uncle, and if the assassin had the strength, they would be leaving to pursue the source of the new magiq that had almost killed him. Kaistam began to walk to the front of the manor house. He was sure the others were in their places by now. They were to take any further signs from him. Until then, he instructed them to remain busy. As he approached the steps leading up to the surrounding porch, someone yelled.

"Hey, you can't be here! Stop!"

Kaistam stopped and turned to see who was yelling. He was using an old staff of his. It wasn't his normal staff of power, but it was still very dangerous in his hands—both as a pole weapon and a magiqal weapon.

A guard came running up to him. "Sir, no one is allowed in the house!"

"Ah, perhaps you could help me then," Kaistam began. "I have heard that my nephew was injured here, and I must locate him."

"Your nephew?" The guard was visibly shaken. "I will have to fetch the captain. Only he can let anyone in to see the injured man. Do you know the man's name?"

"Of course, he's my nephew. His name is Caryl. I must be let in to see him. His mother is so worried about him! I need to be allowed in!"

The soldier stood there, not knowing what to say. One second turned to five.

"Off you go, lad! Fetch your captain. I must see my nephew now!"

Kaistam-Laq was not a man known for his patience. When the soldier had not yet moved, the sorcerer began to become aggravated. "Did you hear me, boy? I said go fetch the man who can help me! I must talk to my nephew *now*!" He emphasized the last word quite loudly.

People turned to see what was going on. The soldier didn't need to be asked again. He sprinted off to locate his superior. Kaistam stood with a smug expression on his face. He did not like to repeat himself about anything, but the soldier seemed to be a bit thick. Within two minutes, the junior soldier arrived with his superior in tow. Kaistam didn't think the junior soldier even took the time to explain the situation because the captain looked annoyed for being dragged over to the old man.

"What is the meaning of this?" the captain asked either of the two. He wanted an answer and didn't care who gave it.

Kaistam spoke up. "I have just traveled from the north to help gather information on my sister's son. I believe he was injured the other evening in this house. I am here to collect him and take him home to his mother."

The captain's eyes narrowed. "Oh, you think so, do you? Who are you to demand that I release our patient? The man you are talking about is injured, and you can't come here demanding that I release him just like that." He snapped his fingers.

"If this is, in fact, my nephew Caryl, I believe I do have the right to ask for his release. Is he being held for any other reason?"

"Well, no, but I will—"

"I apologize for my interruption, Captain, but unless you are holding my nephew for any other reason, I believe this conversation is over. Please take me to my nephew now, Captain!"

The captain was not happy, but he knew the old man was correct. There was nothing he could do to keep him away from his nephew if he had done nothing. The captain turned red as he led the way into the first-floor room. Kaistam was glad that he didn't need to employ any magic yet. Still, he held tight to his staff and followed. As badly as he had heard that his assassin had been hurt, Kaistam was surprised to see that the stories seemed to be exaggerated. His man was sitting in bed with a nearly mended face. There was some severe scarring, but it might heal over time, and of course, some magiqal healing would help as well. Within a couple of minutes, the soldier and what Kaistam assumed was his superior returned to meet him. The captain did nothing to greet the sorcerer. He was not cordial nor even polite.

"You, old man, my soldier says you are here to see the injured man."

"Indeed, I am, sir," Kaistam replied as politely as the situation called for. "There are to be no visitors, by order of the major. The only person allowed to see the injured person," he said with dislike, "is the healer. All others are prohibited from entering."

"But surely there must be exceptions. I have traveled a great deal to see my nephew. I have come at my sister's behest. A promise I do not intend to break. Doubtlessly, I should have an audience with your major to speak about my nephew's release."

"Release? You must have misunderstood me. The wounded man will not be released until he can be questioned by the head of our militia concerning the death of the magistrate and his wife."

"But certainly, you don't think Caryl had anything to do with that tragic event. He himself was wounded trying to protect your leader."

"That remains to be seen, and until the details of that night become clearer, this *Caryl* will be enjoying the hospitality of our village's militia."

"I am afraid I am going to have to demand to speak to the person in charge then," Kaistam said, the edge beginning to set in his voice.

"You are in no position to demand anything, old man. I'm not sure who you are, but if you continue to demand things from me, you will find yourself in a cell faster than you can say—"

"What seems to be the issue here?" asked a man decorated in medals across his chest.

Kaistam figured this must be the major.

"No problem, sir!" the captain said quickly, not looking at the sorcerer.

Kaistam-Laq took this moment to speak up. "The captain here was just telling me that I would not be able to see my nephew. He is the man injured that was injured helping your magistrate. Major, I have traveled a great distance at my sister's insistence to make sure my nephew is alive and well. I was told by this man that I would be locked up if I continued to press the matter!"

The major and the captain were as different as night and day. The major asked the captain. "Is this true? Did you threaten this man, even after he identified himself as the wounded man's relative?"

"Sir, we can't be too careful. Anyone could say they are related to him. I was just being—"

The major cut him off. "You were being a pompous, inconsiderate prat! You had no right to treat this gentleman the way you have!" The major's voice has raised to a dangerous level.

The captain turned red and hung his head in shame.

"Sir," the major told Kaistam, "I would like to apologize for the way this man has treated you. I want you to know all of the people of Vennex do not behave in this manner. I will take you to see your nephew directly."

He turned to the captain and told him to go back to the billets. He would deal with him when he had finished taking the old man to see his nephew. The captain turned without a word and walked away.

Kaistam smiled knowingly. "It is okay, Major. He doesn't seem to be having a very good day."

"Truth be told, he never does," the major said, smirking at Kaistam-Laq.

The two of them made their way into the downstairs room where Xyrfed was being kept. The healer was just finishing another healing session on his face.

Chapter 29

Kuired Gÿann was approximately halfway back to his home and healer shop in Yelliton when he got the feeling that something wasn't right. Birds had been singing in the trees just minutes before, but now the forest was silent. At first, he just put it down to his presence on the trail. But as he walked, the silence grew louder. He stopped his cart that he was pulling and looked around. There were no animals darting through the underbrush; no birds to be seen in the canopy. He didn't even see any insects buzzing around. It was as if someone had just turned off the sound. Everything but the soft noise of his footfalls was gone. The trees were close enough together to hide something small, but he wasn't worried of an attack from anything large.

He circled the cart several times, listening for anything. Nothing. To be safe, he removed his hunting knife from its sheath and held it in his hand as he picked up the handle of his cart with the other. Even the sound of the wheels squeaking sounded dim. After a couple more moments of listening, he shrugged and continued his trek back toward his home. He had only been gone four days, but he knew that there would be a large workload upon his return. More people always seemed to get sick when he was away than when he was home.

As he continued his trip, he became more concerned. There was still no wildlife anywhere. Surely, by now, he should have heard the warble of a bird or seen the flapping of a butterfly's wings. Kuired stopped the cart again. This time, he walked off the trail and into the forest. He was certain that something wasn't right. At one point, he thought he had seen something cross the path ahead of him, but by the time he focused on it, there was nothing. Again, he picked up his cart handle to go, keeping his knife close to his body. He hadn't taken ten more steps when the shapes materialized out of the forest in front of him. There were eleven of them. All human. Two of them very familiar.

"What is this?" he asked, sounding braver than he felt at the moment.

"This," the leader said, coming forward, "is your very own personal escort home."

"I don't understand. What is going on?"

Kuired recognized the leader as the old man from Vennex, the one who claimed to be the wounded man called Caryl's uncle. That was when he noticed Caryl standing in the group of people as well.

"Caryl, what is the meaning of this? Would you mind telling me what is happening?"

The assassin looked to the leader for direction. When Kaistam nodded to him, he spoke, "We will be escorting you to your home in Yelliton. I believe you told me that you have some guests staying with you. The parents of the healer of Vennex? Isn't that what you told me?"

"What do you want with them?" he asked frantically.

"We wish to speak to this healer," Kaistam-Laq took back over the conversation. "I was worried he might not come if I just asked nicely. I feel I need another form of persuasion."

"Who are you?" demanded Kuired.

"There are some who know me as Kaistam-Laq, the leader of the sect of assassins known as Murtair Amagii. Have you heard of me?"

Kuired could feel the blood drain from his face. Everyone in any sizeable town or village had heard of this man and of his people. Kuired blanched at the thought that he had been treating the man who, in all likelihood, had killed the magistrate and his wife. He now understood what he was saying about being attacked in the room. The healer was ready to bet anything that it was Tÿr'Ynyn that had gotten to him. Now they were looking for her.

"I know you," Kuired replied to the sorcerer.

"Then you know that I'm a man of my word. You will not be harmed if you cooperate with us. We are *going* to find your houseguests, and we are *going* to use them to invite this magiq user I have tried in vain to locate. Once I have this person in my custody, you will be released."

"How do I know what you tell me is true?" Kuired asked, scared to anger the sorcerer.

"Because I have just told you. I am a man of my word. However, if you try to fight us or betray my trust, you will be killed immediately. You will not be given a chance for forgiveness or to plead your case. I do not tolerate betrayal of any type from *anyone.* I do not take it from anyone in my organization, so please do not think I will tolerate betrayal from you. Whether you live or die is inconsequential to me. I will get what I need and be gone. If you choose to be released, that will rely solely on you. Have I made myself clear?" The sorcerer has a crazed smile on his narrow face.

Kuired knew at this point that he was a dead man no matter what he did, so he would attempt to help Tÿr in any way he could before being found out. He still had some magiq that he could use to warn her. From the sides of Kaistam, the other eleven assassins surrounded the cart. One moved so quick Kuired wouldn't have had time to do anything with his knife anyway. The assassin struck him roughly on the side of his head. It happened so quickly the healer didn't have time to do anything other than to drop his knife and bring his hand up to his face. The assassin laughed raucously and moved in to hit him again, but the sorcerer stopped him.

"That is plenty! You may relieve him of his knife, but there is no need for further violence. He has done nothing to you. If it happens again, you will answer to me!"

The junior assassin smiled and bent to pick up the knife. "You won't be needing this anymore!"

Kaistam spoke again, and Kuired could hear the sincerity in his voice this time, "Healer, I wish to thank you for caring for my assassin while in Vennex. Your skills are very admirable. Thank you."

Kuired didn't know what to say. He was disgusted with this whole situation, and having taken care of his former magistrate's murderer left a bad taste in his mouth. Instead of saying anything, he simply nodded his acknowledgment. It seemed good enough for the assassin leader as he didn't say anything one way or the other. To keep Kuired from escaping, the sorcerer made an enchanted rope that he tied to the cart and the other end to the healer's wrist.

"This rope will come right off," the sorcerer told Kuired, "but if it does, I promise you will do everything in your power to put it back on. It is enchanted to beat with your heart. When it is removed, your heart will not beat so well. I would keep it on if I were you."

The small caravan of assassins, with the healer at the front, began moving through the forest again. Still there were no sounds of wildlife. Kuired thought of how he could get out of this situation. He thought of leading them to another place altogether, but now there were other people's lives at stake. What the healer wanted to know more than anything was why the Murtair Amagii were so interested in his friend Tÿr'Ynyn. Had they figured out that she was the one who had attacked their assassin back in Vennex? Surely, they couldn't have known that. They didn't even know she was a girl. As far as he could tell, they assumed that Tÿr was male. These types of people never gave credit to females when it same to learning and doing things as well as men. They were as close-minded as most of the planet. Kuired was going to let them keep thinking it too. If they underestimated the enemy, it would not work in their favor—that was for sure.

From his spot in the front of their caravan, Kuired could hear the assassins laugh and joke with the man he had called Caryl back in Vennex. He kept his mouth shut and listened as well as he could. Bits of conversation floated up to him, things like the details of the magistrate's death and how the assassin—now called Xyrfed—had turned his knives on the Siolad's wife because she had laughed like a psychotic fool. He had decided that she didn't deserve to live either. It was then that the entity had blown him into the wall, leaving him for dead. Xyrfed told the story that he was just getting ready to execute the son to eliminate all witnesses. He described the glowing arms and back that lit up the room and the balls of energy that shot out of the hands. His story ended there as he was blasted off his feet and nearly died.

Kuired now wished he had known who this man was when he went to heal him. The outcome might have been significantly different. Kuired had never taken a human life before, but in his mind, he didn't know what he would have done had he been presented with all the facts at the time. There was still over a day's travel before they reached Yelliton. Kuired had no way to warn Tÿr's parents. There were tending his house while he was gone. They had told people that they were visiting relatives to throw people off their trail in case something just like this happened, but unfortunately, Kuired knew just where they were.

"I need to eat," Kuired called out to Kaistam as it neared dark. "I haven't eaten anything since morning. Please, may we stop?"

Kaistam didn't seem too keen to stop. He wanted to push on through until they reached Yelliton yet that night. He could tell that the healer was getting weak and ordered everyone to stop. Kuired fished around in his cart and grabbed some food that he had packed back in the village. He sat down to eat it. Several of the assassins looked at him eating. They, too, were hungry, and Kuired could tell that they hadn't packed any food for the trip. He thought about sharing some, but it could take more time than he had planned. These people were supposed to be survival specialists, but Kuired hadn't yet seen anything that would suggest that it was true. A few of the sect had dried meat to chew on while he sat and ate. He wanted to ask if they were full, but quite honestly, he didn't really care. The more he could wear them out, the worse their morale would become. Never let your troops' morale dip! When that happened, troops began to do irrational things.

The next thing on Kuired's list to do was to sever his connection with the line that bound him to his cart. It was true that the cord wasn't really hurting his arm at all, but it was more the indignity of being held against his will. He needed to cut the bond and disable the sorcerer. The problem was what he was going to do then. There were ten other assassins just itching to remove him from this situation, even though he was still needed if they truly wished to find Tÿr.

That also brought a lump to his throat. What was going to happen when he got to his home? He assumed they didn't plan on asking nicely. Kuired wasn't worried so much for himself as he was for Tÿr's parents. They knew she was gone, but even they didn't know where she went. The wyverns thought it was safer if they didn't know. The healer's head reeled with concern.

Travel was slow as Kuired was tired. He was the only one on foot. The assassins used horses to travel and therefore weren't wearied by walking the great distance between Vennex and Yelliton. It wasn't that it was so far, but travel was made difficult by rough trails and blue, rocky ground. Even with boots on, pieces of broken crystals dug into the bottoms of his feet, causing him to step even slower, choosing his footfalls with care.

It was nearing nightfall when the trees began to thin out, and the signs of a village became evident. Fields of crops laid in between clearings of trees. It was the cool-weather, growing season now, and the crops were as high as a man's boot. Even here near the fields, Kuired would have expected to hear signs of wild boars, or any wild-life for that matter, but the area was still. It was almost as if the sound had been shut off.

Just past the field they were crossing, the group would come to a valley where the Ajenti River took a tight turn and curved in and back out again. It made an excellent area for growing *votrys*, a water-type tuber that was served with many meals, mashed up and sprinkled with herbed salt. Beyond the valley laid the lazy village of Yelliton. It wasn't a large place, only twice the size of villages like Vennex, but it was peaceful and a pleasant place to call home. Kuired's shop and house lay on the western outskirts of Yelliton. He only had a short time to figure out what he was going to do. Despite the laughter and talking behind him, he could feel their eyes watching every move that he made. They were not about to lose the only link to the magiq user that the sorcerer was so eager to get his hands on. Before the small caravan reached the outskirts of the city, Kaistam-Laq called a halt. He walked to the front near the healer and looked him straight in the eyes.

"Healer, we are nearly here. You can save your friends needless pain and suffering by simply telling me what I wish to know." Kuired stared at the sorcerer without moving. "I understand you feel a type of loyalty to them, and that is admirable. I value such qualities in my own people. However, this is something that is not going to help them. I need information about a magiq user, one who may be stronger than even myself. I must be able to speak with this man. Preventing me will only hurt yourself and your friends. Do you understand me?"

Kuired nodded slowly.

"Good, good! What can you tell me about this magiq user? Who is he? Where is he now? I must be allowed to speak with him! I will have my way, healer!"

Kuired said nothing. He could see the frustration on the sorcerer's face. He also knew that this was not a man to be trifled with. He could and did follow through on any and all threats he had ever made. Kuired also knew that there was no way that he could give up his friend Tÿr to this tyrant.

"Say something!" the sorcerer almost screamed.

The other assassins came to a halt with whatever they had been doing. No one dared speak.

"I have nothing to say," Kuired said to the man.

Kaistam-Laq's staff began to glow. Kuired felt like someone had stepped on his chest. He couldn't breathe in. The only thing he could do was exhale, and each time he did, his lungs emptied more and more. Kuired tried to gasp for air, but he couldn't draw breath. His heart beat hard in his chest cavity, but there was no air to feed it. He fell to the ground, holding his throat and trying to breathe. His face turned from red to purple, and his eyes bulged to twice their normal size. He was dying and couldn't do anything about it. Kuired would have tried magiq but wouldn't have known what to use as the magiq being used on him was unknown. He didn't deal with harmful magiq. Despite the fact that his eyes were wide open, he could see a dark cloud begin to fall across his area of vision. Slowly at first, and then he was in the dark. Fear overtook him as he realized he was going to die. Kuired fell to the ground in a heap. Then it stopped. As quickly as it came, it was gone, and the blessed, cool air flowed back into his lungs. He had to force it at first, as if he was reteaching them to breathe. The red left his face, and his head quit spinning.

"Do you believe I could kill you?"

The sorcerer was asking him another question. "I believe you could if you chose to. But don't you need me for something first?"

"Do not press your situation. The next time you will not be getting up. The next time I expect an answer."

Kuired waited for the question to come again, but it never did. It took several moments for the dizziness to wear off, but the sorcerer didn't care. They were off and walking before it went away. They were nearing the village now. Kuired could see the southern edge of Yelliton with its neat, single-story buildings. The taller government buildings were in the center of town near the town center. Most of the homes had blue tile roofs made from the blue clay of a marsh nearby. They were all small cottages painted white to look alike.

Kuired's shop was one of the only buildings in town that was not white. He had wanted it to stand out so it was easy to find. He hoped it would not be a drawback now. His home, however, was white like all the others. One thing that was to his advantage was that his home was not next to the shop. It was one street over from the shop, sandwiched between two larger cottages. Since it was just himself, he didn't need a large place, just two bedrooms a kitchen and living space. He used his kitchen to make many of the potions and ointments that he sold at the healer's shop. Kuired was still frantically trying to figure out how to save Tÿr's parents. He thought he might have an idea, but the end was not happy for him. Also, he didn't have his staff with him, so his magiq was limited. He would only be able to conjure or perform one or two small acts, and they would have to count. If he didn't act at the correct time with the proper spell, it would all be for nothing.

The healer knew that he was up against eleven trained assassins, who could all conjure and probably move faster than he could. He also had to deal with the tether that bound him to the cart that he drew behind him carrying his belongings. A diversion. He needed a large diversion, and then he needed to be gone. If he could find a way to lose the tether. He glanced back to see how close the assassins were following behind him. Most were following closely around the cart he was pulling. This gave him an idea.

He stopped walking and told Kaistam-Laq that he needed to get a drink from his pack. Kuired had stored extra water in goat-skins in the cart for emergencies. He also had several potions made with alcoholic bases, which meant that they were highly flammable. Kuired had his plan. It wasn't going to work out so well for him, but he needed to protect his friends at all cost. The sorcerer looked at the healer with skepticism when he halted the convoy.

"I must get a drink," the healer said earnestly.

Kaistam-Laq was impatient by this time but allowed the short rest. Kuired got into each of his packs, pretending to look for his goatskin. Inside the packs, he opened the alcoholic elixirs and allowed some to spill in the packs. Others he just uncorked. All he needed to do was cause a spark large enough to set fire to it. In the last pack, Kuired feigned finding his goatskin and then removed it. He took a long drink and then hung it around his shoulder. He would not be allowed another stop for a drink. After sating his thirst, he turned and took the handle of his cart and began to walk to Yelliton. It was now or never!

If these were going to be the final breaths he took, he was going to make every last one count. Instead of doing one huge bit of magiq, Kuired decided he would use smaller, smarter magiq. The first would be to sever his bonds. When that was done, he would only have a few moments to keep his heart beating. It was a huge risk. He was a good healer and could do this on others at any time. He had never performed it on himself, but he figured that the mechanics were the same. Once his heart was beating again, he would create the diver-sion with the alcohol by exploding his cart. He hoped that it would cause enough confusion to let him get enough of a head start to make it to his home and warn Tÿr's parents. He figured he would collapse by then, and it would be all over for his part. If he was still alive, he would try to make it to his shop to draw off the assassins. He didn't think he could ask for more than that.

The rope was still tight around his wrist. It grabbed tighter the harder he pulled to get away. Magiq was not his forte. He was a classical healer that used magiq to his advantage, but he knew he could pull this off. Kuired conjured the first of his spells. Silently he cast a severing spell on the rope. At first, nothing happened. He pulled, and the rope pulled back at him. Then there was a quiet, sizzling noise near the handle of the cart. The spell didn't work exactly where he had planned it to, but then the rope dropped off the cart handle. The spelled was severed. Kuired could feel his chest stop. There was no beating from his heart. Without panicking, he cast his second spell, which sent a jolt through his chest. And then again. He hoped that none of the assassins were paying attention to him. The healer had to slow to almost a stop for a moment. It took longer than he had planned to start his heart again. He began to feel light-headed but tried again. This time, there was a completely new sensation as his heart began to beat again. It wasn't beating like it normally did, but he was still on his feet and moving, so that was good enough for him. Part two of his plan had worked.

Kaistam-Laq was about to ask what was causing the delay when the cart began moving again. The assassins had bunched up momentarily, which gave the healer the perfect opportunity to set off his third spell. Right on cue, Kuired ignited the alcohol in the packs, which flamed and exploded in a fireball, sending the assassins running in all different directions. Kuired made his move and sprinted forward. He didn't look back, even when he heard the enraged sorcerer screaming orders to bring him down. The healer had already reached the first row of homes and weaved between them, trying to confuse the pursuers as best he could. He ran for a short distance in the opposite direction from his home. If he could lead them away from his cottage, it could buy him some time to warn Tÿr's parents so they could get a message off to her.

Kuired could feel his chest pounding under his ribs. Breathing was hard to do, but he couldn't give up yet. He had managed to give the assassins the slip for the moment, but they had magiq on their side, and they were far more practiced at it. Kuired could hear yelling from behind, so he dove into a bunch of shrubby plants growing at the side of one of the houses near the corner of the street. He needed to cross but couldn't tell where any of the enemies were. He risked a quick dash across the intersection of the brick-covered street. Farther down the street, he heard angry voices. It didn't seem that all the assassins had split up. With his breath coming in short gasps, Kuired still had several streets to go to reach his cottage and Tÿr's parents.

The healer heard footsteps ahead of him, so he stopped and flattened himself against the cottage he was hiding behind. Chancing a glance around the corner, he saw it was not the assassins. This made his heart drop. There were other people out in the village, and he didn't want them to be used as bait. Hopefully, the assassins were too busy chasing him they would leave the residents of Yelliton alone.

Before moving out, Kuired chanced a rear glance to see if he was being followed. He could see smoke in the sky from where he had set off the explosion. With any luck, the residents wouldn't go to see what had caused it. The healer could hear calls being relayed between the assassins, letting each other know where the other were. This helped him tremendously. So far, none had gotten in front of him. They had taken the bait and had gone in the wrong direction. He was still five streets away from his cottage, and his heart was beginning to give out. He could feel it skipping beats. It was harder to breathe. If he didn't go now, he would never make it. Kuired ran for all he was worth. He could barely breathe now, and catching his breath was next to impossible. When he reached his cottage, he didn't look behind. He threw open the door and fell to the floor, gasping. Elmky Tÿr was in the sitting room when Kuired came crashing through the door.

"Oh my! Kuired! What is going on?!"

"Must listen!" He gasped. "Get message to Tÿr'Ynyn. Murtair Amagii are searching for her in Yelliton. You are in danger! Must get out!"

Elmky rushed down to Kuired and tried to help him up, but his gasping had stopped. His face was turning redder as he tried to draw breath. "Kuired! What can I do? You've got to breathe! Kuired!" she screamed.

Seryth Tÿr came running into the room. "What is going on?" he yelled.

"He's dying!" cried his wife. "Help me get him up."

The two of them tried to move Kuired to a chair, but he had already been dead for over a minute. His body was limp.

"What just happened?" Seryth asked his wife.

"He rushed in here and said that we had to warn Tÿr. The Murtair Amagii are looking for her here in Yelliton. We've got to tell her to stay away!"

Seryth didn't waste any time. He found a small piece of parchment and scrawled a quick message:

Tÿr,

You are being hunted by the Murtair Amagii. They are here in Yelliton. Kuired is dead! Do not come back here! We will try to get out, but no matter what you hear, do not come back here! It is not worth it!

Dad

Seryth rolled up the note to fit it into the säqyr wyvern's note tube. He ran outside to find Sëvyq. The little wyvern was perched on the corner of the roof in the back of the house. Seryth's hands shook as he tried to get the note into the tube. After a quick moment of fumbling, he managed to get it in and urged the wyvern off to find his daughter.

"Take this to Tÿr as quickly as you can! This is an emergency!"

The little wyvern lifted off the ground and sped off toward the mountains. Seryth watched him for a bit until he remembered that they would probably be having unwanted guests before too long. He got an idea.

"Mother! Come quickly! I have an idea."

"What is it?" she asked, rushing up to him. "Help me move his body!"

"Where are we moving it?"

351

"We're going to take it out to the street."

"What? Why?" she asked. "If we can get his body out into the street, we can use it for a diversion. If they can't find his cottage, maybe they won't be able to find us."

Tÿr's mom understood what they were going to do, but it was clear that she didn't like the idea. She felt very bad that their friend had died, and they weren't going to be able to give him a proper burial.

Kaistam-Laq was following Xyrfed as they searched through the village. They were no longer dressed as paupers, the way they had presented themselves in Vennex. The sorcerer strode throughout the village in his finest robes, carrying his staff. This was an intimidation tactic. He wanted everyone in the village of Yelliton to know that he and his assassins were there and that anyone who stood in the way would be dealt with severely. Villagers who saw the assassins turned purposefully out of the way to avoid any conflict. Too many rumors and stories had been told about the sect to keep the people out of the way.

The search lasted a short while before Kaistam finally broke down and asked where the healer's shop was located. A terrified woman wasn't able to find the words to tell them; she only pointed in the direction and ran off as fast as she could, dropping some bread that she had just purchased for dinner from the bakery. At least the assassins had a direction to begin searching. The hunt narrowed, thanks to the frightened lady's assistance, but there was still much ground to cover.

Only after they found the body of the healer himself were they able to close in on the shop even more. Tÿr's parents were already moving through the town to try to make it back to Vennex when a pair of the assassins caught them leaving the village. They were brought back to the healer's shop to answer questions of the leader of the most-feared sect on both planets. Kaistam was actually in a decent mood. This was the closest they had been to finding his magiq user since the very first sign of their magiq. He let the couple sit in the room and wait, imagining what horrors to expect, while he prepared.

Chapter 30

Tỹr had just gotten finished eating and was having a pipeful of herb weed. She took several puffs, feeling the slight intoxicating effects of the thick smoke relax her. She offered the pipe to Sämir, who took it and drew deeply on the quartz pipe. He choked and coughed, still not quite used to the thick, velvety smoke. He and Tỹr both laughed. Their chuckles were interrupted by the piercing screech of the säqyr wyvern arriving. Tỹr knew something was wrong immediately. Sëvyq wasted no time bringing the note. Usually, he would go and see Rævii or Ghra'zhenn, but not this time. When he didn't see the paragon, he flew directly to Tỹr and sat at her feet, nudging her leg with his head.

"Okay, okay, little man! I'm getting it!"

Tỹr bent down and grabbed at his collar. The tube with the note in it opened easily, and Tỹr recognized her father's penmanship immediately. Already a sense of dread came over her. She knew that her dad was not one to panic or ask for help unless the situation was dire. Tỹr unrolled the parchment and read it quickly. Her face blanched.

Where was Ghra'zhenn? He had been gone since she had awakened.

"Is everything all right?" Sämir asked.

"No, it isn't. I'm afraid there has been more trouble. Now the trouble has moved to Yelliton. Did you happen to see Ghra'zhenn before he left this morning?" she asked the boy.

Sämir shook his head. "I only got up just before you did."

Tỹr's only hope to finding the paragon quickly was the little wyvern sitting at her feet. Sëvyq hadn't moved since she had removed the note from the little tube at his neck. He appeared to be waiting for her to respond.

Tÿr got down on his level and looked the säqyr wyvern in the face. "Little boy, I need Ghra'zhenn to come back here as soon as he can get back. Can you go let him know this?"

The little wyvern stared at her intently as if he understood every word that she said when she asked, "Can you do this for me?"

Sëvyq didn't wait to exit the cave. He took off right there, making Tÿr's short hair blow in the breeze of his wings. Tÿr couldn't believe it. Kuired was dead. What had happened? Why did the assassins want her parents? She knew that her dad had warned her against returning, but there was no way she could leave them in the hands of the Murtair Amagii. They were monsters. She had seen what just one of them could do. The apprentice began to pace the cavern while she puffed on her pipe. Her cousin watched her with growing concern.

"Is there anything I can do for you, Tÿr?"

She barely heard him as she paced. "I'm waiting for Ghra'zhenn to return. He's the only one that can probably help me right now!"

Sämir seemed crestfallen. His cousin had done so much for him in the last few hours he wanted to help her. It was then that he realized that he, Sämir, was magistrate of Vennex. Unless, of course, there was an uprising going on. He was in charge of the militia. All these things were a blur in his mind. The system of government in Vennex was different from many other places. Until the family was voted out, they continued ruling. He felt that he wouldn't last long now that his father was gone. He knew that had his mother taken over, unrest would have grown, and the people would have ousted her. She was a cruel lady and only enjoyed the power. Even at his young age, he knew his mother was not what the village needed. Thinking about his parents brought a lump to his throat. He still had not had a chance to grieve their loss. The situation was still so surreal. He knew one day it would hit him, but right now, Tÿr seemed to be in trouble, and if he could help her, that was his personal priority.

Tÿr continued to wander around the cavern, full of nervous energy. She couldn't sit still. The thought of her parents out there possibly being hunted or worse made her insane. Ghra'zhenn just had to be nearby. After only ten minutes, Tÿr heard the familiar flapping of wyvern wings, accompanied by the shrill cry of Sëvyq. It had only been ten minutes, but it had seemed an eternity. The little wyvern had found the paragon. Tÿr rushed out to meet him, barely letting him land before telling him about the letter.

"Hold on, Tÿr. Sëvyq has briefed me a bit on the flight back. He told me that your parents are in trouble? What is happening?"

Tÿr brought out the letter and began to read it to the paragon as they moved to the cavern.

Ghra'zhenn paused a moment before he spoke. "This might be a better matter for the wyverns. You are too close to this situation. They will use your parents against you should you go."

"I respect you, Ghra'zhenn, but I cannot just let my parents sit there at the mercy of these animals. I've seen what they can and will do. I have to go! Please don't ask me to stay!"

"I understand your concern, young one, but will you be able to separate yourself from this matter? There may be very difficult decisions that need to be made. Will you be able to do this with a clear head?"

"I can't honestly say," Tÿr told him. "I've never had to do something like this before, but I must be allowed to try. I cannot let those monsters harm my parents."

"Thank you for your honesty. It is the best I can ask of anyone."

Tÿr breathed a sigh of relief. She didn't want to go against her paragon, but she would have to save her parents. "When do we go? I just need to tell Sämir what we are doing, and then I am ready to go!"

"We must wait for a bit," Ghra'zhenn told her. "We can't just go there with the two of us unprepared. We need reinforcements! When we left Ÿkkynnÿk, I instructed twenty of my older dynasty to fly out to meet us here for this very reason. The youngest wyvern is two hundred and ninety, and the oldest is five hundred. They are just a short distance from here. I am going to instruct them to meet us here, and we will proceed to Yelliton. We will even the odds exponentially by waiting."

"But my parents could be in trouble right now!"

"Patience, Tÿr. We will get there as soon as we can. They need your parents alive to lure you there. It is my opinion that they will not harm them yet anyway. They want you! If they harm your parents, you have no incentive to go!"

Tÿr wanted to argue, but what Ghra'zhenn said made sense. If they harmed or killed her parents, she would have no true reason to show up there. Well, other than revenge. Of course, she didn't put anything past these psychotic murderers. Right now, it was time to plan until the other wyverns of the dynasty arrived. She would try to plot out some magiq that she could use, things that they might not be expecting. She really wished she had time to use her invisibility salve again. This time, however, she would be traveling with her staff. She, too, would be facing one of the planets' most powerful sorcerers and several of his lackeys. She wasn't sure how many there were, which was why she wished she could go in the town with her invisibility potion. She could reconnoiter and report back instead of going in blind. Unfortunately, there probably wasn't enough time. They needed to get in and get her parents out with as few injuries to the dynasty as possible.

"Ghra'zhenn, would I have time to use the invisibility potion? It would be good to send me in to spy."

"I'm not sure that it would work so well this time, my young friend. I believe that Kaistam-Laq himself is in Yelliton, and he is dying to get his hands on you. Rumors say he is looking high and low for the powerful, new magiq user, and I believe he will be trying to sense any type of unknown magiq that gets close. Imagine his surprise when he finally meets you. From the rumors I have gleaned, he believes you to be a male. He does not believe a woman can be as powerful as you are, and that will to be his downfall. He doesn't underestimate a wyvern, but I believe that he won't treat you as an equal. In fact, I believe your power actually exceeds his, and he will not be prepared for that."

Ghra'zhenn chuckled at that. Tÿr was too nervous to laugh but smiled politely. "How long before the others arrive?"

"I sent Sëvyq before he could even land. He can reach them in about fifteen minutes' time. It won't take them much more than that to get here. Let's prepare your harness so we can go as soon as they arrive," he told the apprentice.

Tÿr went over to Sämir and explained what was getting ready to take place. She explained that Ghra'zhenn could take him back to Vennex if he wished to go back and remain there as magistrate. She then told him that she could see the good in him and that he would make a good and just leader with the right help. Sämir hugged her. It was clear that he was not used to receiving kind, loving care. He hugged her close to him, as if he was scared he would lose her too. Tÿr was filled with emotion for her cousin for the first time. She left him on the bed with instructions to care for Rævii. The fox came over to him and nuzzled his leg, her blond tail twitching playfully. He had made a new friend already.

Tÿr didn't know what to take. She would have her staff, and that was all she really needed. Then she thought for a moment. When she found the assassin, he had lachtrys with him. He had used it to form blades from. While she waited, she wanted to try something. There were several medium pieces of lachtrys on one of the shelves that she used for potions. She went and took two pieces, one she put in a pouch on her belt, and the other she held in her hand. The assassin had changed the shape of the stone into a thin-bladed dagger. It had just melted into that shape. Surely, if he could do it, she could. Tÿr concentrated on the stone, imagining it becoming a knife. The stone became liquid in her hand. It wasn't hot but remained cool. At first, it just looked like a blob, but after a short time, she was able to get it to form a crude-looking knife with a very thick blade. She'd never slice or cut anything with it like this.

It took about ten minutes before she had made a respectable blade. Then she did it over. It happened faster this time. She did it again. Each time became quicker and quicker. She had just started to do it once again when a deafening, flapping sound approached from the distance, growing louder and louder. Tÿr dropped the second piece of lachtrys into her pouch and ran out to meet the wyverns.

The sky above the mountain was darkened with the large creatures as they approached their destination. Ghra'zhenn, too, was there to meet them. One by one, they landed on the plateau. Tÿr looked and saw Sämir by the cavern entrance, watching the spectacle of the wyverns landing. She could see there was fear in his eyes. It was hard to say what he had been told about them from his mother. He looked like he wanted to come out, but instead stayed where he was. Rævii, on the other hand, rushed out to greet them all, running from one to the other. They would pat her head, and when she was done greeting one, she moved on to the next. The wyverns knew of Tÿr's pet and welcomed her as they welcomed her master.

The wyverns gathered around Tÿr and Ghra'zhenn to be briefed of the situation. Ghra'zhenn spoke in Cmok to save time. Tÿr was able to follow the conversation but still had trouble catching all the words. The wyverns were visibly agitated by the news that Ghra'zhenn had given them. They did not favor humans using magiq against others to cause harm. The fact that Kaistam probably had Tÿr's parents riled them even more, so they were quite anxious to get underway.

Tÿr ran back to Sämir and hugged him again. She told him that everything would be okay and that if he chose, he could come to stay with her when this was all over. There were tears of fear on the boy's face as they split apart. Tÿr gave him a brave smile and then turned to go. It was time to find her parents.

Ghra'zhenn leaned down to help Tÿr mount the harness on his back. He gave a mighty roar, which was echoed by the others of the dynasty. In a flurry of wings, the wyverns took to the air, darkening the skies as they turned and headed toward Yelliton. Ghra'zhenn took the lead, and the rest fell into a wedge formation behind him. Tÿr held the staff flat against the paragon's back, and then she too flattened against his neck. The wind blew over her with less drag when she rode lower on the huge, flying lizard.

Chapter 31

Pacing in the cottage of the former healer of Yelliton, Kaistam-Laq was becoming more and more agitated. He had expected results by now, and so far, there had not been anything. No message, no anything. Usually, in this type of situation, he would lose his composure, but he couldn't do that yet. The people that he was keeping in the cottage could not see him go into a rage quite yet. As long as his people did as he had instructed, he would not have any issues. The people he had invited to stay with him were too scared to try anything foolish, so he would remain calm as well. He did wonder though, why had no one come? Did their son not care about them at all? Why had he not made contact? Kaistam was sure that there was going to be an attack, and he would use these people as shields if he needed. They meant nothing to him. He also figured this magiq user was very intelligent too, so maybe the attack would not come, and there wouldn't be any fight. The sorcerer really did not like to be unprepared. He preferred to always have to upper hand in all situations. He went out the front door to check to see if there had been any movement or any sign of anything. It was on his third time checking that one of his assassins came running into the cottage.

"Sir! We have movement coming in from over top of the trees from the direction of the mountains."

"Movement? What kind? What do you mean?"

"Wyverns, sir, at least fifteen, maybe more. I'm not sure if this is what you're looking for, but it's the only movement of anything we've seen in a while."

"No! This is it!" Kaistam said positively. "Get out and tell everyone to be prepared. I think we're going to be dealing with a long, costly fight this day. We are not taking prisoners! Kill them all!"

The sorcerer turned to the couple he had taken hostage. He had a maniacal gleam in his eye. "It seems your son cannot refuse to stay away. I assume you warned him to do just that. I have been counting on him to show up to help you. I knew he couldn't stay away."

Tÿr's parents had puzzled looks. "You keep talking of our son. I'm afraid you are mistaken. We have no son."

The air seemed to have been let out of the smug face of the sorcerer. "But, of course, you do. Who else could be doing this magiq? Your son is the healer!"

Both Tÿr's parents almost laughed in shock. They realized how dire their situation was, but this man obviously had the wrong end of the stick. "You are terribly mistaken. We have one child. She is the healer in Vennex, and when you meet her, you won't forget it! She won't stand idly by and let you harm anyone!" Seryth Tÿr told Kaistam-Laq.

The sorcerer turned the color of a ripe dragon fruit. It was obvious that he was not used to being corrected. His face became unusually calm. "Even if what you say is true," he said in a deadly tranquil voice, "I will have them join me, or they will not see another day."

"My daughter would never agree to join anyone who spends their life murdering innocent people. You had my brother killed! It will be you that pays for your crimes today, sorcerer."

Kaistam laughed out loud at this proclamation. Many people had made this claim in the past, and most had ended up in graveyards spread all over the planets. "Your offspring may have power, power that rivals even me, but I assure you, if they"—he still refused to acknowledge the gender of Seryth's child—"attempt to fight, they will perish like all who have come up against the Murtair Amagii in the past. We do one thing in our sect, and we do it better than all others. We kill. To attempt to fight us will be fatal to anyone."

"You underestimate my daughter, and that is where you will fail."

Kaistam wanted to argue, but at that moment, one of his assassins ran up to him. "They are here!"

Kaistam turned to his *guests*. "You will be bound in this house." He did a few movements with his staff, which glowed, and a ribbon of red light shot from it to wrap around Seryth and his wife. It disappeared as quickly as it had appeared. "You will not leave this house," Kaistam said matter-of-factly to the couple. "You may move about freely, but if you attempt to escape, the spell I just wove will stop your heart, and you'll be dead before you can take five steps out of this cottage."

Seryth ran forward and hit the wizard in the face before anyone could move. In one second more, the assassin in the cottage with them formed a blade from lachtrys and went to slice at the man.

"Enough!" roared Kaistam-Laq. He rubbed his face where he had been hit, smiling at the man who had just assaulted him. Then he turned on the other assassin. "You! Out! Now! I can care for myself! Return to your position."

The sorcerer moved his tongue around in his mouth. He could feel a loosened tooth. The man had hit him so hard it had knocked one of his back teeth loose. He reached into his mouth and, with a sharp snap, broke the offending tooth off at the gumline. He looked at it for a second before tossing it to the floor. Seryth waited for some form of retribution, but it never came. Tÿr's mom was shaking; her nerves were so bad after her husband struck the sorcerer. They watched as the robed man took his staff and strode out of the cottage, leaving them alone. As soon as the sorcerer was out of the cottage, the couple ran to the windows to look out. They went from one to the other, trying to see if they could see anything that was going on. Finally, Seryth went to the front door and opened it.

Elmky screamed, "Seryth, no!"

He turned to face her. "I'm not going out. We'll be able to see better if we open the door. Just stand back!"

The sorcerer was standing out front and glanced back. He smiled at the couple in the doorway, almost daring them to step out. From inside the cottage, Elmky and Seryth could hear shouting of orders being given. From the distance, they could hear the sound of flapping wings, and they tensed knowing that Tÿr was on her way. Seryth knew that she had not followed his orders. She would never have left them to be harmed by the assassins. The man moved closer to the doorframe to see if he could see anything in the sky, but he didn't dare get too close. He wasn't sure if the sorcerer's curse was real or not, but he wasn't about to find out now. Eventually he and his wife moved back to a window to watch what they could. The sky above was full of wyverns flying over the village. Both he and his wife had knots in their stomachs, knowing that their daughter was up there somewhere.

Chapter 32

The wedge formation began to split apart as they reached the periphery of Yelliton. Ghra'zhenn was shouting orders to the dynasty to circle the village. They were looking for any signs of the hiding assassins. Tÿr scanned the landscape ahead to see if there were any signs of the forthcoming trouble. From the view above, she could tell that the village looked almost deserted. The normal hustle and bustle of everyday life was at a standstill. Tÿr could see the other wyverns circle around the city. They were calling back to Ghra'zhenn in Cmok to ensure that no listeners would understand what was being said.

The sight of the wyverns above Yelliton was beautiful and quite incredible. Tÿr knew that the village was on great terms with the dynasty, so they wouldn't expect an invasion. She expected they were having enough trouble with the assassin force already hiding out in the town. Ghra'zhenn had warned the dynasty to be cautious of the assassin sect using citizens as shields. They were cowards and would do anything it took to save themselves. Tÿr, too, would have to take extreme care when employing her magiq. Her goal was to keep the injuries down to as few as possible. The leader of the sect was going to pose the most trouble as he seemed to want to get his hands on Tÿr'Ynyn more than anything. She had no idea why.

Ghra'zhenn called the other wyverns back to him to reform the wedge, and when they returned, the dynasty began their descent into the village. The blue-tiled roofs grew closer, and Tÿr could make out each individual tile now—that was how low they were. Ghra'zhenn still remained aloft, looking in all directions, checking for traps or surprise attacks, but they didn't come. When he was satisfied, he landed the group in a field just outside town.

Tÿr dismounted and stood in front of the dynasty. In the bravest voice she could gather, she spoke, "Zhyxxy drx'xy'lagt graaxxa xjyk Zïya klÿllum hokkxt xjyk."

Roughly translated into the wyvern tongue, it meant, "Thank you so much for your help. Please be careful."

Tÿr was getting better at speaking the language, but it still didn't sound the same as when a wyvern spoke it. A wyvern didn't have the same mouth parts that a human did. The wyverns all acknowledged Tÿr's appreciation. And then Ghra'zhenn readied them to move into the village. He told some of the wyverns to protect them from above and to watch out for surprise attacks. A wyvern's eyes were incredible, and they would serve those on the ground well. Before moving out, Tÿr cast a spell of protection over herself, a powerful incantation that would help to keep bolts of energy from striking her unexpectedly.

With her staff held as a walking stick, she began to walk in the lead, followed closely by the earthbound wyverns. The others had lifted off already and were looking for any signs of assassins lurking behind buildings. Tÿr and the wyverns made it to the south end of town without seeing so much as a soul. Neither an assassin nor any Yelliton resident was out. In one way, this was a good sign. It would hopefully keep the civilian casualty toll down. Tÿr knew this was probably wishful thinking as these assassins were cowards and would even use the civilians to hide behind if the situation called for it. Tÿr had only been to Kuired's shop once before, and she wanted to run straight to it to help her parents, but she knew she had to be patient. If she ran there first off, there were too many assassins running around, and her parents or others could get hurt. They needed to eliminate as many of the threats as they could before going after her mum and da.

Almost immediately warnings were called back to the group on the ground. The assassins were in the houses. This would make things much more difficult. Already the enemy was using the innocent villagers and their homes as protection. Ghra'zhenn gave strict orders not to attack anyone hiding in the cottages. These cowards now had the upper hand, and they would have to devise a plan to change that without destroying the homes of the villagers. Tȳr could tell that the paragon was frustrated.

"We must find a way to get those cowards out of the people's homes." He spat in disgust. "They cannot think that we would attack them now. What are they waiting for?"

It was then that the cry from a lone wyvern broke the silence. Tȳr only understood part of what was said.

"The sorcerer" and "he comes now" were the things that she was able to make out. Ghra'zhenn did not move the land-bound wyverns. He sat in place next to Tȳr and waited. Tȳr had an idea that she knew what was happening. Tȳr waited with the others, barely breathing. She wished that Varanus had come, but Ghra'zhenn had instructed him to stay with the brothers and continue their classes. She missed her mentor and wanted him to be there for this, but the paragon had opted to take the elders of the dynasty. They were more experienced and had seen battles before. Varanus was still very young for a wyvern; and although he could protect Tȳr very well from most anything, they were facing an unknown amount of trained, magiq-using assassins. Ghra'zhenn wanted those experienced in battle to be here with him. Varanus would have plenty of time to learn the art of warfare over a long lifetime.

For many long moments, nothing happened. Tȳr counted the houses and looked to see where the roads cut into the village. Yelliton sat on a large hill so she could see much of it from where she stood. Any villagers that were outside seemed to be rushing to get to their homes. They could tell that there was trouble brewing in the village, and they didn't want any part of it. That was why they had moved to Yelliton in the first place. It was a quiet, peaceful place, and now that was being threatened.

From the bottom of the city and a bit to her right, Tȳr spotted some motion. Three figures had appeared. She had been looking around and didn't know if they had walked up or had just appeared out of thin air. All three figures were tall, but the one in the middle was especially so. He carried a staff, so Tȳr figured him to be the infamous sorcerer, Kaistam-Laq. To his right was an extremely tall woman; she was dark and completely bald. On his other side was the man Tÿr had attacked back in Vennex. She couldn't believe her eyes. How had he survived the attack? She had seen him fall and not get up. No one should have been able to withstand an attack of such ferocity, yet there he stood. When the sorcerer had reached the edge of the field that Tÿr and the wyverns were gathered in, he halted.

"Tÿr'Ynyn!" he called out.

Tÿr froze in place. How did he know her?

"I have come with a proposal for you. Before you think to react, let it be known that I have your parents in my care. If you or your…" He paused with a look of dislike on his face. "Your companions. Should you think to try some type of hopeless heroism, you will not see them alive again. Should you anger me by not hearing my proposal, you may never even find their pathetic bodies. Do I have your attention, young lady?"

Tÿr felt as if she had been slapped across the face. No one had ever spoken to her like this before. Even her uncle and aunt—may they find peace—never threatened her like this. The sorcerer had continued speaking, but Tÿr hadn't heard the first little bit because she was still in shock from the man's audacity.

"Before we can do anything, we must find out where he keeps your parents, Tÿr," Ghra'zhenn had whispered as quietly as was possible for a wyvern.

Tÿr nodded her head and tried to hear what the madman in front of her was saying. "For you to join us. You have great powers, and we wish to tap into your great magiqal resources. You will have all you could ever want or need. You and your family would be—"

"What! You have come out here, killed my uncle and aunt, kidnapped my parents *and* threatened to kill them, not to mention make them disappear, just to *invite* me to become one of your paid killers! Gaunts, man, are you completely insane?"

A maniacal smile cracked the face of the sorcerer. "Are you refusing my offer without even thinking it over? Think it over! You could be wealthy beyond your dreams! You could have anything you—"

"Gaunts, you are insane!" Tÿr said, cutting off the leader of the killing sect. "Of course, I'm refusing. Shit, I'm thinking I'm crazy for not killing you right now for simply threatening my parents!"

Kaistam-Laq took this as a serious threat and began the attack on Týr. The other two assassins prepared to attack as well but waited for the word from their leader. Týr and the wyverns had been prepared for the attack. In unison, they cast a shielding spell that surrounded the whole troupe of them. Kaistam launched a large fireball that sped at Týr. It never got close before it disintegrated against the invisible shield that had been cast well before it was launched. The sorcerer was not happy to see his magiq stopped so easily. He cast again, and then again. Each time the attack grew more robust, the fire turned lighter, the last fireball actually white hot like a star. Each time the fire just hit the invisible shield and then was destroyed harmlessly.

The sorcerer was growing more frustrated with each attack. He hadn't planned on such a difficult encounter. He howled with exasperation and finally stopped hurling fire at the girl. He would have to figure something else out, and fast. The group of wyverns, with Týr leading them, began to walk toward the village. The sorcerer had made his opening move, so now it was time for Týr to show him her power. With the wyvern paragon at her back, she felt like there was nothing that couldn't be done. Now she would return the attack. Hopefully, she didn't miss this self-serving fool. She couldn't afford to miss him and hit any of the homes. The land was dry, and the homes were close together.

As she prepared to conjure, the wyverns from the air dove in low and created a cloud of dust around the sorcerer. Týr took that opportunity to send a ball of highly concentrated energy that split into three and shot at the enemies in front of her. She could tell that at least one of the dynamic orbs had found its mark by the sudden string of curses emitting from the blue cloud of dust that the flying wyverns had created. The swift lizards soared back into the heights to avoid any quick retaliation from the assassins on the ground.

As the dust cleared and Týr readied another spell, she could see the two assassins on either side of Kaistam-Laq, attempting to regain their footing. The sorcerer had raised his staff in preparation to outcast her. She suddenly had an idea. She sent off another dynamical ball of electricity, but this time, Týr hid it under the cover of invisibility. Kaistam waited for her to cast. He wanted to let go his spell the moment her spell left her staff. During the split second that she let her attack go, she would be occupied and unprepared for his. He hoped to hit her with his blast during this time, but it didn't happen. He didn't have time to think to cast. He never saw her attack. The only thing he saw was a movement in the dust on the ground in front of him, the mere moment before he was lifted off his feet and blasted back thirty feet. Tÿr was ecstatic that her plan had worked.

Ghra'zhenn congratulated her and told her to climb on his back. "We cannot simply shoot back and forth at each other all day," he told her. "Eventually someone will get hurt or end up dead. We need to sneak up on them. The element of surprise seems to work better on these fools."

Tÿr climbed into his back, and the rest of the wyverns, along with Tÿr and Ghra'zhenn, took to the air. They headed to the north side of Yelliton. The spies above had not seen any of the assassins hiding on that side of the village. As soon as Ghra'zhenn landed, Tÿr jumped off and headed in the direction of Kuired's shop. She knew the general direction she needed to travel to arrive there.

The last thing Tÿr heard before they took off was the sorcerer cursing at the two assassins to get to their feet. The sorcerer himself had still been on the ground, with smoke billowing from his robes. Tÿr sprinted toward the healing shop but came to a stop when she was confronted by a young man holding a woman around the neck, obviously a poor lady that hadn't gone inside when the assassins had come into town.

"Lay down your staff now!" he told Tÿr. "I have no trouble killing her."

"Let her go!" Tÿr yelled back at him. "You will be the one who suffers if you do not."

The man laughed. "Do you know who we are, healer?"

"Please, please don't let him hurt me," the lady pleaded. "My children are at home alone. My husband is dead, and they will be…"

"Save it, lady!" The assassin shoved her roughly to the ground and held a lachtrys blade at her throat. Tÿr watched as the short blade morphed from a thick, stocky blade to a long, thin dagger with pushed into the skin at the side of the woman's neck.

"Please help me!" she cried.

"I will ask you one last time, healer, lay down your staff and step away. I will kill this woman, and her blood will be on your hands."

Tÿr laid her staff on the ground. "I have done as you asked, but no matter what you say or how you talk yourself into this, her blood is on your hands, you twisted freak. Now let her go. You want me. Come and get me."

The assassin thought about it for a second before he roughly shoved the woman to the ground. She crawled away as fast as she could before getting to her feet and then running away from the scene. Tÿr walked slowly to the young assassin. He held the dagger out as she moved gradually in his direction. Then she stopped.

"What are you doing?" he asked almost hysterically.

"I think I've changed my mind," Tÿr said. She turned and began to walk back in the direction of her staff.

"What! Get back here!"

"No, I don't think so. If you want me, you will need to come and get me," she taunted him. "I guess you let your hostage go a bit too soon!"

The assassin lunged and began to run after Tÿr. She cast a spell, and her staff shot back into her hands. The man was yelling in rage, his arm was raised with his lachtrys dagger in his hand. Tÿr turned and hit him hard with the bottom of her staff. The blow knocked him senseless for a moment, giving Tÿr a second to get a head start away from him. If she was going to fight him, it wasn't going to be fair, and it wasn't going to be in close quarters. She was going to open the distance as much as she could. The assassin had fallen to one knee, but he was regaining his footing with a wild look in his face. Tÿr had managed to get a good distance away when she heard a string of unknown words being shouted from behind her. In a second, something large and hot collided with her in the back, knocking her over. She rolled to the side to see what it could be but realized that it could only be magiq. Something that fast had to have been a spell.

"Damn," she said out loud, "what the hell was that?"

She was already getting back to her feet. Tÿr didn't glance behind her until she had a chance to duck around the corner of a cottage.

"You won't get far, little lady," the young man said, taunting her.

She listened for any sound of his footsteps, but like any good assassin, he walked silently. Tÿr was getting ready to stick her head around the edge of the cottage she had taken refuge behind when she saw the assassin's shadow pass over the window on the other side of the house. He was moving her way. The healer apprentice had no time to think. She half-guessed and then cast her spell, hoping that it would hit true. It was a trap and an illusion, and she hoped it worked. She would know in three...two...

"Ahh!"

It had worked exactly as it was supposed to. Instead of trying to harm the boy, she had constructed a quick trap, which she had hidden with a quickly crafted illusion. In essence, it was a deep, circular hole made to look like the ground around it. The assassin was so busy sneaking around and looking for Tÿr he didn't bother to watch where he was walking. The loud yell was him falling into the twelve-foot-deep hole. It was wide enough to keep him from trying to shimmy his way back out, but close enough to keep him from trying to run and jump. It was a perfect spot to keep him safe until the battle was over. Tÿr glanced over into the hole and found the boy sitting on the bottom, holding his ankle.

"You bitch! I just broke my ankle when I fell in your little pit. When I get out of here, I will slit your throat."

Tÿr smiled at him and said, "That's pretty good motivation for me to keep you down there then, isn't it? I'll be back to fetch you later. Don't go anywhere!"

Tÿr used a small bit of magiq to smooth over the pit and make it turn back to a flawless piece of roadway. The young man yelled loudly before the road covered him over, and it was silent again. He had started to call her another name, but she had cut him off before he could finish. Elsewhere, the apprentice could hear shouts of curses and spells being shouted, as well as the wyverns above, shouting down directions in Cmok to keep the assassins from understanding. Tÿr looked up to see Ghra'zhenn and two other wyverns circling down to land on the street behind her.

"Are you all right, Tÿr'Ynyn?" he asked, voice full of concern.

"I'm fine for now. I need to find my parents. I believe they will be in Kuired's shop or in his cottage. I presume it will be heavily guarded, so I will use care when I approach."

"We are here to join you on your trip to the cottage. It is way too dangerous to attempt on your own. This is Zajj." Ghra'zhenn indicated a huge wyvern to his left.

The wyvern's coloring was similar to Ghra'zhenn's, except he appeared to have an orange tint to his scales in the light. Tÿr remembered seeing him back on Ÿkkynnÿk and remembered how beautiful his scales were back there. Now, up close, they were even more amazing. The other wyvern was introduced as Bysÿsaa. He, too, was very large and would be able to protect the apprentice with the greatest of ease. Tÿr felt safe for the first time since arriving in Yelliton, but she knew that her feeling could evaporate as quickly as it had come on. They had only seen a couple of the sorcerer's henchmen, and she had no idea how many they would be facing. Right now, she had to trust in her training and hope that she had prepared herself properly. Tÿr wished that the sorcerer, Kaistam-Laq, would show himself—her philosophy being, if she could remove the head of the organization, the rest of its members might fall apart. She knew in her heart that the evil man was with her parents, making sure they couldn't escape and also making sure that she would have to face him before this was over.

The thought of coming face-to-face with the sorcerer did not give her a good feeling. Everyone on the planets knew of him and knew of his powers. She would have to fight smart, let him exhaust himself first and then strike when he was worn out. This was the plan, but plans rarely went as envisioned. She knew he would do his best to see to that. Tÿr and Ghra'zhenn led the other two down the street and then turned west toward the shop. They were still several streets away, but they were on high alert as nothing had happened. It was too quiet in the streets, and Tÿr was on edge.

"Something isn't right, Master. It's way too quiet. There should have been something by now!"

"Agreed," Ghra'zhenn said. He, too, was looking around warily. He called the small group to a halt. "Keep on a lookout for an ambush! We should have run into someone by now," he told Tÿr and the two wyverns.

They were just preparing to move again when the smashing of windows came from all sides. Five assassins in black came leaping out of three of the houses, surrounding the little group. One of the assassins, the bald black lady, had leapt up on the back of the paragon and attempted to drive her lachtrys dagger into the area between where his wing connected to his body. Ghra'zhenn shrieked and thrashed as the assassin flew off his back. The dagger had shattered on his hard carapace. A wyvern's scales were much harder than they appeared, and the dagger stood no chance. The assassin hit the ground hard and rolled back to her feet. The three other assassins aimed spells at the other two wyverns. The first hit the back of Zajj and bounced off, slamming into the wall of the house next to him. A huge fireball erupted, and the cottage caught fire quickly.

Tÿr'Ynyn spun around her staff held at the ready. She drew on her energy, and this time, she began to glow, her arms and back alight with magiqal fire. She aimed her first attack at the closest assassin. The dark, bald woman saw Tÿr light up and warned the others, but the assassin called Qatÿll never saw it coming. He was preoccupied with his attack on the paragon, and his back was still turned to the apprentice. Tÿr shouted as her fireball flew at the assassin. It picked him up in the air for the briefest of seconds, and he looked as if he were trying to scream, his body shocked by the intensity of the pain. And then he was no more. He literally evaporated in a burst of red energy that exploded around him. The assassins stopped for a moment. They couldn't believe their eyes. They had never seen the type of power that they had just witnessed.

"The girl!" screamed the bald lady. "Take her out now!"

The remaining assassins that had attacked the little group stopped their attack on the wyverns to focus their effort on the healer. Tÿr'Ynyn's glow grew brighter as she prepared to battle the remaining four assassins. The wyverns also had a chance to catch their breath as the focus of the attack shifted from them to the little girl with the staff. Tÿr didn't realize how strong her glow had become. It had begun to burn her tunic from her back and arms. She didn't have time to care. She was under attack and needed to focus.

Owonnyn, the bald assassin, threw her lachtrys blade at Tÿr, hoping to catch her off guard, but Tÿr's shield was glowing around her, and the knife blew into a million pieces of harmless dust. The assassin tried again with the exact same results.

She screamed in frustration. "Don't use your ranged weapons! They are useless! We will have to combine our attacks and break her down!" the dark-skinned lady yelled out to the remaining assassins.

Two of the assassins carried their staff bolines—deadly pole weapons with an upside-down, half-moon-shaped blade used for slashing, stabbing, and many other types of attacks. They ran at the healer, allowing Owonnyn to shoot energy beams at the healer as a distraction. The whole time this was taking place, the last assassin was attempting to sneak behind the healer to try and incapacitate her. If she could be knocked out or distracted for just a moment, she might be able to be taken down. The problem with this logic was that they had completely forgotten about the wyverns sending balls of energy in their direction while this was taking place. Balls of fire and energy flew back and forth between the two sides.

The wyverns seemed to be hitting their marks more often than the assassins. The wyverns didn't allow the assassins to get close to Tÿr. They shot energy balls as fast as they could, sending clouds of brick and blue dust up all over the roadway. Tÿr used the distraction to continue her way toward Kuired's shop. Owonnyn couldn't see the healer to shoot at anymore. The wyverns were causing so much dust to be blown around she needed to move to get a better position. She, too, ran to the west. She figured out that was where the healer was most likely to be heading. Tÿr continued to hide behind buildings, checking to make sure that the path was clear before sprinting to the next one. At one point, she saw two villagers attempting to flee the battle, and she screamed for them to get back inside.

"It's too dangerous out here!" she yelled. "Stay in your cottage, and don't let anyone in until I come to tell you it is safe to come out!"

The villagers quickly turned back and slammed the door closed, their faces filled with horror. As Tÿr rounded the corner of a cottage on the south side of the building, she saw another assassin trying to silently slide out of the back window of the small cottage. He looked up in time to see her point her magiqal staff at him. He didn't have the chance to utter one single word. Tÿr cast a simple freezing spell on him. It wasn't pretty, but it was made powerful by her intercalation and staff. The assassin froze in place. One leg was sticking out of the window, as were both hands, which were still grabbing the frame. His head was in an awkward, ducking position. She saw his lachtrys blade fall to the ground and bounce in the dusty blue earth. He would remain in that position as long as she left him like that or until she died and the spell broke. From above, Tÿr heard a warning cry.

"Zjyyllat!"

In Cmok, it was the warning for someone being behind you. Tÿr spun with her staff up. It was the one thing that saved her life, though it did leave a long cut down her forearm. The tall black woman had managed to somehow sneak up on Tÿr without a sound and had almost stabbed her in the neck. Had Tÿr not turned when she did, her story might have ended there. But she, too, was very fast and managed to elude the worst of the attack. In a smooth, fast motion, the healer brought up the bottom of the staff and hit the assassin in the hands, knocking both lachtrys daggers loose. Owonnyn cursed and tried to dive for the daggers.

Tÿr laughed even though she was in pain. "What would your boss have said if you have just killed me? I thought he wanted me alive?"

"He would have gotten over it. I believe he still will. You will not last more than two minutes, little girl. You are not a match for me. I will destroy you, and I *will* be rewarded for it."

Owonnyn was still searching the dirt for the daggers. She was turning in circles but couldn't find them.

"Are you looking for these?" Tÿr asked, holding out the two blades.

Owonnyn screamed in frustration. Then she started to conjure. She meant to try something Tÿr was famous for, but unfortunately for her, it wasn't in her cards. The assassin drew on her magiqal power to attempt to fire in rage at the young girl standing in front of her.

At the same time, Tÿr was reforming the lachtrys into two long bolts. She would wait for the precise moment when the assassin was at her weakest to make her attack.

The attack came just moments later. Tÿr could feel the hair on her arms begin to stand on end, a surefire way to tell that energy was on its way. As soon as the dark-skinned woman opened her mouth to cast, Tÿr sent the two bolts flying directly at the assassin's chest. Owonnyn felt the initial hit, which was like being hit in the chest by a blacksmith's hammer. The force knocked the wind out of her so that she couldn't find the words to cast at the healer. The energy needed somewhere to go and exploded around her with loud, crackling paroxysms of deadly energy. The bolts didn't stop in the woman's chest. They were moving with such speed and power they shot through her and out her back and into the cottage twenty-five yards away.

Tÿr stood in amazement as she watched the assassin slump in front of her. She fell to her knees first and then over onto her face. She was dead by the time her head hit the ground. The wyverns above let out a victorious scream and continued their search. Two more assassins dressed in black rounded the corner in time to see Owonnyn, their comrade, hit the ground. The assassin called Kÿr'zhed stopped cold. He had been training under Owonnyn and had felt as close to her as he had ever felt to anyone in his life. Anger coursed through him at the sight of his mentor laying on the ground, her corpse leaking blood from the chest. Rage like he had never felt in his life took over his mind, and he sprinted after the healer.

Tÿr was surprised that this assassin had lost control so easily. She held out her staff as he approached and drew on her power. Her arms and back were bare from where the tunic had literally burned off her because of her intense, magiqal power. Krÿ'zhed was sprinting at Tÿr as fast as he could physically move, the assassin behind him casting a spell to help him move even faster. Tÿr was ready for him, and in his blind fit of rage, he wasn't prepared to deal with a force like the healer. His boline spun around his body like a baneful fan blade, lethal to most that it came too close to. The apprentice healer's staff glowed with a light brighter than the planets' suns. She took one step forward and stuck out her staff, stopping his spinning blade instantly.

The vibrations that shot down the handle caused his hands intense pain, making him almost lose his grip. Still, he managed to keep hold of the ancient weapon. He heard a shout from behind him and realized that the other assassin was running to join him. They could not fight this healer fairly. She had already defeated one or two of their party, and they couldn't allow her to whittle down their already-low head count anymore.

The other assassin, a female with short black hair and dark eyes, came running to help Kÿr'zhed. She, too, put on an extra boost of speed to cover the forty yards quicker. She arrived right behind her partner, her boline raised to attack. Tÿr's arms and back glowed brightly. The assassins could see the light shining on the buildings behind her. The male attacked again while the woman gasped for a breath of air. He slashed with the boline, aiming at Tÿr's neck. Her senses helped to move her out of the way, and she brought up her staff to block. The resulting collision of weapons caused a huge ball of sparks to shower down around the two fighters. When the assassin pulled back the staff boline to make another attack, he saw that the blade had been bent sideways.

The female assassin called Mynnÿ Sï made her attack at the same time the weapons collided. Tÿr only had time to bring her arm up to defend her head. She added another gash to her already-bleeding arm.

"You are outnumbered, healer," the assassin told her, readying another attack.

Tÿr didn't give her a chance. She attacked swiftly with another freezing spell. She didn't want to kill if she could avoid it. Mynnÿ Sï was frozen in place with her blade in front of her. Tÿr used her staff of power to burn it to ashes, leaving the assassin holding nothing but air. She quickly turned to face the other assassin. He had tossed his boline to the ground and was conjuring two lachtrys blades. In the air behind her, Tÿr saw a wyvern fly over. It dropped something in the square between the houses. It took her a moment to realize that it was a body. She heard the sickening crack that it made when it landed on the street nearby. She turned to freeze the male assassin, but he was already moving at her with such incredible speed.

Tÿr only had time to bring up her staff to block him. Sparks of energy shot out of both ends, covering both the assassin and healer. The male recovered quicker and tackled Tÿr, knocking her staff away. He had both hands above her, one aiming at her throat and the other at an eye. She had all she could do to keep him off her. Her arms were still alight with magiq, and with her hands around his wrists, she sent as much power as she dared into her hands. She felt them heat up to temperatures that she could not have endured otherwise.

The man began to yell from the searing pain as his wrists began to blister under her grip. He tried to shake her, but she held on as tightly as she possibly could, knowing that if she let him go, one or both of those daggers might very well find their marks. As the man was thrashing around, trying to get loose, Tÿr used his momentum to reverse their positions. She flipped as hard as she could and rolled him onto his back, with his arms above his head as she straddled him. Her hands became so hot the lachtrys blades that he was holding shattered into thousands of pieces on the ground around them.

Tÿr felt safe enough to get up, so she put a quick knee to the bottom of his chin, slamming his teeth together and making him see stars for a moment. With his hands as blistered as they were, she knew he wouldn't be able to hold the pieces of lachtrys to reform the daggers. She doubted that he would be holding anything for a while.

Tÿr's main concern was staunching the flow of blood from her forearm. She had two deep cuts and were bleeding quite profusely. She needed to check and make sure that there were no other assassins nearby for the moment. Tÿr looked up and saw several wyverns circling above. She figured that they would let her know if anyone was close enough to harm her at the moment. She ran over to the frozen female assassin and ripped at her shirt, pulling two strips of cloth from it. The healer used the cloth strips to ebb the flow of blood and tie off the cuts, and then she used a couple of her own spells on them. They were spells that mended from the inside, stopping the bleeding in the tissues and keeping the wound from gushing. She would still use the strips of cloth to cover the wound to keep it as clean as she could until she could wash it out and treat it properly. There were still assassins to deal with.

Chapter 33

Ghra'zhenn scanned the village below. He didn't want the apprentice to have any surprise attacks if he could help it. He would lend as much assistance as he could from the air. The others wyverns scanned the village with the paragon, passing messages back and forth when they saw the assassins move between the buildings below.

Ghra'zhenn was mainly looking for the leader of the Murtair Amagii, Kaistam-Laq. He knew that the sorcerer wanted to get his hands on the healer for some reasons known only to him, and Ghra'zhenn was going to keep that from happening. The sorcerer had made himself unseen since his original arrival. Ghra'zhenn figured that he was either in Kuired's shop or his cottage. He wanted to go down and check, but he also knew that he would never be able to get in either building, and it would probably put Tÿr's parents at an unnecessary risk.

Several times during their flights over the city, assassins had tried to hit the wyverns with curses, but the magiq that they used was not that strong. Ghra'zhenn doubted that even the sorcerer himself would have been able to do any damage to him. The other wyverns were younger than Ghra'zhenn, but they still had very strong hides, and their magiq was extremely strong as well. The circling wyverns were ordered not to attack the assassins as long as they hid near the cottages and other buildings in the village. The paragon did not want to harm any buildings if he could help it. The citizens of Yelliton had not asked for this fight. The assassins had involved them, and Ghra'zhenn was going to keep the loss of life and property as low as he could.

Ghra'zhenn could see Tÿr down in the street, dealing with two assassins at the same time. Normally, he would have been concerned, but she was so powerful and had become so intuitive she would easily defeat these two with little trouble. That was when he spotted a third running at top speed toward the fray that Tÿr was still involved in. The assassin never saw the wyvern drop from the sky. Ghra'zhenn purposely glided down without a sound from his huge, leathery wings. The man below never heard a thing, even when the paragon opened his huge jaws and grabbed the man by the head. The man only yelled for a couple of seconds because after the wyvern lifted off the ground, the man struggled so much he caused his own neck to be snapped. Ghra'zhenn felt the assassin go limp in his grip but still climbed to a safe height to drop the man from.

So far, as much as Ghra'zhenn could tell, they had not had one single casualty. The other side had not been so lucky. He wasn't sure what had happened, but there was one man sticking out of a window, frozen in time, not moving at all. He had seen Tÿr kill one or two assassins herself, and he had killed one too. He didn't have an exact count, but he thought there were around eight to twelve assassins in the village, and he would not rest until they were all accounted for.

He glanced back down at Tÿr, and it appeared that she had done away with another. He wasn't sure, but he was going to join her. It was time they tighten the noose and get to the sorcerer. The longer he had the apprentice's parents, the more he could find ways to use them or reasons to get rid of them. Ghra'zhenn wanted to end that now! He turned at the back of the village and looked for Tÿr. It was time to remove this madman from power!

The paragon touched down where Tÿr was addressing her wounds. They weren't life-threatening to a healer. She had closed them properly and would probably not have much of a scar. Ghra'zhenn saw the other male assassin rolling around on the ground. His hands were burned beyond recognition. There weren't even stumps left to indicate where fingers had once grown.

"You bitch, how could you do this to me? I'll kill you!" he screamed, cradling his hands in his arms.

Tÿr walked slowly over to him. Ghra'zhenn stood back to watch the interaction between the wounded assassin and the gentle healer.

"Why do you call me such things?"

"You just burnt my hands? You ruined my hands, you little bitch!"

"You *did* try to kill me!" she said to him, moving close to his face.

"Look what you did! You bi—"

Ghra'zhenn cut the assassin off. "If you refer to her as *that* once more, I shall make you regret it. She attacked you only after you had attacked her. Does any of this sound familiar to you? What is your name? I can't just call you, you."

The assassin looked like he had swallowed something very bitter. It was as if he had been insulted by someone who was way beneath his station. He began to speak to Ghra'zhenn. "Who are you to lecture me, you freak! That bitch took my hands, and she will pay! I will have my revenge! My master will heal me, and that little bit—"

Smash!

Ghra'zhenn had turned and thrashed the man with his powerful tail. The man went sailing over fifty feet before landing on his shoulders; his neck had been broken from the blow of the wyvern's tail. Ghra'zhenn looked at Tÿr. She could tell that he was angry.

"I did warn that coarse man to shut up. He just continued to talk! I had enough of him and his language."

"It was fine, Ghra'zhenn. I wasn't upset. I've been called worse."

"Really! Well, no one will do it when I am around. I warned him. I warned him more than once. The world will not mourn the loss of another assassin," he said, sounding completely disgusted.

Tÿr didn't like to agree but felt that he was probably correct in this case. She had done nothing but protect herself, and this man had not seen it that way. *Some people*, Tÿr thought, rolling her eyes a bit. She shook it off quickly though. Her parents' faces appeared in her head. They had to get to them before that madman got into their heads and caused real problems, things that she might not be able to heal yet.

Ghra'zhenn called into the sky. Tÿr understood that he was bringing some of the wyverns down to join them. Two were already swooping down to land near them. Tÿr and Ghra'zhenn began to carefully walk in the direction of the healer's shop. They would check there first. Kuired's house was just up the road, and they could reach it in minutes. Tÿr hoped that they were in the cottage as opposed to the clinic. The healer's building was bigger and could hold more people. She was worried that Kaistam-Laq would have more assassins waiting in hiding in the shop. If they were in Kuired's home, there was literally no place to hide anyone, but the chance of Tÿr's parents getting caught in the crossfire was higher as well. Tÿr was thinking about things like this and almost missed the black-clad assassin who had been lying in wait for her.

Tÿr jumped back in surprise as he made a quick slice at her with his boline. Her magiq sprung back to life in an instant, arms and bare back aglow with magiq energy. The assassin was obviously used to impressing his marks before killing them. He twirled the boline around his body and above his head, hoping it would have an intimidating effect on the healer. Instead of menacing the apprentice, she used this time practically. She cast another heating spell, this time on the spinning pole of the boline as the assassin showed off his weapon skills, moving closer as he spun the boline around his waist and neck, keeping his eyes glued on Tÿr and not focusing on his weapon. A shortcoming that Tÿr noticed of all the assassins she had faced—they loved to show off but were never prepared to face the possibility that someone might be more skilled in the art of killing than they were. Tÿr had always been able to distract them or allowed them to be distracted enough to get in one fatal shot. With any luck, the sorcerer had been the one to teach this precedent. Tÿr was agitated by now and didn't care to deal with a long dialogue. She didn't need to see any more of his ridiculous weapon-handling.

"You will move, assassin, or you will pay the price. You have two seconds to comply. One—"

"You do not frighten me, little girl. I have killed so many—"

Whack!

The man fell over. Tÿr didn't know if he was dead or alive. She had struck him in the temple, and he had dropped straight down. He didn't even grunt.

"I did warn him," she said under her breath as she and the wyvern entourage continued walking toward the shop.

She looked to see two more wyverns circle overhead and come to land behind the growing parade that they had formed as they marched onward to Kuired's shop.

"I may be incorrect, but I believe we probably will not encounter any more attackers until we reach the sorcerer and your parents." The wyvern stopped walking abruptly. "Tÿr, I want you to know that there is a possibility that your parents may be injured or worse. This sorcerer that we are dealing with is psychotic, and he is doing something horrid to the people that you love. I want you to be prepared for every possible situation that you could encounter when you open the door to meet that madman. Do you understand me?"

"I do, Ghra'zhenn. When the time comes, I will pay each and every person that has caused my family pain. I will be fair. I will treat them with dignity even though it will not be reciprocated should they catch me."

"You may not have the chance to do that, Tÿr'Ynyn. They might make it a case of you do what you must to survive. I will support you in either case. You have made me very proud, my young apprentice. You will do better than anyone today because you know what to do, and I need not worry about you being fair, but I know you will be just, and you will see that the sorcerer pays for his injustices. Thank you for being such an incredible student."

"Ghra'zhenn, we're just going to fight a sorcerer. Don't be so dramatic! Tell me all of this when I capture him."

Ghra'zhenn nodded. "I just want to be prepared in the case that anything should happen, and we don't—"

"Ghra'zhenn, you are doing it again! Tell me when it's over. I don't need to be nervous for this! Please!"

Ghra'zhenn stopped and hung his head in mock shame. "I *am* sorry, Tÿr. Please forgive me."

Tÿr saw what he was doing. Now she giggled. "Thanks, Ghra'zhenn! Let's go get my parents."

The wyvern followed the apprentice's lead, and they walked toward the old healer's shop. The wyvern had cast another spell earlier that allowed him to detect any amount of magic from any source close to him or the healer.

"Master, I can tell that there is someone in the building ahead of us!"

"Yes, I believe there is only one. We will have to deal with the others at the shop or the cottage. I can tell that the rest are ahead of us, but I cannot pinpoint them yet. Let us take care of this one before we go any farther. I don't want him sneaking up behind us."

Together they cautiously approached the cottage from the back. Ghra'zhenn determined that the assassin was alone in the cottage. He could not detect any other life-forms in the building with the assassin, which was hard to say if it was good or bad. Had the assassin killed the people inside, or had they already vacated the place before the assassin had arrived? Tÿr truly hoped it was the latter!

Ghra'zhenn performed a simple spell that caused the front door to shake in its frame. If this distraction worked as the paragon hoped, it would cause the person hiding in the cottage to run out the back. The two waited. Tÿr tried to listen for any sound from inside, but it had gone silent. Ghra'zhenn caused the door to rattle again. This time, Tÿr heard scurrying inside; it was coming near the back door, and then the door burst open! Out ran a young man, carrying a bag filled with items from the house. Tÿr realized that he was no assassin. He didn't have the build of a killer nor did he move like one. She also realized that he didn't own the cottage that he had just come from, and the belongings in the bag were very likely stolen. Tÿr almost laughed at the look on the boy's face as he sped from the meager house into the waiting arms of two wyverns and her. She had a feeling that he was near to passing out.

"Who are you?" asked the paragon. "What were you doing in this house?"

The boy looked at Ghra'zhenn with defiance written all over his face, but when he opened his mouth to give the paragon attitude, all that came out was a squeak.

"I suggest that you put back everything that you have taken that doesn't belong to you, or you will answer to me. Do I make myself clear?"

"Um, I, um." The boy finally just nodded.

"If I find out that you have not given back all that you have stolen today, I will make it my life's goal to plague you until one of us is dead. Now get out of here before you end up getting hurt! It is not safe to be here!"

The boy turned and ran as fast as he could. Tÿr smiled despite the severity of the situation. The boy's face had told her that he had expected to see almost anything else at the door than what had greeted him. Tÿr chuckled again, remembering the look of complete and utter terror.

"Okay, on to Kuired's shop," Tÿr said.

She and Ghra'zhenn weaved their way through the cottages without any incident. Tÿr figured that the rest of the assassins were with their leader at the shop. They didn't bother sneaking around this time. The time for that was done. They rounded the corner of the street and could see the shop ahead of them. There was only one black-clad figure standing in front of the door. Tÿr called up her magiq. Her arms and back glowed with power, and she wasn't worried about anyone seeing it. Maybe if they saw it, it would act as a warning, and the enemy would stand down. This was not the case however. As Tÿr and Ghra'zhenn arrived at the door, the assassin seemed as if he was ready to duel, even after two more wyverns dropped out of the sky behind Ghra'zhenn.

"This is between me and the healer. If she chooses to come quietly, no one will be harmed."

The assassin looked like he could harm too. He stood almost seven feet tall and was all muscle. Tÿr doubted that in a dragged-out fight that she would last one punch. This was not going to happen though.

"Where are my parents? I will only speak to the sorcerer when I have seen that my parents are alive and unharmed."

"You will do as I instruct. You are in no position to demand anything. Kaistam-Laq will decide when he wishes to speak with you. He is in charge now."

"I think you will find it is you who is mistaken. I will give you five seconds to live. I am sick of these insane games your leader likes to play. Now where are my parents?"

"You do not frighten me, little girl," the assassin said, but there was a note of doubt in his voice. "You will follow my instructions, or your parents will—"

The large man raised his staff boline as a defensive move against the apprentice and the wyverns. Tÿr cut him off mid-sentence.

"One!" she said, voice raised.

"You do not frighten me. I have killed people like you with no—"

"Two!"

Tÿr pointed her staff at the huge man, and he began to lift off the walkway in front of the shop. "What the hell? Put me down, you bitch!"

There was that word again. "Three!"

The man rose higher. "You don't have it in you to kill. I've seen what you did to Krÿ'zhed. You left him frozen in a window. Didn't have the guts to even kill him. You make me—"

"Four!"

The man hung in the air at least forty feet up now. Tÿr spoke to him. "This is your last chance. Where are my parents, assassin? I won't ask again! When I let you down, you will be wyvern food."

The assassin let out a hysterical bark of a laugh. He knew she wasn't kidding anymore. She had just shot him up fifty more feet. "Okay, okay, they're in the healer's cottage, but you'll never save them, bitch. Kaistam will kill them before you have the chance. He won't let them live if you kill me!"

"Why do all of you refer to me by that word? I must really have gotten under your skin, huh? Do you really think your boss cares whether you live or die?"

"Get me down, you *bitch*!" he screamed the last word. "I told you what you wanted. Now let me down. I'm going to teach you a lesson."

"Really? You haven't learned a thing, have you?" Týr asked.

She shot the man another hundred feet into the air and then, with her staff, shot a large ball of energy that collided with him mid-air. Sparks showered all around as his body came falling back to the ground, hitting with a sickening thud. *There*, Týr thought, *that's the last time you will call me or any other woman that ugly word*. She didn't usually let things like this bother her, but for some reason, every assassin she had come across had thought to call her that today. Enough was enough! She turned to Ghra'zhenn.

"Well done, apprentice!"

"Did you hear where he said they are keeping my parents?"

Ghra'zhenn nodded. "Then we move to the cottage. We must use extreme caution. The sorcerer is not going to be as easy to subdue. Do you need to rest first? You have used a lot of power!"

"I am fine," she told the paragon. "I will find the power I need to save my parents no matter how tired I am!"

Týr and the three wyverns turned and walked the short distance from the shop down the cobbled street, across the open yards, and up the next two streets to the small, innocent-looking cottage, where her most challenging fight lay waiting for her.

Chapter 34

The cottage door was open when she arrived with the three wyverns. She could see her parents standing to the side of the door. Her father was trying to wave her away.

"No, Tÿr'Ynyn! It's a trap. The sorcerer is here!"

Tÿr smiled at her father. "I know, Da. He's been waiting for me. We have some business to deal with."

"You aren't going to have anything with that madman, are you, Tÿr?" her mother asked.

"Oh, we have business, but he won't like it." Tÿr gave a quick wink to her mother to try to ease her worrying. She doubted it helped. Her father stood near the door, and Tÿr wondered why they didn't come out. "I'm here now, Da. Come out of there. Let me deal with Kaistam-Laq. You don't need to be here anymore."

"We can't," her mum said. "The sorcerer said we will die if we leave the cottage. He has some kind is magiqal curse on us."

Tÿr finally understood. They were bound to the cottage. If they left, they would die...while the sorcerer lived or was conscious. If he could be knocked out or killed outright, the curse would be removed, and she could get her parents out.

"Ah, the girl who would be healer." The voice of Kaistam-Laq came from the back corner of the cottage. He strode into view. "Have you changed your mind? Will you join the Murtair Amagii? We would be honored to have a magiq user of your caliber in our ranks."

"Your dwindling ranks, you mean," Tÿr said. "Before the day is out, there may only be one or two left in your killing club. Who will lead the group once I remove you from power?" she asked casually, as if they were talking about the weather. She knew she had struck a nerve.

The sorcerer's mouth twitched. How dare this insolent child talk to him like this? Who was she? There were two other assassins in the room, and they joined their master as he stood talking to the healer.

"Let my parents go, and I will listen to what you have to say," Tÿr told the sorcerer. "If you continue to hold them as hostages, these talks will be finished, and I will leave, but not before I remove you from power. You have a choice to make, and I will not wait. You could ask your large assassin, but I'm afraid he chose to ramble on and call me names instead of seeing reason. He now lay in the field. You may join him if you desire."

Kaistam's face split into an evil grin. "I'm afraid you don't understand the gravity of your situation, apprentice. For that is all you are. Isn't that correct? You are a healer apprentice?"

"What I am is completely immaterial. You have now threatened me and my family. I will not tolerate that from you or anyone! I will see you fall today sorcerer!"

"How dare you! You little bitc—"

At that moment, Ghra'zhenn stuck his head through the door. "Kaistam-Laq, you may wish to rephrase your next thought. The last person who said that is now out in a field, ready to be eaten by my dynasty. If you would like to become a meal for wyverns, please continue with what you were saying."

The sorcerer had stopped short. He had a good idea that the wyvern was telling him the truth. He didn't know who in his sect were alive or dead. He wanted to be here when the girl arrived. The two assassins took it upon themselves to move at Tÿr's parents. The first one grabbed Tÿr's mother roughly by the arm and morphed a piece of lachtrys into a dagger at her throat. The other one meant to grab Tÿr's father, but her dad used the assassin's momentum against him; and as he ran toward him, he reached back with all his strength and hit the man with a good, old-fashioned, bar-fight punch. The assassin stopped in his tracks. His eyes rolled up into his head, and he fell backward onto the floor. The other assassin with the razor-sharp blade on Tÿr's mother's neck pressed it in deeper, cutting the skin. Blood began to pool up around the edge of the blade.

"Hey, healer," the assassin mocked Tÿr, "here's something you can heal." He went to pull the blade across her mother's throat.

Tÿr's magiq surged with the rage she felt at the sight of the blood on her mum's neck. It wasn't deep, but that monster had hurt her. The blast that came from the staff was so large it made Tÿr take a step back. It hit the assassin in the torso. The ball of energy evaporated him where it touched him, blowing straight through him and out the back of the cottage. Tÿr didn't dare look to see how far the energy had gone. The assassin's head and arms, including the one at her mother's throat, hung in the air without a body before they fell to the floor with a sickly splat. One leg stood in place while the other fell over.

Kaistam-Laq stood where he was, anger flooding through him. "Enough! If you continue this, I will kill your parents now!"

"You will let them go, or you will suffer the same fate, sorcerer!"

Tÿr held her staff up, ready to cast another spell.

Kaistam-Laq took a step back. He had seen what the girl could do and was not looking for a repeat performance. "If," he started, "if I let them go, will you hear what I have to say?"

"I want nothing from you. I am not interested in joining your murderous gang. I am not interested in healing you when you are injured in the line of killing innocent people. What I want is my parents returned to their home, uninjured, and unbothered ever again. If I do not get your word right now, you will end up as this poor soul here." Tÿr indicated the legs and arms and head in a pile on the floor.

Kaistam had the look of soured milk. He had paled, and Tÿr could tell that he was trying to think of a way out of this hopeless situation. "And what guarantee do I have that you will not pursue me?"

"I give you no guarantee, just as you give me none. I want nothing to do with you nor your type."

Outside Ghra'zhenn was listening to the progress inside the cottage. He told the other two wyverns that he and Tÿr would be fine and that they could go. "Help round up the bodies of the assassins and bring them to the field outside of the city. These poor people should not have to clean up this mess," Ghra'zhenn told them.

The two wyverns flew off to relay the paragon's message to the others still circling the village. Ghra'zhenn was feeling pleased. So far, the battle had gone very well, and they hadn't lost one wyvern. He still had uneasy feelings about the healer inside with the sorcerer. Something wasn't right. Tÿr's parents were terrified for their daughter. They didn't trust the sorcerer. They thought him a psychopath and that he still had something up his sleeve for Tÿr. Tÿr, on the other hand, was beginning to be able to tell when a person was losing their power. Though the sorcerer was a powerful man, he had dissipated much of his power on needless spells. The problem with being a powerful person comes with paranoia and the fear that everyone is out to get you. It causes you to spend way more energy than you need to protect yourself because you always fear that someone is sneaking up on you. However, if you treat people well, you need not worry about being attacked by everyone you know.

Kaistam had alarms of one kind or another all around the cottage, so he knew when anyone was nearby. He also knew when they left. He was about ready to let Tÿr's parents go when he felt the presence of another assassin cross into the alarm zone. Kaistam knew that the paragon was now alone, so it was just the one wyvern and the healer. He also knew who the assassin was. There was only one assassin who gave off this much power. It was Xyrfed Mai.

The sorcerer continued to keep the healer occupied while he watched his assassin sneak around the side of the cottage toward the paragon wyvern. Yes, the wyvern was huge, but Xyrfed was the strongest and most highly trained assassin Kaistam had collected for the sect. Xyrfed Mai was the one who trained all the other assassins in the art of murder, stalking, and the art of fighting to the death. If anyone could kill the beast at the front of the cottage, it was Xyrfed. Kaistam was suddenly hopeful.

Xyrfed snuck up quietly along the side of the cottage, hoping that his master had seen him. With any luck, he would be provided with a diversion, and he could attack the wyvern before it even knew he was there. If luck was with him, he would be able to jam the special dagger he had crafted into the beast's throat and kill it quickly. A wyvern was large and difficult to kill, but if you knew its anatomy, it would go down like any other creature. The trick of the wyvern was that the major blood vessels from its heart to the brain ran along the back. The heart was protected in a double rib cage, and then the veins that ran to the brain were also housed in a circular type of bony cage that ran up the neck. A regular knife had very little chance of penetrating the cage. Xyrfed had formed a dagger from two pieces of lachtrys, and the cross section of the blade was a cross. The wound it inflicted would be very difficult to heal.

It was then that Kaistam made a racket, yelling and hollering, drawing the attention of the wyvern to him. Xyrfed was able to slip around the corner of the house and drive the blade into the side of the wyvern's neck. Týr jumped as Ghra'zhenn let out an almighty shriek. She turned to see Xyrfed trying to stab her paragon again, but Ghra'zhenn was thrashing around in pain, and the assassin had gotten stepped on. Xyrfed cried out as the wyvern broke his leg, shattering his shin bone. The assassin fell over, trying to escape the flailing wyvern. Týr could see blood pouring out of Ghra'zhenn's neck and ran out the cottage to tend to her master. Her parents watched in horror as the wyvern lost blood all over Týr's hand as she was casting a spell to ebb the flow.

"Ghra'zhenn, I need you to stay still! I have to stop the bleeding!"

The wyvern stopped moving, and Týr's hands were coated in deep-red blood as she cast spell after spell. Finally, the blood oozed to a stop. She turned to the assassin on the ground.

With her parents watching in horror, she pointed her staff at Xyrfed. "You won't escape this, you butcher!"

A ball of white-hot energy hit the assassin on the ground, and he vanished in a flash of sparks and smoke.

"Týr!" her mother cried.

"It's almost over, Mum!" she told her.

Týr looked up at the doorway. She knew what had to be done. Kaistam had his staff held out, pointed at the healer as she strode in the cottage. He sent a fireball at her, which she easily deflected away from her parents. He was trying to get her to harm them. He sent another and then another, and she bounced them back at him.

Kaistam hadn't expected this. The last fireball had come too close for his liking. His long cloak was left smoking. He threw it off and was about to cast another spell when the healer had finally had enough. Tÿr was angrier than she had ever been before. This man was trying to make her hurt her parents by using his spells against her. Enough was enough. She gathered every bit of power she could find. Her arms and back lit up like it was daylight of the sun. The sorcerer realized his mistake too late. When she cast, she screamed with every bit of fury she felt. She used her magiq to hide the bolt of energy to keep the sorcerer from blocking it. He never had any warning other than her scream of fury. The windows all blew out of the cottage as her invisible bolt of energy shot out at Kaistam-Laq.

The leader of the sect known as Murtair Amagii had just enough time to bring his staff up in front of himself, but he didn't have the speed to cast any spell. He could feel the energy a split second before it blasted him through the wall behind him. He lost consciousness instantly and lay in a heap outside the little blue-roofed cottage. Immediately the link between the sorcerer and Tÿr's parents was severed. They ran to catch her as she staggered. She had expended so much force to take down the sorcerer she was left weakened. She leaned against her staff as her parents each grabbed an arm.

"It's okay. I'm okay now," she said, trying to get her legs to work. Her dad helped her to sit down where she was.

"Is he..." Her mum hesitated to finish.

"I'm not sure. I don't care right now. I do know he won't be bothering anyone for a while. I don't think he can even move. I'm not much better if the truth be told," Tÿr said with a weak smile.

Her mother rushed down to embrace her with tears in her eyes.

"I'm okay, Mum, really. Please go check on Ghra'zhenn. He lost quite a bit of blood!"

"I am fine, young lady!" came a rasping voice from the doorway.

Tÿr turned to see Ghra'zhenn poking his head through the doorway. She smiled at him. "Can I get you anything? Are you okay?"

"I will be fine. I just need a little rest before I get you and your parents back to Vennex."

"You can't fly, Ghra'zhenn! You've been wounded! You're hurt, and you lost a lot of blood, remember. This isn't dragon fruit wine on my hands!"

"I've been wounded much worse than this before and lived to fly hundreds of miles immediately after. I will be fine!"

Tÿr just turned and shook her head. She knew there was no sense in arguing with the wyvern. She turned back to tend to her parents. "Are you all right?" she asked her father.

"We are fine," he told her. "They didn't really bother with us too much. It was you they wanted the whole time, only that madman thought you were a boy." Her father chuckled as he told her this.

"Thought I was a male? Why would he think that?"

Her dad thought for a second. "You know," her father said, "that idiot probably didn't think a girl could do what you can do. I believe that was his undoing. He underestimated you. People have been doing that your whole life, and you have been proving them wrong at every turn."

"Oh, thanks, Da!"

"I'm damn proud of you, Tÿr'Ynyn!"

"We both are!" her mother chimed in.

"As I told you when I first met you," Ghra'zhenn said, "there is something special about you. You have not made me out to be a liar, for which I am very grateful. You are going to be a great healer and so much more. I've said it before, and I stick by my word."

Tÿr was as happy as she could possibly be. She just needed to sleep because she was as tired as she was happy. She could wait to get back to her normal routine. She had only been gone a short time, but she missed Varanus and the boys. She also had to decide what to do with her cousin. He had asked to stay with her for the time being, and she had agreed. She still hadn't told her parents. The looks on their faces would be priceless. *Family*, Tÿr thought fondly. She had been adopted into a huge one.

The militia in Yelliton listened in disbelief as Tÿr and Ghra'zhenn explained what had happened in their village. They had been completely unaware that anything was going on. One or two of the soldiers said that they wondered what the wyverns were doing above the city but didn't give it a second thought. The wyvern and the healer told the soldiers where the bodies of the dead and injured and unconscious assassins were located. The militia sent out soldiers to round up the assassins and put them where they belonged.

Tÿr stayed long enough to see Kaistam-Laq being carried into a prison cell, where she hoped he would spend a long, long time. She did warn the men in charge to destroy the sorcerer's staff. Tÿr had an idea that Kaistam might not need the staff for all his magiq, but she felt it was best to make sure he never had it again. It was too dangerous in his hands.

Tÿr and Ghra'zhenn met the rest of the dynasty and her parents at the edge of the field. They were all anxious to be gone, but there was one thing they wanted to do before leaving. The paragon had asked for the wyverns to search through the forest and the area surrounding Yelliton to find the body of Kuired. He was a friend of all of them and deserved a proper burial. The wyverns had managed to locate him and had prepared a grave for him. It was located at the edge of the forest near the road heading into Yelliton.

"He would have liked it here!" Tÿr said absently.

"I knew him for many years, and I believe he would have," the paragon agreed.

"Let's go home, Ghra'zhenn. I want to get back to my normal life."

Ghra'zhenn smiled. "I don't believe there is any such thing as normal with you, Tÿr'Ynyn."

The End

Epilogue

Tÿr was finally back in her healer's shop, seeing patients again. She was doing the job she had trained to do. Even though she had only trained a relatively short time compared to others who had trained for this same position, she was far advanced from her contemporaries. The job came easily to her, as did the magiq, which aided her in the healing.

The people of Vennex loved their healer and thought of her as a hero. Word had quickly spread of the battle that had taken place in Yelliton and of the healer's heroics. Tÿr was sure that half the people that came to see her only wanted to catch a glimpse of her. Many were not sick or injured, but she was happy to see each one of the people.

The assassin sect, Murtair Amagii, was no more. Tÿr'Ynyn and the dynasty of wyverns that had gone to Yelliton to save her parents had removed the sorcerer and the rest of his assassin sect from power, killing many or putting several in the custody of the militia of Yelliton to stand trial for damage to the city and harm to the people. Tÿr also found herself with new responsibilities here in Vennex. Her cousin, Sämir, had become magistrate by default. Both his parents had been killed by an assassin, who was sent there to murder his father on a contract put out by his mother.

Sämir realized that he was not cut out for a life of politics. He had barely seen his father, and his mother had become so manipulative in the days before their deaths. The boy did not want to end up like them, so he asked his cousin if she would consider running the town until a proper magistrate could be appointed.

Tỹr thought about it for a long time and eventually agreed with the condition that her father be allowed to help with some of the decision-making. Her father balked at the idea at first. He said that he wasn't cut out for politics and didn't have the head of a politician. It turned out that that was exactly what the village was looking for in their next magistrate. The people of Vennex were truly happy for the first time in ages. Seryth Tỹr would go on to rule the village of Vennex for over fifteen years.

Tỹr was thinking about all the events that had taken place in the past few months. Varanus had named her a full healer, something that usually took years to happen, but he and Ghra'zhenn had both agreed that she had earned it. No one in the history of the planets had ever done something like this as quickly. She had also become a guardian to her cousin, Sämir. He was now studying to become a healer under her and Varanus's teaching. He had certainly changed in the few months he had been with her. He had gone from being a demanding, hateful prat of a child to a giving, loving human who had devoted his life to healing the sick, like his cousin, who he looked up to and wanted to emulate.

Tỹr was so proud of the young man he was becoming. Sämir also helped to fill the void left by Tỹr's two best friends, who had stayed on the wyvern island to study magiq under the paragon Ghra'zhenn and his dynasty of wyverns who had adopted the boys as their own. There was even talk of the boys receiving the sacred intercalation that Tỹr had been given. Tỹr was prouder than she could ever express of all the boys. How they had matured and grown.

She and her cousin still had dinner every day with her parents, and her mother still fussed that she hadn't made enough food each meal. Varanus still went out to hunt every night, but was told that the village hunters would be happy to bring him back food anytime he asked. They loved Varanus and treated him just like another citizen of the village. Varanus told Tỹr that he preferred to hunt for his food so he didn't sit around and get oversized. Tỹr did notice that he never turned down the piles of dragon fruit the villagers left him when they traveled to distant places.

"It would be rude not to accept such thoughtful gifts," he would tell the apprentice.

Tӯr would just shake her head and smile.

Tӯr and Rævii could be seen walking around Vennex at any time. The healer with her quartz pipe lit with herb weed and her cousin and fox in tow. The farmers never complained about the fox with the blond tail. In fact, more often than not, instead of harsh words, Rævii was greeted by bits of cooked meat left near the farmers' doors. Rævii, too, was a hero; and the farmers, along with the other villagers, treated her like one.

Life was good for the trio, and the village of Vennex thrived happily. The wyvern Varanus was always close at hand for any situation that could not be handled by the healer. Luckily for the wyvern, those situations rarely arose. The paragon visited Vennex at least twice a month. He kept an eye on the situation, making sure Tӯr had everything she needed in her shop. Quite often Gordian and Danior came with him to see their mother and their best friend.

Tӯr's dad, as magistrate, declared an anniversary party for his brother and for the day Tӯr went to Yelliton to rid that village of the oppression of Kaistam-Laq and his sect of murderers. Tӯr and her cousin were busy closing down the shop. Varanus was out back, tending to their ever-growing flock of birds. Tӯr still allowed any form of payment to be seen at the clinic. They had amassed quite a collection of fowl and other barnyard creatures, which truly helped. When she and Sämir were done in the shop, they would get their pipes out and have a smoke before heading over to her parents' place for dinner. She smiled at the thought. *What*, she wondered, *would happen next?* She didn't have any clue, but right at this moment, she felt ready to take on the world!

Pronunciation

Tÿr'Ynyn: Teer Eye-nun
Aaxtagara: Aj tah-gar-ah
Siolad Tÿr: She lahd Teer
Elmky Tÿr: Ehlm Kee Teer
Seryth Tÿr: Sehr uth Teer
Varanus: Vahr an us
Danior: Dahn EE or
Gordian: Gord EE an
Ellysse Tÿr: Ellus Teer
Murtair Amagii: Mur Tire Ah maj ee eye
Kuired Gÿann: Kee red Guy Ahn
Kaistam-Laq: Kī stam Lahk
Rævii: Reevee

About the Author

Brent Snyder lives in Central Texas with his wife and two sons and his French bulldog, Steve. He enjoys reading, having a nice cigar, and spending time with his granddaughters. You can often find him playing video games and listening to music. He also collects rocks and has an extensive collection of crystal skulls.

Printed in the USA
CPSIA information can be obtained
at www.ICGtesting.com
LVHW051027171023
761280LV00001B/2